... she enjoys small-game hunting, ...ing, cross-country ski-ing and cooking.

...er first Paris Murphy novel, *Clean Cut*, is available in ...me Warner Books.

COLD BLOOD

THERESA MONSOUR

TIME WARNER
BOOKS

TIME WARNER BOOKS

First published in the United States in 2004 by G. P. Putnam's Sons

First published in Great Britain in 2004 by Time Warner Books
This paperback edition published in June 2005 by Time Warner Books

A CIP catalogue record for this book
is available from the British Library.

ISBN 0 7515 3387 4

Printed and bound in Great Britain by
Mackays of Chatham Ltd, Chatham, Kent

Time Warner Books
An imprint of
Time Warner Book Group UK
Brettenham House
Lancaster Place
London WC2E 7EN

www.twbg.co.uk

This book is dedicated to my sons,
Patrick and Ryan,
with all my love.

Acknowledgments

I'd like to thank David for his continued support; Ryan for his expertise on knives; Patrick for rescuing me from computer problems; Marilee Votel-Kvaal, Ann Norrlander and Rita Monsour for their medical knowledge; Tom Dooher and Joseph Monsour for their auto tips; Kristina Schweinler of city licensing for background on St. Paul bars; and Esther Newberg and Leona Nevler for their hard work.

COLD BLOOD

Learning Curve

Two of them pinned the tall boy's arms against the wall of the school building. Two others did the punching; one would step back and take a breath and the other would take over. They started with the head and worked their way down. Steam boiled out of their mouths as they whispered curses in the fall air. He wouldn't have hollered for help. Wouldn't have given them the satisfaction. They gagged him anyway. Stuffed his mouth with a jockstrap. It tasted salty with someone else's sweat and urine and made him feel filthy. A dirty animal. Down the hill behind them, the bonfire crackled and sputtered, and teenagers talked and sang. A radio blared the Talking Heads. "Burning Down the House." The tall boy tried to concentrate on the music and on the sparks darting into the air, send his pain floating into the night sky.

They punched him in the crotch, and he felt as if a flaming log had shot up the hill and buried itself in his gut. He gulped. Almost swallowed the jockstrap. The one holding his right arm laughed. "Not the balls. That's lower than low." They let go of him. He folded in half and fell to the ground. He coughed up the gag and a tooth chip and a mouthful of blood. Don't cry, he told himself, but he did. Big, heaving sobs.

1

One of them kicked him in the side. "Woman. Should have earrings in both ears. Fucking baby."

"No," said another. "He's a f... f... f... fucking b... b... b... baby." The four of them laughed.

He curled up on the ground, covered his head with his arms. The grass felt cool on the side of his face. He wished he could bury his whole body in the coolness. Disappear into it. Melt away.

"I think he peed in his pants," said the fat one. He bent over and took the tall boy's baseball cap off his head and put it backward on his own.

"He always smells."

"No. He did. He fucking pissed all over himself."

"Let's call his old man to mop it up."

That hurt him more than the punches and kicks. He propped himself up on his elbow. He lifted his head; it felt heavy. A block of concrete on his neck. He tried to open his eyes; they were already swelling shut and all he could see through the slits were shadows. He wanted to tell them something. Get one insult in. What came out was a growl. "You b... b... bastards."

The fat one pushed the tall boy's head down with his shoe and kept it there, as if he were propping his foot up on a rock. "Did you s... s... s... say something, d... d... d... dickhead?" They all laughed again.

Someone down the hill saw them. A teacher's voice: "Hey, what's going on up there?"

"We're outta here," said the fat one. He took his foot off the tall boy's head. "Come on!" He threw the tall boy's baseball cap on the ground.

Three of them ran to the car. The fourth, the one with the most arm patches on his letter jacket, leaned over and whispered in the tall boy's ear: "Listen good, Motorhead. Talk to her again and I'll kill ya, you creepy son of a bitch." He grabbed the ear. "One more thing. You're fuckin' out of uniform." He ripped off the earring, tossed the gold loop in the grass and went after the others.

2

On Monday, the tall boy went to school. His hand repeatedly went up to his left ear to finger the bandage. That tiny part of him, the torn earlobe, throbbed more than his entire body. He kept to himself all day; he always did anyway. Nothing had changed, really, except now he had a burning hate where once there was emptiness. He preferred the hate to the emptiness; it filled him up and gave him purpose. He had to find a way to get back at them. Sweet Justice would be patient and clever; he was a smart motorhead. Whatever happened would be their fault.

What goes around comes around.

He knew she was sitting there during lunch, at her usual table with her girlfriends. He longed to look at her. Longed to let her know that he blamed her. She must have said something to them. Maybe she told them to do it. Yes. She was also guilty. At first he thought she was different from the others. Thought she was good. Another Snow White. He was wrong; her beauty had fooled him. Bitch. She was as mean and shallow as the rest of them. Sweet Justice would nail her someday, too.

What goes around comes around, beautiful.

"Jesus. What happened to him?" asked one of the girls in between bites of a sandwich. "He get hit by a truck, or what? At least he lost the jewelry. Band-Aid's an improvement."

The other girls at the table laughed. All but one. The tallest, and the only one with black hair. "Leave him alone," she said.

The girl with the sandwich: "Got the hots for him? He make ya cream your jeans? Thought you had better taste than that."

"The creep asked her to homecoming," said one eating yogurt with a carrot stick. "I heard him. During choir. You should've seen his face when she turned him down. I thought he was gonna bawl right there on the risers. Right during 'Ave Maria.'"

"Shut the hell up," said the dark-haired one. She grabbed her lunch bag and left the table.

The other girls watched her go. The one with the yogurt ran the carrot around the inside of the carton. "She broke up with Denny.

3

Big fight. This morning. Saw them in the parking lot." She paused for drama, and to take a lick off the carrot. "She ain't going to homecoming."

The bell rang and the students got up, some leaving their trash on the table. A janitor pushed a broom into the lunchroom. He picked up apple cores and napkins and tossed them into the garbage cans as he went along. The tall kid stared at the custodian until their eyes met. The man nodded. The boy got up, threw his lunch sack into the garbage. He walked past the janitor and said in a low voice, "Later, P... p... pa."

1

Bunny Pederson would be alive today if her best friend hadn't picked peach for the bridesmaids' dresses.

"I'm a fucking pumpkin," said Bunny, standing in the ladies' room at the bar and scrutinizing her hips in the mirror. She swayed drunkenly, grabbed the countertop for support and burped. Something fruity came up; too much Asti. She swallowed it back. Raised her arms and sniffed under her pits. Damn deodorant was quitting on her. She turned around and looked over her shoulder to scan her butt.

"Peach is good on you," said Katie Stodel, the other bridesmaid and a twig of a woman. She brushed a few strokes of blush into the hollows of her cheeks and dusted between her breasts.

Bunny grabbed the dress at the hips and tugged down. It crawled up again and bunched under her bodice. "Black would have been better. Slenderizing."

"Black? For a wedding?"

"A fall wedding. Everyone does it."

"Not in Moose Lake."

"This town should join the twenty-first century." Bunny hiccuped.

Katie dropped the blush compact in her handbag and tightened the drawstring. She and Bunny had matching purses made from the same material as the dresses. "She went cheap on the flowers, but the music was nice. I love J.D." She started humming "Sunshine on My Shoulders."

"John Denver's a wuss. She should've gone with my pick."

"The vocalist didn't know it."

Bunny loosened the string on her bag and reached inside. She pulled out a folded piece of paper and waved it in Katie's face. "I got the words right here." She opened the paper and started singing "Can't Help Falling in Love," but stopped after "fools rush in" to burp.

"Was Elvis as drunk as you when he sung that?"

"Shut up." Bunny hiccuped again, dropped the paper on the wet counter. She picked it up, shook it off, folded it. Tucked it back in her purse. "Chad and me, we had that song at our wedding dance. Made the DJ play it four times."

"Yeah, and look what it done for you. How long you been divorced?"

Bunny flipped her the bird and pulled a tube of gloss out of her bag. She leaned closer to the mirror and applied another layer to her lips. She stepped back and saw the wet counter had left a waterline across her abdomen. "Great. Now I'm a soggy pumpkin. Screw this. I'm sliding into some jeans. Drive me home?"

"Stick your stomach under the hand dryer. Come on. Do it and let's go."

Bunny ignored her, kept looking at her reflection. Someone had slapped a NO FAT CHICKS bumper sticker to the top of the mirror. Bunny's eyes kept wandering to the sign, as if it was meant for her. "This hairdo she picked out. Jesus Christ. What porn magazine did this come from?"

6

Katie was offended; she'd helped pick out the do. "It's from *Modern Bride*."

"Try *Modern Slut*." Bunny reached up, pulled out a few bobby pins. The brown pile atop her head came cascading down. She bent over and shook her hair and stood up again. She looked in the mirror and groaned. Medusa. "Gimme your brush."

"Didn't bring one. Use your comb."

"It'll never get through this mess. Take me home. Please?"

"They're cutting the cake. German chocolate. Can't you wait?"

"Forget it. I'll walk."

"The dress is fine. Stay."

"I'd stay if it wasn't peach. Peach in October. Might as well be orange."

"What should I tell Melissa?"

"That she has shit taste."

Bunny shivered and held her sweater close as she clicked through the parking lot. Should have worn a coat, she thought. Shouldn't have had that fourth glass of Asti Spumante. She felt sick. She ducked between two pickup trucks, bent over and vomited. She straightened up, leaned her back against one of the trucks and reached into her purse for some Kleenex. She wiped her mouth, blew her nose, tossed the tissue to the ground. The night air was hazy. Neighbors were burning leaves in their yards. Something else was smoking. What was it? She sniffed. Bratwurst. Burning leaves and brats. She loved the smells. They smelled like Friday night in a small town. Bunny inhaled deeply and immediately felt better. She brushed some hair off her face. Hoped she didn't get puke on it. She considered turning around and going back into the bar, but she couldn't stand the dress a minute longer. She wrapped her sweater tight around her body, shoved her evening bag under her armpit and kept going. A short walk, she told herself. Less than a mile.

Halfway there the heels started to hurt. She kicked them off and picked them up. Peach pumps. When would she wear those again? Waste of money, and she didn't have money to waste. Two kids to support on a crappy waitress job. Chad was late with his child support. Again. He should have shown up Thursday morning with the money and to take the boys duck hunting. Here it was, Friday night. No Chad, no check. Come morning she'd have to drive down to St. Paul and bang on his door. She knew he was struggling. Still, he had money for a new snowmobile. Why couldn't he pay on time for his sons? She was always short of money and the boys always needed things. They were growing out of their sneakers faster than she could buy them. Winter was around the corner. They'd need new boots and coats and snow pants, thought Bunny. Hockey skates. What about hockey skates? Last year's wouldn't fit either one of them. Little Chad was going to need new goalie pads for sure. Both boys' helmets were still good. The sticks, too. Where did she put those sticks? They weren't in the garage. The basement?

Home was a couple of blocks away. She could see the porch light. That dim bulb teenager she'd hired to baby-sit was probably out there smoking. Better not be her pack he was puffing. A cigarette would be good right now, thought Bunny. She couldn't fit her Marlboros and matches into the stupid little bag Melissa made her carry down the aisle. Another waste of money. Won't they all be pissed when the matron of honor returns in jeans and a sweatshirt? Tough shit. Tacky bar reception anyway with tacky bar food. Who

8

serves onion rings and buffalo wings at their wedding? Besides, thought Bunny, it's all Modern Bride Melissa's fault for picking peach. Peach dresses. Peach shoes. Peach purses. Even peach nail polish.

Some women turn thirty and panic because their lives aren't headed in the direction they'd hoped. When Bunny hit thirty earlier that fall, she hardly noticed. Her life was exactly what she'd expected. She saw it unfold ahead of her years ago, in high school. She could pinpoint the exact time and place and circumstances of the epiphany: between second and third period, in the girls' bathroom, while she was sitting on the pot reading the instructions from a drugstore pregnancy kit. As long as it took for her to pee on the stick and wait for it to change is about how long it took for her to let go of any grand plans for the future. She married a month before she gave birth and was pregnant again before she turned twenty. She lost the third; that didn't surprise or upset her. Got her tubes tied at twenty-five—smartest thing she ever did, she told friends. She didn't tell herself that working at the restaurant was temporary, until something better came along. Bunny knew nothing better ever comes along, especially in small towns.

Her low expectations were always on the money. She expected Chad to take off and he did. Anticipated the heartache and was relieved when it finally came. He was too much for her. Too handsome. Too decent. Too well built. Too desired by other women. Bunny never got what everyone else wanted, only what no one else wanted. Leftovers. Some nights she'd be in bed next to him, listening to him snore, watching his chest rise and fall with each breath. She imagined she actually loved him and he loved her. Then she'd snap out of it, wonder if she should kick him out and get it over with.

She let him dump her instead because kicking him out would have taken planning and Bunny wasn't good at planning. She was better at watching things head her way and letting them happen.

Open. *Chink*. Close. *Chink*. Open. *Chink*. Close. *Chink*. He couldn't keep both hands on the wheel. Too nervous. Too jumpy. Not too high, though. He steered with his left hand and with his right pushed the switch on his stiletto. The blade shot out of the handle. A snake's tongue. Pointed and straight and narrow. He closed it and the snake's tongue darted back inside. He loved the *chink* sound it made. Metallic and mechanical at the same time. Open. *Chink*. Close. *Chink*. Open. *Chink*. Close. *Chink*. His forehead itched under his baseball cap. He reached up and scratched it with the knife handle. Scratched and scratched until it burned.

"Dammit," he muttered. He dropped the knife in his lap and turned the cap around so it was backward. On the back of the cap in embroidered script: *Elvis Has Left the Building*. He picked up the knife. Open. *Chink*. Close. *Chink*.

When he spotted her walking on the side of the road, he had that thought he always had after a bad day. After too many pills. After too many nights on the road. Alone and driving, driving, driving. A white-hot thought that burned his brain and warmed his body. The thought went this way: a small movement of the wrists and hands. No greater than the effort it takes to wave good-bye. Shoo away a wasp. Twist the gas cap off a car. Flip open a jackknife. A small, controlled movement. That's all it would take to flatten someone. A quick jerk of his steering wheel to the right and they would be finished. Gone. All they ever were. All they ever hoped to be. All their high-and-mighty dreams.

10

Crushed. Erased with the slightest movement of his hands. So breakable, the human body. Doesn't take much to do a lot of damage. Cripple. Kill someone.

Open. *Chink*. Close. *Chink*. She could be that someone. Open. *Chink*. He saw her weave a bit. She was drunk. He liked drunks. They made it easier. She dropped something. Shoes? She picked them up and kept walking. The dress was a perfect target. When his lights hit it, it glowed. A walking neon sign. HIT ME! He passed her slowly, took a right down a side street. He wanted to circle the block and drive by her again. Do a little calculating. Close. *Chink*. Open. *Chink*. Give it more consideration. Pop another pill. They always made him smarter. Braver, too. He closed the knife for good, shoved it in his pants pocket. He flipped on the interior light and looked over at the passenger's side. Shit. The top had come off the bottle. Pills all over the seat. He eyed the mess, hunting for the yellowish Adderall tablets. He picked out one and popped it in his mouth. Chewed. It tasted nasty, but chewing worked the amphetamines faster than swallowing whole. He grabbed his Coke cup and sucked on the straw. Watery dregs. How many was that tonight? Two? Three? Doesn't matter, he thought. As long as he felt wired for action. Gotta fly high this weekend to make up for the week. The week had been a black hole. Most of his work weeks were black holes; his life disappeared into them. Vanished without a trace. He flicked off the dome light.

He wouldn't think about flattening someone in a car. Cars were weak. Couldn't be trusted to handle even the smallest smack. His Ford truck could take it. It had taken it before. Trucks were his safe world. Didn't matter if he was driving them or working on them. Trucks recognized his talent. Bent to his will and skill. His red F150 had an extended cab and eight-foot box covered by a sturdy

11

topper. Brush guard across the front that protected the lights and grill. There'd be limited damage to the vehicle. Nothing he couldn't fix himself. If she went up on the hood, she might take the windshield with her. Again, no big deal. He'd get the hell out of town quick. Fix it when he got home. The surface conditions were right. Hard, dry road. There'd be no tracks. He'd drive away. Check the papers in the morning for her name. She probably deserved it. He figured most people deserved to get run over for one thing or another. Maybe it was for something they did that morning. Maybe it was for something mean they did years ago. Could be they forgot what they did wrong; that didn't make it right again. He wondered what she did. Decided he didn't care.

It would be a good night for Sweet Justice, coming as it did on the heels of a black hole week filled with mean people.

"The shop's limited on floor space."

"We're vendor downsizing."

"Does anyone wear dress shirts anymore?"

"Got flannel? Don't bother me if it ain't flannel."

"Read the sign. No solicitors. Take your shitty shirts outta here."

They were shitty shirts, and he knew it. That's what the side of his truck should read, he thought. GET YOUR SHITTY SHIRTS HERE. He pulled at the collar of his oxford. Stiff and new and scratchy. He hated wearing his own merchandise; all the salesmen had to pay for their own samples and it was a drain even at cost. He was too tall for most of the stuff and it never fit right, but he'd run out of clean clothes and didn't want to waste quarters at a Laundromat. He undid another button at the neck and the button came off in his hand. He tossed it onto the seat with the pills and muttered, "Shitty shirts."

He circled the block and saw her in his lights again. Fat ass taking up more than its share of the road. That dress. What was she, some old prom queen? Probably thinks she's hot shit. She deserved it, all right. He was coming up on her fast. His only hesitation was checking the rearview mirror to make sure there was no one behind him, and there wasn't. He clenched his teeth, tightened his grip on the steering wheel. Then something amazing happened. She stumbled and fell flat on her face. He couldn't believe how much she was helping him. "Now!" he said out loud. He gunned it and yanked the wheel to the right. He smiled at the satisfying *thump-thump* as the front right wheel rolled over her. Then the back right one. Another *thump-thump*. Solid sounds. He could feel them through his steering wheel. He said, "Perfect!"

He slowed and checked his rearview mirror. A smear on the side of the road. He punched off his lights and peeled away. He took the next right, drove a mile down the country road. He pulled over and turned off the engine. "Damn!" he said, and pounded the steering wheel with his fists. "Damn!" He threw his head back and exhaled while a shudder started at the top of his head and rippled down to his toes. He was panting. His heart was zooming. Patching out. Burning rubber. Such a rush. Such a high. Better than the best blow. Better than racing down the highway with all the windows rolled down and the needle pushing past eighty. Past ninety. Past a hundred. The prom queen didn't even squeal. Didn't have time. Lying drunk on the road one second, squished dead the next. He wondered how her face looked right as he nailed her. Longed to see that surprise. Mouth hanging open and pressed into the tar. He wished he could have heard her last words. Wondered what she squeaked as the life was pressed out of her. "Shit!" or "Help!" or "Fuck!" or maybe, simply, "No!" Did she

13

cry out for her ma or her pa or her lover? The eyes. He bet her eyes were so wide when he rolled over her they looked pure white, as if the pupils had popped out. He figured the prom queen had to be dead. Get back on the road and keep going, he told himself. Keep driving. Stopping is never smart. Someone could see him, see his truck pulled to the side. He hadn't checked carefully; there might be something caught on the tires. A bit of material. Someone could spot it. He told himself to savor the moment only a couple of minutes longer.

He wondered what else ever gave him such a high. Thought back to the last time he felt this good. Wasn't about pills or the road or his wheels. God, that was fun. An even bigger high than this high. That was glorious. He was a real fuckin' superhuman superhero. On top of a mountain on top of the world. He'd never get that back. Or could he? Maybe the dead prom queen could pull double duty. He punched his steering wheel again. "Hell, yeah!" he said. That'd serve Sweet Justice fine. He popped open the glove compartment and fished around for his sharpest knife. Decided the wire cutter would work better.

He pulled on some gloves. Worked quickly but carefully; he didn't want blood on his clothes. Kept his eyes peeled for other lights. If someone stopped, he'd tell them he found her there and was taking her to a hospital. Only two cars drove past. One right after the other while he was sliding her into the back. Their headlights scared the shit out of him, but neither car slowed. He figured the whole town was sleeping or out drinking. That was all there was to do in small towns late at night. He took out a bag of sand, part of the truck's winter gear. He emptied it over a spot of blood on the road. He pulled off the gloves. Checked the road one

14

last time with his flashlight. He'd almost left her shoes. He picked them up and tucked them inside the tarp with the body.

He didn't sleep at all Friday night. The Adderall did that. He gassed up the truck at a station off Interstate 35. Used the bathroom to wash his hands, wash the wire cutter, check his clothes. Grabbed a Coke. Paid for it and the gas. The tired clerk hardly gave him a look when she rung him up. He stepped outside and walked around the truck. He didn't see any blood or cloth on the tires. Noticed a sub shop next door to the gas station. He wasn't hungry. The Adderall did that, too. He leaned against the side of his truck, unscrewed the cap off the Coke and took a long drink. He had the driver's window opened a crack; a Judas Priest CD was pounding inside the car. Every once in a while he patted his jacket pocket to make sure her finger was still there, wrapped in plastic.

2

He wanted to hear what people were saying about the prom queen. Did they assume she was dead? Kidnapped? He decided to spend Saturday morning making sales calls in town. He wouldn't be an unusual figure; he'd called on most of the shops before. He walked into a clothing store with a box of individually packaged shirts and asked the clerk if he could see the store owner. The girl went into the back office. Toward the front of the store, two women were picking through a rack of Halloween costumes and talking about the missing woman. He listened while taking the shirts out of the box and stacking them on the counter.

"Spider-Man," said the fat one, holding up a nylon outfit of red and blue. She checked the price tag. "On sale. Twenty bucks. Size ten. Could fit your youngest."

"He was Spider-Man last year," said the skinny one. She kept shuffling through the rack. "What do you think happened to her?"

The fat one pulled out a Batman costume, stared at it for a few seconds and put it back. "Sleeping it off somewhere. I heard she got drunk as a skunk at the reception."

16

The skinny one held up a skeleton costume. "This one's got a rip. Maybe they'll knock off a couple of bucks."

The store owner came out of the office and shook her head. "Sorry. Not unless it's wool or flannel. Winter's on the way."

He scooped up the shirts and dropped them back in the box. "Thanks anyway." He slipped out the door and went to the truck.

By Saturday afternoon, he was congratulating himself. Hauling the body around with him was brilliant. The body would keep. He'd wrapped it in a tarp and it was cold enough outside to prevent it from rotting right away. The topper kept everything dry and out of the open. He wouldn't bury her until the cops had searched the area. Then he'd put the prom queen someplace they'd already covered. A place they'd never find her.

Bolstered by the amphetamines, he even had the guts to stop at a diner for coffee. He watched from the restaurant window while a sheriff's deputy walked down the sidewalk toward the truck. He held his breath and squeezed his coffee cup with both hands. The deputy walked right by without a glance. He exhaled and loosened his grip around the mug. He saw the waitress heading toward him and busied himself with the menu.

"How about a warm-up?"

He slid the cup toward her and she filled it. He raised his eyes as far as her name tag. "Thanks, B... B... Bonnie."

After his coffee he got a room in a motel outside of town. Water stains on the ceiling. Matted shag carpet. Sagging bed. Television with free cable that didn't work. Reminded him of every other motel he had ever stayed at while working sales. His first job was right after high school, peddling wholesale party goods. Plates, cups, napkins, streamers, balloons, piñatas. Great samples. Cheap

17

for him to buy and useful. He didn't do dishes the whole time he had that sales job. He and his old man would laugh as they sat down to dinner. "What are we celebrating tonight?" his pa would ask. They'd pull out birthday party plates or baby shower plates or Halloween plates. Then a string of other sales jobs, each ending with him getting fired or quitting. The one right before the shitty shirts was the worst—commercial cleaning supplies. He'd stand in bathrooms and squirt urinals with blue liquid or pink goop in an effort to convince janitors that his chemicals cleaned piss off porcelain better than some other guy's products. He would never be a good salesman no matter what he sold. Didn't have the personality for it. Couldn't look people in the eye and bullshit with them. Backed down as soon as someone said "no." He stuck with sales only because he loved riding around in his truck.

He threw his suitcase on the bed, opened it, rummaged around inside for her purse. He'd left her shoes wrapped up in the tarp with her body, but he wanted to check her handbag. Wondered what secrets were contained in a dead woman's belongings. He loosened the drawstring and tipped the bag upside down on the bed. Bobby pins. Lipstick. Kleenex. Comb. Couple of quarters. Three tiny vials; perfume samples. He opened one and sniffed. Lily of the valley. He put the cork back in and threw the bottle on the bed. Something was stuck in the bottom of the bag. He reached inside and pulled out a square of folded paper. Finally, he thought, a little mystery. He opened it. Immediately recognized the lyrics. "Can't Help Falling in Love." He'd come all this way to run over an Elvis fan when he could have had his pick of them back home. He refolded the paper and slipped it back in the handbag. He thought about throwing away the lipstick, perfumes and bobby pins, but instead returned them to the purse. He

18

put the quarters and comb in his pocket. He inspected the Kleenex. Clean. Put that in his pocket, too. He tightened the drawstrings on the purse and stuffed it into a dirty sock. He threw the sock back in the suitcase and closed it.

He went back into town for an early dinner; he finally had an appetite. By then, the flyers were up. He walked past the drugstore and saw the pharmacist taping one to the window. He read it through the plate glass. MISSING, it said. Below that was her photo and right beneath her photo, her name: *Bunny Pederson*. He hadn't heard her name while walking around town and it never occurred to him she had a name other than the nickname he'd given her. The poster gave her height and weight—no wonder he'd strained to lift her into the truck—and age. Only thirty? He thought she was older than that. Time hadn't been kind to Bunny Pederson's face or figure. Were she alive, she'd probably be one of those loser women who'd consider sleeping with him. A washed-up prom queen. The poster said she was dressed in a peach bridesmaid's dress and shoes. Carried a peach purse. Television is going to love that, he thought. A disappearing bridesmaid. That would be her new nickname: the bridesmaid. She was last seen leaving a wedding reception at a bar. That's where the whole town was Friday night, he thought. CALL THE MOOSE LAKE POLICE OR CARLTON COUNTY SHERIFF'S OFFICE. Below that, what he was waiting for: volunteers were meeting in a church basement to prepare for a Sunday morning search of the woods and fields in the area. He checked his watch; he could still make it.

* * *

19

He steered the truck into the church parking lot. Jammed with news vans; he'd read the media right. His heart raced. Already, it was starting. He patted his jacket pocket; the finger was still there.

3

"Pull!" said a husky female voice.

The clay pigeon thrown from the trap veered to the right. She aimed the barrel over the orange saucer and swung to the right, getting ahead of it. She counted to three in her head and squeezed the trigger. The disk exploded into a black cloud.

"Nice hit," said her shooting partner. The crack of other guns and the smell of gunpowder warmed the cold fall air. A busy Saturday at the range.

"Your turn," she said.

"Pull!" he said. His pigeon flew to the left and seemed to hang in midair for a moment, as if caught in an updraft. He pointed the barrel over the target and squeezed. The shot nicked off a sliver of orange and the rest of the disk fell to the ground. "Finally. A hit," he said.

"Barely," mumbled the teenage boy behind them. He was sitting in a chair keeping score. He ran the trap by pushing a button on a box he held in his palm. An extension cord connected the box to the concrete bunker that expelled the clays.

21

The man looked over his shoulder. "What'd you say, kid? Working on your tip?"

The boy grinned and started to say something, but it was lost in the rattle and whistle of a train crossing the nearby tracks.

"A chip's still a hit," the woman said over the noise. She slipped a shell into the chamber and pumped it forward. "Pull," she said. Another throw to the right. She started the barrel pointing behind the pigeon and swung it smoothly ahead until it was past the disk before squeezing the trigger. It shattered; another square hit.

The man slid a shell into the chamber, pumped and raised his shotgun. "Pull." He followed the target with the barrel. He closed his right eye and squeezed the trigger. A miss.

"Lost," said the scorer.

"What am I doing wrong here, Paris?"

She took off her safety glasses and shoved them into the pocket of her shooting vest. "First off, are you shutting one of your eyes?"

"Yeah. Sometimes."

"Don't. This is a shotgun, not a rifle." She pulled out her earplugs.

"Okay," he said. "What else?"

Paris Murphy walked over to the gun rack behind the teenager, leaned her gun against it and went over to her husband. A gust of wind rattled the trees on either side of the range and sent more leaves floating to the ground. Murphy regretted leaving her gloves at home and tucked her numb hands under her armpits.

"You're behind the pigeon when you should be in front of it." She stood behind him. Jack Ramier was tall, but his wife nearly matched his height. She was slender, with a narrow waist and hips, but had large breasts and a runner's

22

well-defined legs. She had long black hair, violet eyes framed by thick lashes and olive skin—traits from her Lebanese mother and Irish father. Her complexion was flawless except for a crescent moon scar on her forehead— a souvenir from her job as a St. Paul Homicide detective.

"And your form is all wrong," she said. She bumped the back of his legs with her knee. "Bend those knees, Jack. Relax. You're not performing surgery." Jack was an emergency room doctor at Regions Hospital downtown. "Put your left foot slightly forward. Keep your feet shoulder-width apart." She put her hands on his hips. "Lean forward a little at the waist."

"You're getting me hot, wife."

"Not in front of the kid."

"This isn't fair. You handle a gun all day long."

"Stays in my purse ninety-nine percent of the time."

"You've had training."

"I've given you training."

"I'll say you have." He turned and winked at her. He had curly brown hair and brown eyes that never failed to get her attention.

"Watch that muzzle control," she said lowly. "Wouldn't want your gun going off prematurely. Save something for tonight."

"I got plenty of ammo," he said, and they both laughed.

"You finished or what?" asked the boy behind them.

"We're finished." Murphy rubbed her hands together. "I'm cold, Jack. Give him a couple of bucks and let's go inside. Sun's going down anyway."

Jack pulled three ones out of his pocket and handed them to the teenager. He set his gun next to his wife's.

"You sure the chamber's empty?" she asked.

He picked up his gun and checked. "Chamber empty. Safety on."

23

"Good."

He set the gun back on the rack. "I'm a quick study." He shoved his glasses and plugs into his vest pocket.

"Yeah. Right. Don't quit your day job."

He smiled and followed her into the South St. Paul Rod and Gun clubhouse, a building that resembled a ranch-style house with a deck attached. The Mississippi River snaked in front of it and railroad tracks cut behind it. It was a block off Concord, a long street connecting the city of St. Paul and the suburb of South St. Paul. The gun club shared the neighborhood with a furniture liquidator, a used-car lot, a beauty shop and a Dairy Queen.

Murphy checked the bulletin board inside the clubhouse door. Covered with handwritten index cards and flyers: "Beretta AL390 Gold Mallard 20 GA. $725." "Custom Docks. Call for an estimate." "4×10 Utility Trailer made by Cargo. ALMOST NEW. Drop down ramp. $900." "Lab choc. M. AKC Exc. bird dog. $2,500." "FOR SALE. Remington 870. Nice clean gun. $450." "German Wire-Haired Pups. AKC. Exc. Blood Lines. MAKE GOOD HUNTERS/FAMILY PETS. $500."

"Decent price," Murphy muttered. She grabbed a bar napkin and wrote down a phone number.

"Shopping for a gun?" asked Jack, looking over her shoulder.

"A dog."

"Since when? You're not home enough. Your place is too small. A dog would go stir-crazy on that dinky house-boat. It'd chew the shit out of everything."

"Stop hyperventilating." She shoved the napkin into the pocket of her jeans. "We'll discuss it over a beer."

It didn't take much to turn their discussions into arguments, and that's why they periodically separated. In their eight years of marriage, they'd lived apart as much as they'd lived together. Jack stayed in the house they'd bought together when they first got married. She had a houseboat on the Mississippi River, moored across from downtown at the St. Paul Yacht Club. They kept trying to make their marriage work and were most successful in the bedroom; they never argued about sex.

All the tables were taken; they found two stools next to each other at the bar. "What can I get you?" asked the bartender. He was a big man with curly red hair, a red beard and a red flannel shirt. He could have passed for a lumberjack.

"Grain Belt," said Murphy.

"St. Pauli Girl," said Jack.

"No imports."

"Grain Belt then."

The bartender set two cans on the bar. "Sign up for the big shoot?" He thumbed toward a flyer behind the bar: MINI JACKPOT TRAP SHOOT.

Murphy took a bump off her beer. "You betcha."

He eyed Jack. "You that ringer she been threatening to bring in?"

Murphy laughed and then coughed and held a napkin to her face; she felt beer coming up her nose. Jack glared at her. She cleared her throat. "No," she said. She blew her nose and took another sip of beer. "This is my husband, Jack. Jack, this is Gunnar."

"Gunner?"

"Gunnar," said the bartender, without smiling. He walked to the other end of the bar.

"Isn't that what I said?"

"No. Gunnar is Norwegian or something. Gunner is . . . I don't know . . . a good name for a hunting dog maybe."

"Back to the dog, are we?"

"I'm the only one in my family without a dog." She had nine brothers, no sisters.

25

"Your siblings are nuts. You can't eat dinner at their houses without swallowing a pound of fur. Rawhide bones everywhere. Yards all tore up. They live in giant kennels."

"I'll be sure to pass that compliment on to my brothers—and their wives." She frowned and brushed the hair from her forehead with her fingertips. She wasn't comfortable with bangs. Jack said he found them attractive, told her she looked like Cleopatra. She used to wear her hair parted down the middle and pulled back. She got bangs over the summer to help cover the scar, a constant reminder of the fight she'd gotten into with a killer.

Jack popped open his beer and took a sip. "Forget the damn dog. Dog's a bad idea."

She didn't answer. She turned in her stool to see who she knew in the bar. The room had paneled walls, a low ceiling and was cloudy with smoke. Four guys in camouflage jackets were at a table playing cards and puffing on cigarettes. She recognized a couple of them. Retired towboat crew. Her family used to run a bar along the Mississippi that served river workers. The two men saw her and nodded. Another table was filled with guys in blaze orange caps. They were hunkered over a map, planning a deer hunt. Murphy was envious. She wished Jack was more of a hunter. Maybe she could get out this season with her brothers.

She turned around to sip her beer. The television behind the bar was turned to the news. Gunnar walked over to switch channels when a female reporter came on. She was standing in front of a church, interviewing a tall man. "Stop," Murphy said. She strained to listen. "Turn it up."

"One of your cases?" asked Gunnar.

Murphy didn't answer. She stared at the screen. The reporter was talking about how the tall guy was a traveling salesman who'd volunteered to join a search party. They were looking for a Moose Lake woman who'd disappeared Friday night after a wedding. "A bridesmaid who vanished," the reporter said. She emphasized the word *bridesmaid* to show it made the story different. Special.

Jack watched his wife's face. "What is it, Paris?"

"I recognize him."

"From where? Work?"

"No. Can't remember exactly. But not work."

"Fuckin' tall as a house," said Gunnar. He grabbed a bar rag and wiped the counter.

Murphy studied the man while he continued talking to the reporter about why he'd volunteered, how he'd wanted to help. His face was pale and smooth and his eyes dark. His lips were full. Almost a woman's mouth. He had black, slicked-back hair. In a strange way, he was attractive. Seductive. He looked like a vampire from a black-and-white movie. His left ear was weird. Looked as if he had two lobes. Some kind of accident? More familiar than his face was his voice. He had a trace of southern drawl, and a stutter. She could tell he was concentrating on his speech, pausing at words that were threatening to turn into a problem. Who did she know with a stutter? No one came to mind.

"Hey!" yelled one of the deer hunters. "How about some ESPN instead of this crap?"

"Yeah. Yeah. Keep your shirt on." Gunnar walked over to the television and switched channels.

Murphy rubbed her arms; she had goose bumps under her sweatshirt, but not from the cold. Talking more to herself than to Jack: "I know him. How do I know him?"

Jack drained his can and set it down. "How about some dinner, babe? Something from that Mexican market down the road. I could go for some beans and rice."

"I've got stuff in the fridge," she said. She took one more sip of beer and slid off the bar stool. "Let's get the guns and get outta here."

4

The school bus rattled down the road, kicking up a cloud that trailed behind like a phantom. The bus lurched to a halt and the dust ghost disappeared into the gravel. Thirty-three people in jeans and sweatshirts filed out, calling out the number each had been assigned before boarding the bus.

"One."

"Two."

"Three."

"Four."

"Five."

Men. Women. Seniors. Middle-aged folks. A couple of teenagers. A few had water bottles strapped to their waists and candy bars shoved in their pockets; they were the ones who'd done this before and knew they'd get thirsty and hungry out in the field. They squinted in the fall light and wrinkled their noses. The air smelled of skunk. All wore coats or down vests over their sweatshirts and some donned mittens and stocking caps. The sunshine was deceptive; it was raw outside. Gusts of wind bent the tall grasses and blew the remaining leaves off the trees. It could have been

December instead of October. Last off the bus was a sheriff's deputy, a short, husky woman. "Number One takes the ditch along the road and the rest of you follow him in order," she said.

The civilians lined up in firing-squad formation at one end of the meadow. They stretched their arms out so they'd be spaced apart evenly. Number One was the tallest in the crowd by two heads. The ditch was knee-deep, but when he stepped into it he still towered over the deputy and half the others in the group. The deputy studied his feet. "Hope those are decent boots," she said. The ditch was swampy.

"Sorels," he said. "I know how to d... dress, ma'am."

"Guess you do," she said. She noticed his baseball cap. A suede brim and *E.P.* embroidered on the front. "Those your initials?"

"Elvis Presley," he mumbled. He shoved his hands into the pockets of his leather jacket and averted his eyes.

He's a weird one, she thought. She turned her attention to the rest of the group, eyed the row of volunteers. She wished she had someone as tall as Number One anchoring the other end, and the middle for that matter. The middle man kept the line straight. No matter, she thought. It was the second day. Missing people cases go bad after two days. Same as fresh fish in the fridge. After two days, the missing become the dead and clues turn cold. It would be a miracle if they found anything useful out here.

"Ready?" They all nodded. "Let's go," she said. The line started moving. The deputy walked behind them, surveying the evenness of the line. The speed. "Slow down, people," she hollered. "This ain't a race. Wait for the middle to catch up while they go through that brush. Take your time." No one talked. They kept their eyes down as they walked, searching for something. Anything. A strand of thread from her dress. Footprints. Bobby pin from her hair.

A crow landed on a tree stump ahead of the line, eyed the humans heading toward it and cawed. A woman—Number Fourteen—looked up. "No bird-watching," said the deputy, and a few in the line laughed. Then another stretch of walking and no talking in the line. The sound of boots crunching down dried grass and leaves. A menacing noise. The sound of an invading army. Halfway across the field, Number Seventeen caught the toe of his boot on a rock and fell on his face. He stood up and spit out dirt and weeds. The line stopped while he brushed off.

"You okay?" asked the deputy.

"Yeah, yeah," he said, red-faced.

The line continued moving. They'd nearly reached the end of the meadow when a yell went up.

"Found something!"

"Everyone stop. Now," said the deputy. She ran to Number One. He had his right hand raised like a kid at school and his left pointed to the ground. Her eyes followed to where he was pointing. She squatted down. Couldn't believe what she saw.

"Shit," she breathed. A finger. Peach polish on the nail.

"Stay where you're at!" she yelled to the line. Then, so only he and those next to him could hear, she said lowly, "Good eye, Number One." The deputy stayed hunched over the finger while she radioed for help.

Number Two, a pretty blond woman, kept her place in the line but turned her back to the finger. Stared up at the sky.

"You okay, ma'am?" Number One asked in a low voice.

"Sorry I'm such a baby," she whispered.

"N... no," he said. "You're doing fine."

She turned to face him and touched his arm. "Thank you."

31

He lowered his eyes and nodded. His heart raced. He tried to keep from breathing fast. Tried to keep from grinning. He covered his mouth with his hand, pretended to cough. Don't grin, he told himself. This wouldn't be the time or the place for grinning. It would peg him as a creep, and it would tip them off.

5

Sunday afternoon Jack relaxed on the deck off the living room while Murphy chopped and mixed in the galley. Every time they had a quiet moment, she wondered if she should tell him about the affair she'd had over the summer. The urge to confess was overwhelming; she blamed it on her Catholic upbringing. That morning she'd gone to the cathedral without him. All during mass she'd thought about their marriage, their problems. She scanned the pews in the cavernous church. Saw couples worshiping together. Families. The fact that he wasn't next to her in the pew spoke of one of their differences.

When she was growing up, Sunday mass and meals were a big deal for the Murphy clan. She and her mother would be up before church preparing the feast. They'd make Lebanese flatbread from scratch. The first loaf out of the oven would be theirs. They'd spread butter on the hot bread and wash it down with mint tea. The smell of baking would fill the house and rouse the males out of bed. They'd all attend morning mass together, filling up two pews. After church came a family meal that seemed to last all day. Jack was raised differently. He was the only child of two University of

Minnesota professors. They seldom went to church and rarely cooked. Jack's childhood memories of Sundays involved sleeping late and going out for brunch at a restaurant. Murphy didn't relish visiting his parents in their upscale St. Anthony Park neighborhood. Their house was too quiet and the copper pots they had hanging in their kitchen were covered with dust. Murphy thought there was something sacrilegious about buying nice cookware and using it solely for decoration. Jack was equally uncomfortable in her childhood home. Holidays were especially crazy with her brothers' wives and children added to the mix. More than one Thanksgiving she'd found Jack sitting alone on the back porch. "Too much noise," he'd mutter.

She watched him sitting on her deck, his feet up on the rail and a Sunday paper next to his chair. She went over to the refrigerator and stood in front of it, hand on the door handle. She ordered herself to go out on the deck and spill her guts. She stood still for a moment, and then pulled open the door and reached for the tomatoes. She told herself she'd unload her conscience on another day. She slammed the door shut and returned her attention to something she could control: the food.

She was glad she had all the ingredients on hand for tabbouleh:

Half cup of bulgur (cracked wheat)
Four cups of chopped parsley (no stems)
Two medium tomatoes, diced
Half cup of finely chopped green onions (including tops)
Quarter cup of finely chopped fresh mint
Quarter cup of extra virgin olive oil
Quarter cup of freshly squeezed lemon juice
One teaspoon of salt
Half teaspoon of pepper

34

She covered the cracked wheat with lukewarm water and let it soak until it was soft—about twenty minutes. She drained it and squeezed it with her hands to get out as much water as possible. She tossed the bulgur with the other ingredients and chilled the salad in a covered bowl while she made the rest of the meal.

They ate in the galley; it was too cold to dine on the deck. After lunch, he sprawled out on the couch to watch the Vikings game while she cleaned up. The galley was separated from the living room by a counter. He scrutinized her camel statues, figurines and pillows. "Where'd you get that big wooden one?" he asked. It had a leather saddle and was nearly a foot tall.

She was loading the dishwasher and froze with a plate in her hand. "What'd you say?" She was glad he couldn't see her face.

"Never mind," he mumbled.

She heard snoring a few seconds later and was relieved. She finished loading the dishwasher. The camel was a gift from Erik Mason, an investigator for the Ramsey County Medical Examiner's Office. She hadn't thought Jack would notice a new addition to her collection.

That night Murphy and Jack sat up in bed; he was in his boxers and she was in an oversized Old Navy tee shirt. She had the remote and switched from one channel to the other. The tall guy was all over the ten o'clock news; every station led with him. He'd uncovered a clue during the search, and now the Moose Lake cops knew it was murder. Murphy stopped at one station. The reporter tipped her head toward the tall guy, as if the two of them were sharing a secret. "And what did you find?" The way she asked the question—slowly and dramatically—made it clear she already knew the answer.

The guy paused and swallowed. The camera closed in on

35

his face. He was looking off to the side, as if he was shy, and rubbing the brim of a baseball cap he held in his hands. "A finger. Her p... pinkie, I think."

"A final question," said the reporter. "Is there anything you want to say to the person or persons who did this to Bunny Pederson?"

For the first time he looked up and into the camera. "Turn yourself in and tell the p... police where you buried her, or you'll never be able to sleep at n... night."

The reporter: "Will you be able to sleep tonight, after that horrible find? Expecting nightmares?"

He smiled, head lowered again. "I'll be fine, ma'am."

"Thank you, Mr. Trip. Back to you in the newsroom, Blake."

"Trip." Murphy said. "Why is that name so damn familiar?" She switched from station to station until she finally caught his full name: Justice Trip. "Bastard's every-where," she said. "Dammit. I wish I could remember."

Jack grabbed the remote and pulled it out of her hands. "Why'd you put a set up here when you've already got one downstairs? I don't like a television in the bedroom."

"Fine. Then don't put one in *your* bedroom." She grabbed the remote back and switched to another channel. Justice Trip on that news station as well. She studied his face; that weird earlobe. She said suddenly, "Wait. I know how I know him. Sweet Justice." She threw the remote at Jack and hopped out of bed.

"Babe. It can wait," he yelled after her. "Who gives a shit?"

She thumped down the stairs. He heard her opening and closing cupboard doors and throwing stuff around while talking to herself. "Where is it? I just had it out." She ran back upstairs and climbed under the covers; it was cold downstairs and her feet were icy. She tucked them under Jack's legs.

Jack looked over her shoulder while she flipped through the slender volume. "What's this?"

"St. Brice High yearbook."

"You went to school with him?" Jack nodded toward the television. Trip was still on the screen, but Jack had hit the mute button.

"Yup." She pointed to his photo. In the sea of grinning teenage faces, Trip's stood out for its dark seriousness.

"What made you think of him? You don't see any of your old high school friends."

"All-class reunion coming up. Anniversary of the founding of the school."

"You're going without me, I hope."

"Without you," she said. "But I would have remembered Trip regardless. Hard to forget. He asked me to the homecoming dance one year."

"Didn't know your standards were so low."

"Funny." She elbowed him in the ribs. "Didn't go with him. Didn't go at all that year." She stopped paging for a minute and stared straight ahead. Remembering. "The guy I should have gone with . . . Denny . . . we had a fight. Made up after homecoming. Were planning on prom. He died that winter. With three other boys. Car accident. They'd been drinking. Roads were slick. Went off a curve and into a lake." She turned to the first page of the yearbook and showed Jack the dedication. A photo of four boys in letter jackets. Grinning. Arms thrown around each other's shoulders. Below that, lines from Longfellow:

We see but dimly through the mists and vapors;
Amid these earthly damps
What seem to us but sad, funereal tapers
May be heaven's distant lamps.

Jack: "Four kids. Big loss, especially for a small school."

"Horrible. I'll always regret missing that homecoming dance with Denny."

"What was the fight about?"

"Denny and his buddies beat up Sweet because he asked me out."

"Sweet?"

"Trip's nickname. One of the nicer ones. Another was Motorhead. Trippy. Freak."

"Nice school you went to."

"Small schools don't have a lot of choices when it comes to cliques. If you don't fit into one of a handful of groups, then you don't fit in at all. Sweet was one of those kids who fell between the cracks. His creepy personality didn't help him out. Check out what he wrote in my yearbook." She turned to the last page and pointed to a neatly printed message in the upper right corner:

What goes around comes around, beautiful. Sweet Justice.

Jack's eyes widened. "Damn."

"Yeah. I'm sure he blamed me for the beating. I never had the courage to talk to him again, tell him it wasn't my doing."

"Maybe the reunion."

"I don't think Sweet's one of those sentimental alums who misses the old gang."

"What was your nickname?"

She turned to the section of the book with individual student photos and pointed to a line under hers: "A.k.a. Camel Rider, Potato Head and Betty."

"I get the first two. What's with Betty?"

"Private joke between me and Denny. He was a closet *Flintstones* fan. He'd shut the door to his bedroom after school and watch. He told me I was his Betty. I gave him a *Flintstones* coffee mug. He kept it in his car. Filled it with change. I know it sounds stupid, but I wanted it back when they recovered his car. It was gone. Probably sitting at the bottom of the lake." She closed the yearbook and set it on her nightstand.

Jack shut off the television and handed her the remote. "Put this away, too. Bedrooms should be reserved for screwing and sleeping."

"In that order?" She threw the remote on her nightstand.

"Bet your ass in that order."

"Talk's cheap, baby." She slid down so she was flat on her back. He reached over and shut off the bedside lamp. He peeled off his boxers and leaned over her and pulled her tee shirt over her head. Jack crawled on top of her. She loved the weight and warmth of him; it was like being buried in sand at the beach. Hot and heavy and wet.

A passing barge pushed waves against the boat, but they didn't notice. The rocking seemed part of the rhythm of their lovemaking.

6

What a rush it had been. Being fawned over. Fought over. "I get the first live shot . . . Bullshit. I was here first . . . I set this up before you got here." Treated with respect. Treated like someone with a mind. Called "Mister" every time he turned around. "You're doing fine, Mr. Trip . . . Thank you for your time, Mr. Trip . . . How can we reach you later, Mr. Trip?" He was finished with all the television interviews by a little after ten o'clock Sunday night. Finally got to pull his hat back on. They didn't go for his hat. Told him to take it off for the on-camera interviews. They said they couldn't see his face when he had the hat on. He took it off to please the reporters. Especially the pretty women. All his life—with one exception—just the homely ones went for him, and then only when they were lonely. He'd slept with a lot of ugly, depressed women. He liked being liked by attractive women, and being liked by more than one person at any one time was a complete novelty.

The only other time he'd been showered with that sort of group approval was when he found that little girl's necklace. A few years earlier. A Wisconsin town, outside of Eau Claire. The maintenance engineer for a manufacturing

40

company said he'd buy a couple of five-gallon buckets of degreaser and a bunch of mops if Trip would help comb a farmer's cornfield for a missing kid. Reluctantly, he went along. A hot August afternoon, and the corn was tall. He'd bent over to tie his shoes in between the rows and found the child's jewelry. Then the cops found the kid. Alive. Then it started. Newspaper interviews. People stopping him on the sidewalk and shaking his hand. Strangers in the bar slapping him on the back, buying him beer. At first he was terrified of the fuss. Tried to numb his nerves with booze and pills. Took someone out one night when he wasn't prepared. He wanted to leave town right away, but there were too many reporters waiting for interviews. He didn't want to raise suspicions. He got scared when a cop noticed his cracked windshield the next day, but a couple of people stood up for him. Said the crack had been there all along. He'd never had anyone stand up for him like that. Not since Snow White. That's when he warmed up to the attention, discovered it wasn't so bad if it was positive. The town's mayor, who owned a trophy shop, even gave him an award with his name engraved on it. A bowling trophy. The message said: *Thank you, Justice Trip. You bowled us over with your help*. Probably a leftover from a bowling tournament, but Trip didn't care. He'd never before won a prize for anything.

Most of his thirty-six years, he'd been afraid of any sort of attention. Self-conscious about his height—nearly seven feet—he walked hunched over. He stared down because looking up never got him anything but whispers and stares. Even in kindergarten he was big, and he was so afraid to draw attention to himself he'd pee in his pants rather than raise his hand and ask to go to the bathroom.

41

He finally trained himself to go without water all day. Everyone expected him to play basketball when he got older, but he got tangled in his own legs. He was smart, but doing well in class would have drawn attention. He worked at mediocrity and kept his grades to Cs. Worst of all was the teasing about his stutter. The more the other kids teased, the worse it got. He'd try to go all day without talking. Then he'd hear: "What's wrong? The c... c... cat g... got your t... t... tongue?" When he'd come home from school crying because of the mean kids, Pa would tell him they'd get theirs. He'd say, "What goes around comes around."

His pa was tall, too, but he carried it well. Trip didn't know what his ma was like; his pa had burned all her pictures right after Trip was born. All he knew was her name. Anna. Whenever he asked about her, his pa would say, "Ran off with your big sister. That's all I know." Same words every time. All Trip knew about his big sister was her name. Mary. Two names. Anna and Mary. The only history Trip ever had of his immediate kin. When he was ten, he found a photo in a kitchen drawer, under the paper liner. Nothing written on the back. He assumed it was his sister. Black hair. Nice skin. Dark eyes. She was in a frilly dress. His pa found him holding the picture, ripped it out of his hands and shoved it in the sink.

"That my s... s... sister? That Mary?"

His pa's answer was to turn on the garbage disposal.

Most days he and his pa got along. They were both neat. Kept the house fine. Neither one could cook worth a damn; ate a lot of TV dinners and instant oatmeal. Certain holidays, such as the Fourth of July and Flag Day and Halloween, his pa dressed in a white jumpsuit and passed out Fudgsicles from the front porch while "All Shook Up" blared from the cassette player. He'd make Trip wear a cowboy outfit: hat, vest, bandanna, spurs, holster, plastic six-shooter. That way his pa had his two favorites on the porch: Elvis and cowboys. The routine was supposed to be for the neighborhood kids, but the women came around, too. Pa charmed them. Called them all "ma'am," whether they were junior-high girls or grandmas. His pa craved an audience the way Trip feared it. He was relieved when he finally outgrew the cowboy clothes.

Trip couldn't decide if his life would have been better or worse if he hadn't spent his childhood in the shadow of Graceland. His pa sold bootleg Elvis Presley paraphernalia at a strip mall in Memphis, right across the street from Graceland. Bumper stickers. Snow globes. Shirts. Hats. Action figures. Backscratchers. Salt and pepper shakers. The shop was a weird place to be when Elvis was alive. Always full of tourists talking about *The King. The King. The King.* When he was real young, Trip thought they were talking about Jesus because he'd heard about The King of the Jews in Sunday school. He thought Jesus starred in *Jailhouse Rock* and sang "Love Me Tender," and wondered if The King was crucified and went to heaven, why was he still living in the big house across the street. The shop got weirder after Elvis died, and busier. His pa struggled to keep up. The stock of souvenirs multiplied nearly overnight; floor-to-ceiling snow globes and backscratchers. The stuff flew off the shelves, but the fans doing the buying weren't happy anymore. They were all bawling when they came into the store, and his pa would bawl with them. Trip didn't like any of it; he hid in the stockroom. His pa would yell for him: "Make yourself worthwhile." The store became a jumbled mess.

Then his pa hired Snow White.

Cammie Lammont had skin the color of eggshells and black hair that reached down to her butt. She walked into

43

the shop carrying a suitcase and wearing sunglasses and a wide-brimmed straw hat; she could have been a starlet on the run from her fans. Her dress was spray-painted on. She was nearly as tall as Trip, but she carried herself like a queen. Nose in the air. Back straight as an ironing board. She ripped the Help Wanted sign they'd posted in the shop window and brought it over to his pa. "Meet your help," she said, and slapped the sign on the counter. When she took off her sunglasses, the expression on his pa's face was strange. A combination of surprise and fear and curiosity. She moved in with them. Took the spare bedroom. She couldn't cook and she didn't know spit about Elvis, but she managed the inventory and did the bookkeeping. She saved the shop. His pa gave her a baseball hat on her six-month anniversary. She eyed the cap with suspicion. "What's this E.P. stand for?" Trip thought his pa was going to pass out.

She was Trip's first crush, and she knew it. She'd laugh and tell him, "For all you know, I'm old enough to be your mama." Cammie was one of those women who slathered on the makeup and kept her age a big secret. She told him she'd run away from home because her ma's boyfriend tried to get into her pants, so Trip suspected she wasn't that much older than he. Still, she didn't dress or act much like a teenager and she had a hard edge. She didn't laugh or smile much, but she was good to him. Called him "Sweet Justice" or "Sweet." She didn't mind his stutter. Told him she used to stutter. He didn't believe her; to his ears, she articulated like a radio announcer. They'd go to movies together. Cartoons. She loved anything by Walt Disney. One night some older kids from school saw the two of them together. She caught them giving Trip dirty looks. She grabbed his ass in front of them and kissed him hard on the mouth. One of them dropped his popcorn. Trip loved her for it. She took him to a motel after the movie. He was fourteen. Not long after, Cammie and Pa had an argument. Trip heard them yelling at each other one night, then Cammie crying. Trip rolled over and went to sleep. Cammie was one for dramatics. He figured the fight was over the bookkeeping. They always fought over the bookkeeping. Pa thought Cammie was doing a little skimming; he kept her on anyway. Whatever she was holding over his pa's head, Trip was glad for it.

She was with them about a year, until she was struck by a car one autumn night while walking home from the shop. She'd left Trip's pa behind to close up. Dark side street. No witnesses. Paramedics said she might have lived had they gotten to her a little sooner. Had the driver stopped and summoned help. The police never caught who did it. The only clues were two quarters wiped clean of prints. One placed on each side of her head. Cops guessed whoever killed her left the money as some kind of final insult, like she was a two-bit whore or something. Trip imagined the accident. Played it over and over in his head. In his mind's eye, she was run over by a car filled with jealous teenagers like the ones at the movie theater. Sometimes they were headed to a dance and other times they were coming back from a football game. Always ended the same, though. Snow White sprawled on the street. Coins tossed out of a car window. Laughter coming from the car as it squealed away.

His pa was as broken up as he was. Trip wondered if they'd had another fight that night and that's why she stomped off. When Trip asked him what had happened, the response was nearly the same as when he asked about his missing ma: "Ran off. That's all I know." His pa shipped her body down to Baton Rouge, where he said she had family. Trip wanted to go to the funeral but his old man told him they were headed in the other direction. They sold everything and moved to Minnesota—about as far north as they could drive without leaving the country. They kept a few Elvis souvenirs. A snow globe with a miniature of Graceland inside. A box of cigarette lighters engraved with a line drawing of Graceland. A clock with The King's swinging legs as the pendulum. A green street sign that said *Elvis Presley Boulevard*. Trip made sure he took her *E.P.* hat; it carried her smell. Herbal shampoo and Charlie cologne.

His pa got work cleaning a Catholic high school in St. Paul. The principal gave Trip free tuition. Wasn't any better or worse than public school in Tennessee. Like back in Memphis, the other students teased him about his stutter. They had the additional ammunition of his pa being the janitor. His accent was the biggest, easiest target, however. Between classes, the meanest ones yelled stuff down the hall in an exaggerated southern drawl. *Yew-all* this and *yew-all* that. *How yew-all doin', b... b... boy? Yew-all eat g... g... grits, b... b... boy?* He worked on it and toned down his accent, but there was nothing he could do about his stutter. He'd had it all his life, since he could remember. Even in his dreams he stuttered. In elementary school, the nurse tried to get Trip some speech therapy, but his pa wouldn't go for it. Said it would be a waste of time because stuttering ran in the family. Nothing to be done about it. Trip wondered what his pa was talking about; he didn't know any relatives who talked like he did.

At home, Trip hid under the hood of a truck. All the neighbors in the trailer park brought their beaters to him and he worked on them until they purred. He loved it. Trucks didn't care whether he could dribble a basketball or what he sounded like when he opened his mouth. All they recognized was his skill and genius at work on their engines and bodies. Behind the wheel of a truck, up so high off the ground, he didn't have to look anybody in the face. The money he earned fixing trucks he spent on his own trucks, and on drugs and knives.

He loved fancy knives. Sharp and flashy, the way he wished he could be in public. His pa thought the knives were a waste, wanted him to get into hunting. "Buy a shotgun. Something worthwhile," he'd tell Trip. His room had piles of catalogs with knives and swords and daggers in them. He ordered hundreds of them so there were always packages with wonderful surprises arriving at his door. Samurai swords. Battle-axes. Throwing knives. Daggers with dragons carved on the handle. Machetes. Folding knives. Stilettos. Bowie knives. A set of jackknives with Confederate officers etched on the handles, including General Robert E. Lee. He surrounded himself with his collection; they were his closest friends since Cammie. They hung on the walls of his room and rested in different wooden cases under his bed. At night, he'd spend hours getting stoned and listening to Black Sabbath and getting those blades sharper. Loved putting a good edge on a blade while listening to his music. Sharp metal and heavy metal.

7

Murphy got up before Jack to go for a run. Pulled on some sweats and a stocking cap and her shoes. Went out onto the dock, shutting the door quietly behind her. While she stretched she searched the decks of her nearest neighbors and saw signs of cold weather preparations. Covers draped over grills. Patio flowerpots emptied. Those who were planning to stay the winter but didn't have well-insulated houseboats were already wrapping their exteriors in plastic. She'd recently beefed up her insulation to avoid doing that this year—one bit of practical maintenance she'd managed to accomplish. She wondered which of her neighbors would tough out another winter on the river and which would lock up their boats and get an apartment downtown. The cold didn't get to them as much as the isolation. Even in the summer, not many people lived on the river full-time. In the winter, the numbers dropped to a hardy few. The wildlife artist and his photographer wife would stay; they utilized the scenery for their work. The architect would stay; his well-equipped boat even had a Jacuzzi in the master bath. She hoped Floyd Kvaal and his three-legged dog, Tripod, would stay another winter. Kvaal was a garage-door salesman and a musician. In the summer, he paddled his canoe around the neighborhood and played the sax. Last winter, the neighbors took turns having him play at their houses.

She finished stretching and thumped down the dock and through the parking lot. Took one of her usual routes. North across the Wabasha Bridge, glancing down at the Mississippi as she crossed it. The leaves on the trees lining the river were orange and yellow and rust. A gray morning. Cold and windy. She ran through downtown to the State Capitol mall. Fallen leaves crunched under her feet. Back south down Wabasha. For variety, she took a left at Kellogg Boulevard and cut through the riverfront park to run across the Robert Street Bridge. She looked downriver as she ran. Jammed with barges. Soon enough they'd be gone, chased south by the ice. She hung a right on Plato Boulevard and watched for trains as she went across the railroad tracks. North up Wabasha and a left onto Harriet Island. A couple of weeks had passed since the Twin Cities Marathon. It had been a good race for her—she'd come in at 3:41—but it left her sore and she was having trouble going back to a regular running schedule.

She started walking when she got to the yacht club parking lot. Thumping toward her boat, she spotted her copy of the *St. Paul Pioneer Press* in the middle of the dock. The paper carrier was getting better; at least it wasn't floating in the water this time. She bent over to retrieve it, stood up, inhaled the river air. What did it smell like today? Some days it smelled like dead fish. Other days, motor oil. On rare occasions, like something fresh and clean. She didn't mind. Murphy loved living on a working river jammed with barges and towboats. Sure there were speedboats and paddleboats and rowboats, but they all knew to steer clear of the metal behemoths that ruled the

Mississippi. She couldn't imagine living on a body of water without the barge traffic. Too quiet and boring. She tucked the paper under her arm, walked into the boat, heard the shower upstairs. Damn. He'd beaten her into the bathroom. She'd have to put a shower in the downstairs guest bath one of these days. She turned on the coffeemaker and scanned the paper while the pot dripped. There he was again. Justice Trip. On the front page, above the fold. She stared at his photo. "Sweet Justice," she said. She poured herself a cup and sat down at the kitchen table to read the story. Trip was a shirt salesman. He traveled around northern Minnesota and western Wisconsin selling shirts to clothing stores in small towns. He'd helped during a search years ago. A Wisconsin town. A missing girl. He found her necklace in a cornfield. The cops concentrated their search and found the child at the edge of the field. Dehydrated but alive. It made him feel good, he said in the story, and he wished this search had the same happy ending. "But it doesn't look good," he said.

"No shit," Murphy said.

Jack walked downstairs while digging in his ears with a Q-Tip. "Talking to yourself? You're losing it, lady." He bent over and nibbled on her neck. He saw the front page spread out on the table. "They're sure making a big deal out of him."

"Something isn't right; these stories aren't the whole story," she said, more to herself than to Jack.

He walked over to the coffeepot and poured a cup. "How so?"

"The way Sweet's portraying himself. It's as if he's talking about someone else. Some character he made up."

Jack leaned against the counter and sipped his coffee. "I'm sure we'd all exaggerate, try to make ourselves sound better in the newspaper."

"Genuine good guys are embarrassed when people call them heroes, especially on the front page. Sweet's wallowing in it. Promoting himself. He was never that way."

"That was high school. People change." Jack took another sip of coffee.

"Look here. He's talking about how he feels a connection to this Bunny Pederson because she was an Elvis fan. Who says she was an Elvis fan? And he hates Elvis. Heavy metal was his music He's constructed this bizarre fantasy world."

Jack set his coffee cup in the sink. "Her music tastes aside, anything else new about the unfortunate owner of the finger?"

Murphy folded the paper and set it down. "They ran out of stuff to say about the disappearing bridesmaid. Sweet's the latest angle, you know."

"On that cynical note, I'm outta here." He pulled on his jacket.

"What about breakfast? I've got omelet fixings."

"Nope. Early shift. By the way, that showerhead is leaking."

"I'll add it to the list," she said. "Right after the paint job and new deck railing and a second shower."

"I've offered to help. I spend enough time here."

She shook her head. "It's my own damn fault." She'd saved for repairs at one point, but blew it all on upgrading her galley. She had to have a great kitchen. "I'm a big girl. I'll figure it out."

He kissed her on the cheek and left. The sound of the door slamming made her feel sad. Another weekend spent together and not a word uttered between them about their relationship. She couldn't remember what they'd talked about. What they'd said to each other that mattered. Lately they both kept moving and doing because when they weren't in motion, they had nothing to say to each other. It used to be the silent moments they shared were intimate and comfortable. Now they were awkward. First-date awkward. Not a good sign for the marriage, she figured. Something had changed, and she decided it was her fault. The affair had hit her harder than she expected. She was spending too much time thinking about it, analyzing the word itself. *Affair*. Had it lasted long enough to be called that? She and Erik had slept together only once. If it wasn't an affair, what was it? She avoided thinking about the other *A* word. *Adultery*. Whenever it crossed her mind, she told herself it wasn't adultery because she and Jack were separated at the time and working on getting back together. Like they were now. It seemed as if they were always working on it. What did Erik say? *If it takes too much work, maybe it isn't there*. She had to admit she missed him. Missed his hands on her. His mouth. She ran her finger around the rim of her coffee cup. "Damn you, Erik." She shivered, cold in her damp running clothes. She'd have to turn up the temp on the boat; winter was on the way.

She ran upstairs, pulled off her clothes and turned on the shower. She stepped into a lukewarm spray; a new water heater moved up a notch on the home improvement list. She heard ringing while she was drying off. She twisted the towel into a turban around her wet hair and went into the bedroom to search for the cell phone. She fished it out from under the covers. "Murphy."

The Homicide commander: "Got a little job for you this morning."

"Let's hear it." She braced herself. Commander Axel Duncan was new to the job but not to the department. He'd worked in Vice for years. Since moving to head Homicide he'd shaved his beard, cut his wild blond hair and stopped dressing to pass for a drug addict, but he was still behaving like a loose-cannon undercover cop. His act wasn't translating well in Homicide; he summoned his detectives at all hours to send them off on strange missions. Some of the other cops called Duncan "Yo-Yo."

"That Moose Lake case," he said. "They haven't been able to reach her ex. Baby-sitter says he took off with the kids Friday night."

"So?"

"So he's a West Sider. Check out his place. See if anyone's seen him or his kids. Sniff around the garage. Maybe he's a sentimental fool and took part of her home in the car trunk."

"They're looking at him for this?"

"Maybe."

"Don't suppose anyone's explored the nine hundred other possibilities." The state had a medium-security prison in Moose Lake with nearly nine hundred male inmates.

"All the naughty boys have been accounted for."

"Good." Then a question for which she already knew the answer: "Have we got a search warrant for the ex's place?" Duncan rarely worried about legalities, rules, jurisdiction.

"For what? We're not searching jack. We're poking around. That's all. Poking around."

She paused and then asked, "Is this official or unofficial poking?" That was code for: *Are you going to get both our butts in trouble with this one?*

He ignored her question. "You're from that end of town. You can canvass it in your sleep. Shit. With that big fucking clan of yours, he's probably one of your relatives and you don't even know it. Get on it, Potato Head."

She didn't want him calling her that, but she let it go. With Duncan, it was best to let it go. He was always ready for a fight. "What's the address?" she asked.

53

8

Murphy didn't need to write down the address. It wasn't far from the Murphy family home, where as a kid she'd claimed the root cellar as her bedroom to escape the rest of the beehive. That's how she'd earned the title "Potato Head." A family nickname. She didn't want anyone using it except relatives and a couple of close friends; Axel was neither one. She thought he was a pain in the ass. A hot dog and a show-off.

She pulled out of the yacht club parking lot and went south on Wabasha Street. She took a right on Water Street and passed the Great River Boat Works, where yachts and speedboats and houseboats were on blocks and lined up behind a fence, waiting for repairs in the yard. She took a left on Plato Boulevard and a right on Ohio Street and snaked up the winding hill. She hung a right on George Street, crossed Smith Avenue and drove into Cherokee Park.

Chad Pederson lived in a compact bungalow off the park. Murphy circled the block once and then drove down the alley. She parked her Jeep in front of a garage a couple of houses away from Pederson's. Before getting out of the car, she opened her shoulder bag and checked her service weapon, a .40-cal. Glock Model 23. When she didn't wear a belt or shoulder rig, her purse doubled as her holster and had a special sleeve to carry her gun. She walked down the alley, surveying the trash cans huddled next to all the garages. The cans were empty; the neighborhood had recently had a garbage pickup. If Chad Pederson had disposed of any evidence in the trash, it was already at the dump. A cedar privacy fence enclosed Pederson's backyard, but there was a gate from the alley. She peeked through a crack between the fence boards and then opened the gate and walked in.

Against the back fence was a garden the size of a doormat; it was a tangle of dead tomato vines. On one side of the yard she saw an aluminum playground set with two swings and a slide. On the other side was a tree with slats of wood nailed onto the trunk; the rungs led up to a wooden platform set between the lowest branches. A fort. Her brothers built lots of them when they were kids. A deck ran alongside the back of the bungalow. Tucked into one corner of the deck was a doghouse—a miniature of Pederson's bungalow—with a sign nailed across the top. *Spike's Place*. A couple of shallow holes in the dirt against the fence had to be Spike's handiwork. There were no suspicious mounds or patches of fresh sod, and she'd expected none. She'd never come across someone stupid enough to bury his ex in the backyard. She remembered one genius who'd dumped his wife in the lake behind their house. Another kept his girlfriend in a trunk in the garage. Better check the garage, she thought.

The service door was open a crack. She put her ear to it and listened. Nothing. She pulled out her flashlight and pushed the door the rest of the way with her hip and walked inside. She sniffed. No suspicious smells. She flicked on the flashlight and ran the beam around the garage. No car. No trunk, either. A snowmobile sitting on a small trailer took up half the two-car garage. Tools hanging from the walls. Kids' bikes and rakes pushed against the side. She shined her light overhead. A plastic snowman and a set of reindeer tucked into the rafters. A bunch of hockey sticks. Couple of shovels. She turned off the flashlight, stuffed it in her purse and went back outside.

Both the garage and the house needed a coat of latex; white paint was flaking off in spots. Murphy could sympathize; her boat needed a paint job. She walked onto the deck and peeked through the sliding glass doors. No signs of movement. She knocked on the back door and listened. No response.

A big voice from next door: "They went duck hunting."

Murphy turned to her left; a man was standing on his deck looking over the fence at her. He'd returned from his own hunting trip. He was dressed in camouflage and had an armload of shotguns in camouflage cases. He was fat and all the green he was wearing and carrying made him look like an army tank.

"How'd you make out?" Murphy asked.

"Got our limit." Three boys in camouflage came up behind him on the deck, their arms empty. He looked at them as he struggled to open the back door. "You lazy turds. Go help your mother unload the car."

"I gotta pee," said the littlest.

"You can hold it. Go help your mother." The three boys turned around and stepped off the deck.

"No school today?" Murphy asked.

"Kids have been off since Thursday. Teachers' convention. They should have been back in school today but I let them play hooky so we could hunt longer."

56

"When did Chad leave for hunting?" Murphy asked.

The man pushed open his back door. Two big dogs ran up the deck steps and shot through the door ahead of him. "He was having a hard time getting off work. Said he wasn't leaving until after work Friday. Was gonna swing by his ex's house and pick up his boys and go."

"Know when they're due back?"

"He was talking about taking today off, like we did. Send them back to school tomorrow." The man set his guns down against the side of the house and looked at her. "You the new girlfriend?"

"No."

He smiled. "Too bad. Chad's a good egg. Deserves a babe." His wife came up behind him, arms loaded with gear. She was as big as he was and was also dressed in camo. She pushed past her husband to get into the house.

"Know where they were hunting?" Murphy asked.

"Chad's buddy has got a cabin. Not sure exactly where. You social services or what?"

Murphy heard barking from inside the man's house, and then his wife: "Fred! Get these filthy animals out of here!"

"Gotta go," he said. He picked up his guns and walked through the door.

Murphy went to the front of the Pederson house, stood on the porch, peered through a couple of the windows. An elderly voice: "Nobody home. Went duck hunting." Then a hacking cough. Murphy turned and saw Pederson's neighbor on the other side of the fence. The elderly black woman was wrapped in a heavy sweater and sitting on a porch swing. In her lap was a white poodle dressed in a matching sweater. Murphy swore to herself she'd never own a dog that wore sweaters.

57

She smiled as she walked up the old woman's steps. "Hello."

"You're a cop," said the woman. She coughed again. Her skin was as gray as her hair. She had a cigarette between her boney fingers and was holding it away from her so the ash wouldn't drop on the dog. She wore red lipstick; it was smeared all over the cigarette butt. "Paris Murphy, right?"

"Yeah. Do I know you?"

"Mrs. McDonough. Recognized you from your mom and dad's joint." More hacking. "I saw you punch a fella after he pinched your ass. You were a tough little shit."

"Tell me about this Pederson. Is he a decent neighbor or a jerk?"

"Chad. He's a nice kid. Moved down here from up north. Juggles two jobs to make his child support."

Murphy took her notebook out of her purse. "Where's he work?"

"Machine shop in Minneapolis. Third shift. Tends bar during the day at that titty club on West Seventh Street."

"I know the place," said Murphy, writing in her notebook. "Ever see him lose it with his kids or his ex or anyone else?"

"Never met his ex." She stopped talking to pick a dog hair off her tongue. "Cute kids. A little wild."

"Does he yell at them a lot? Slug them? Hear any racket over there?"

"That stupid monster, Spike. Barks at everything that moves. Scares the living shit out of my baby." She scratched behind the poodle's ears and kissed his head; she left a lipstick mark on his fur.

"What else about Chad?"

"Quiet. Shovels my walk in the winter. Won't take a dime from me. Sent tomatoes over all summer. Big Boys. Real meaty." She paused to take a drag off her cigarette, coughed, took another pull. Then it occurred to her: "Christ Almighty! That's his ex on the news, isn't it? You're not thinking he killed her. No way he did it."

"Know how I can reach him?"

"He's at a friend's cabin. No phone. No electricity. Outdoor crapper." She coughed so hard she dropped the cigarette. A gust of wind made her shiver and pull her sweater tighter around her thin body. "I think he's nuts. Especially this time of year."

"He ever mention the friend's name? Where the cabin is located?"

"Nope. If he did, I'd remember." More hacking, then: "The body's going, but the mind still works. Your folks, Sean and Amira, they still alive?"

"Alive and kicking," Murphy said.

"Tell them Tootie says hello."

"I'll do that. You take it easy, Mrs. McDonough." She closed her notebook and slipped it back in her purse.

"Try tonight on Chad," she said as Murphy stepped off the porch. "He'll be back tonight. Probably bring me a duck all cleaned and ready for the oven." She bent over and picked the cigarette off the porch floor and took another puff. "No way in hell he killed her."

Murphy checked her watch. Close to lunchtime, and she could go for a bar burger and fries. She took Smith Avenue and crossed the High Bridge over the river. She hung a left on West Seventh and drove a couple of miles. There used to be several strip joints in St. Paul, but one by one they were shut down by neighborhood activists. One on the East Side was now an Embers restaurant in the front and a bingo hall in the back. Another on University Avenue had been converted into the police department's Western District Office. The West Seventh club was one of the last two left in town.

59

She took a left and pulled into the parking lot, turned off the Jeep and slipped her keys in her purse. She slid out of the car and shut the driver's door. Surveyed the parking lot. Not many cars. From what she remembered, the place had the biggest lunch crowd on Fridays. She hiked her purse strap over her right shoulder and walked to the entrance. The front windows were painted black with white silhouettes of nude women. After stepping inside, Murphy stopped for a few seconds so her eyes could adjust to the dark. The place looked the same as she remembered from her days as a uniform. The bottom half of the walls were covered by wood paneling and the top half by barn-red paint. Large oil portraits of nude women provided the main decoration for the place. The bar was on one end of the room and was circled by stools. The other end was the stage. Murphy saw a nude dancer swaying to Tina Turner. A boney blonde with dark pubic hair shaved into a narrow V. A glass wall separated the performers from the rest of the bar. The city didn't allow establishments with nude dancing to serve liquor. As a way around the rule, the strip joints divided their clubs and put up the walls. They had separate outside entrances for the performance and bar areas. So the women could still receive tips, slots were cut at the bottom of the glass walls. Men slipped the bills through like they were sliding deposits to bank tellers.

Murphy took a stool at the bar. Unzipped her jacket and set her purse on her lap. Most of the dozen customers were sitting at the foot of the stage. A guy in a booth against the wall was getting a lap dance from a skinny brunette in a bikini. Murphy didn't see anyone she recognized; it would be easier to ask questions. She didn't expect trouble regardless. Strip clubs tended to have middle-aged patrons—including lots of married men—and those customers kept a low profile. Rarely made trouble. The police got more complaints about bars frequented by the younger crowd; they'd spill out of the clubs and pee and puke on people's lawns.

An older woman with big arms and a pink face walked to Murphy's end of the counter. Her silver hair was braided and coiled in a circle on top of her head. She wore a tee shirt that read: *Cleverly disguised as a responsible adult.* "What can I get you?"

"Burger and fries."

The woman scratched the order on a pad.

"Anything to drink?"

"Diet Pepsi."

"No Pepsi."

"Diet Coke?"

"Coke we got. Want that now?" Murphy nodded and the woman turned around to fill a glass with ice.

"Chad not working today?" Murphy asked.

The woman poured the pop and slid the glass to Murphy. "Duck hunting. That's why I'm up front instead of in the kitchen." She nodded toward the dancer onstage. "I'm not big on this stuff." She left to hand the order off to the kitchen. Murphy looked at the stage again. The dancer's routine had switched from simple swaying to squatting with her knees splayed wide and then standing. Squatting. Standing. Squatting. Standing. The bartender returned with a towel. Started wiping the counter.

Murphy sipped her Coke. "I suppose Chad deserves a day off."

"That he does," said the woman. "Works his hind end off for those boys of his. Hockey equipment ain't cheap. The older one is a goalie. Know what goalie pads cost? My daughter's got two goalies. Thank God her husband makes good scratch."

Murphy took another drink. Set it down. Stirred it with the straw. "You'd think Chad's ex would help out more."

"Don't know a thing about her," said the bartender. "Never heard Chad say a word against her. Who knows? Maybe she's playing him for a sucker." The woman stopped wiping and eyed Murphy. "You Chad's new squeeze?"

Murphy: "No."

"Friends, huh? Chad's got plenty of those. He needs a woman who can cook for him."

Murphy tipped her head toward the woman onstage. "Doesn't he socialize with any of the ladies here?"

She wrinkled her nose. "The dancers? No way. Not his type."

A guy in a suit took a stool to Murphy's right. He had a drink in his hand. It smelled like whiskey. Strong stuff for lunch, Murphy thought. His eyes were bloodshot. Tie askew. He had short red hair and freckles. Old enough to be in the bar, but too young to be hitting the booze so hard so early in the day. He raised his right index finger. The bartender eyed him. "I think you've had enough," she said.

The guy turned and said to Murphy, "The responsible adult thinks I've had enough."

"I'd have to agree," Murphy said. She sipped her Coke.

He stared at Murphy's chest. "You should be up there, baby." He thumbed toward the stage; the boney blonde had been replaced by a chubby blonde, also with dark pubic hair. She turned her back to the crowd and bent forward, looking between her legs while hanging on to her ankles.

"No," said Murphy. "That's not my kind of dancing."

"You wouldn't have to dance," he said. "All you'd have to do is get naked and stand there and they'd slide you wads of cash. Know why?"

"Why?"

" 'Cause you got a rack." With the word *rack* he slammed his right hand on the bar.

"Thanks," Murphy said dryly.

"No. I mean it. I could talk to the manager. I know the manager." He threw his left arm around her shoulders and leaned into her right ear. "Listen. Here's the plan." He stopped talking and frowned. "I forgot what I was going to say."

Murphy pushed his arm off her. "You were going to ask the bartender for a cup of coffee and a sandwich."

He nodded. "Good idea." He raised his finger again. A male bartender—a tall black guy in a square haircut—approached him. The drunk pointed to his glass.

"No way, buddy. You're done," the bartender said, and walked to the other end of the bar.

The female bartender set a plate of burger and fries in front of Murphy, and a bottle of ketchup. The drunk picked up the bottle and squirted a puddle of ketchup on Murphy's plate. Set the bottle down.

"Hey!" said Murphy. He picked a couple of fries off her plate, dipped them in the ketchup and started eating them. She slid the plate in front of him. "Put this on his tab," she told the female bartender. "He needs it more than I do."

"I'm sorry," said the woman. "I'm gonna get someone over here to deal with this joker." She walked over to the tall bartender and whispered something in his ear. He nodded and picked up a phone under the bar.

"I got what I need," Murphy said to herself. She pulled some bills out of her purse, threw them on the bar and

63

hopped off the stool. Threw her purse strap over her shoulder and went out the door. She was reaching in her purse for her keys when she heard someone behind her. She turned. The drunk redhead. He had ketchup on his chin. "What the hell do you want?" she asked.

He stepped toward her. "I think you know." He pressed her against the side of the Jeep and cupped her left breast over her jacket. "You gotta be a hooker, coming into a place like this by yourself. With tits like these. What do you charge for a knob job, huh?"

She pushed him off of her and he fell against her again. Reached around and cupped her buttocks with his hands. "Come on, baby. This your day off or what?"

"My friend," Murphy said. "You picked the wrong ass to grab." She pushed him off of her with both hands, stepped behind him and slammed him face-first into the Jeep. She grabbed each of his wrists in each of her hands and pulled his arms behind him.

"Murphy. Need some help?"

She looked over her shoulder. Two uniforms. She recognized both of them. The male bartender must have called them. "Yeah. Take this asshole to detox." She stepped away.

The bigger of the two uniforms held the drunk's arms behind his back while his partner cuffed the guy's wrists. They flipped him over so he faced them. He looked at Murphy. "Why'd you call the cops, baby?"

Murphy was wiping the front of her jacket with a wad of tissue. The guy had ketchup on his hands and had gotten some on her. "I am the cops," she said.

"Shit," the drunk muttered.

The two uniforms walked him over to their squad. They eased him into the back while Murphy watched with her arms folded in front of her.

"Wouldn't have squeezed her tits if I knew she was a cop."

"You squeezed her tits?" said the big uniform. "Jesus Christ. You're lucky to be breathing. We saved your life, dumb shit."

9

Chad Pederson wasn't a wife killer. Murphy did more checking when she got back to the station. Made a few phone calls from her desk. He had nothing in the way of a record. "Damn waste of time," she muttered as she threw down a pen and leaned back in her chair.

Chuck Dubrowski and Max Castro walked into the office. They were veterans in Homicide and had been partners so long they looked alike—big arms, bushy eyebrows, gray hair, thick necks that seemed sunburned even in the middle of winter. When Dubrowski learned he needed glasses, he went out and got the same wire-rimmed frames as Castro. He said it was a coincidence, but Murphy enjoyed giving him grief about it. Today they wore matching sweatshirts under their blazers.

"Wild-goose chase," Castro muttered, tossing a notebook on his desk.

Dubrowski poured himself a cup of coffee and collapsed into his chair. "Yo-Yo and his bullshit."

"What happened?" Murphy asked.

"Get this," said Castro, sitting down. "Duncan hands us this address on the North End. Some guy getting death threats."

"The North End?" asked Murphy. "I know where this is going."

"Yup," said Dubrowski. "Anyway, I tell Yo-Yo who we're dealing with, that we all know this head case. He says there could be something to it; maybe somebody is really threatening the guy this time. I tell Duncan to send a uniform. Castro says we should call head case's social worker. The asshole says if we don't take the call, he's gonna write us up. Fuck him."

Castro: "So we drive out there to make Duncan happy. The head case is sitting in his front room with a crucifix. He's got his noggin wrapped in aluminum foil so the aliens can't tap into his mind. Waves his cross around and says he won't talk to us because we're part of the conspiracy. Says we're ghosts from another planet and we're helping UFOs abduct people."

"Ghosts? That's a new twist in his story," Murphy said. "But then why does he keep calling us?"

Dubrowski: "Hell if I know."

Murphy: "Ghosts don't go out during the day, do they?"

Dubrowski: "I didn't write this guy's script for him."

Castro got out of his chair and walked over to Murphy's desk. "Anyway, we're coming back to the cop shop and Duncan calls us." He folded his arms across his chest. "Guess what he says? Says to make sure we do up a detailed report. That's the word he used. *Detailed*."

Murphy: "You're shittin' me."

Castro: "I shit you not."

"Think it would do us any good to talk to the boss?" Murphy asked.

"He's got his own problems," said Castro.

Murphy knew he was right. Months earlier, Chief Benjamin Christianson had been accused of hindering her investigation into a prostitute's death. The murderer—the

67

man who'd given Murphy the scar—was a surgeon and a cousin of Christianson's wife. The doctor killed himself before his arrest, but that didn't end the mess. The mayor wanted the chief's resignation and Christianson was fighting it. Adding to the tumult: a city council plan to move police headquarters from downtown to the lower East Side.

"What about going to the union?" said Murphy.

"We already talked to Sandeen," said Dubrowski. Pete Sandeen, another Homicide detective, was a union steward. "He says we should hold off. Give Yo-Yo time. I say it's time to kick his ass."

Castro walked back to his desk, sat down and waved Dubrowski over. "Come on, Casper. Let's put our alien heads together and do up a *detailed* report on Reynolds Wrap Man."

Murphy had to give them a hard time about their shirts before they went to work. "Hey, cute sweats. Where can I get one? Then we can all match."

Castro opened his desk drawer. "I already grabbed one for you."

Murphy thought he was joking, but he pulled a shirt out and threw it to her. She caught it and held it up. The upper left side of the shirt was embroidered with a St. Paul Homicide detective's badge and circling it, the words: *To the living we owe respect. To the dead we owe the truth.* "I like that," she said. "Where'd this come from?"

Castro: "The union. Sandeen made them up. Says it'll promote unity and team spirit and all that other crap. He's trying to come up with a different one for each division. If he can't get rid of Yo-Yo for us, at least he can dress us pretty."

* * *

Murphy wanted to find out if her mission was Yo-Yo's idea or if the Moose Lake cops had asked for help. She walked into Duncan's office before going home that night. He was on the phone with his feet up on the desk. He motioned for her to sit down in the chair across from his desk, and she did.

"Did he have anything on him when you picked him up?" While cradling the phone between his ear and shoulder, he was playing with a paper clip. Unbending it. A mound of straightened paper clips on his desk, as well as foam coffee cups, piles of paper, a half-eaten bagel and a copy of *Popular Science*. "No kidding? Any of them been fired?"

He wore an oxford shirt with sleeves rolled up, dress pants and a tie—Christianson ordered all his commanders to wear ties—but his clothes looked as if Duncan had slept in them for a week. He had sneakers on his feet. Murphy recognized the brand. Pricey running shoes. The tread was worn. Did the slob actually exercise? The blazer he'd brought to work was on the floor next to his desk and there was a dirty stripe across the back; he'd run over it with the casters of his chair.

"I'll ask my detective. She's back from the house. Sure. Sure. Happy to help out. Glad the s.o.b. turned up."

Murphy realized he was talking about Chad Pederson. She couldn't believe Moose Lake was seriously looking at him for this. Everything she'd learned about Pederson told her he wasn't the killer. What did they have on him? She got a sick feeling in the pit of her stomach. Had Yo-Yo cooked up some theory and sold it to the cops up north? Duncan craved being in the middle of all the action. She hoped he hadn't dragged her into the middle with him.

He picked up a cup and speared it with a paper clip. "Tell you what. Here's an idea for you." He pulled his feet off the desk, knocking a pile of papers to the floor. "Why don't I send her up there?"

"Shit," Murphy said under her breath.

"She's the best we've got. Real easy on the eyes, too." Duncan winked at her and Murphy smiled. He swiveled his chair around to glance out the window while he talked and she flipped him the bird behind his back.

"No. No. Not a problem." He spun his chair back around and hung up the phone. "Pack your bags, Potato Head."

Murphy: "What did you tell them? I haven't even briefed you yet. Jesus Christ. I don't think he did it. Doesn't have a record. Neighbors love his ass. Works like a dog. He was duck hunting with his kids."

"That's the bullshit he laid on the authorities up there. Here's what really happened: Pederson shoots his ex after she leaves the wedding reception, dumps the body, grabs the kids and takes off. Maybe he really does take them duck hunting; it's a good excuse to disappear for a while. He brings them back to the ex's house days later and acts all broken up, pretends he didn't know she got croaked."

"Motive?"

"Hated paying child support."

"Why did they find a finger? Where's the rest of her?"

"Animals probably snacked on her; one of them ran off with a hunk of her and dropped it. The rest of her is out there somewhere."

"This is the story you've sold to the Moose Lake police?"

"Carlton County sheriff. But the police up there are on the same page." He picked up a sheet of paper and started folding it into an airplane.

Murphy got up from the chair and paced in front of his desk. "You've got nothing to base this on."

70

"Pederson had a trunk full of shotguns when he pulled into Moose Lake this afternoon. A couple of them had been discharged." He tossed the paper airplane toward a wastebasket in the corner and missed. "On top of that, he had a vicious dog. Almost took a deputy's arm off. I would've shot the thing."

She stopped pacing, stood behind the chair she'd been sitting in, grabbed the back of it with both hands. She knew he was waiting for her to go ballistic; she saw the expectant expression on his face. She sat back down and rubbed her forehead with her hands. She caught his eyes locking on her scar and she brushed her bangs down to cover it. In a low voice she said, "He was duck hunting."

"If he's innocent, it'll all come out. He's got major fucking holes in his story. If you think you can plug them with what you got down here, go right ahead, if that's what you wanna do." Duncan leaned back and put his feet up on the desk again. "But if that is what you wanna do, it makes me wonder. That little bump on the head. That making you soft, Murphy?"

She sat up straight in the chair. Her eyes narrowed and darkened, seemed to go from violet to black.

He smiled and took another shot at her: "They got an opening in the Public Pretender's Office."

That's what Homicide called the Ramsey County Public Defender's Office. She wanted to bolt out of the chair and tell him to go fuck himself. Leave the room. Slam the door behind her. He'd love it, though. A big scene in the office. She didn't give it to him, but she was disappointed with the weak argument that finally came out of her mouth: "This is out of our jurisdiction."

"Don't worry about jurisdiction."

"It's not our case."

"Now it is. Get your butt up there, Potato Head."

71

10

He'd decided not to weave any lies because he feared he'd lose track of them. Instead, he left out the bits of his life that were unsuitable for a savior. He didn't tell them he lived in a trailer park or that his father was his roommate or that he was considered a loser in high school or that he'd never gone to college. No one questioned the missing details; all the reporters wanted to concentrate on was his previous hero experience.

He met one last newspaper reporter for an interview over lunch Monday. She said she was doing a feature on him for the next day's paper. He ordered a burger and fries and she bought herself a Diet Coke. He was grateful for the food; it gave him something to fiddle with. He kept stumbling over what to call her because her last name sounded like a first name—Jill or Jane or Jan—and her first name was a fella's name. Terry or Tommy. He gave up and called her "ma'am." His pa had taught him to fall back on "ma'am." She was barely five feet tall and couldn't have weighed ninety pounds. Cute. Smelled good. Lilacs. He tried to imagine himself in bed with her and decided they'd look ridiculous. He was clumsy at sex no matter who he was with, but it was the most awkward with the short ones. He was having trouble concentrating on the interview itself. Exhausted after the weekend, he'd hit a wall and needed to pop another pill. The body in back of the truck was another distraction. Minnesota Octobers were unpredictable; any day the cold snap could give way to a warm spell. He had to get rid of the bridesmaid.

An hour into the lunch interview he was staring at his plate and repeatedly dipping the last fry into a spot of ketchup. "What p... paper you with again?"

"*Duluth News Tribune.*" She sounded irritated. She closed her notebook, clicked her pen and shoved both in her purse. "I got everything I need. Why don't you get some sleep? You're wiped out." She slid out of the booth and threw enough cash on the table for her drink. Trip watched her leave and tiredly ran his fingers through his hair. A few strands fell into his plate.

His cell phone rang. He'd shut it off Friday night and had turned it on again that morning. He pulled it out of his jacket and flipped it open.

Wade Murray, his regional sales manager: "Hey, big shot. Why the hell haven't you been picking up?"

Trip: "Busy."

"Yeah. I noticed. Why didn't you give the company a plug?"

"B... b... been wearing the shirts on TV."

"So what? Who knows where they came from? Next time they shove a camera in your mug, the first words outta your mouth are *Pinecone Clothing Distributors.*"

"Sure."

"How'd you do up there?"

Trip: "Great."

A pause. Murray knew Trip was lying; he never did great. "When you heading back to the Twin Cities?"

"A couple d... days. Thought I'd d... do some cold-calling south of Duluth."

"We got a sales meeting early Thursday. I want you here for it." He hung up.

Trip closed the phone, shoved it back in his pocket. He threw some bills on the table and slid out of the booth. Went out the door. On his way back to the car he heard sirens. He stopped in the middle of the sidewalk and scanned both ends of the block. His heart raced; three squads were coming down the street. His eyes went to the truck and back to the squads. Were they on to him? How? They zoomed past him. He wobbled as he walked the rest of the way to the Ford. He wondered where they were going; wherever it was, he wanted to steer clear of them. He pulled his keys out of his jacket and dropped them in the street while opening the door; his hands were shaking. He picked them up, opened the door, slid into the driver's seat. As soon as he shut the door his cell phone rang again. Should have left the thing off, he thought. Probably Murray again. He pulled it out and flipped it open.

"Yeah."

"Son?"

"Pa."

"When you coming home?"

"Soon. How you f... feeling?"

"Horseshit."

"How's your blood sugar?"

"Too damn high."

"How high? Nurses b... been there yet?"

"Come and gone. Bitches. Especially that fat blond one you favor."

They *were* bitches, but he and his pa couldn't pick and choose. The free homecare service was contracted by the county. The fat blonde, Keri Ingmar, was a longtime neighbor in the trailer park who'd enrolled them in the program. She was ten years older than Trip. Stupid as a rock. She'd been supplying him with his drugs since he was in high school. She'd been sleeping with him since then, too. It used to be the drugs were separate from the sex. Over the years, as Keri grew older and Trip grew less willing, the sex became part of the payment for the drugs.

"Hang in there, P... Pa. I'll try to cut it short." He felt guilty for being gone and at the same time was glad he wasn't there. His pa wasn't a well-behaved diabetic. He ate what he wanted. Didn't keep up with his insulin shots. Ignored the sores on his feet until he had to have a big toe amputated. The nurses fought with the old man to get his socks off during their visits. His pa didn't want them to check his feet because he was sure a leg would be the next to go, and he was probably right. His eyesight was failing—another side effect of his refusal to cooperate with medical treatment—and the old man wouldn't admit it. Pretended he could see perfectly well. All the while he kept pissing in the bathroom wastebasket instead of the toilet.

"Sweet."

"Yeah?"

"You look real sharp on TV."

"Thanks." Trip was amazed his old man had taken a break from his western channel to catch the news.

"They pay you anything for that?"

"No."

"Don't worry about me. Take your time up there. Sell some shirts. Make some money. Do something worthwhile."

"Later, P... Pa." He closed the cell phone and tried to put home out of his mind. The whole scene in their trailer was getting too depressing. The fat blond nurse was getting to be the highlight of Trip's week, and that in itself was pathetic. He wished she didn't live so close; sometimes he felt trapped by her. His pa knew Trip was sleeping with her; he'd asked Trip to keep the bedroom door open so he could listen. The old man said it was the only action he'd get for the rest of his life, but Trip knew that was a lie. His pa was sleeping with her, too. That's why his old man told him to take his time. Trip didn't care. He couldn't leave Moose Lake yet anyway; he had work to do that night.

Trip went back to the motel room after lunch and relaxed on the bed with some magazines and a six-pack. He popped open a can, took a gulp and paged through a couple of knife catalogs to see if there was anything new. The bowie knife with a running stag etched on the six-inch blade was nice, but the handle was imitation antler and he wanted the real thing. The gladiator swords didn't interest him; he already had a whole rack of those. He wondered if his pa could use the cane; the carved cobra head pulled out to reveal a sword. He pictured his old man tooling around the trailer park with a sword cane and laughed.

The motel room was chilly. He cranked up the thermostat, peeled off his clothes and stepped into the shower. Good and hot. He ducked his head under. He massaged his scalp with his fingertips; his pa told him he needed to get the blood circulating in his head. When the stream turned lukewarm, he turned off the water. Trip saw black strands in his palms and tangled around his fingers. More hair on the shower floor. He'd been losing hair since he graduated from high school. It depressed him; he figured he'd be bald by the time he hit fifty. Just like his old man. Didn't seem fair.

The room was warmer by the time he toweled off and collapsed into bed. His feet hung off the edge of the mattress. He tried to turn on the television with the remote. The screen stayed black. Batteries were dead. He got up and turned it on manually and fell back against the pillows. He was surprised and happy to see what was leading the six o'clock news. Bunny Pederson's ex-husband had been picked up for questioning on her disappearance and suspected murder. Trip never imagined someone else would get blamed, and so quickly. He figured they'd eventually find the body—she'd be a collection of bones. There'd be weeks of investigation while they followed tips and leads that led nowhere. Then they'd give up. Beaten. They'd never say the word. *Beaten*. But that's what they'd be. That's how it had worked before. This was even better. "Perfect," he said. He popped open a second can and took a long drink. He studied the man on the screen. Handsome. Well built. Probably a jock in high school. Captain of the football team or some such shit. Chad was his name, according to the television reporter.

"I didn't do anything," he said into a microphone, and he slid into the backseat of a sheriff's car. In the background, the cops were loading a bunch of shotguns and a barking dog into a van. A deputy was holding a couple of crying boys by the hands. Trip figured they were the Pederson kids.

He thought: *Things are looking up for Sweet Justice*. He wondered if he should dump the body where the cops could find it and really seal the jock's fate. No. They took the jock's guns; they thought he shot her. If they found the body and figured out she'd been run over, that might somehow exclude the ex-husband as a suspect. The cops would probably figure out that it was a truck that did it and maybe this Chad didn't have a truck. No. Better play it safe. He'd bury her that night while the cops were focusing their attention on the jock. He took another sip of beer and popped the top off his pill bottle. Fished around with his finger until he found what he needed. His favorite. The

77

Adderall. Full of energy. He'd need energy tonight. He chewed the pill and washed it down with another sip of beer. He was hungry. Knew he'd better eat before the amphetamines did their thing and took his appetite away. He decided to go back into town for dinner. Load up on some food. More energy for tonight. He'd try that bar where the wedding reception was held. Where Bunny Pederson was last seen alive.

11

"Public Pretender's Office my ass. Stupid jerk." She drove home from the station Monday night muttering to herself while making a mental list of who she needed to call before leaving and what she needed to pack for Moose Lake. She pulled into the parking lot and saw a sapphire Jaguar convertible. Erik Mason's car. "Not what I need," she said to herself as she shut off the Jeep and pulled her key out of the ignition. She slid out of the car with her purse and slammed the driver's door hard. As she ran to her boat she heard Tripod, her neighbor's three-legged dog, barking like crazy. He was the yacht club's fail-safe alarm; he went off whenever there was a stranger on the dock. She thumped down the dock and saw Erik standing by her boat. She would have recognized his figure from across the river: tall, athletic, short walnut brown hair. Jack was a rower and had a muscular upper body. Erik, a runner, was a bit trimmer—and more preoccupied with his own looks. He spent a lot of time in the gym. He was also more interested in money. Spent too much time at the track. Murphy figured the horses paid for the Jag. She liked that dangerous edge to Erik, and his looks matched his personality. She thought he resembled an older James Dean. Her husband—safer and more playful than Erik—looked like a younger James Caan.

"Horseshit timing," she said, and rushed past him to open her door. He followed her into the galley; his arms were filled with flowers. "What if Jack was here?" she snapped. "You can't just show up. Jesus Christ." She threw her keys and purse on the kitchen table and turned to glare at him.

"I checked first. No silver Beemer in the lot. Got a vase?"

She pointed to a cupboard and ran upstairs. "I've got to go out of town for work," she yelled from her bedroom. "I appreciate the thought, but they're going to be wasted. And what if Jack sees them?"

"Tell him they're from your mother." Erik set the flowers on the table and followed her upstairs. She was stuffing a tangle of bras and panties and socks into a duffel bag that was sitting on her unmade bed. "When are you going to tell him what happened over the summer? You should. Get it all out in the open."

"No," she said flatly. She went into her closet and pulled a jean skirt off a hanger. Some running gear—stocking cap, sweats, shoes—were in a heap on the closet floor. She picked them up. Maybe she could squeeze in a workout; Moose Lake had some great trails.

"That's it? No? Didn't it mean anything?" Erik was on her heels and she almost knocked him over when she turned around. "Answer me."

She stepped around him and tossed the clothes on the bed. "I don't have time for this." She yanked open a dresser drawer and pulled out three sweaters and two pairs of jeans and tossed them on the pile. She went into the bathroom, scooped a handful of toiletries out of the medicine cabinet and went back to the bed with them. Her cell phone rang. "Dammit!" She dumped the toiletries in the bag and rifled around the sheets for the phone. She found it under a pillow and picked it up: "Murphy."

Jack: "Babe. Want to meet for dinner at that Italian joint on St. Peter Street?"

Murphy frowned at Erik while she talked to her husband. "I can't. They're sending me up north. Moose Lake."

Jack: "Why?"

"Long story," said Murphy, cradling the phone on her shoulder while shoving clothes into the bag. "Call my folks. They're expecting us for dinner tomorrow night."

"You won't be back by then?"

"I don't know. Maybe not." She tried to close the bag; the zipper was caught on a bra strap. "Gotta go. I'll call you."

Jack: "Love you."

She paused. Erik was staring at her; he knew who was on the other end of the phone. "Me too," she said. She hung up and threw the phone on the nightstand.

"Want some company for the ride up?" Erik asked. "I've got a couple of days off."

"No," she snapped. She disengaged the bra strap and finished zipping the bag shut.

Erik sat down on the bed. "Stop moving and talk to me." He put his hand on the bag to keep her from leaving. "What about us?"

She hated that pleading tone in his voice and the hungry look in his eyes; she thought he might as well wrap his arms around her ankles. "I don't know. I told you a couple of weeks ago I don't know. I'm no closer to figuring this thing out. Jack and I are still married, you know. I still have feelings for him."

"You have feelings for me." He grabbed her wrist and

pulled her next to him on the bed. She opened her mouth to argue and he planted his mouth hard over hers. His left hand cradled the back of her head and his right moved down to her left breast.

"Damn you," she breathed, trying to push him away with both hands. "Don't tie me in a knot right before I have to leave town." He released her and she stood up. The smile on his face. Smug. Self-satisfied. He knew how to stir her up.

"Admit it," he said. The smile disappeared. "You care about me."

From manipulator to wounded puppy; Murphy didn't know which made her angrier. "Give me some time. Breathing room. Space." She pulled the bag off the bed.

Erik stood up and shoved his hands in his pants pockets. "That's the line I usually use."

Murphy ran downstairs and took her keys and purse off the kitchen table. She opened the fridge and took two bottles of spring water for the road.

Head lowered and hands still in his pockets, Erik walked downstairs. "I'll leave the flowers in some water. They'll last. Call when you get back."

"Fine," she said. Suddenly, leaving town for a few days seemed a wonderful idea. She opened the door to leave and turned to toss him her spare key. "Lock the place up behind you." He caught it and grinned. "Don't get any ideas," she said. "I want that back."

As she walked to the parking lot, she wondered what was going on with Erik. They'd known each other for years. She was familiar with the sly, dangerous side of him; it was what first attracted her to him. The timing had been good for them, too. They'd both been assigned to the prostitute's murder—she as the lead detective and Erik as an investigator for the ME's office. Erik supported her through the tough case and believed her when she first raised the surgeon as the main suspect. Jack, who hated her job anyway, thought she was nuts. He went out of town for a medical conference in the middle of things. Part of her was still angry with Jack for that. Erik stuck by her, too, in the internal affairs investigation that followed the surgeon's suicide. The doctor had killed himself with her gun. But this clingy, needy stuff with Erik was new and unsettling. If that was her lover's flip side, she didn't want any part of it. What did they have in common anyway? Good sex. They'd trained for the Twin Cities Marathon together. They both enjoyed cooking. Sex and running and food. Not enough for a long-lasting pairing. Sometimes she feared all she and Jack had in common was sex.

She opened the back of the Jeep, tossed the bag inside, slammed it shut hard. Sliding behind the wheel, she took a deep breath and told herself to relax. She went through downtown and turned onto Interstate 35E heading north. She'd missed rush hour; traffic was light. Moose Lake, a town of two thousand on the way to Duluth, would be well under a two-hour drive. She slipped a compact disc into the CD player. Billie Holiday's "Night and Day" filled the interior of the car with smooth horns. She took a long drink of water and felt better. Time to forget about Erik and Jack and her leaky showerhead.

As soon as she got out of the metro area, the drive took on a north woods feel. She passed a few red barns and white farmhouses, but mostly the highway was lined with hardwoods and pines. The interstate sliced through lakes and rivers and towns with names that conjured up the forest: Pine City. Snake River. Willow River. Sturgeon Lake. Moose Lake would be coming up after all those. What did she know about Moose Lake? She'd passed it a hundred times while headed to the North Shore. She'd taken the exit into the town on a few occasions. Once to interview an inmate at the state prison. Another time she ran a 10K there. A weekend in May. Moose Run, it was called. Rock hound Jack dragged her there one July weekend for Agate Days. The town dumped 150 pounds of agates and $100 in quarters in the street mixed with gravel; with the blast of a siren, everyone dove in to dig for rocks and money. The silliness of the event charmed her. She'd been in enough small towns to know she'd never work in rural Minnesota. The odd missing bridesmaid case aside, there wasn't enough murder and mayhem to keep a cop busy. If she had to pick a place to retire to, however, Moose Lake would top the list. It was one of those places that had at least one of everything. Flower shop. Pet store. Dentist's office. Doctor's office. Funeral home. Drugstore. JCPenney catalog store. Hardware store. Grocery. Hospital. Movie theater. The community was nestled in an area checkered with lakes, streams, rivers and forests. She couldn't see what else a person needed.

She was south of Moose Lake when her work cell phone rang. She looked over at her purse sitting on the passenger's seat. Let it ring, she thought. She didn't want to talk to Erik or Jack. Maybe it was her mother. It might be the cop shop. She reached over, fished it out and answered. "Murphy."

Duncan: "Don't sound so excited."

After the scene she'd left behind on her houseboat, talking to Duncan didn't seem so bad. "Actually, I'm looking forward to this little trip," she said.

"Know where you're staying?"

"Not yet." She planned on scoping it out when she got to town.

"I do. I already made reservations for you at the Americ-Inn right off the freeway. Got you a room with a Jacuzzi."

"I'm afraid to ask why."

"My way of trying to apologize. Plus they had a weekday special. Okay?"

Odd but well-meaning gesture, she thought. Yo-Yo wasn't such a jerk after all. "Okay."

"Sorry about that crack about your head. Actually, that scar gives you an air of mystery."

"Cut the crap, Duncan. Should have quit while you were ahead."

He laughed. "My life story."

She took the Moose Lake exit. The hotel was part of a growing tourist development right off the highway. A gas station and sub shop shared the intersection. She parked the Jeep, took her bag out of the back and walked in. A blaze crackled in the lobby fireplace. The clerk at the front—a skinny blond woman with hair pulled back into a ponytail—slid the key card across the desk to Murphy. "Breakfast in the morning. Served right here in the lobby. Coffee. Juice. Cereal. Toast. Fruit. Waffles. Danish. The whole nine yards. Comes with the room."

"Thanks." Murphy took the card and grabbed a trail map from the counter. A quick run at dawn would be good.

"You can get on one of the trails right off the parking lot," said the clerk.

Murphy pointed toward the moose head mounted over the fireplace. "That real?"

"Who knows? I hate it regardless. Scares me at night. His eyes follow you."

"Which way to the pool?" Murphy asked, and the woman sent her down the hall. Murphy poked her head into the room. Hot and humid. High, wood-beamed

85

ceiling. Through the sauna window she saw two fat men sweating it out. Two fat women sat in the hot tub; probably the fat guys' wives. The pool was unoccupied. She'd have to go for a swim later. She walked to the edge of the pool and peered into the water. At the bottom of the pool, written in tile: MOOSE LAKE. She went to her room, slipped the key card into the lock and pushed open the door. She turned on the light and gasped. A two-room suite with a whirlpool and a fireplace. "Shit," she muttered. She threw her bag and purse on the bed, a four-poster. The setting gave her an idea. *Why not?* She pulled the cell phone out of her purse and punched in his phone number. "Hey, babe," Murphy said into the phone. "Are you up for a one-night vacation?"

Murphy pulled down the bedsheets, turned on the gas fireplace, filled the ice bucket and set it next to the tub. She called the front desk. "A tall, handsome guy is meeting me here."

The woman laughed. "Does he have a brother?"

"His name is Jack Ramier. If he gets here before I get back from dinner, give him a key card."

"Gotcha."

Murphy checked her watch. It would take nearly two hours for Jack to drive up. He'd already eaten and she was hungry. She grabbed her jacket and purse. Remembered a bar off the main drag that served dinner.

12

Murphy spotted Trip the instant he stepped into the bar. His height caught her eye first, then his gait. Eighteen years had passed and she still recognized his walk and posture. Slow. Hesitant. Head down. A giraffe tiptoeing past the lions. He was by himself; that hadn't changed with the years either. In high school, he'd sat alone. In the library. At the lunch table. In his truck. Never a friend at his side. She saw him turn his head away when the hostess started talking to him; he was still having trouble looking people in the face.

The woman led him to a table toward the front. A round table with six chairs around it. The hostess probably figured she was doing him a favor, giving him legroom. The big table made Trip seem even lonelier. Murphy was in a booth in back. A few other tables and booths were occupied. A young couple. A middle-aged couple. Three men in jeans and flannel shirts. Probably farmers. Four duck hunters in camouflage loudly replaying the day's shoot. A family celebrating Grandma's birthday. Home-made cake in the middle of the table. Pointed hat on the old woman's head.

The room was dark, long, narrow and had a low ceiling. She figured she could order and eat dinner and he'd never notice her, but that would make her feel like she had something to hide. She contemplated standing up and walking over. Extending her hand. Joining him for dinner. Would he remember her? Sure he would, she told herself, and that's why she was hanging back. He would remember that she turned him down at homecoming. That her boyfriend and his pals beat the hell out of him for talking to her. That she never offered an apology. Could he still be holding a grudge? Would it mean anything if she said she was sorry now? Pushing her even more than her guilt was her curiosity. What was he trying to do by reinventing himself? Was he after attention or something else? She had to know. She grabbed her purse and jacket, slid out of the booth, stood up and walked over.

His back was turned to her. His posture when he was seated was as bad as when he was standing. As crooked as a comma. His black mop was worse than she remembered; she could see his scalp through the thin hair at the back of his head. She walked to the other side of the table to face him. He was paging through a menu, bending over it like a man huddling over a campfire.

"Hello, Sweet." She extended her hand.

He glanced up. Ignored her hand. His eyes widened and then narrowed. In the span of a few seconds, she could see his expression go from recognition to surprise to hate. After all these years, he still blamed her. That made her sad and uncomfortable, but above all else, curious. What kind of man was Sweet Justice?

"D... d... do we know each other, ma'am?" Trip asked. His gaze shifted back and forth between her face and the menu.

He's playing a game, she thought. She lowered her hand

but flashed him her biggest smile. "Justice Trip. I can't believe you've forgotten me. Paris Murphy. It's been eighteen years, but I thought you'd still remember. St. Brice's?"

"High s... school. Sure."

His mouth was half open, as if he wanted to say something more to her. Murphy braced herself. Expected him to finally rip into her after years of stewing over the beating and her imagined role in it. Trip only stared. Not at her. Past her. She decided not to say anything about it. Let it be for now.

"How've you been, Sweet? You look good."

His eyes fell again. "So d... do you, Paris."

"I'm eating alone," she said. "Mind if I join you?"

"Suit yourself," he said.

Not an enthusiastic reception, but she'd take it. She draped her jacket over the back of a chair, set her purse on the floor at her feet and took a seat across from him. Despite his thinning hair, she still saw a trace of his high school handsomeness. Dark. Brooding. But that earlobe. Two gobs of flesh hanging down like teardrops from the side of his head. Why didn't he have that fixed? Was it some kind of badge?

The waitress came by. A skinny young woman with short hair the color of strawberry Jell-O and a silver stud in her nose. She handed Murphy a menu. "You changed tables."

"Is that okay?" Murphy asked.

"Whatever. Separate checks?"

Murphy was going to buy Trip dinner but decided against it. "Yeah. Separate."

"Something to drink?"

"Glass of red wine," said Murphy. "House Merlot is fine."

The waitress to Trip: "What about you?"

He was fingering the menu. "Whatever's on t... tap."

"Miller? Bud? Pabst?"

"Miller."

The waitress left to get the drinks. Murphy propped her right elbow on the table and rested her chin in her hand. Waited to see if Trip could manage a question. His head was bent down. He was studying the menu again. Finally he glanced up.

"You m... married? Kids?"

She was surprised that was his first question. Figured there was no reason to lie about it. "Separated. No kids. What about you?"

Head down again. "No. I'm not m... married." A long pause, then he asked the question she thought would have been his first one: "What you d... doing up here? Live in Moose Lake?"

If she wanted to get the maximum amount of information out of him, she had to hide what she did for a living. "No. Still live in St. Paul. Come up here every year for the fall colors. A little vacation. What about you?"

He set down the menu and picked up the salt and pepper shakers. "Work. Up here for w... work." He had a shaker in each hand. Tapped one against the other. Looked at them instead of her.

"So what do you do for a living?" she asked.

"Sales."

"Oh, yeah. I read that in the paper. Shirts, right?"

He set down the shakers. "Dress shirts."

"You've certainly been big news lately."

"Guess s... so." He raised his eyes and smiled.

"You're a regular hero," she said. The waitress brought their drinks. Murphy took a sip. "How does it feel to be a hero?"

"Good," he said. He took a sip of beer and set it down. Stared at the stein. Ran his right index finger around the rim. "Actually, feels g... great." He added what sounded to Murphy like a hollow afterthought. "I like h... helping the c... c... cops." He took a long drink. Wiped his mouth with the back of his hand.

It wasn't about being helpful, she thought. It was about getting attention. He was as puffed up as a rooster. She took another sip of wine. "Must have been horrible when you found that poor woman's finger."

He leaned back in his chair and stretched his legs out underneath the table. "I've g... got a mighty s... strong stomach." He finished off his beer and looked her straight in the eyes for the first time. Grinned. Murphy found it a creepy, self-satisfied smile. An idea darted into her mind. Trip and the missing bridesmaid. Was there something more to it?

The waitress returned with her order pad poised. "Walleye's on special. Fried or baked. Comes with fries or baked potato and coleslaw or garden salad. All you can eat. Seven ninety-five. Ready or should I come back?"

Trip jumped in before Murphy could answer. "Fried chicken."

"Half or quarter?"

"Half. Fries. Coles... slaw."

The waitress looked at Murphy. "For you?"

"The baked walleye, please. Baked potato and garden salad."

The waitress left. Murphy took another sip of wine and drummed her fingertips against the side of the goblet. Even though he had already ordered, Trip was back fiddling with the menu. She'd have to keep the talk flowing. Slide in some questions without arousing his suspicion. "Newspapers said you helped find a missing girl, too."

He saw the waitress, set down the menu and raised his empty glass. "Found her n... necklace. That led the c... cops to her."

"Alive?"

"Yeah." The waitress set another stein in front of him.

"What do you suppose happened to that bridesmaid? Who'd do such a thing? She's got a couple of little kids."

Trip took a long drink of beer. Set the stein down but kept his hand wrapped around the handle. "The ex d... did it."

She took a sip of wine. Tried to act surprised. "What? You're kidding?"

"Saw it on the n... news tonight." He took another long drink, almost finished the second stein. "Guy looks like a s... stupid jock."

Trip still hated athletes. Another leftover from high school, she thought. The waitress slapped their salads and a basket of rolls on the table.

"About t... time," Trip grumbled to no one in particular. He pulled the rolls toward him, took three of the four, put them on his bread plate. Slid the basket in Murphy's direction. He started spooning the coleslaw into his mouth. Murphy thought he was swallowing the stuff without chewing.

She unfolded her napkin and set it on her lap. Picked at her salad. Took a sip of wine. Tossed out a chilling question: "How does it feel? I wonder."

He bumped off the rest of his beer and raised his glass toward the waitress. "How does what f... feel?"

"Killing someone. Murdering someone. Wasting them. What's that like?"

He ate a roll in two bites and as many chews. Nodded toward the table of men in camo. "Ever go h... hunting?"

"Think it's like shooting birds?"

"No. Not d... duck hunting." The waitress brought him another beer. He grabbed the mug by the handle and lifted it. "Ever go d... deer hunting?" He took a long drink and set the stein down. "Ever hit a d... deer with your car?" That creepy grin again.

Murphy was ready to jump up and leave. She needed a break. She pushed her chair away from the table. Took her napkin off her lap and set it on the table. "Got to visit the ladies' room. Be right back." She grabbed her purse, stood up, walked to the bathroom.

He watched her go and thought: *Bitch. Beautiful bitch responsible for the worst beating I ever had.* He reached up and touched his earlobe. Seeing her gave him the same jolt as the one he'd gotten once while he was wiring a new light switch in the trailer. He'd touched the hot lead and felt a charge that ran right up his arm. Pain and excitement mixed together. After that shock from the light switch, he'd been tempted to touch it again. Had it really been that bad or had he imagined it? Of course, he was too smart to touch it again; he was too smart to fall for her again.

Trip pulled his pills out of his jacket pocket and, under the table, emptied them into his left palm. Surely he had something left for Paris Murphy. He couldn't see in the dim light of the bar. He reached over and slid the votive candle closer. Better. He poked around the tablets and capsules with his right index finger until he found the white ones. Scored on one side. Stamped with the word "Roche" and an encircled "2." He'd paid Keri about five dollars apiece for them. They came in a bubble pack, but he'd popped them out and dumped them in with the other pills. He hadn't tried them on himself yet. Keri told him they went great with beer; took the drunk to a new high. He couldn't

93

remember the drug's real name. She called it a lot of different things. "Roofies." "Roachies." "Date rape pills." He didn't want to rape Paris Murphy; but if he got her stoned, maybe someone else would. He'd heard it made women lose their inhibitions, practically rip off their own shirts. Even if it didn't do that, it would make her dizzy and drowsy. Maybe she'd get behind the wheel. Pass out. Crash her car. He scanned the room to make sure no one was watching. A table of people had started singing "Happy Birthday" to an old woman and everyone else in the bar seemed to know her. Turned to watch and sing along.

Happy birthday to you. Happy birthday to you.
Happy birthday, dear Hazel. Happy birthday to you.

He reached across the table and dropped a tablet in her glass of wine. The drug had no taste or odor. He'd wolf down his dinner and leave. She'd get sick after he was gone. Blame it on the food or the flu. She'd never suspect a guy from high school. A guy she hadn't laid eyes on in nearly twenty years. She had no idea how much he hated her. Was one pill enough? What would two do? Three? He picked two more tablets out of his palm. Dropped a second one in the glass and then, to be sure, a third. That should do it, he thought. Keri had told him the pill was ten times more powerful than Valium. He poured the rest of the pills back in the bottle, screwed the lid back on, shoved the bottle back in his pocket. Slid the candle back to the middle of the table. He studied her wineglass and prayed the pills would dissolve quickly.

The waitress set the chicken and fish dinners on the table. "Will the lady need another glass of wine?"

"Doubt it," Trip said with a small smile. "I think that'll b... be enough for her."

Murphy washed her hands and splashed water on her face. Eating dinner with Trip was making her sick. He had the table manners of a pig and the conversation skills of a rock. The few full sentences he'd managed to utter gave her the creeps. She dried her face with a paper towel and looked in the bathroom mirror. How had she held up since high school? She leaned closer to the mirror. Except for the stupid scar on her forehead, her face was good. No lines yet. She took a brush out of her purse and gave her dark mane a few strokes. No gray hairs yet, either. She dropped the brush back in her purse and hiked the strap over her shoulder.

She walked out of the bathroom. She looked across the room and saw Trip pick up her glass, swirl the wine around and set it back down. What the hell was he trying to pull? He didn't see her watching him; he'd started attacking his food. She stepped next to the table. Set her purse on the floor. Trip was tearing off strips of chicken with his fingers and rifling them into his mouth. She sat down. Put her napkin back on her lap. Picked up her fork and knife, cut off a piece of fish and popped it in her mouth. Chewed and swallowed. She glanced at her glass. She wanted to ask him what he'd been doing with his hands on it, but decided to get some conversation going first. What in the world did she and Trip have left to talk about? Then it came to her: "Going to the all-class reunion?"

He set a chicken bone down. "What?" Licked his fingers.

"Didn't you get an invite in the mail? I can send you a copy." She put her hand on the wineglass, saw him nervously eye the goblet.

"No. No. I saw it. I d... don't know. I wasn't p... p... planning on it." He picked up a leg. Cleaned the meat off in a couple of bites. Threw down the bone.

She started to lift the wine to her lips. He looked at it again. She pretended to sip and set the glass down. Had Trip slipped something into her drink? "You should go. Everyone will want to hear about how you helped up here. If it was me, I wouldn't miss a chance to wave it in their faces." She saw he was studying her face. Searching for signs that she'd tasted something odd or that whatever he'd slipped into her drink was working.

His eyes fell again. He wiped his mouth with the napkin. "Maybe I will g... go. When is it?"

She wrapped her hand around the goblet again. Picked it up. Put it to her lips and then set it down again. His eyes followed the glass like a dog's eyes following a steak bone. "Saturday night," she said.

"This Saturday? You g... g... going?"

She smiled. "Wouldn't miss it." She wanted to throw the wine in his face and slap some cuffs on him, but she had no proof. She didn't see him do it. He could always say someone else had altered her drink. His behavior was also making her wonder about his involvement with the missing bridesmaid, and she didn't want to get his back up until she could poke around that case more.

She wanted to say something about the past to see if he really had held a grudge for nearly two decades. If he did, the scars went deeper than the torn earlobe. Could one beating change someone, turn them into something they wouldn't have otherwise become? Maybe it triggered something that was already there, waiting to surface with the right provocation. Perhaps other traumas had marked him after high school. Regardless, there was a dangerous edge that wasn't there eighteen years ago. The Trip she knew wouldn't have doctored a woman's drink.

She wrapped her hand around the goblet and watched him watching her do it. "Sweet. I always wanted to tell you."

"Tell m... me what?" He wasn't listening to her; he was preoccupied with her wineglass.

"What those boys did to you. It wasn't my fault. I didn't know until afterwards. When I found out, I felt horrible. Didn't have the courage to say anything. I always wanted to say—"

"I d... don't know what you're t... t... talking about," he said, interrupting her. For an instant, his eyes left her glass and locked on her face. He knew exactly what she was talking about. He didn't want to give her the chance to apologize.

"You know, Denny wasn't so bad if you'd gotten the chance to know him. He was just another kid. Not so different from you."

"I wasn't a b... bully. I wasn't a big b... baby. Didn't still like stupid c... cartoons in high school."

Murphy was stunned. How did Trip know Denny watched *The Flintstones*? Only she knew that. She stared at him but he wasn't paying attention to her anymore. He was scanning the bar for the waitress. He spotted the strawberry head and waved her over.

The young woman walked over to the table. "Another beer?"

He pointed at Murphy's glass. "On second thought, m... maybe I should l... let the l... lady catch up. Why don't you p... polish that off and I'll buy the n... next round?"

Murphy checked her watch. "Know what? I gotta go. I'm supposed to meet someone." She pushed the wineglass away. Stood up, pulled on her jacket. Picked up her purse, opened it, pulled out some bills and threw them on the table. "I'll see you on Saturday." She turned and left.

The waitress was still standing over him. "Another beer?"

"No. The check."

The waitress ripped it off her pad, set it on the table and walked away. He stared at the wineglass. She hadn't had enough. Waste of good drugs. He checked his watch. Still early. He'd go back to the motel and rest before his late-night errand.

13

Murphy was never so relieved to dump a dinner date. She practically ran to her car while digging her keys out of her purse. She opened the driver's side, threw her purse on the passenger's seat, got in, slammed the door shut. She started up the Jeep and shot out of the parking lot, turned onto the main drag. She slipped in a CD. An upbeat instrumental by Leo Kottke. The twelve-string guitar massaged her nerves during the short drive back to the hotel. She rolled into the parking lot and her cell phone rang. She hoped it wasn't Jack backing out of their romantic evening. She turned off the CD and pulled the phone out of her purse.

Duncan: "Don't get too comfortable."

"Don't tell me I have to turn around. I'm all settled in." She didn't want to tell him her husband was on the way up.

"No, no. But you might be spending less time there than I thought."

Something's up, thought Murphy. She guessed the theory he'd sold to the sheriff was beginning to unravel.

Duncan: "The ex-hubby's story is starting to check out. The cops up there finally caught up with this friend of his."

Murphy smiled to herself; she was right. "The buddy with the cabin?"

"Name's Ozzie something. Starts with a Y." Duncan shuffled some papers on his desk. "Yates. Ozzie Yates. Claims he was in the car with Pederson from the time he left St. Paul until he picked up his kids and went hunting."

"Where's this Yates been this whole time?"

"Still at the cabin. Pederson left him there to take his kids back home. Yates had a motorcycle he was working on up at the lake. Was gonna ride it back to the cities."

She couldn't resist: "Told you so."

"The sheriff's got more checking to do. Could be Oz is lying for his pal."

"I'll bet you lunch he's not."

"You're on. Give Carlton County what you got, see what you can do to help. Might as well spend the night. Here's the plan. Unwind tonight. Go to work in the morning, then head back. How's that sound, Potato Head?"

"Duncan." She thought about challenging him on the Potato Head issue, then reconsidered. Leave well enough alone. "I'll check in with you before I leave town. And hey, thanks for the nice room."

"No problem. Enjoy."

"I will." She hung up and shoved the phone back in her purse. She spotted the silver Beemer in the parking lot and checked the Jeep's clock. She didn't want to think about how fast he'd driven to get up there. She pulled her keys out of the ignition, shoved them in her purse, slid out of the car and slammed the door. Told herself to punch out of the job for the night. Put Trip and that horrible meal they'd shared out of her mind. Jack sure as hell wouldn't want to hear someone may have tried to poison her. She walked through the lobby.

The clerk was behind the front desk, leaning on the

counter and flipping through a magazine. "Your hubby *is* a looker. Sure he ain't got a brother?"

Murphy smiled. "Sorry. Only child."

"My luck. Most of my dates look like that." She nodded toward the moose head.

Murphy laughed and went to her room, slipped her card in the lock. Pushed it open. Jack was standing in the middle of the room with a bottle of champagne in his hand and a big grin on his face. He'd just walked in himself. Under his jacket, he was still in his scrubs. Murphy shut the door.

"Where were you?" he asked. "I was getting worried. Thought you'd dragged me up here to stand me up."

"Went out for some dinner." She looked at his crotch. "Wasn't it uncomfortable driving all the way up here with that in your pocket?"

"I've had a continuous hard-on for you since we got married. I hide it well is all."

"How many traffic laws did you break on the way up here? Add any new speeding tickets to your collection?" She pulled off her jacket and purse and tossed them on a chair.

"Believe it or not, I even had time to stop by your boat and grab a couple of accessories." He pulled a champagne glass out of each pocket. "I saw flowers in the galley." He said it in a way that required an explanation.

"My mother," she said, and immediately hated herself for the lie.

"What's the occasion? Did I miss something?"

"You didn't miss a thing." She wanted to get him off the subject. "When are we going to get a new set of flutes?" She pulled the glasses out of his hands and set them on the nightstand.

He took off his jacket, threw it on a chair. He saw the

ice bucket on the floor next to the tub. "How'd you know I'd bring champagne?"

"You're that kind of fella." She walked over to the tub and turned on the water. It would take a while to fill. She peeled off her top, dropped it on the floor and walked toward him.

"The kind of fella that will drive for two hours with a hard-on to meet his wife?"

"Exactly." She pulled his shirt over his head and threw it on the floor. "Know what I love about doctor duds?"

"What?" he said.

She loosened the drawstring on his pants and slipped them down. "No buttons or zippers."

They finished undressing and fell into bed. He kissed her, his tongue darting past her teeth. His mouth moved to the hollow at the base of her throat, and then to her left breast. When he bit her nipple, she arched her back. He entered her. Moaning, she wrapped her legs around him and gently raked his back with her nails. He saw her eyes were half shut and slowed the pace of his thrusts. "I don't want you to come too soon," he breathed in her ear. "I had to wait. So do you."

They saved the champagne and Jacuzzi for last.

14

Trip knew the park was open year-round, but he was counting on the office being empty late at night. The entrance was a half mile east of Interstate 35 at the Moose Lake exit, off County Road 137. He pulled down the road that ran next to the building and saw a sign posted out front that made the campground an even better hiding place: DUE TO STATE BUDGET CUTS, OVERNIGHT CAMPING HAS BEEN ELIMINATED FROM THE DAY AFTER LABOR DAY UNTIL MEMORIAL DAY WEEKEND NEXT YEAR. He left the truck running, got out and walked up to the park office window and peeked inside. Dark and empty. He got back in and drove around the arm blocking the entrance. He drove a few more yards straight ahead. A right would take him to the picnic grounds and beach. A left to the campground and boat landing. He took the left. Headed for the south end of the park.

The campground was made up of three loops coming off the west side of the road. The east side of the road was lined with woods and a farmer's field. Even if the campground was open, it would probably be near deserted on a cold Monday night in October. Still, he decided to be safe and make sure no campers had ignored the sign and pitched a tent. He took the first right off the road and drove past campsites 1 through 10. Empty. He took a right turn and exited the first loop. The second right off the road rounded past sites 11 through 18. Again, not a single car or tent. He hung a right and got off the second loop. He went down the road toward the last and largest loop. The third right turn circled 19 through 35. A dull glow radiated from a building containing the showers and toilets. No one around. He hung a left and took the road back to the first set of campsites.

He pulled the truck into number 5, the closest to Echo Lake. He punched off the lights and turned off the engine. He wanted to pop another Adderall, but his stash was getting low and he needed to ration the stuff until he got home. He wished the park was more uniformly wooded. It used to be old farm fields and it was in the process of turning back into a forest. Many of the trees looked more like tall bushes. The few mature hardwoods had dropped most of their leaves. The rest of the park was pines.

He thought about the options. If he drove around he could probably find a garbage dumpster or a big trash can for day visitors. Chances were there wouldn't be anyone in the park until the weekend. Still, there could be a weekday visitor, or the dumpster pickup might be anytime during the week. No. He wanted the body to stay well hidden for as long as possible. Until it rotted. He could walk to the end of the fishing pier and dump her into Echo Lake. He had chains and bags of sand and salt—the truck's winter equipment—that he could use to weigh the body down. What if it wasn't deep enough at the end of the pier? No, the lake was too risky. The pond in the northern half of the park? No. Definitely too shallow, and there were beavers living there; they might disturb the grave. Better to bury her in the woods. He had a shovel, another piece of winter gear. Flashlight. Where'd he put it? He reached over to the glove compartment, flipped it open and felt around. Sunglasses. Owner's manual for the truck. Couple of jackknives. Bowie knife. Stiletto. Wire cutter. His one-hitter kit. Damn. No flashlight. He grabbed the stiletto and shut the glove compartment. He played with the stiletto while thinking. Open. *Chink*. Close. *Chink*. Open. *Chink*. Close. *Chink*. He reached under the driver's seat and felt some highway maps and a phone book. No flashlight. Leather gloves, though. He'd need those. He grabbed them and sat up. "Fuck. Now what?" he muttered. Open. *Chink*. Close. *Chink*. He couldn't bury her using his truck lights; he wanted to walk the body into the woods so he wouldn't leave a trail of tire marks. Come morning, the tracks he'd left around the closed gates could be blamed on teenagers screwing around. Tire marks going into the woods would raise suspicions. He peered through the windshield. The moon was full. Maybe he could manage without a flashlight. He shoved the stiletto in his jacket pocket and pulled on the gloves.

As he opened the driver's door and got out, he heard rustling in the bushes surrounding the campsite. Holding his breath, he gently closed the truck door. He pulled the stiletto out of his pocket. Open. *Chink*. More rustling. Son of a bitch, he thought. Had someone followed him there? He turned, flattened his back against the truck, held the stiletto in front of him. In the moonlight, he couldn't distinguish substance from shadows. An icy gust rattled the trees. Had it been a breeze he'd heard? The wind settled down. He stood still. More rustling. No. Not the wind. He exhaled slowly and tightened his grip on the knife. A ball of fur on four legs waddled out of the bushes. It stopped, sat up on its haunches and stared with beady eyes. "Fucking 'coon," Trip said. He picked up a rock and threw it at the animal. It didn't budge. He threw another. It growled at him and bared its teeth. "Get the f... f... fuck out of here." It turned and went toward the road.

Trip closed the stiletto and slipped it in his right jacket pocket. He walked to the rear of the truck and opened the back. A flashlight rolled out and hit the ground. "Great," he said. He picked it up, turned it on and shined it over his cargo. Under the pile of boxes and packaged shirts he saw a corner of blue plastic. The tarp. He set the flashlight on the tailgate, grabbed the edge of the tarp with both hands and pulled. It hardly moved. Bunny Pederson was a cow, all right. He pulled harder and the body inched out. Was the tarp caught on something? He gave a good yank. The blue cocoon slid out and fell to the ground with a thud. A pile of boxes and shirts tumbled out after it. He picked up the boxes and shirts and threw them back. He shined the light on the ground to make sure nothing else had fallen out. He reached inside the truck, pulled out the shovel and threw it next to the body. He trained the flashlight on the tarp. A good wrapping job, he thought. Nice and tight. A giant candy bar. He bent over and sniffed. No stink yet; he could thank the cold spell for that. He wondered if she'd bled all over the truck bed, or if the plastic had contained it all. He ran the beam up and down the tarp and didn't see any dark stains. He'd check the truck later. He shoved the light in his jacket pocket, wrapped his arms around the middle of the cocoon and hiked the body onto his right shoulder like a rolled-up carpet.

"Oh, man," he grunted. He held the body in place with his right hand and with his left pulled out his flashlight. He shined the flashlight in front of him and walked three steps before he realized he'd forgotten the shovel. "Fuck." He set the body down and went back for the tool. He picked up the shovel—a wooden-handled spade—and wondered: *How am I going to carry all this shit?* He thought for a few seconds, shoved the flashlight back in his pocket. He unbuckled his belt, ran the end of it through the shovel handle and buckled it again. The shovel dangled down the side of his leg and banged against him when he walked, but it worked. He went back to the body. Awkward with the shovel, but he managed to bend over and hike the cocoon back up on his shoulder. He stood still for a minute, making sure of his balance. He pulled the flashlight out of his pocket and started walking again. He'd visited the park before, even camped there a couple of times to spare the expense of a motel. He had a pretty good idea of where he wanted to bury her. He walked north on the road out of the campground. Every ten minutes or so he had to stop and adjust the body's position on his shoulder. The gusts of wind seemed to grow stronger and last longer. He was grateful for the gloves but wished he'd packed a wool cap. His *E.P.* hat wasn't warm enough. The Minnesota fall felt worse than any Tennessee winter. The hat belonged back in Memphis as surely as he did. After less than a quarter of a mile on the road he took a sharp right and went east into the woods, where there were no trails or other attractions for fall visitors. The ground was hard. The digging was difficult and he worked up a sweat. Even had to take off his jacket. He buried her, tarp and all, in a shallow grave.

Trip was throwing the first shovel of dirt over the body when ranger Bob Kermitt turned in to Moose Lake State Park. Clueless tourists who hadn't been reading the newspapers didn't know many state campgrounds were closed until Memorial Day weekend. They'd pull up to the office, read the sign, get pissed off and drive around the arm. Some didn't even read the sign. They stuffed money in the self-registration lockbox and drove around the arm, never questioning why the thing was down. Since the day after Labor Day, park staff had been monitoring the campground, even during the week. If someone had pitched a tent or parked an RV, they were told to leave. If they left money in the lockbox, it would be returned. Kermitt wanted to check his live traps for raccoons as well; the day staff had probably forgotten to do that and he didn't like leaving the animals caged for an entire day.

He didn't mind working the night shift on occasion; it broke up his week. His day hours were filled with what he called "glorified housekeeping and baby-sitting." He scrubbed the outhouses around the picnic grounds and trails—there were still a lot of hikers taking in the fall leaves. Picked up trash. Sold souvenir tee shirts. Cut the grass. Gave directions. Asked park guests to *please* stop leaving food out for the raccoons. *Please* stop dumping trash down the outhouse holes. *Please* don't rinse diapers in the lake. *Please* leash your dogs. *Please* don't let your kids run wild on the dock. He told his wife he should change his name tag to *Ranger Please*. He looked forward to November, when the visitors would taper off and he could catch up on some of the maintenance he never had time to do in the summer and early fall. Painting picnic tables. Repairing broken grills and fire rings. Removing dead wood. The park would get busy again after the first good snowfall, when winter visitors came in with their snowshoes and cross-country skis.

All in all, Kermitt thought he had a good job. He enjoyed being outside; it kept him fit and trim and tan. The state benefits were great, especially the pension. A few more years and he could retire. Spend time with the grandkids. Do a little fishing. Make more trips to Vegas with the old lady. Maybe they'd even make it to Hawaii.

Kermitt pulled up to the office, got out of the pickup. He dug his keys out of his pants pocket and opened the lockbox. He shined his flashlight inside. Empty. He slammed it shut and locked it again. As cold as it was, he didn't expect any illegal or clueless campers. Monday nights were dead even before the cutbacks. Still, there was always the odd slacker and screw-off. He looked up at the sky. A full moon, as white and as bright as a snowball. Full moons brought goofballs out of the woodwork. He decided to take a tour of the campground and leave the live traps for last. The raccoons could wait a little longer.

Free of his load, it took Trip a fraction of the time to get out of the woods. He ran most of the way—shovel in one hand and flashlight and jacket in the other. He wanted to get back to the motel for another hot shower, another beer. Unwind. Treat himself to a couple of tranks. Those baby-blue Valium tablets. He came out of the trees and got on the road. A raccoon darted across his path and startled him. "Fucking 'coon," he said. He stopped and followed it with his flashlight as it crawled into the weeds. He leaned against the shovel to catch his breath. He inhaled; the night air smelled of dry leaves. A blast of wind chilled his body, still damp with sweat. He shivered and put his jacket back on. He picked up the shovel and started jogging again. He took a right turn off the road and started down the loop containing campsite 5. Then he saw it. A pickup with its headlights on, parked behind his. A park ranger walking around Trip's truck, shining a flashlight into the cab windows. The ranger had his back turned and didn't see the beam from Trip's flashlight. Trip flicked it off, shoved it in his left pocket and crouched behind a low bush on the edge of the adjoining campsite. Trip heard the ranger yelling as he peeked inside the truck. He couldn't make out the words at first; they were muffled by the breeze. The wind died down.

"Hello? You can't spend the night. Campground is closed." The ranger walked to the back of the truck.

"Fuck," Trip said under his breath. "Fuck. Fuck. Fuck." He'd left the gate open. If there was blood on the bed, the ranger could find it.

The ranger reached inside the truck, rifled around, pulled something out. He held it upside down by the heel while he trained the flashlight on it. Trip's palms felt cold and wet under his gloves. He wasn't breathing anymore. He was sure his heart had stopped beating. He thought: *Is this how it feels when you're drowning?* He couldn't believe he'd missed it; it had fallen out of the tarp. Her shoe! The ranger found her fucking peach shoe! The entire town of Moose Lake—the entire state—knew what the bridesmaid was wearing when she went missing. Peach dress. Peach purse. Peach shoes.

The ranger was still rummaging around in back of the truck. What else was he grabbing? How long had he been snooping around? Trip studied the ranger's figure. No one was ever as tall as Trip, but most men were thicker. Stronger. The ranger was big. He couldn't see his face; he was probably some young guy. Trip wondered if he could take someone stronger and younger. The ranger headed back to his truck with the shoe. Trip figured he was going to radio for help. Couldn't let him do that.

Another gust came up, whistling around the bushes and pines. Trip dashed out from his hiding place. The ranger's fingers were wrapped around the door handle of his pickup when Trip came up behind him and bashed the back of his

110

head with the shovel. The *clang* of the spade rose above the sound of the wind in the trees. The ranger's head bounced once against the driver's-side window of the pickup. He dropped the shoe and the flashlight and fell against the door. He slid to the ground. Facedown in the dirt and moaning, the ranger blindly raised his right hand and brushed it against the side of the pickup. He was trying to pull himself up. Trip raised the shovel up over his right shoulder and brought it down hard with a *thud*. The ranger wasn't moving, but Trip struck his head a third time to be sure. Gray hair was matted with the blood. He wasn't a young guy. He was old, same as Trip's pa. That made him angry. An old man shouldn't be out here, he thought. He raised the spade and brought it down again. A sickening sound. Crunching and soft at the same time. Trip dropped the shovel and stood over the still figure.

Trip had never killed someone this way before. Had never gotten so close to one of his victims while they were still breathing. Still moaning and groaning. Fighting for life. This wasn't like running someone over with a truck, so high off the ground and impersonal and efficient. This was messy and personal. Hard work. Scary. Trip was perspiring under his hat. His armpits were clammy. He was panting. Couldn't get air into his lungs quick enough. That drowning feeling again. He wanted to get the hell out of the park. Get away from the mess. He hopped over the body and ran to his truck and pulled the door open. The shovel and the shoe. He forgot the shovel and the shoe. He ran back and picked them up. Rubbed the back of the spade against the dirt to get the worst of the blood off. Wondered if there were brains on it. The ranger's pickup lights were on. Should he shut them off? No. Leave it alone, he thought. The ranger's flashlight was next to his body and it was still shining; the beam illuminated the man's bloody head. Trip was spooked by it; the flashlight was accusing him. He kicked it and it rolled away; the beam flickered and died. He remembered his own flashlight. Where was it? Did he drop it? He reached into his jacket pockets. His right one. Empty. His left. There it was. On the way back to his truck, he stumbled over the ranger's leg and fell in the dirt, right next to the body. It freaked him out; he made a startled noise that sounded like a pig's squeal. He scrambled off the ground, picked up the shovel and the shoe. He checked his pockets. Flashlight still there. Checked his head. Hat still there. Did he drop anything else? He scanned the ground with the beam and saw only the ranger's body and the ranger's flashlight. Good. He flicked off the light and shoved it back in his jacket. He ran to his truck and threw the shovel and shoe in back and shut the gate.

When he pulled out of the campsite he managed to back up without hitting the ranger's pickup, but he did run over the ranger himself.

15

He was shaking as he sped out of the park. Vibrating like a car going faster than it could handle. He wanted to escape the sound the shovel had made with that last hit. It reminded him of something. A kitchen sound. An egg cracking? A mallet hitting a tough steak? No. His pa used to buy fryers whole because they were cheaper that way. He'd chop them himself into serving pieces with a meat cleaver. Sloppy and messy. That was the sound. Meat and bone being broken. Crunching and squishing. It'd be a long time before he could handle a raw chicken again. He needed to downshift. Needed his pills, and they were in the motel room. He'd calm himself with the next best thing: his music. His discs were in a case on the front passenger's seat. He grabbed one without looking at it, popped it in, cranked the volume. When he realized the CD he'd picked, he had to laugh. *The Grave Digger*. Dark and evil German power metal. The guitars and drums pushed the broken bones and meat out of his mind. His first instinct was to keep driving. Keep the pedal to the floor and tear out of town. What about his stuff? He couldn't leave his stuff in the motel room. The purse was in his suitcase. Should have buried the bag with her, he thought. The risk hadn't been worth it to get a peek at a handful of her cosmetics and the lyrics from an Elvis song.

He headed for the motel; he'd pack his stuff and leave. Then he remembered he hadn't paid the bill. Skipping town without paying would attract attention. The motel owner, an old woman, lived in back of the office. Trip checked his watch. Midnight. Too late to wake her; that would arouse suspicions. He could slip the money under the door. No. That would seem odd. He could check out at dawn; the owner kept early hours. He pulled into the motel parking lot and sat behind the wheel with the lights off and the music on and his brain working.

The purse and her shoe. The only objects tying him to her. The shoe was in back of the truck. The purse was in the suitcase. He'd left no witnesses. No one saw the truck run her over and no one saw him in the park except for the ranger, and he was dead. What had changed since he buried her? Had he dropped any clues that could steer the cops in his direction? He'd gotten rid of the biggest piece of evidence—her body—and it was well hidden. He'd left another body behind in plain view. He should have buried the old guy. Still, they would have found his car and probably a mess of blood and brains on the ground. Once the ranger's body was discovered, the cops might set up roadblocks. Stop cars and trucks. Couldn't let them see the shoe or the blood on the shovel. The shoe would be easy to lose. He'd clean up the shovel. Washing the entire truck bed wouldn't be a bad idea. Check everything out. Make sure the bridesmaid's body hadn't leaked anything while it was bouncing around back there. Something to do while waiting for sunrise; he sure as hell wasn't going to get any sleep. He turned his lights back on, pulled out of the motel parking lot and headed to town. He knew there was a self-service car wash in Moose Lake adjacent to a gas station.

Three bays, all of them empty. He steered the truck into the middle one, punched off his lights, turned off the engine. He opened the driver's door but before he hopped out, he took off his baseball cap and set it on the passenger's seat. He didn't mind if he got his clothes wet, but he didn't want to mess up his hat. Didn't want to ruin his leather gloves, either. He pulled them off and threw them on the seat. He got out of the truck, slammed the door behind him. Walked behind the truck and pulled down the bay door. The streets were empty and the gas station was closed for the night, but he didn't want to chance anyone seeing what he was doing. He opened the truck gate. The shovel and shoe—partners in crime—fell out together. Lying on its side against the gray concrete floor, the peach pump resembled a dead tropical bird. How to get rid of it? He looked around the bay and saw a trash can. Too obvious. The drain might work. A narrow trench that ran nearly the entire width of the floor and was covered by sections of grate. He bent over, wrapped his fingers around one of the sections and tugged hard. It didn't budge; screwed in. He tried the next grate. It lifted out easily. He set it aside. Using two fingers, he picked up the shoe by the tip of the heel and carried it over to the drain. He dropped it in, watched it settle in the muck, replaced the grate.

The shovel. He lifted it up by the handle. Wet spots all over the spade. Blood. A few clots of something red and raw and glistening, like bits of uncooked liver. He dropped the shovel on the floor directly over the drain and walked to the power hose mounted on the wall. He scanned the sign over the hose. It listed spray settings: *Tire*

Cleaner. Engine Cleaner. High-pressure Soap. Suds 'n' Brush. High-pressure Rinse. High-pressure Wax. At the end of the list: *Warning. Grip wand tightly due to 1000 lbs. pressure. We are not responsible for damage.* He turned the knob to *High-pressure Soap* and plugged the machine with a dollar's worth of quarters. He pulled the wand over to the shovel. Sprayed the blade with soapy water. Pink dripped down the drain. He kept shooting the blade until the water ran clear. He flipped the shovel with his foot and sprayed the other side. Ran the wand up and down the handle. His time ran out. He walked back to the knob. Turned it to *High-pressure Rinse.* Four more quarters. He sprayed the blade and handle until the water shut off. He picked up the shovel and inspected it. Clean as a spoon out of the dishwasher. He set it upright against the wall. Plugged the hose with more quarters and took the wand over to the gate and sprayed it down to give him a clean working surface.

Now the hard part. He started reaching in and pulling his merchandise out of the truck. The unopened boxes filled with individually wrapped shirts were easiest. He slid them out of the truck, held them up, examined the cardboard cubes on all six sides for bloodstains. Each of the five sealed boxes was clean. He threw them inside the cab. He leaned in and grabbed the two opened boxes out of the truck. The cardboard was clean on the outside. He carefully lifted out the polybagged shirts inside and held them to the ceiling light. Clean. He put the shirts back inside, folded the box tops shut, set the cubes inside the cab. Now all the loose stuff. One by one, he pulled out two dozen packaged shirts. The shovel must have rested on top of them because six of them were smeared with dirt and traces of blood. It looked like red food coloring against the clear plastic. He set the clean ones on the floor, propping them upright

116

against the wall, and stacked the dirty ones on the gate. Then one by one, he picked up each bloodied package with his left hand, holding it by a corner. With his right, he worked the wand. He used the gentle *Tire Cleaner* setting. The high-pressure sprays could rip the polybags and he didn't want to ruin his samples; he'd already paid for them. As he finished each package, he propped it against the wall to dry next to the clean ones. By the time he was done, he had a row of shirts sitting upright on the floor as if on display. Instead of a garage sale, he thought, it would be a grave digger's sale.

He had to crawl inside to reach the truck's winter gear: jumper cables, a set of chains, a towrope, one bag of rock salt, six sacks of sand. As he pulled out each item, he held it up, examined it from all angles. Set the clean stuff against the wall next to the shirts. The edges of two bags of sand had dirt on them; he couldn't tell if it was plain dirt or dirt mixed with brains and blood. He washed the edges with the *Tire Cleaner* setting and propped the bags against the wall.

The truck bed itself. Should probably spray the sides and ceiling of the topper, too, he thought. He plugged the hose with coins and turned it to *High-pressure Soap*. He shot foamy water inside the truck and watched as it poured out of the bed and ran down the floor drain. He didn't see pink. Only dirt. When his time ran out, he plugged the hose again for the rinse. When it stopped, he hung up the wand and scanned the bay, hoping for a towel dispenser. Nope. He wished he had some rags to wipe the bed dry. He studied the row of shirts, picked out the ugliest one. He ripped the package open and took out a yellow oxford with navy blue and white vertical stripes. He pulled out the stickpins, removed the plastic from around the neck and the cardboard from the back. He ducked under the topper and leaned in to wipe the bed. When he was finished, he balled up the wet shirt and its packaging and threw them into a corner of the truck bed. He wanted to get a good look. Where was his flashlight? He checked his jacket. Still in his left pocket. He took it out and turned it on and ran the beam around the inside of the bed and ceiling of the topper. Clean.

The winter gear went back into the truck first; he shoved it all against the rear of the bed, including the shovel. He stacked the merchandise on the bed. Did it in rows so it appeared neat and professional. Sealed boxes in back. Then the unsealed. Then the loose shirts. He ran the flashlight around one more time. Satisfied with his job, he flicked it off and shoved it in his left pocket. He slammed the gate shut. Might as well wash the outside of the truck, he thought. He reached into his pants pockets. Bills. No more quarters. He peeled three one-dollar bills off and fed them to the change machine mounted against the wall. Twelve quarters. Enough for a wash, rinse and wax.

When he was finished, he stepped back and admired his truck. It always looked so good after a wash and wax. Shiny and new and invincible. He wiped his hands on his pants legs. Went behind the truck. Opened the bay door. Scanned the street. Still quiet and empty. Went to the driver's door, opened it, got behind the wheel, slammed the door shut. He turned the ignition and started to back out of the bay. As he pulled out he saw a sign on the outside of the car wash: *Thank You for Your Dirty Business.*

He checked the clock on the dashboard. Still too early to wake the motel owner. He felt safe and calm after washing the truck and sorting through his merchandise. He thought he could snooze a little and still get out of town at dawn. He pulled into the motel parking lot exhausted. He

118

pushed open the door to his room, dropped his jacket on the floor and collapsed on top of the bed, his shoes still on.

At first light, he rolled out of bed and shuffled into the bathroom. He unzipped his pants and peed for what seemed like half an hour. As he was zipping up, it occurred to him that he could have gotten blood on his clothes. He looked down at his pants legs. Didn't see anything. They were dark so if there was any blood, it wouldn't be visible. He checked the bottom of each shoe. Clean. If they had had any mud or blood, it had probably come off while he was washing the truck. Satisfied he was clean, he decided against changing. Better shave, though. He looked like a bum. He turned on the television and watched the early morning news while he lathered. Nothing on the ranger. Either his body hadn't been discovered or it had been found, but the media hadn't yet learned about it. He shaved in front of the bathroom mirror with an ear still keyed to the news. He toweled off his face. Packed up his stuff. Switched channels a few times. Still nothing on the ranger. He turned off the set and walked out of the room with his suitcase. He set it on the floor of the cab on the passenger's side; he didn't want to mess up his neat merchandise arrangement in back. He peered through the office window. There she was behind the counter, wearing the same polka-dot dress as when she checked him in Saturday. Hair still knotted in a bun at the back of her head. He rapped twice on the door with his knuckles.

"Come in," she said. She had a singsong voice.

He turned the knob and opened the door.

"Watch your head," she said.

Trip walked inside. He was used to people reminding

119

him to watch his head. Ducking through doorways had become second nature. His posture was so bad, he didn't have to duck too much. "Morning," he mumbled.

"You're an early bird," she said.

The coffee was still dripping into the crusty pot she kept behind the counter. "Smells g... good," he said. He was hungry; his stomach growled. She pulled the pot out even though the coffee wasn't done dripping. Some splattered on the warmer and sizzled. She poured some into a foam cup and handed it to him.

"Thanks." He sipped. Exactly what he needed. Hot and strong.

"Sorry to see you go." She set a box of gas station donuts on the counter and lifted off the cover. "Help yourself."

He took a chocolate glazed. Ate it in two bites.

"Take more," she said, hands on her hips. "Sure was fun having a celebrity around."

He popped a powdered sugar one into his mouth. Chewed three times. Took another sip of coffee to wash the donut down. He set the cup on the counter, licked his fingers.

"Do me a favor, Mr. Trip?" She pulled a newspaper out from under the counter. The Minneapolis *Star Tribune*. "Sign your picture? Please?"

He grinned. "No p... problem." He checked his pockets for a pen. She slid one across the counter. He picked it up and signed at the bottom of the front-page color photo: *Good luck. Justice Trip.* She took the paper from him. He tried to hand the pen back to her.

"You keep it, Mr. Trip. It's got the name of the motel and the phone number. You're always welcome here."

He pulled out his wallet. "What d... d... do I owe you?"

"Got a special rate for heroes," she said, and winked at him. "Half off."

He took three twenties out of his wallet and thought: *God I'm going to miss the attention.*

He started up the truck, turned on the radio, pulled on his baseball cap. He searched the stations and hit one with the news. A male voice: "The Carlton County Sheriff's Office has not named the park employee, but may identify him at a press conference set for later today. It is the first murder of a state park worker in decades. In other news this morning . . ." More station scanning, and then a female reporter: "Moose Lake authorities have refused to release the apparent cause of death. The Ramsey County Medical Examiner's Office is conducting the autopsy. More information may be released at a press conference today. We'll be there with a live report. Now for the weather . . ." He switched stations again and found nothing more on the ranger. He turned it off. He wondered what the cops were up to, why they were holding back. He opened the glove compartment to take out his worry beads. His stiletto. He rifled around; it wasn't there. Then he remembered he'd shoved it in his jacket after the raccoon encounter in the park. He reached inside his pockets. Flashlight still in his left. He pulled it out and threw it on the passenger's seat. Dug around inside his pockets. Nothing more in his left. Nothing in his right. Where was it? Had he dropped the knife somewhere in the park? "Fuck no!" he moaned, and beat the steering wheel with his closed fists. "No!" He remembered checking his jacket for the flashlight after he fell over the ranger. His stiletto was gone from his pocket by then. Had it fallen out when he tripped? No, he'd checked the ground around the body. So where had he dropped it? Probably near the grave when he took off the jacket. He had to go back for it. The dead ranger would draw an army of cops to that park; one of them could eventually come across the bridesmaid's grave—and his knife right with it. He'd used gloves that night, but his prints would be all over the knife from the hundreds of other times he'd handled it. Might as well have wrapped his signed confession in the tarp along with the dead woman. He had to get the knife back. He could feel that panic starting again, that clammy drowning sensation. He'd packed his pill bottle with his clothes, but had shoved the remaining few of his favorites into his pants pocket. He fished out two Adderall tablets and popped them in his mouth.

He took Highway 137 and drove past the park without slowing. The cops were still there, of course. Yellow tape crisscrossed the entrance and there were sheriff's and police squads parked along the highway. Only two television news vans so far. He went a couple of miles past the park and pulled onto the shoulder. He checked his rearview mirror. No one behind him. He shut off the engine. The pills were working; his mind was racing around an idea. Parts of the park were bordered by private farmland. He could cut through a farmer's field to get to the woods. Sneak in while the cops were in the south end of the park gathered around the campground. It would take them a while to start spreading out, work the rest of the park. He'd be in and out in no time. Could he do it in broad daylight? No. Stupid idea. Someone would surely see him. Wait until dark? No. He'd probably get lost. Plus the cops would still be sniffing around the park. If they caught him sneaking through the woods at night, they'd really have reason to suspect him. He thought about the knife again. His prints were the only identifying mark. Otherwise it was a mail-order piece. Cheap. Mass-produced. Could belong to anyone. They needed to suspect him and get his prints to compare them to those on the knife. He'd never been arrested for anything before. Never had his prints taken. The big question: Did they have a suspect? If he was lucky, there was another Chad-type scapegoat waiting in the wings. He heard a helicopter overhead and looked through his windshield. A Twin Cities television station. He could see the call letters from the ground. A news van shot past him on the highway on the way to the park. He wanted to get the scoop on what was going on. He'd wait a bit and then swing back to the park. Give the news crews time to get there, get some inside information. He'd stop and chat it up with them. They all loved his ass. Maybe he could get on television one more time. Yeah. He was starting to get pumped.

16

In the morning Jack went out into the lobby and loaded a tray with bagels, cream cheese, fruit, juice, coffee. He saw a box in the foyer and bought her a *Duluth News Tribune*. He went back to the room. She was still sleeping. He laid the food and newspaper out on the table and turned on the tub faucet; the sound of the water didn't wake her. He sat on the edge of the bed, kissed her eyelids. "Paris," he said in a low voice. "Time to get up, my desert flower."

Her eyes fluttered open. He looked down at her and traced the scar on her forehead with his index finger. "Maybe you should see a plastic surgeon. You're so beautiful."

She pulled his hand away from her face. "But not with the scar."

"That's not what I meant."

"What did you mean then?"

"Nothing." He stood up. "I'll get out of here."

"Wait. I'm sorry. I'm super sensitive about that stupid mark. Can't you stay a little longer? Talk? How about some breakfast? I can't eat all this."

"Quicker you get your day going, quicker you can get

back." He leaned over, kissed her on the mouth and crossed the room to shut off the tub. "Thought you'd want to get another soak in before you check out of the Taj Mahal."

"Thank you." She sat up. Felt bad about snapping at him. "Don't forget to phone my folks about tonight. Tell *Imma* we'll make it another night," she said, using the Lebanese term of endearment for mother.

He pulled on his jacket. "Why don't you call?"

"Too early to call now and I'll be too damn busy later. Besides, my mom enjoys visiting with you over the phone."

"And visiting and visiting." He pulled his car keys out of his pocket. "Sure you won't be back in time for dinner?"

"Even if I am, I'll be tired." She lied. Murphy suspected her folks had invited the two of them to dinner to meddle. Whenever she and Jack split, her parents made it their mission to get them back together. Sometimes their interference made reconciliation harder instead of easier. He walked to the door. She rolled onto her side and watched him leave. "Love you."

He was in a hurry, didn't answer. Pulled the door open and walked out.

She flopped onto her back, stared at the ceiling, replayed the night. As usual, the sex had been great. Afterward, she'd tried to talk but he'd rolled over and gone to sleep, so she'd turned on the television. That was becoming their routine as well, and it pained her to see it happening. They used to cuddle. Rehash the day with each other. Lately, the list of what they could discuss without fighting had shrunk. Some days, she thought the neutral topics could fit on the back of a postage stamp. He'd grown to hate her job. Feared any day she'd be the next patient wheeled into the ER. She'd start describing an especially tough case or problem at the cop shop. He'd raise his arm as if he were fending off a blow and say, "Give the Cliffs Notes version."

She respected his work as much as he resented hers. He was a top doc in town. Led the effort to make Regions Hospital a Level 1 trauma center. Still, he hoarded the details of his day at Regions like they were buried treasure. If he was especially stressed out over something, she'd ask and he'd say, "You don't want to know." They'd stopped talking about the future; planning was a wasted exercise since their life together was uncertain. The subject of children was a land mine. If the timing seemed right to one of them it was wrong for the other. She suspected the real reason neither was ready for kids was they didn't want to bring children into a marriage destined to end in divorce. She knew one night of spontaneous romance wouldn't fix everything, but she'd hoped to see a glimmer of their old relationship when she invited him to join her at the hotel. Instead, she saw more of what was wrong with her marriage.

She kicked off the covers and sat up, swung her legs over the side of the bed and stood up. She glanced at the breakfast table. Typical Jack. Neat. Methodical. Precise. Bagels stacked into a tower on one plate. Cream cheese stacked on another. One of each kind of fruit in a bowl. One of each kind of juice and milk, cartons lined up in a straight row like soldiers. She wished the time he took laying out the food had been spent in bed with her, talking. She was surprised she'd been able to lure him up to Moose Lake at all; he didn't like messing up his routine. The bed was what drew him, she thought. He'd never sleep with another woman, but in a way she felt he was cheating on her by having sex and bolting for St. Paul. On the other hand, there was a part of her that wanted to get rid of him first thing in the morning. Maybe they were both only in it for the sex. She turned on the Jacuzzi and stepped into the bubbling hot water. While she was soaking, she wondered if there was a way she could fit a whirlpool on her boat, along with a fireplace. She leaned back in the tub and her cell phone rang. "Go away," she said. It stopped ringing and then started again. Had to be Yo-Yo. She stepped out of the tub, wrapped a towel around her wet body and took the phone off the nightstand. "Murphy."

Duncan: "Morning, Potato Head. Catch the news?"

"Damn," she said. She grabbed the remote and turned on the television. "Now what?"

"I think we can completely rule out our pal Chad."

Murphy stopped channel hopping when she got to the news. A helicopter shot showed a body in the woods being lifted onto a stretcher. Murphy turned up the sound. The cameras switched to a male reporter standing at the entrance to Moose Lake State Park. The gate was blocked with yellow police tape. She turned up the sound and all she caught was: "Back to you in the newsroom."

"Who's the dead guy?" Murphy asked. She reached for a cup of coffee and took a sip. Cold and bitter. She downed it in a couple of gulps and shuddered.

"Park ranger. Robert Kermitt."

"When? How? Who found him?"

"Got croaked last night. Head bashed in. Body run over. Couple of other parks workers found him this morning. I would have called you earlier, but the cops up there haven't asked for our help on this one, especially since the one St. Paul connection is heading south."

Duncan was talking fast; he always talked fast when he was on to something big. Murphy knew he was saving the best for last. "What else?" she asked.

"The parks people found something with the body. Inside the ranger's jacket. I talked to the sheriff and police chief up there. They're keeping it out of the news."

"Something tying the ranger's murder to Bunny Pederson."

"That's my girl," said Duncan. "How does a peach shoe sound?"

"Sounds like the ranger caught someone dumping the bridesmaid. Couldn't have been the ex and his pal?"

Duncan: "Not unless there's a third person involved. The cops were keeping an eye on Pederson and his buddy all night."

"Good." Murphy had never laid eyes on Chad Pederson, but she found something endearing about a man who took his kids duck hunting and gave elderly neighbors tomatoes out of his own garden. "Still want me to talk to the cops here?"

"Sure. Give them what you got as long as you're up there. It'll reassure them Mr. Chad ain't their man. Then it's not a wasted trip."

Murphy thought the last twenty-four hours had been a waste personally and professionally. She ran her fingers through her tangled hair. Tried to move her mind from her marriage to work. "I'll head on over to the park. They'll still be processing the crime scene. Scouting around for the bridesmaid's body." She picked up a bagel and took a bite.

"You okay?" he asked.

Was her voice betraying her turmoil? Was Duncan that perceptive? She decided it didn't matter. Time to get down to business. "Fine," she said shortly. "Tired."

"Make sure you call before you head back to St. Paul, in case something else pops."

"Sure, Yo-Yo." She bit her lip; it had slipped out.

"What?"

"No. No. I won't leave before I call. Later." She hung up before he could say anything else. Shoved the phone in her purse. She dropped the towel and stepped into some

128

panties and a sweater. She'd brought the union sweatshirt with her; it was huge. She'd wear it over her sweater instead of her jacket. Her stomach growled. More food. She walked over to the breakfast table and saw the *Duluth News Tribune*. Unfolding it, she wasn't surprised to see yet another story on Justice Trip. She sat down at the table and read it. Still making a big deal about volunteering for the search party. More fluff about how he felt an emotional tie to Bunny Pederson. Had he known her, he said in the story, they could have been friends. "Give me a break," she muttered, folding the paper. She grabbed another bagel and took a bite. She wondered if a dead ranger would finally push Trip off the front page. She thought about the uncomfortable meeting with him the night before. The way he'd picked up her glass and swirled the wine around. The way he'd repeatedly glanced at her drink and quickly averted his eyes. She was sure he'd dropped something in it. She should have challenged him on it, but all she wanted to do was get away from the creep. Trip and the bridesmaid. She kept thinking there was something more there. A connection, and not the bullshit kind Trip was selling to the newspapers.

Checkout time wasn't until noon, so she left her things in the room. She wanted to get to the murder scene. The park entrance was a half mile east of the hotel. On her way in, Murphy passed a caravan of squad cars and television news vans parked along the shoulder of Highway 137. She knew the call letters from the Twin Cities and Duluth stations, but there were several others she didn't recognize. The murder was big news, and for good reason. She couldn't remember the last time a park employee was murdered on the job in Minnesota. Rangers wore uniforms, but their work wasn't supposed to be as dangerous as cops' jobs. When she pulled up to the office, Murphy spotted a familiar beat-up pickup truck parked in the lot adjacent to the building. She scanned the back bumper of the heap to make sure and saw the telltale sticker reflecting the owner's attitude toward most other human beings: "Some People Are Alive Only Because It Is Against the Law to Kill Them." Cody, the *Pioneer Press* police reporter. Murphy drove up to the police tape blocking the road and flashed her badge out the window. A deputy stepped up to the driver's side of the Jeep and right behind him was Cody, with his shoulder-length brown mop and John Lennon glasses. He wore a down vest over a sweatshirt, but Murphy figured his signature Hawaiian shirt was under there somewhere. He was at the deputy's elbow while the officer checked her ID. "Murphy. What are you doing here? Got a St. Paul angle to this ranger slaying? Tell them to let me in. Come on."

The deputy looked to be in his late twenties, about Cody's age. Even with his hair shaved into a crew cut, it was obvious he was a redhead. Freckles spattered his face like measles. He handed Murphy's badge back and turned to yell at Cody. "Get lost!"

Cody was wired. Too much coffee and news. He had a notebook in his right hand and a pencil in his left. "She knows me. She can vouch for me. We work together in St. Paul. Tell him, Murphy. Tell him you know me."

The deputy: "I don't give a shit who knows you. Go away. Go far away. Take that piece-of-shit truck with you."

Murphy: "Sorry, Cody. Stay behind the tape with the rest of the pack." The deputy untied the tape to let Murphy through. "Who's here? BCA up yet?" she asked, referring to the Minnesota Bureau of Criminal Apprehension.

"Everybody and his uncle. BCA. Sheriff. Police chief. Bunch of squads. Ramsey County ME is doing the autopsy. In fact one of their guys happened to be up here on vacation. Came by right away. Nice of him."

She paused. Rural communities often asked Ramsey County to do autopsies in murder cases. Murphy figured Erik wouldn't be on the case, though. He was off work. "Yeah. Nice." Damn Erik, she thought. He'd followed her up and then heard about the ranger. Figured she'd be here. He must have spent the night in town. She didn't want to imagine what could have happened if he'd ended up at her hotel.

"Which way?" she asked.

"Hang a left after the office," he said, pointing toward the road. "You'll pass a boat landing. Keep going. Watch the signs. Campsite five. First loop off the road. Can't miss it."

She noticed the deputy's eyes were red. "Knew him?"

The deputy leaned inside her window and spoke in a low voice; he didn't want Cody to hear. "He worked hard. Treated people fairly. Hell of an angler. Pretty good poker player, too. Taught me a few things. Couple more years and he could have retired. The whole thing sucks. I want to personally nail the bastard's hide to a tree."

"You'll get him," she said.

He noticed her Homicide sweatshirt. "Catchy slogan."

"What's your mailing address? I'll send you one. Our union rep came up with them." The deputy's face brightened. He reached into his jacket pocket and handed her a card. "Sean Mahoney," she said. She tucked the card in her purse. "My dad's name is Sean. A good Irish name. I'll ship you a shirt as soon as I get back to the cop shop."

"Appreciate it." He stepped back from the car, waved her through. Murphy looked in her rearview mirror as she pulled away and saw Cody following the deputy inside the office, yammering the entire time and waving his notebook around.

Murphy pulled over to the side and parked the Jeep on the road leading to the campground. Figuring it was already jammed with cars, she didn't want to park at the campsite itself. She walked south for several yards, took a right off the road. Headed down the first loop into a sea of uniforms. BCA's crime-scene team crawling around the ranger's truck. A guy snapping pictures of the ranger's body. Another guy kneeling in the dirt making a cast. Cops and deputies poking around bushes and weeds. A couple of parks workers standing around, probably the ones who found the ranger. Then she saw him. He was the only one crouched next to the ranger. She contemplated turning around and getting back in the car. Too late. He looked up and saw her. He smiled. She told herself she was a coward for wanting to run from him. He stood up and walked toward her, peeling off his gloves as he went. He moved slowly and deliberately. His eyes never left her face. He reminded her of a lion who'd spotted his next meal. She hated to admit it, but that predatory quality intrigued her. Excited her. She didn't want that right now; she was already confused.

"Surprise," Erik said, and stuffed his gloves into his jacket pocket.

She crossed her arms over her chest. "Are you trying to piss me off? I can't believe you followed me up here."

He stopped next to her and leaned into her ear. "This isn't the space you wanted?" he whispered.

She took a step away from him. She didn't want his hot breath on her neck; she enjoyed it too much. "I'm not going to be here too long," she said, pulling some sheets of paper out of her purse. "I'm handing over a few notes and then I've got to check out of my room. Head back to the cop shop. Where did you spend the night?"

"Not with you, unfortunately. Lunch?"

"Don't have time."

"Not even for lunch?"

"I've got to get back." She looked past him. "The sheriff around? Who's in charge?"

"Come on. I'll introduce you to Mr. Warmth." He led her to a big man standing next to the ranger's pickup truck. "Detective Murphy from St. Paul PD," said Erik. "Sheriff Winter." He looked like his name. White hair. White mustache. Ice-blue eyes.

He extended his hand—as big as a catcher's mitt—and she shook it. "What you got for me on this Chad Pederson?"

Murphy could tell he was impatient. He had better things to do than listen to a detective from St. Paul with a marginal connection to the case. She handed him her notes. "Here's everything I got. I'm sure you've already cut him loose."

Winter grunted. "Probably halfway home by now. Tore up about his ex and madder than hell we picked him up for questioning, especially in front of his boys."

Murphy: "How are his kids?"

"Unglued. They're staying up here with Grandma. For now. Pederson wants them, but child protection is giving him the third degree."

"Why?"

"Why the hell do you think? 'Cause we thought he killed their mama. Hope we didn't mess things up for him." Winter's eyes narrowed. "Tell your boss thanks for all his assistance."

133

Murphy opened her mouth to apologize for Duncan, but felt strangely defensive. "He was trying to help. You must have bought into it if you picked Pederson up."

Winter's face reddened. "Yeah. Well." He looked at the notes she'd handed him. "Good. This is good. County attorney thought we were too quick to rule Pederson out. This clears the decks on that issue."

She had questions about the ranger's murder and the connection to Bunny Pederson, but she figured Winter wasn't the one to ask. She handed him her card and he stuffed it in his jacket. "Call me if you want anything else," she said, and turned and headed to her car.

Erik went after her. "Thought you couldn't stand Yo-Yo. Why'd you pass up a chance to slam him?"

"Duncan's not so bad."

"Since you're in such a generous mood, how about granting me an audience?"

"This isn't the time or the place."

"I'll meet you at the hotel," he said. "We've got to talk."

"What about your dead guy?"

"He's got his own ride down to St. Paul. Where're you staying?"

They stopped next to the Jeep. Murphy wasn't ready to talk about their relationship—she was still angry he'd followed her to Moose Lake—but she did want to hear what Erik knew about the case. "Fill me in on the ranger's murder?"

"Sure."

"AmericInn," she said. She opened the driver's-side door and hopped in. "Meet me in the lobby. Under the moose head." She slammed the door.

On her way back to the hotel, she saw Trip standing by the side of the highway talking to Cody. A news van parked in front of Cody's beater truck pulled away and she steered the Jeep into the space. She turned off the car and shoved the keys in her purse. Looked down at her sweatshirt. Ran her fingers over the embroidered badge. Now Trip would know what she did for a living. Good, she thought. Let's see what kind of reaction that gets. She opened the door, hopped out, walked toward Cody's truck. Trip and Cody were leaning against the side of it, talking. She noticed the reporter wasn't taking notes; this wasn't an interview. Trip's back was turned to her, but she could see Cody's face. He was aggravated. Seemed Trip was finally wearing out his welcome with the press.

"Hello again, Sweet," she said. Trip turned and looked at her face and then glanced down. He didn't notice her sweatshirt, she thought. She'd have to talk to him a little longer.

Cody checked his watch. "I'll leave you two to catch up. I've got a press conference." Murphy and Trip stepped away from Cody's pickup. The reporter got in his truck and pulled away, following a stream of other cars and television vans headed to town. The two of them were alone next to her Jeep. They stood three feet apart—closer than strangers stand, but not as close as friends.

She forced a tight smile on her face. "Was Cody trying to wring one more quote out of you?"

"I was on my way out of t... town. Saw all the reporters. Thought I'd check it out."

"They all know you now."

"Yeah, yeah."

He was still looking down, but she could see he was blushing. He loved all the attention, she thought. This didn't feel right. Not any of it. The way he enjoyed the publicity. His behavior in the bar.

Another breeze rippled the trees and sent leaves falling between them. She pulled one out of her hair. Trip's gaze

135

moved up to her face and then her forehead. The scar. She thought she detected a small smile on his face. Then she saw Trip take in her sweatshirt. Watched his eyes widen and his face whiten. He quickly looked down. Fiddled with the baseball cap in his hands. She'd rattled the shit out of him and she was glad.

"You d... didn't tell me you're a c... cop last night," he said.

"Didn't think you'd be interested," she said. "Sometimes it puts people off."

"So you're a d... detective. In St. Paul. Interesting work?"

"Has its days."

"What b... brings you to the park?" He was pushing a rock around with the tip of his right shoe, trying hard to act casual.

"I heard the Moose Lake cops had a murder. Thought I'd check it out. I know a couple of the deputies."

He stopped pushing the rock around and froze. "The r... r... ranger? Know anything more about it?"

"I can't talk about it."

He started pushing the rock around with the other foot. He was trying to hide it, but he was nervous and afraid, and it had something to do with the ranger's body. She didn't believe he'd stopped outside the park to bullshit with the reporters. Killers return to the scene. Could Trip be the killer? Her amorphous suspicions jelled into a theory, and it sent a chill through her body. It all added up. The fact that he found the bridesmaid's finger. The way he enjoyed all the attention. His presence outside the park. His startled reaction when he saw her sweatshirt. She tried to beat down her own theory. Couldn't be Trip. Not somebody she went to school with, somebody she knew. In the same instant she warned herself that she didn't know him. Not really. That business with the wineglass proved it last night.

Last night! Did he have time to do it last night, after their dinner? She needed more. She had to make sure he showed up at the reunion. She pulled her keys out of her purse. Saw her business cards, pulled one out and handed it to him. "Call me if you can't find your invitation."

He took the card, put it in his pocket. "Sure you'll b... b... be there?"

"Absolutely." She glanced at her watch; almost checkout time at the hotel. "Gotta go. How far away you parked? Need a ride to your car?"

"Got my wheels right here," he said, pointing at his Ford parked across the road.

"Nice," she said, and took a mental photograph of the truck.

"Was good seeing you again, Sweet." She walked up to her car door, opened it, threw her purse inside. Over her shoulder she said, "Should have asked you last night. Can I still call you Sweet, or did you outgrow that nickname?"

He'd pulled the baseball cap on his head. "No. Pa s... still calls me Sweet."

"Good." She got in, shut the door, turned the ignition.

As he watched her drive away, he studied the make and model of her car. He said under his breath, "What goes around comes around, beautiful."

137

17

Erik was pacing impatiently under the moose head when she walked into the lobby. He looked pointedly at the clock behind the front desk. "Sorry," she said. "I saw Justice Trip on the way back and stopped to talk."

He frowned. "Why does that name ring a bell?"

She sat down on the couch in the lobby. She was overheating in the sweatshirt. She pulled it off, tossed it on the arm of the couch, ran her fingers through her hair. Had she forgotten to brush it this morning? Pretty soon she'd be coming to work looking like Duncan. She rubbed her forehead with her fingertips. A headache. She needed to eat something. The bagels in her room would be hard as rocks by now and they'd already cleared the breakfast food from the lobby. She saw a basket of fruit at the front desk.

"Toss me an apple," she said.

Erik carried the basket over and set it on the coffee table in front of her. "Told you we should have had lunch. I'm starving, too." He sat down next to her, peeled a banana, ate it in three bites. He tossed the skin on the coffee table and grabbed an orange. "Who's Trip Justice?"

She picked up an apple, wiped it on her sweater and took a bite before she answered. "Justice Trip," she said, wiping juice from her chin with her hand. "He's that tall guy who's been on television and in the newspapers for finding the finger."

"Oh yeah."

"I went to school with him. I bumped into him at a bar last night; we ended up having dinner together. Listen to this. I leave to use the john and when I start heading back to the table, I see him messing with my wineglass."

"You think he put something in your drink?"

"I wasn't sure last night. Didn't take any chances. Didn't touch it. Now I'm sure he tried to slip me something. He's acting so bizarre."

"How so?"

"Hanging around outside the park for no good reason this morning. Then his eyes bug out when he sees I'm a cop. On top of all that, he isn't the person he's pretending to be in all the news stories."

"Rewriting his own history?"

"More like giving himself a personality makeover. In the stories, he acts the part of this noble do-gooder. Volunteering for this search party and that. Helping the cops by finding clues. He's really a mouse. He's doctoring up even dumb little stuff about himself. Claims he's a lifelong Elvis fan, same as the bridesmaid. But he never—"

"Whoa. What did you say?" Erik stopped peeling the orange.

"The bridesmaid. Bunny Pederson. He says she liked Elvis and so did he and they could have been soul mates or some stupid crap like that." She took another bite of apple, chewed, swallowed.

"Paris." He touched her arm. "That's a tidbit only the cops up here know."

"What?"

"She had the lyrics to an Elvis song stuffed inside her purse when she went missing, but that's not general knowledge," said Erik. "As far as I know, nothing that was in her bag has been made public. A couple of her friends from the wedding party know what she was carrying, but that's about it."

"Shit," she said.

"Think he's the one?" Erik shoved an orange section in his mouth.

"I've been thinking he could be," she said in a low voice. "Explains the finger turning up minus the rest of her."

"He planted it."

"Kills her, cuts off the pinkie, ditches the rest of her somewhere. Then he volunteers for the search party so he can 'find' the finger. Could have been carrying it. Waiting for the right time to drop it."

Erik nodded. "The condition of the pinkie. Pretty damn pristine for sitting out in the woods. No insect bites. No animal bites. Winter wondered if the finger had been removed by a raccoon or something. No way, I told him. The cut was clean. Baffled the hell out of us. Who would have suspected the guy who found it? Brilliant and ballsy in a way."

Murphy: "Brilliant and ballsy. Two words I'd never use to describe Justice Trip."

"But why? What's the motive?"

"So he could be king for a day? I read the stories about him. He played hero before and loved it. Helped hunt for a missing girl outside Eau Claire."

"Think he killed her, too?"

"No, no. They found her after Sweet found her necklace."

"Sweet?"

"His nickname." She took another bite out of the apple. Chewed and swallowed. "Which song?"

Erik: "What?"

"Which Elvis song in her purse?"

"Why?"

"Curious. Bet it was 'Can't Help Falling in Love.' "

"How'd you know?"

"Every couple has it at their wedding."

"I wouldn't know. Never been married." He stared at her and she quickly looked away. "You'll need more than an Elvis song. Hell. He could say he overheard somebody in town talking about it." He popped two orange sections into his mouth.

"I know." She took another bite of the apple, chewed, swallowed. "What about that cast they took?"

"Tire tread. A partial. They're trying to figure out if it's the killer's or whoever camped there last."

"I saw a sign. Thought camping was done for the year."

"A few people have been sneaking in anyway." He picked up a second orange. Started peeling, adding to the garbage pile on the coffee table.

Murphy: "Car?"

"Looks like it was a truck." He pulled an orange section off, stuffed it in his mouth, chewed twice, swallowed, wiped his mouth with his hand.

"Sweet drives a truck," she said.

"So does half the state." He rifled more orange sections into his mouth. Chewed and swallowed.

"What else they find?"

"A print. On the bridesmaid's shoe. Some black hairs. The BCA lab boys are doing their thing." He shoved the last piece of orange in his mouth.

"Sweet's losing black hair a strand a second," she said. "But if he's as devious as I think he is, he's never been

141

caught doing anything. His prints and DNA aren't in the system." She chewed her bottom lip. "My only question is timing. I saw him last night. We had a late dinner."

"How late?"

"Seven or so."

"He would have had plenty of time to do the ranger." Erik swept the mound of orange and banana peelings off the coffee table and into the wastebasket. "What's your game plan, lady? Gonna run your theory by the locals?"

"I'm not saying anything to that prick Winter until I've got more. That's for damn sure." She ran her fingers through her hair again. "God. Somebody from high school. How weird would that be if he is the killer?"

He wiped one hand on his pants. "A guy I went to high school with is in prison."

"Murder?"

"Nah. Big-time embezzlement. Credit union."

She tossed the apple core in the wastebasket, picked up a pear. Polished it on her sweater sleeve. "When do you suppose we stop keeping tabs on the kids we went to high school with?"

"What do you mean?"

"You might not stay in touch, but you're always keeping score in your head. *I hope I'm doing better than he is. I'll bet I look better for my age than she does.* It's only four years out of your life. What's the big deal about high school?" She took a bite and chewed. The pear was hard and green.

"Here's my theory on that: High school's important because the person you become then is the person you stay for the rest of your life."

Murphy: "Bullshit. People change. Grow."

"Not all that much. Some traits and habits amplify or lessen when you become an adult. But the whole package is still the same."

142

"That guy you went to school with. Was he a thief in high school?"

"Bet your ass he was. Stole my calculator. Was this Justice character a creep in high school?" She didn't answer. "I'll take that as a yes. See what I mean?"

She shook her head. "I still don't know if I buy it."

He threw up his hands. "Hey. That's my theory. Take it or leave it."

She sat back in the couch with the pear in her hand. "I'm wiped out."

"Me too," he said. He leaned back and shut his eyes.

Both sat still on the couch for a moment. Murphy wondered when she'd last had a conversation this long with Jack, especially about work. She'd even forgotten about the stupid bangs covering her forehead. She touched them. They were all screwed up, but Erik hadn't once looked at her scar. She had to keep reminding herself that he'd followed her up there and that it pissed her off.

Murphy nudged him in the side with her elbow. "Wake up. We better get our butts moving." She stood, tossed the pear in the wastebasket. Picked up her sweatshirt and purse off the couch. Erik opened his eyes and yawned. "Talk to me while I pack," she said, and he got up and followed her down the hall. She was excited. Someone interested in her job. In her ideas. She slid the key card into the lock and pushed open the door. Threw her purse and sweatshirt on the bed.

"Nice room," he said, and sat on the edge of the four-poster while she stuffed her clothes into the duffel bag on the end of the bed.

"Tell me more about the case," she said, bending over to pick up her socks and jeans off the floor.

"First tell me about last night," he said. She stood up with the clothes in her arms. Erik was holding a champagne glass

143

in each hand. "Jack?" he asked, searching her face for a response. She dropped the clothes and nodded. "Jack," he said again. Not a question this time. A statement. Then angrily: "Jack!" He hurled one of the glasses against the fireplace. It shattered against the brick. He dropped the other glass on the floor. Bolted from the bed. Grabbed her hard by the arms. "You didn't want my company last night but you were happy to summon Jack. Run to me when you need a shoulder to cry on. A pal. Then go fuck Jack. Is that how it works?" His voice was low and deep. He was struggling to contain it. "Stop doing this to me. Stop doing it to Jack. Make up your mind."

She'd never seen him this furious. She struggled to push his hands off her, but he only gripped her harder. "You're hurting me," she said.

"No," he said. "You're hurting me." He pulled her to him and kissed her roughly on the mouth. He cradled the back of her head with his left hand. With his right, he pressed the small of her back; he wanted her to feel his hardness. He eased her backward onto the bed and fell on top of her. His mouth covered hers again and then moved to the curve of her neck. His left hand stayed tangled in her hair. His right moved up under her sweater. Cupped her left breast over her bra. Slid under her bra. He pushed her knees apart with his and moaned as he rubbed his crotch against hers.

She could still smell Jack's cologne on the sheets. "Erik," she said. "Please."

His hand moved from her breast to her stomach. Slid under her jeans and panties. "Please keep going?" He sounded groggy. Lost in the passion.

She raised her voice. "Stop. Get off me. We can't do this."

"Sure we can." He pulled on her left ear with his teeth.

Even louder: "No!"

"Damn," he muttered. He withdrew his hand from her panties. "*No* forever? Or *no* right now?"

"I don't know," she said.

"Let me help you make up your mind," he said into her ear. His right hand moved back to her breast; he squeezed it as hard as he could over her sweater. "Break it off with Jack or I'll do it for you." The lion coming in for the kill. "I'll tell him we slept together. So help me God I will."

"Bastard!" she said. She tried to push him off with both hands but he grabbed her wrists and pinned them against the bed. He kissed her on the mouth while she cursed him. "Bastard!" He released her wrists. She rolled him off of her and stood up. Her legs felt weak and wobbly; she grabbed the bedpost for support. He sat up on the bed, smiling. She drew her right hand back and slapped him. The smile was still there. So was the lion. She drew her hand back again and he grabbed it and pulled her onto his lap and kissed her on the mouth. He wrapped his arms around her and she buried her face in the crook of his neck.

"You son of a bitch," she murmured. "I hate you."

He rested his head between her breasts. "Paris. I have to know if we have anything together. Life's too short. I want to enjoy you in public. I want to look ahead with you. Make plans. I'll tell him if you don't. I mean it."

"Tell him what? That we slept together once?"

"There's more to it. More to us. I know there is."

She wrapped her arms around his neck. There was more, but she couldn't put a name to it. Maybe it was simple lust. Whatever it was, it made her guilty and miserable. Behind his back, she held up her left hand. She half expected the gold circle to crack and fall off her finger right before her eyes. She untangled her arms from his neck and got up off his lap. Turned her back to him while she talked. She

145

couldn't look into his hazel eyes. Not while the lion was awake. "I can't write off eight years of marriage so easily."

He got up off the bed and walked over to her. Stood behind her. Twined his arms around her waist. "Give it up, Paris. If it's this much work, it ain't there. Move on."

She tried to push his arms off her but he wouldn't budge. She gave up and rested her arms over his. "I have to try."

"Try what? Try hoping for a miracle? Let me ask you. Is he trying as hard as you are?"

She didn't respond.

"Is he?"

In a voice that was barely audible, she answered, "No."

"That's what I thought." He dropped his arms from her waist and walked to the door. She turned to watch him go. "I'm heading back to St. Paul. Ranger Bob pulled the plug on my little holiday. If they find the bridesmaid, she's on my plate, too. I'll be a busy man this week." He put his hand on the door handle. "Make a decision." He opened the door and left.

She went to the bed and finished packing her duffel bag. She picked up the surviving champagne glass off the floor, tossed it in the wastebasket. She'd have to get a whole new set. What good was one champagne flute? She'd never find a match for it. Then she sat on the edge of the bed and buried her face in her hands. The glass was from their wedding day.

18

While he sat in the truck watching all the news vans pull away, he took the pill bottle out of his suitcase. Trip hadn't learned anything from the reporters. They were all cold to him. Too busy to talk to him. They'd used him up; on to the next big thing. Fuck them all. Every last one of them. See if he'd ever give them another story. With shaking hands, he fished a couple of downers out of the bottle and swallowed them. He needed to come down after seeing her outside the park. She had a scar on her forehead; he hadn't noticed it last night in the bar. That mark pleased him. Something had caused her pain and damaged her and he was glad. She was still stunning, though, and that disappointed him. All these years he'd imagined she'd turned into a dried-up hag with gray hair and yellow teeth. Worse than seeing that beautiful face in the light of day was seeing that detective's badge printed on her shirt. She was lying about being on vacation. If she was working on the Moose Lake case, there had to be a Twin Cities angle since she was a St. Paul detective. The bridesmaid's ex was from St. Paul. Maybe that was it. That didn't explain why she was at the park after the ranger's body was discovered. Did the police see a St. Paul angle in that case as well? Or had the cops somehow connected the two cases? How? If they had, it wouldn't be good for him. It could mean he'd left something else behind. He'd picked up the shoe the ranger found. What about the other shoe? No. He'd shined the flashlight around before he pulled out of the campsite. Had he dropped it in the park while carrying the body? No. He would have noticed. The shoes were big, bright objects. Not like the dark, compact stiletto. He was sure the other shoe was buried with her in the tarp. He'd left nothing else behind besides the stiletto, and maybe they wouldn't even find that. Even if they did, it wouldn't immediately lead to him nor would it tell the cops the two cases were related. If they found her body, then they'd figure out why the ranger had been killed. That still wouldn't lead them to him. He decided he was safe.

He started the truck and pulled back onto the road. He was afraid it would take too long for the downers to kick in. While he drove, he opened the glove compartment with his right hand and pulled out his one-hitter kit. The wooden container was the size and shape of a pack of unfiltered Camels. He flipped open the hinged top with his thumb. Inside, a stash of Colombian weed on one side of the divided box and a brass smoking pipe on the other. He shifted the box to his driving hand and with his free hand pulled out a pipe the size of a cigarette. He dipped the pipe into the weed, ground it in, pulled it out, put it between his lips. He pushed in the truck cigarette lighter. When it popped out, he grabbed it with his right hand and lit up. He inhaled deeply. The end of the pipe glowed. He held the smoke in his lungs as long as he could. He coughed and the truck swerved a bit. The buzz was starting. "You don't cough, you don't get off," he muttered to himself. He put the pipe back in the box, closed the kit, returned it to the glove compartment. He felt much better.

He checked the gas gauge. Might as well top off the tank before hitting the highway, he thought. He drove to the station off the interstate. He looked up and down the road as he held the gas pump. No police blockades or anything. He was relieved. Maybe the cops figured whoever did it was long gone. He went inside and paid for the gas. Went next door to the sub shop and bought a couple of sandwiches and a pop. He slid into a booth and ate so fast he didn't taste anything. Still hungry. He bought a bag of chips and a third sandwich and shoveled the food in. His cell phone rang while he was wiping his mouth. He pulled it out of his jacket.

"Yeah."

His pa: "You sound tired, Sweet."

"I'm ready to c... come home."

"How'd you do? Sold a bunch of shirts?"

He lied: "G... g... got all sorts of orders."

Pa: "I knew that job would be worthwhile. So when you heading back?"

Trip figured his old man wanted to schedule one last blow job from the fat blond nurse. "I should be home before d... dinner."

"Dinner tonight?"

"Yeah."

A pause. "Good. Okay then." He hung up.

His pa sounded let down. Tough. Trip wanted to get home. Get his head together. Find out about this reunion thing. Perfect opportunity for Sweet Justice. He started sucking down the last of his pop and turned his head to glance out the window. A state van had pulled into the parking lot. He tried to read the writing on the side. Minnesota Department of Corrections. The van was empty. How long had it been there? Where was the driver? He heard a voice at the counter and tried to check it out without being obvious. Two men in navy blue uniforms with DOC patches on their shoulders and a bunch of hardware hanging from their belts. Prison guards getting sandwiches. Big sons of bitches, Trip thought. Almost as tall as he and a lot more muscular. Military haircuts and hard-set mouths. The bigger of the pair eyed Trip while he was waiting for his sub. Trip wondered if he was close enough to smell the pot. He dropped his eyes and picked at some stray lettuce on his tray. He pictured himself behind bars. Imagined that all the in-between stuff could be skipped—arrest, charges, trial, conviction, sentencing—and that the two guards could grab him and take him back with them. The guards paid for their lunches and went back outside. The big one glanced at Trip's truck, got back in the driver's seat of the van. The other one got in, slammed the passenger's door. They pulled out of the parking lot and headed toward the prison. For a second, Trip thought he was going to vomit. He sat in the booth staring straight ahead, empty pop cup in his hand. Time to get the hell out of town, he thought. He'd pushed his luck long enough. He slid out of the booth and went to his truck.

Trip leaned back in the driver's seat as he got on I-35 heading south. Traffic was light. He steered with one hand. Wished the other had the stiletto in it. He slipped a disc into the CD player. *Master of Puppets* by Metallica. The screaming guitars provided balance to the downers and the one-hit. The sensation was similar to sitting on a seesaw with someone who weighed the same. He and Snow White did that in a park. Sat on an old wooden seesaw. Each took an end. Sat perfectly still. Held their knees up so their feet were inches off the ground. He didn't know how long they were there; could have been a minute or half an hour. They looked straight ahead at each other; she was the only female he could ever stare at for any length of time. She broke the spell. "No sudden moves, Sweet," she'd said. She quick hopped off and his end slapped down on the ground. Landed hard on his ass. She laughed and laughed. So did he.

"No sudden moves," he said, and pounded the steering wheel to the beat of the drums. He'd make a sudden move on Paris Murphy. Knock her hard on her ass at the reunion. So hard she'd never get up again. How would he do it? He had to be careful. Taking down a cop would be dangerous. He'd already taken down one uniform. How different was a ranger from a cop? The ranger didn't have a gun, but a cop always carries one. He didn't see one on her. Probably under her sweatshirt or in her purse or even strapped to her ankle. He'd seen that in the movies. No. He couldn't take her up close the way he'd taken the ranger. Fooling with her Jeep Grand Cherokee was a possibility. Still, that was complicated. Took planning. He'd have to find out where she lived. Could he simply do it his usual way? He'd just nailed Bunny Pederson; flattening someone else so soon was risky. He liked spacing them out more. His face had been all over the news. If he showed his face at the reunion and someone at the party died the same way as the bridesmaid . . .

No. He'd have to do something different with Detective Paris Murphy. He eyed the pill bottle sitting on the passenger's seat. He hoped the fat nurse was still hanging around when he got home. The plan he'd almost executed in the bar wasn't such a bad idea. Next time she'd drink her drink; he'd make sure of it.

19

Her cell phone rang while she was loading her bag into the Jeep. She pulled it out of her purse. "Murphy."

Duncan: "Jesus Christ. Every time you pick up the phone you sound worse than the last time."

She silently cursed his perceptive ear. "Need to crash in my own bed."

"You sure that's all?"

"Let's not go there right now."

"That dick Winter give you a hard time? Something else going on?"

She appreciated Duncan's concern, but wasn't ready to spill her guts about anything personal. They didn't know each other well enough. "Winter was a jerk. I gave him what I had and hit the road. Throwing my stuff in the Jeep right now." She slammed the back gate and walked around to the driver's door. Opened it, got in, shut the door. "Please tell me I can head back to the cop shop. I already checked out of the hotel."

"Go straight home. Catch up on your Zs. Drag your butt into the station house tomorrow. You put in your eight and then some."

She leaned her head back in the car seat. "Thanks."

"For the record, Potato Head, Winter said you put together a real nice package for him. Stuff from the neighbors. Stuff from his work. Confirmation there were no cop calls to his place. The whole bit. Backs up his duck hunting story and shows he's no homicidal maniac."

She wondered if she could run her theory by him. "Speaking of homicidal maniac, I've got a wild idea about who the killer could be."

"Love wild ideas. Hit me with it."

"Tell you what. Let me present it in person. I'll get cleaned up at home and then come in with it. How late you gonna be there tonight?"

"Late as you want. Is your suspect for real? Should we run it by Winter? Maybe they should pick him up."

She regretted saying something to him this early. "Slow down, Duncan. I don't have enough yet. Got some legwork to do. Besides, my suspect isn't going anywhere. In fact, I expect to see him Saturday night."

"It's somebody you know? I can hardly wait to hear this. Only thing is, if it ain't a burning emergency, maybe you should save it for the morning."

"Why?"

"You sound like shit."

She decided he was right. She needed to pull her thoughts together, write it all down. There might be some holes in her theory. Her brain wasn't completely focused on work right now. "Know what? I think I will sleep on it."

"Good. Catch you tomorrow in the A.M. Later, Potato Head."

She hung up and slipped the phone in her purse. One of these days she'd have to tell him to lay off on the Potato Head talk. She started the Jeep, pulled out of the parking

153

lot and turned onto the interstate. She was on automatic pilot during the drive home. For once she wished she had a partner so she could ask him to take the wheel. She inserted a compact disc into the CD player. Nat King Cole's "Unforgettable" filled the interior like warm bathwater.

Traffic was light coming out of Moose Lake, but got heavier as she got closer to the Twin Cities. She checked the clock on the Jeep. A little early for rush hour. She took a downtown exit. Cut through downtown. Crossed the Wabasha Bridge and went home. She saw Jack's car in the yacht club parking lot. What was he doing there? She wasn't ready to tell him anything. She pulled into a parking spot, turned off the engine and sat for a minute. The beginnings of three different speeches ran through her mind. *I'm sorry I cheated on you. I'm sorry but if you don't try harder, we're through. I'm sorry but I'm tired, need to be alone tonight.* That last one sounded the best. Gave her some time. Okay, she thought, speech number three. She had no idea what she'd say after that first sentence, but figured something would come to her. She grabbed her keys and her purse and slid out of the driver's seat. Slammed the door. Went around back and opened the gate to get her bag. She walked down the dock and noticed a pair of mallards bobbing in the water. She had some stale flatbread. She'd toss it out to them later. She opened the door to her houseboat and walked in, her mind a jumble of Jack and Erik and ducks and bread.

He was standing in the living room looking out the patio doors. He was still dressed in his scrubs. Some days she wondered if he had any other clothes. She dropped her bag on the galley floor and tossed her keys and purse on the kitchen table. He didn't greet her. Something was wrong. "You lied," he said, his back still turned to her.

154

"What?" she asked.

"The flowers. I called your mother. Told her we weren't going to be over for dinner. I asked why she sent the flowers."

Murphy looked at the bouquet on the kitchen table. Covered her mouth with her right hand. With her left, she grabbed the back of a kitchen chair for support. She didn't say anything. Not one word came to mind. None of her speeches would work. Her brain was a blank sheet of paper: white, flat, flimsy, useless. The house was silent. Outside, she heard the sound of a speedboat. She wished whoever was piloting it would stop by, interrupt this, take her away.

Jack: "Who?"

She didn't hesitate; no point in hiding it any longer. "Erik Mason."

His back stiffened. He knew Erik. They'd worked together on different medical committees and projects over the years. "How long?"

"Does it matter?" She didn't want to go into details. This was too painful.

He turned around to face her. He poked his right index finger in his chest. "It fucking matters to me. How long?" She didn't answer right away. Louder: "How long?"

"Since the summer. That night you left for the medical conference. It was just that once. I was so wound up over that case . . ." Her voice trailed off. She didn't want to give excuses.

He took a step toward her. "Are you blaming this on me? This is my fault somehow?"

"No," she said in a low voice.

He took another step toward her. "Do you think I ever cheated on you? Slept with another woman, even when we were separated?"

"No," she said.

155

"Did I ever hit you, abuse you in some way?"

A mean, spiteful question that stung her. She shook her head. "No. Of course not."

"Was I a lousy lover?"

She looked into his eyes. He was genuinely concerned that their sex life was the problem. It mystified her. Didn't he realize it was the one thing that wasn't at issue? "You're a wonderful lover. You know that."

"I don't know anything anymore." He ran his fingers through his hair. "Why, then? Why?" She didn't answer. A long silence. Then: "Do you love him?"

The one question she dreaded. She looked down. Covered her forehead with her right hand and with her left still held onto the chair back. She felt as if the kitchen chair was the only thing keeping her from falling through the floor into an abyss. A special hell reserved for unfaithful wives. "I don't know," she said. She looked up with tears in her eyes. Then the only words she found useful from her prepared speeches: "I'm sorry."

He rubbed his face with his hands and said through them, "Me too."

She let go of the chair back and was surprised to see her legs still worked. She walked across the galley into the living room. She tried to wrap her arms around him but he pushed her away and turned toward the river again. The fall sun was starting to fade on the water. Come night, the Mississippi would be as black as ink. She spoke to his back and found the words easier than when she faced him. "I still love you and I think you still love me," she said.

"Nice words," he said.

She ignored it. "But we don't get along. We can't even live under the same roof. What kind of marriage is that?"

"One I thought we could save," he said sadly.

"We still could," she said. "You . . . we need to work harder at it."

He turned and faced her. He grabbed her shoulders. "Tell me something. Did you fuck him upstairs, in the same bed where we made love? On the same sheets? Or did you have the courtesy to change them?"

Hateful words that made her cringe and feel even guiltier. Dirtier. It had been in the same bed, on the same sheets. Her only response was a plea: "God, Jack. Please. Stop."

He pushed her backward onto the couch and leaned over her. She dug her fingers into the cushions, bracing for another verbal assault. "You and Erik can both go to hell. We're through. Take this souvenir with you." He pulled her to him, kissed her hard on the mouth. She tried to pull away from him; he was frightening her. He grabbed each side of her head with his hands and held her mouth to his. Almost a minute went by. He withdrew his mouth, but not before biting her bottom lip.

She yelped and fell back against the couch. "Jack!"

He stood up and walked out, slamming the door so hard it shook the galley cupboards.

She touched her mouth with her right hand. Looked at her fingertips. Blood. Jack was usually a steady, calm man. Whenever they fought, he usually walked out before things got ugly. What he'd done was mean and angry, and his parting words unnerved her. Were they really finished? Was it really over? She got up off the couch and went to the kitchen table for her purse. Pulled out her phone. Took a deep breath and exhaled before punching his number.

"Erik?"

"Calling with good news?"

"Jack was here."

"You told him?"

"Yes." She pulled out a chair, sat down, rested her elbows on the kitchen table. "He went ballistic."

"You surprised?"

"I'm worried. If he shows up at your office, could be a scene."

"If he wants a battle to the death, this is the right place for it."

"Not funny."

"Don't worry. I'll behave."

She touched her bottom lip again; it was starting to swell. "You're not the one I'm worried about."

"Jack will behave, too. I know him; he's a gentleman."

She didn't want to tell Erik that the gentleman bit her. She stood up and went to the refrigerator, opened the freezer, dug around inside. Grabbed the ice cube tray. Empty. Pulled out a Popsicle instead. Shut the freezer door. Sat down again. "Be careful. He's not himself."

For the first time, he sounded serious. "I'd be a changed man if I lost you, Paris."

"He's the one who did the dumping, Erik," she said in a low voice. "He told me we're finished."

"Good. Somebody had to make a decision."

It wasn't the decision she'd wanted or expected, but she didn't want to tell Erik that. She peeled the paper wrapper off the Popsicle. Covered with crystals of frost. She licked it. Banana-flavored. The thing was probably six months old. She put it to her lip.

"Want some company tonight?" he asked.

She didn't want to see Erik. She was still trying to grasp the idea that her husband had just walked out. "I need to decompress. This thing with Jack, it was pretty intense."

"All the more reason I should be there, lover."

"No." She didn't like him calling her "lover." Suddenly everything he said was wrong. "Besides, I've got work stuff to keep me busy. Got to collect my thoughts on the Moose Lake case. Put something down on paper to show to Duncan."

"The tall creep still your man?"

"Yeah." She glanced at her duffel bag sitting on the kitchen floor. "I haven't even unpacked yet."

"Call if you change your mind."

"Okay."

"I love you, Paris." She didn't respond. He didn't seem to mind. "Call if you need anything."

She hung up and set the phone down on the table. She wasn't sure she'd ever be able to say those three words to Erik and mean it. She stood up and tossed the Popsicle in the sink. Felt her lip. Still swollen. Her cell phone rang. She answered quickly, hoping it was Jack calling. "Murphy."

Her mother: "Honey. Are you back in town?"

"Yes, *Imma*." Murphy leaned against the kitchen counter. Concentrated on steadying her voice. The last thing she needed was her mother's meddling.

"Why couldn't you and Jack come to dinner tonight if you're home?"

"Ma, I'm dead tired." That wasn't a lie; she was drained.

"Who sent you the flowers?"

"I don't need this right now."

"That's why you're not coming. You and Jack had another one of your fights."

"No, no." She turned around and rested her head against a cupboard. "Everything's fine, Ma."

"Bullshit."

Murphy stood to attention. Her mother never swore. "*Imma*." Murphy paused, holding the phone to her ear. They'd have to find out eventually. Might as well spill it now. "Jack found out I saw someone over the summer." She couldn't find the courage to say she "slept with

159

someone." Her mother would know what "saw someone" meant.

"Someone. Who is this someone? Another cop?"

"Not a cop. A guy I work with from the ME's office."

"A guy you work with? You're risking eight years of marriage for a guy you work with?"

"Ma, don't make it sound like that."

"Like what? What does it sound like? Cheap? Come over and let's talk about this, daughter."

"Ma. *Imma*. There's nothing to talk about. It's over."

"You and this guy?"

Here comes the explosion, thought Murphy. "Jack left me. For good."

Amira gasped. "Jesus, Mary and Joseph!"

Murphy knew her mother was making the sign of the cross. She heard her father asking questions in the background. Heard her mother say the word "divorce." Suddenly he was on the phone: "Get your ass over here pronto young lady!"

Her father's language didn't jar her; he swore all the time. "I can't, Papa. I'm bushed." She knew that wouldn't satisfy her father, so she pulled out another excuse. "I've still got to go to the station. Tie up some loose ends from a case. File a report."

"File tomorrow. We got supper all ready for you. We'll talk about it over *koosa*," he said, referring to a Lebanese dish of zucchini stuffed with rice and lamb. "There's not a problem that can't be solved over *koosa*."

Murphy's shoulders sagged. She couldn't fight both of them. Besides, her refrigerator was nearly empty and she was famished. "Okay. Give me an hour." She hung up and shoved the phone back in her purse. She picked up her duffel bag and carried it upstairs. Threw it on the bed. She wished she could collapse on the mattress next to it and sleep for twelve hours. She peeled off her clothes, walked into the bathroom, turned on the shower, stepped into the stall. She reached for the shampoo, squirted a gob in her hair, lathered and rinsed. She tilted her head back, let the spray hit her face and sting her lip. While she was toweling dry, she checked her face in the bathroom mirror. The swelling was barely noticeable. She studied her reflection. Wondered if she looked any different now that she'd been dumped. Did she look like a woman about to go through a divorce? Her mother once told her she could spot divorcées on sight. Said they had a tightness around their mouths. As if they'd tasted a bitter herb. Murphy thought that was a bunch of nonsense. She examined her own mouth. Searched for new lines. Nothing yet. She walked out of the bathroom, dropped the towel on the floor and got dressed in her jeans and a flannel shirt.

She went downstairs and opened a few cupboards searching for something to take to her folks' house. Nothing but canned goods and crackers. She needed to go grocery shopping. She hated showing up at their doorstep empty-handed. Made her feel like she was back in college, coming home to mooch a meal. She scanned the counter. Her eyes fell on the wine rack. Two bottles left. She pulled one out and held it up. Champagne. Hardly appropriate. She slipped it back in the rack. Pulled out the other bottle. Good. A clear Lebanese liquor. *Arak*. Distilled grape juice flavored with anise. One hundred proof. Perfect with any Middle Eastern meal. She twisted the cap off and sniffed. The licorice scent belied the drink's strength. She screwed the top back on. Peeled off the price—her parents never approved of how much she paid for anything—and set the bottle in a paper bag. She pulled on her leather bomber jacket, grabbed her purse and keys and the bag and left. While she was shutting the door behind her, she wondered if Jack was going to give back her keys. She walked to her car and thought about all the clothes and toiletries he'd left at her place. Would he want photos back? She slid into the driver's seat of the Jeep. On the floor of the passenger's side, his travel coffee mug. Something else that needed to be returned. She turned on the ignition and pulled out of the parking lot. His sunglasses were dangling from the rearview mirror by a strap. She thought: *This must be what it feels like when someone dies and their stuff keeps turning up. Memories to be boxed up and stored—or thrown away.* As she turned south onto Wabasha to head toward the West Side, she looked at the gold band on her left ring finger. She stifled a sob.

20

He pulled into the trailer park late Tuesday afternoon. At the entrance: MANUFACTURED HOME COMMUNITY. He thought the sign made the place sound nicer than it really was. Adding to the deception: the decorative boulders and fall mums planted at the base of the sign. This was not a neighborhood filled with flowers and rock gardens. The community was a collection of mobile homes with attached decks that were often as wide as the trailers themselves. Metal garden shed in every yard. Satellite dish on every roof. Patches of grass in place of big lawns. The only flowers were the plastic ones in some of the window boxes. The trailer park was on the northern fringe of the city. He parked in front of the house, got out with his suitcase. He decided he'd empty the back of the truck later. He was wiped out and wanted to crash for a couple of hours. The last half hour of the ride home, even his music couldn't fight the fatigue.

He pushed open the front door with his shoulder, stepped into the front room and almost knocked over Keri. She was bending over, trying to pull the old man's socks off. Frank Trip was sitting on the front room couch in his standard weekday attire—drawstring pajama bottoms decorated with cowboys riding horses, white tee shirt with a pack of unfiltered Lucky Strikes rolled up in the left sleeve, Vikings ball cap pulled over his bald head. On one side of the couch was the TV tray his pa used for every meal. Today it was covered with an ashtray filled with cigarette butts, Grain Belt beer cans, a jar of salsa, a bag of tortilla chips, a can of beef jerky strips, an empty ice cream pint. Rocky Road. In the middle of the mess was a Mason jar with his pa's dentures; they were soaking in their usual disinfectant of Jim Beam bourbon whiskey. The television was blaring; his pa couldn't see the screen clearly but seemed to think he could compensate by increasing the volume. *TV Guide* was on the floor at his pa's feet; it was from last summer. Trip had canceled the subscription and kept handing his pa the same issue; his old man didn't know the difference and the money Trip saved he used to order more knives.

"Jesus Christ! Get away from me! You're killing me! They're fine, goddammit! Leave 'em be! Tell her, Sweet!"

"I got to check them tootsies, Frank." Keri looked over her shoulder at Trip. Her hair was her biggest asset; she had a blond braid that ran halfway down her back. Even though she was in her late forties, she only had a few strands of gray. "How ya doin' there, Mr. Big Shot Hero? Long time no see." She looked at his crotch and then up at his face. She winked at him and he looked down, adjusted his grip on the suitcase.

She returned her attention to the patient. Frank was hanging onto his cane with both hands and jabbing at her like he was harpooning a whale. She played the running back, deftly dodging him. The right sock was already half off and dangling from his toes; the left one was around his ankle. They played the game every time she came over and

164

she always won. She outweighed Trip's old man by a hundred pounds.

Trip sighed. "P... Pa, let the lady do her job. Let her check your f... f... fucking feet."

He waved his cane in Trip's direction. "You can both go straight to hell in a handbasket!" The tip of the cane grazed the Mason jar. It fell over and spilled whiskey on the tray and the rug.

"Shit, Pa." Trip dropped his suitcase in the middle of the front room and went into the kitchen to get a towel. The front room was in the center of the trailer. On one side of it was the kitchen and then Frank's bedroom. On the other side was a hall that led to Trip's bedroom, the bathroom and a spare bedroom. The ceiling was higher than in lots of trailers—nearly seven and a half feet—but Trip still felt perpetually cramped in the place.

Keri took advantage of the spilled jar as a diversion and pulled the right sock off all the way. "Gotcha!" She grabbed the left one and got it in one yank. Waved it victoriously over her head. "Hah!"

Trip walked back in with the towel and got on his knees to blot the carpet dry. Close to the floor, he could smell urine and wondered if his father was having incontinence problems on top of everything else. Next he'd be taking a dump in the middle of the front room.

Keri was on her knees next to him with Frank's feet in her lap. "They're good," she said, patting them. "As usual, all your fussing was for nothing. Toenails could use a trim, but I ain't doing them. You got to get to a podiatrist." Her sweatshirt had crawled up her back. Trip could see a white flash of flesh dotted with pimples and above the waist of her jeans, a tattoo of a frog. He was well familiar with the frog, as well as the lily pad a couple of inches below it. The sleeves of the sweatshirt were cut short, revealing her fat upper arms.

Frank: "Sweet can clip my nails."

"He can't trim shit," Keri said. "He breaks the skin and you're back in the hospital."

Trip looked at his pa's toes and grimaced. The nails were yellow and thick and curling under. That empty spot where the big toe used to be bummed him out. He had no intention of touching those feet. He stood up with the wet rag, righted the Mason jar. The teeth were under the bag of chips. Trip picked them up with two fingers and dropped them into the jar. He looked for the whiskey bottle; his pa usually kept it within arm's reach. He found it on the couch behind a throw pillow. Trip picked it up and emptied the remainder into the Mason jar. He'd have to make a liquor store run later. Pa had to have his Jim Beam.

Keri: "Got to check your blood sugar."

"You ain't poking me," Frank said.

"The hell I ain't." Keri set Frank's feet down and stood up. She folded her arms over her chest. Trip thought she had small breasts for such a large woman, and they were heading south with the rest of her aging body. She nodded toward the TV tray. "What's this crap?"

"Breakfast. Lunch. Probably dinner, unless my son gets his ass in gear."

"You can't keep eating crap. Gonna kill yourself."

"Good. Then I won't have to listen to your nagging." He turned the volume even higher on the television.

She shook her head and walked into the kitchen to get the glucose monitor. Trip followed her with the wet towel. Threw it into the sink on top of the pile of dirty dishes. The counter was covered with empty beer cans, opened bags of chips, half-empty cereal boxes. Hardened spatters of something orange. The remains of a fried egg sandwich rested in a skillet on the stove. His pa's housekeeping had declined along with his health; the place was always filthy

166

when Trip returned from the road. He worried his old man would burn the place down on top of it. Trip suspected his pa couldn't see well enough to tell if the range was off or on. Trip had arranged once to have some neighbor ladies come in and cook while he was out of town, but his pa had refused to open the door for them. Told Trip they were trying to poison him with slop called "tuna hot dish."

Keri was bending over the kitchen table, fiddling with the blood glucose monitor. "He can't keep drinking like a fish, especially with his diabetes. You're gonna come home one day and he's gonna be dead on the couch."

"I know," Trip said tiredly. He started moving plates and cups from one side of the sink to the other so he could plug the drain and start filling the sink with water. The dishes were going to have to soak; he saw dried egg yolk from the week before. A couple of the whiskey glasses had Keri's lipstick on the rim. How could she lecture about his old man's drinking one minute and tip a glass with him the next? She was a two-faced bitch not to be trusted. How could he ask Keri about which pills to use on Paris Murphy without telling her what they were for? Maybe he'd have to stick with a known quantity. The date rape pills. He plugged the drain, squirted some dish soap in the bottom of the sink and started filling it with hot water. He swayed as he stood over the counter. He wanted to sleep for a week. He turned off the tap when the suds reached the top and transferred one mound of dishes into the water. Wiped his hands on his pants. Keri's back was turned to him; she was sorting his pa's pills on the kitchen table. Putting them in the plastic box with the different compartments. One compartment for each day of the week. Trip came up behind her, massaged her shoulders. Leaned into her ear. "G... got any stuff for me?"

"Later, Romeo," she whispered. "Let me finish up with that old bastard in there first."

He hated that nickname. Romeo. The way she always said it—with a little smile on her face—made him feel as if she was making fun of his abilities in the bedroom. He walked back into the front room, picked up his suitcase. On television, cowboys were shooting up a town. He didn't know why they owned a remote; the set never left the western channel. "P... Pa. Lower that shit." His pa waved him away.

Trip walked down the hall to his bedroom and threw his suitcase on the bed. The trailer was a steam bath. His pa must have cranked up the heat to eighty degrees without realizing it. Trip unzipped his jacket and pulled it off and tossed it on the bed. Took off his hat. Set it on the dresser. His head itched. He scratched it with his fingertips; a few strands fell into his face and he picked them off. Unbuttoned his shirt down the front and at the cuffs. One of the cuff buttons came off in his hand. "Shitty shirts." He tossed the button in a wastebasket. Peeled off the shirt. Tossed it on top of the bed. He was sleeping in the same twin-sized bed he'd had since he was a kid, with his legs hanging off the edge every night. He didn't care. A full-sized bed would take up too much space and he had to have room for his stereo and his knives. The mattress was covered with a bedspread from childhood. Cowboys herding longhorn. One of his pa's picks. The bedroom curtains carried the same pattern. So did the sheets and pillowcases. While the linen was little-boy Old West, nearly everything else in the room was heavy metal Medieval. Wall rack with four samurai swords mounted horizontally. Spiked mace, South African bush machete and battle-ax, each displayed on its own wall shelf. Metal shield etched with a writhing dragon hanging on the wall over the headboard. Two U.S. Cavalry Artillery Officers' sabers mounted crossways over the dresser. On top of the dresser, an assortment of daggers and knives. On the nightstand more daggers and knives, as well as a pewter dragon with a round clock set in its belly. He checked the clock. If he fell asleep now he'd probably get up in the middle of the night. Better to stay awake for a few more hours. Besides, he still had to fuck Keri to get his pills. Trip hated the way she made him pay twice: by giving her cash *and* sleeping with her. He figured his pa was paying *her* for the sex, and he found that ironic. Some days he'd like to pay her more for the pills to get out of the sex.

He decided to unpack and hit the shower; a shower would wake him up. He popped open his suitcase. The sock stuffed with the peach purse was sitting on top. He reached inside the sock and pulled out the bag. He'd look at it one more time and dump it later that night.

"Hey, Romeo. Playing with yourself in there or what?" Keri was standing in the bedroom doorway.

He threw the purse in the suitcase, slammed it shut and turned toward her. "All finished with P... Pa?"

"Frank's passed out on the couch. Sawing logs to beat the band." She walked over to him and wrapped her arms around his waist. Her biceps were bigger than his; her head barely reached his chest. She pressed her body into his crotch. Cupped his butt with her hands. "Feeling frisky?"

"Let me shower. I reek."

She buried her face in his tee shirt. "I like you kind of smelly and dirty," she said into his chest.

"I d... don't," he said, and untangled her from his waist. Her arms were sweaty. He was being mauled by a sticky bowling ball.

"Why don't I join you then?"

He took a couple of steps back from her. "What about P... Pa?"

"Told you. Sound asleep. He'll sleep for a few hours." She pulled something out of the front pocket of her jeans. Held up a pill bottle and shook it. "Timed it right. Gave it to him after he told me you were on your way home."

He snatched the bottle from her hand and looked at it. He didn't recognize the name of the drug, but he could see it wasn't his old man's pills. The pharmacy label had another patient's name on it. In all their years of doing business he'd never asked her how she got the pills she sold him. He figured she stole the bulk of them from her patients.

"Don't worry. Only gave him one," she said.

"What if we g... gave him a few more? What would that d... do? Make him sleep through the n... night?"

She threw her head back and laughed. "Sweet Justice! What have you got planned for us tonight, Romeo?" She stepped toward him and plucked the bottle out of his hand.

"Wait," he said, trying to grab it back.

"No freebies," she said, pulling the bottle out of his reach. She stuffed it back in her pocket. "I don't give a damn if you fuck me till the cows come home. Still gotta have some cash to go along with it." She put her hands on her hips and looked around. "Speaking of bedroom, I'll say it again. This is the weirdest room I have ever laid eyes on. What you planning to do with all this stuff? Start your own war?"

He didn't like anyone criticizing his collection. He lowered his eyes. Wanted to hit her in the worst way. Instead, he shoved his hands in his pockets. "N... n... nothing wrong with a few knives. Man can have a f... few knives."

170

She frowned and shook her finger at him. "Don't tell me you ain't got the cash to pay for the pills when you got all this expensive hardware."

He looked up. "You d... d... didn't answer my question. What would more p... pills do?"

"Tell ya what, Romeo." She pulled her sweatshirt off and dropped it to the floor. Underneath: a white cotton bra and a bulging white midriff. Over her right breast, another frog leaping over a lily pad. Her hair wasn't showing her age, but her neck was. More lines in it than he could count. "We'll discuss pharmaceuticals after the shower."

"How you g... got time for that? Don't you got more p... patients to see?"

"Frank was my last. I'm punched out. Taking some compensatory time off. Got the rest of the week free, clear through the weekend. Plenty of time for fun." She raised her right arm, revealing the puff of blond hair buried in her armpit. "Got a razor I can borrow? If you ask real nice, I might let you watch me shave." He didn't say anything, shoved his hands back in his pockets and looked away. "Why don't you start up the shower while I slip out of the rest of these duds? Unless you want to help me undress." She reached behind her back and started unhooking her bra. Trip left to start the shower.

The steam enveloped them and boiled over the shower door, filling the compact bathroom. The radio hanging over the shower arm was turned on. They couldn't make out the song because of static, but Keri swayed as if she could hear music. Goofy woman, he thought. Trip wondered what the two of them looked like, crammed together in the stall. The tall, thin man and the short, round woman. She stood in front of him, her back to him, while

171

she hogged most of the spray. He didn't care. Wanted to get it over with. She wanted her back scrubbed. He used a loofah sponge; he didn't want to touch her wet skin with his bare hands.

"Don't forget Mr. Froggie," she said. "He needs some bubbles, too."

Trip moved the sponge down to the small of her back and scrubbed back and forth a couple of times.

"A little farther south," she said.

He sneered and ran the loofah in large circles around her left buttock and then her right. Her rear end was starting to sag. He could hardly stand touching her when she was lying down with her body spread flatter. Even then he kept the sheets pulled up, the lights off, the shades drawn.

"The shampoo, Romeo."

He cracked one eye open and spied the bottle on the shelf above the showerhead; too high for her to reach. He put the loofah on the shelf and took down the shampoo.

"Squirt some in," she said, and she bent her head back so her wet hair hung straight down in front of him. He tipped the bottle upside down and squeezed a gob the size of a quarter into her hair. She reached behind her head and scrubbed; he was fiercely jealous of all the hair she had. Wished he had a fraction of it. "What kind is it?" she asked.

He put the bottle back. "Baby shampoo. G... generic."

"Baby shampoo? Ain't you old enough to use big-boy suds?" She laughed at her own joke and then choked and coughed on some water.

"Supposed to be g... gentle."

She kept scrubbing. "Nothing gonna save your hair, Romeo."

She was right. He saw a tangle of black hair accumulated over the drain from the last couple of showers he'd taken. Not a single blond strand had fallen since she stepped in.

"You're destined for a rug," she said, stepping closer to the shower stream and rinsing off the shampoo. "I got a girlfriend who works at a wig store. I'll ask her to keep her eyes open for a deal."

"No," he said. A wig would be an admission of defeat. The last slam against his virility. Might as well get castrated and get it over with. "No rug."

"Sure?"

"Yeah."

"Whatever. Where's that razor?"

He paused. He didn't want to be so close to her when she shaved her armpits. "G... got one in the medicine cabinet." He stepped around her, pulled open the shower door, stepped out, pulled it shut. He opened the cabinet over the sink, grabbed a disposable razor. Handed it to her over the shower door.

"Shave cream?" she asked. He took a can off the shelf and handed it to her over the door. He heard her squirt some. "Ain't you gonna watch? How about I shave my pussy for you?"

He shuddered at the thought of witnessing that. "I hear P... Pa banging around the kitchen." He yanked a towel off the bar, wrapped it around his waist, walked out of the steamy bathroom. He exhaled with relief as he shut the door behind him. He went down the hall and poked his head into the front room. His pa was still snoring and the television was still blaring. He wanted to shut it off or at least turn down the volume, but that might wake his old man and it was more peaceful when he was asleep. He went back to his bedroom, threw the towel in a hamper. The dirty clothes were piled high, plus he had a suitcase full of dirty underwear and shirts. He'd have to go to the Laundromat damn soon. He opened his top dresser drawer. Three pairs of clean boxers left and no tee shirts. He stepped into a pair of boxers. Opened the second drawer. One pair of clean jeans inside. Stepped into those. Third drawer. Two sweatshirts left. Grabbed the one with the oval Ford logo across the front and yanked it on over his head.

"Sweet! Sweet!" His pa bellowing from the front room. He sounded groggy, but he was awake.

Trip shuffled out of his bedroom and saw Keri in the hall, walking naked out of the bathroom. "Jesus Christ. Get s... something on. Pa's up. So much for your b... bullshit p... p... pills."

"I'm still waiting for a little help with the razor," she said.

He looked down at her crotch. Shave cream covered it. The sight made her even more repulsive to him.

She saw him frowning. "Don't like it? Fuck you then." She flipped him the bird, went back into the bathroom. Slammed the door behind her.

More yelling from the front room. "Sweet!"

Trip walked into the front room. "What you want, P... Pa?"

"Supper! I'm getting light-headed! All woozy."

Damn pills, Trip thought. All they did was make his old man tired and crabby.

"Okay, Pa. I'll whip you up s... something." He walked into the kitchen. The floor was sticky on his bare feet. For all he knew, he was stepping on dried piss. He needed his shoes. They were in the bedroom. He walked past his pa into the hall, started to step into his bedroom and stopped. Heard something in the bathroom. Stepped next to the closed door and listened. What he heard coming from the other side made him freeze. What he heard told him that after he'd left his bedroom to start the shower, Keri had opened the suitcase. What he heard was Keri singing. "Can't Help Falling in Love."

He opened the bathroom door a crack. She stopped

174

singing. "I knew you'd come back for some action," she said. "Hurry up. Hot water won't last forever." She returned to her singing.

The two-faced bitch was going to use the purse against him, he thought. "B... be right there," he yelled into the bathroom and shut the door. Trip went into his bedroom and pulled open his top dresser drawer. Under his boxers was a small cardboard box. He took it out and set it on top of the dresser. He lifted off the cover. Inside, a straight-edge razor. One of his antique finds. He picked it up, unfolded it, ran the edge across his thumb. Sharp. Hiding the straight-edge behind his back, he walked down the hall and looked in the front room again. His old man had fallen back asleep. He went up to the bathroom door. He set the straight-edge down on the floor and stripped, leaving his clothes in a pile in the hallway. He picked up the razor and opened the bathroom door a crack. All he heard was the water running and in the background, some indistinguishable music coming out of the shower radio. He slipped into the bathroom and closed the door behind him, locking it. She was still singing, but a different Elvis song. What was it? "Jailhouse Rock." She was playing with his mind, he thought.

She heard him and stopped singing. "Come on, Romeo. Hop back in. The water's still fine." He pushed open the shower door with his left hand and with his right held the straight-edge behind his back. "Got a surprise for me?" she said, turning to face him and putting her back to the shower. She had shaved her crotch clean, but there was some lather in spots.

He snapped the door shut. "B... better rinse off one more time," he said. She turned around to face the water. He wrapped his left arm around her body and with his right, brought the razor to her throat.

"Sweet!" she screamed. "Sweet!" Then no more words. Only shrieking and frantic struggling. She locked both her hands around his right arm and tried to pull it down. He feared he would lose his grip on her fat, wet body. He pressed the straight-edge hard and sliced it across her neck, from his left to right. She yelped and then gurgled. Blood sprayed across the shower walls and dripped down her front. He looked at the shower floor and watched the red liquid snake down the drain. She went limp. He backed up and let go of her. She collapsed on her back. A wet heap of blood and water and shave cream. Knees bent. Arms out. Eyes wide open. Mouth partially open. Raw rip across her throat. He stood over her, panting. His legs felt weak. He dropped the razor; it fell to the shower floor with a clatter. He pressed his left palm against the door and his right against the wall for support. He ducked his head under the shower. Let the stream massage the back of his skull. The water had turned ice cold, but he didn't notice. For several seconds, the only sound he heard was the shower. A gentle rain washing the blood down and around her neck. A red necklace. More blood. Still more. When would the blood stop? Then through the static, he heard a DJ on the shower radio: "*Only twelve hours left of our twenty-four-hour Elvis marathon. Phone or fax your requests for songs by The King. Here's one of my favorites off his . . .*"

She hadn't discovered the purse or the lyrics inside it. She wasn't playing with his mind. Keri had been singing along with the radio. Trip reached up and pulled the radio off the shower arm and slammed it against the wall. Batteries and plastic pieces scattered on the shower floor around her body. He pounded the wall with his right fist. "Nothing. Killed her for n... nothing." He looked down. One of the plastic pieces had landed on her right breast. Covered the frog so only the lily pad was showing. Didn't

176

look right. He bent over and picked up the shard. Now both were visible. The frog and the lily pad. He stood up and studied the plastic shard. Wrapped his right hand around it. Squeezed until it hurt. He let go of the plastic and it fell into her hair. He checked his arms. Blood on his arms. He'd gone from neat kills with his truck to bashing a man's head in with a shovel to this mess. A woman's bare body pressed against his while he sliced her throat. Her blood on his skin. Too personal and up close and intimate. On the shower floor, blood was collecting around her body and under his feet. Her body was blocking the drain. He envisioned the shower stall filling with blood and water, drowning him. Imagined the two of them floating together in the chamber of pink water. Dead.

Banging on the bathroom door jarred him from his waking nightmare. "Sweet? Sweet? What the hell is going on in there?"

His pa. What could he tell his pa?

21

For a family of six, it would have been roomy. For a family of twelve, it was a sardine can. Now with everyone gone and her parents alone, it seemed cavernous. She worried it was too much for them to maintain, but the place was immaculate whenever she visited. Murphy parked on the street in front of the two-story Victorian and immediately noticed how even in the fall, the lawn was golf course green. All the leaves were raked and bagged and sitting in the driveway, waiting for a trip to the city compost site. Orange and maroon mums lined the sidewalk leading up to the front steps.

Murphy shut off the Jeep and sat behind the wheel for a minute. She pulled the keys out of the ignition and jiggled them in her right hand. Talking to them about it was going to be tough, she thought. Almost as tough as talking to Jack. Her parents loved their son-in-law. Loved the whole idea of him. A big, handsome doctor. Catholic. The son of college professors. No Lebanese blood in him, but a smattering of Irish. Native of St. Paul. Helpless in the kitchen, as was proper for any self-respecting male. What could she tell them about Erik? He was a big, handsome

Lutheran from Minneapolis. German and Irish and Norwegian and God knew what else. Sliced open dead people for a living. Drove expensive cars. Spent too much time at the horse track. Too much time at the gym. Could cook circles around the best restaurant chefs. No. They weren't going to be impressed with the résumé of the guy she'd slept with. The guy who'd helped end her marriage.

She put her keys in her purse and got out of the car with the paper bag. She walked up the front steps, opened the screen door. She scanned the porch, which ran the length of the front of the house. The aluminum lawn chairs were folded and leaning against a corner. The terra-cotta planters were empty and cleaned and stacked in a row against the wall. Her father hadn't yet taken the hammocks down in preparation for winter. When she was a kid, many hot summer nights were spent sleeping on the porch. Swinging from the three hammocks her father strung from hooks in the walls. She and her brothers did rock, paper, scissors to see who got to use them. The losers slept on the wood floor atop sleeping bags or—if they were crybabies about it—were banished inside. She was usually one of the winners; the rock was her good-luck charm. She walked up to the front door. Her parents hated when she knocked or rang, said the doorbell was for strangers, not family. She turned the knob, pushed it open, walked inside. Inhaled. Garlic and onions and lamb and tomato sauce.

"Hello!" she yelled. She looked around. As usual, wood floors spotless enough to eat off of. Furniture shiny and aromatic with lemon oil polish. Overstuffed front room furniture with crocheted doilies draped over the arms and backs. Starched lace curtains hanging from the windows. She noticed a basket of clean clothes on the floor at the bottom of the stairs. Without complaint, her mother continued to carry clothes baskets from the basement to the second-floor bedrooms. The Murphy sons had offered to turn the pantry into a main floor laundry, but Amira refused to surrender an inch of kitchen storage. She had to have shelves for her home-canned goods. Tomatoes. Green beans. Grape leaves. All grown in the backyard. Murphy pulled off her jacket and set it and her purse and the bag on the front room couch. She picked up the clothes basket and put her right foot on the first step.

Her mother walked out of the kitchen, wiping her hands on her apron. "Put that down, young lady." Like her daughter, she was large-breasted. Unlike Murphy, her hips were wide after carrying ten children and her skin leathery from years spent tending to her garden. She stood a little over five feet tall to her daughter's five feet ten inches. Her dark hair, streaked with silver, was in a bun behind her head, but tendrils were loose around her forehead. Her face was red and beaded with perspiration from the kitchen heat.

"I can carry it up for you, *Imma*."

"I'm not crippled." Amira pulled the basket out of her daughter's hands and started walking upstairs with it. "I'm going to hop in the bathtub," she said over her shoulder. "Sit down and make your father wait on *you* for a change."

"Sure smells good in here," Murphy said after her.

"Yeah, yeah," said her mother as she reached the top of the stairs. Amira Murphy wasn't good at accepting compliments.

Murphy hung her jacket and purse in the front hall closet, picked up the paper bag, walked to the back of the house. She passed through the dining room, noticed the table was set. Not a good omen for the evening. The clan ate their casual meals in the kitchen at a table made of rough-cut oak and surrounded by a dozen mismatched wooden chairs. Formal family meetings—to plan a

180

wedding, announce a pregnancy, settle a sibling spat—were held in the dining room at a long mahogany table surrounded by matching upholstered chairs. The kitchen table was suitable for a backyard picnic; the dining room furniture belonged in a castle. She counted the place settings. Five. Who else had they invited? She was afraid to ask. She pushed open the swinging door into the kitchen. Sean Murphy was sitting at the table drinking coffee and flipping through the *Pioneer Press*. He looked at her over his reading glasses and smiled. "Daughter."

"Papa." Murphy crossed the linoleum floor, set the bag on the table. She threw her arms around him, planted a kiss on top of his head. He still had a full head of hair, though it had long ago turned from black to gray. He smelled of Aqua Velva aftershave and cigar smoke. He loved cigars. The cheaper, the better.

He pulled the paper bag toward him. "Hope this ain't some of that overpriced wine you waste your money on." He pulled the *Arak* out and smiled. "Good girl. Get us a couple of glasses."

Murphy went to the cabinets above the sink, opened a door and took down three juice tumblers—recycled jelly jars with cartoon characters painted on them. She set them in front of her father. He filled each a third of the way. "Should we wait for Ma?" she asked.

A dismissive wave with his right hand. "We'll be dead before she gets out of the tub. Get the water and ice for ours. She takes hers neat anyway."

Murphy took a bottle of spring water out of the refrigerator and a bag of ice cubes out of the freezer and set them in front of her father. He poured water into two of the glasses; the transparent liquid turned a cloudy white. He slowly slipped two ice cubes into each milky tumbler. She sat down next to him and each raised a glass.

Sean: "May neighbors respect you, trouble neglect you, the angels protect you and heaven accept you."

Murphy loved her father's Irish toasts made with Lebanese liquor. "Thanks, Papa." While they sipped, Murphy studied her father. Searched for signs of old age beyond his gray hair. As always, he seemed the same to her. Bushy brows jutting over blue eyes. Lantern jaw. Barrel torso. Big arms. Big hands. Big nose broken on three separate occasions when he stepped between fighting patrons at the family bar. Still, with every visit he seemed to move slower and reminisce more. He missed the bar. Talked with increasing frequency about opening another. Murphy knew it would never happen. Not at his age.

He pointed to the refrigerator. "Your mother made some *kibbee nayee*," he said, referring to the Lebanese dish of raw ground beef, bulgur, onions and spices. "Let's have a nibble before dinner." Murphy got up, put the ice and water back and took a plate out of the refrigerator. The *kibbee* was patted into a large round like an oversized hamburger. She set the plate on the table and went to a cupboard below the sink for a bottle of olive oil. She set the oil on the table. With the side of her right hand, she pressed a cross into the *kibbee* and poured olive oil into it. "Daughter. Where's the garlic?" The dip was a sort of mayonnaise made of lemon juice, garlic and oil.

"I didn't see it."

"It's there."

She pulled open the refrigerator and dug around. Found the thick, white sauce in a glass bowl covered with plastic wrap. Took it out. Set it on the table. Peeled off the plastic. Immediately got a whiff of garlic.

"Flatbread's on the counter," he said. Murphy turned to get the bread and her mother walked into the kitchen.

"Papa," snapped Amira. "Why is my daughter running around the kitchen like a maid?" Her hair was damp; she didn't believe in blow-dryers. She worked her long mane in a bun behind her head while she talked. She always chastised Murphy for wearing her hair long, but never wanted to pay for a haircut for herself. So she kept it knotted behind her head. "I told you to wait on *her*."

"I am," he said. "Now I'm waiting on her to get the bread."

"We're eating in the dining room," Amira said.

"This isn't eating," he said. "It's nibbling."

Murphy put the plastic bag on the table, reached inside, pulled out a round, flat loaf. Ripped off a couple of pieces. She sat down next to her father and each used a hunk of the bread to scoop up some oil-drenched *kibbee*. Amira tucked a couple of strands of hair behind her ears and took a seat across from them. She was wearing a short-sleeved housedress that zipped up the front. Even while working in the garden, she wore dresses. She believed ladies never wore slacks. In a bow to comfort, however, she always wore knee-high nylons and flat-heeled shoes. Amira tore off a hunk of bread, scraped some *kibbee* off the plate and dipped it in the pool of oil on top of the meat.

The three of them chewed silently for a couple of minutes. Murphy's father took another sip of *Arak*. "That'll put hair on your chest." Another sip, then: "What's this bullshit about a divorce?"

Murphy swallowed her food, took a sip of *Arak*. "Can't we save this for after dinner?"

"No," said her mother. She lifted her glass, emptied it, slammed it down on the table. "I don't want to ruin the digestion with bad talk. Let's settle it now."

"Nothing to settle, *Imma*. It's over. Jack and I are finished."

Her mother dragged her right palm over her left, as if she were dusting flour off her hands. "Finished. Like that. Eight years of marriage. Use it, crumple it, toss it in the toilet."

Murphy rubbed her forehead with her fingertips. "It's not like that. We tried, Ma. I tried."

"Have you talked to a priest?" Amira asked.

"Should have had babies right off the bat," said her father. "Kids are glue. Stick people together."

"I'm glad we didn't have kids," said Murphy.

Amira: "Bite your tongue, daughter. You should go to confession."

"If we had kids, then a split would be messy."

"So that's how it is?" Her father took off his spectacles, folded them and pointed them at her. "This is gonna be one of those nice, modern divorces? Send each other Christmas cards and birthday cards? What a load of crap. No such thing as a nice divorce."

"It won't be nice. Jack is pissed." She touched her bottom lip.

"Here's to Jack," said her father. He set down his spectacles, raised his drinking glass and polished off the *Arak*. Rattled the ice around. "Balls the size of an elephant."

Murphy was indignant. "Whose side are you on?"

Amira: "The marriage's side."

Murphy stood up. Her father pulled her back down by her arm. "Okay, okay. Tell us about Mr. Wonderful."

Amira: "The home wrecker."

Murphy finished her drink and poured herself and her parents another. Going to be a long night, she thought.

The doorbell. Sean ripped off another piece of bread and used it to scrape more *kibbee* off the plate. "Who the hell is bothering us now?" He shoved the meat and bread into his mouth and chewed.

Amira folded her arms across her bosom. "What's his name, this guy you work with?" The doorbell rang again. "He Catholic?"

Murphy stood up. "I'll get it."

Sean swallowed. Motioned her down with his hand. "Sit. Probably kids selling magazines for school. We could stock a library with the crap we ordered from your brothers' kids."

Murphy walked to the front of the house and opened the door. Two men in their early forties were on the porch, each carrying a six-pack. They stood well over six feet tall, had their father's fair skin and blue eyes. "Why'd you clowns ring?"

Her older brothers looked past her into the house.

"We figured you'd answer the door," said Ryan.

"Fireworks over yet?" asked Patrick. He was nervous, ran the fingers of his right hand through his hair. Both men had wavy ink-colored hair like their sister.

She stepped onto the porch and shut the door behind her. "Hell no," she said. "Haven't even started." She rubbed her arms; the sun was setting and it was cold outside. The early evening air smelled of burning wood from neighbors' fireplaces.

Patrick pulled a bottle out of his pack of Beck's and held it up. "Got an opener, Potato Head?"

"Yeah. Keep one on me at all times."

He set the six-pack down. "Was that sarcasm?" He took out a second Beck's, turned it upside down and used the top to pry the cap off the first bottle.

"Our orders were to talk you out of this," said Ryan. Patrick took a bump off his beer and nodded.

"Can't believe they called you bozos," she said.

"They figured we'd stand up for Jacko because we wear the same uniform," said Ryan. He and Patrick were both orthopedic surgeons and had a practice together.

185

Patrick raised his bottle. "To the medical brotherhood." He took another sip.

"I got a news flash for you guys," said Murphy. "I'm not the one who did the walking."

"I'm sorry, Potato Head," said Patrick.

"*Imma* told us it was your doing," said Ryan.

"I guess it's my fault," she said. "No. There's no guessing. It *is* my fault."

Patrick picked up his six-pack and tucked it under his left arm. "Let's assign blame inside, where it's warmer. Besides, I'm starving."

"Go ahead," said Ryan. He pulled his sister by the elbow toward the first hammock. "We're gonna go for a swing. Be inside in a minute. Don't eat all the *kibbee*, you sow." Patrick made an *oink* noise, went inside, shut the door behind him.

Murphy opened her mouth to protest but then closed it. Ryan was two years older than Patrick and much more serious. He undoubtedly took to heart his parents' request to intervene. She'd have to hear him out now or he'd hound her later.

They lowered themselves into a hammock. Ryan set the six-pack down between them. "Want one?" he asked. She nodded. He picked up a Rolling Rock, twisted off the cap, handed her the bottle. Picked up another one, opened it. They sat for a few minutes, their feet flat on the porch floor. They moved the hammock back and forth by bending and straightening their legs. She wrapped her arms around herself. He set his beer down, took off his jean jacket and draped it over her shoulders.

"Thanks."

He picked up the beer, took a bump. Cupped the bottle between his palms. "What's the deal with you and Jacko?"

All her brothers called him that; Jack hated it. Another thing about her family that aggravated him. She took a sip of beer. Switched the bottle to her left hand and ran her right index finger around the mouth of the bottle. "We're finished. He found out I saw someone else. Over the summer."

"Is that why you're finished?"

She paused. At first she felt insulted, then she told herself it was a fair question. "It didn't help. That's for damn sure. But you know we've been having problems for a long time. Haven't been able to live together without fighting."

He stopped moving his legs. "I know. I figured. I don't know."

"You figured we'd keep limping along." She switched the beer back to her right hand. Lifted it to her lips. Took a long drink. Wiped her mouth with the back of her left hand. "That's what I figured, too. But Jack's really mad. Hurt. This might be it for us."

"So who's this guy? Is it serious?"

"Erik Mason. Investigator with the ME's office."

Ryan nodded. Took another bump off his beer. "What about the second half of my question?"

She took a sip of beer. "I don't have an answer right now. I don't know. All I know is Jack walked out and I think this time, we're split for keeps."

Ryan finished his beer. Set it on the floor. Started swinging the hammock again. "Maybe that's not so bad," he said in a low voice. "Lately, when I've seen you with Jacko, I haven't been so sure about the two of you. I've watched you watching him. Reminds me of someone sitting on the edge of their seat in a movie theater."

"Waiting for the next scary scene," she said. She took one last sip, set the bottle down, pulled her brother's jacket tighter around her shoulders.

He stood up. "Let's go in. It's cold out here and I'm hungry." He started for the front door. She bent over, put

187

the empties in the six-pack carton, stood up and followed him. Still cleaning up after them, she thought. He was holding the door open for her. She walked through and he leaned into her ear to whisper, "Let me do the talking or Ma will throw us all out before we get to the *koosa*."

She smiled and nodded, even though she had no intention of letting anyone do the talking for her. They were still trying to take care of her.

22

He stood in the shower with icy water needling his body and creating a puddle of diluted blood at his feet. His pa kept pounding on the door with his fist. Pounding, pounding. Trip wished the pounding would stop. Wished the bleeding would stop.

"Sweet! Sweet! Open up, goddammit!" Now a sharp sound. He was hitting the door with his cane.

Trip looked at his arms. The cold water had washed the red off. His feet were wet with blood and water. He reached for the shampoo. Squatted over her body. Wedged the bottle under her hips so it propped her up and cleared the drain. The blood and water started running down the hole. He stood up and rinsed his hands under the shower. Pulled open the stall door as much as he could with her body blocking it. Hung onto the door with his left hand. Lifted his left foot into the cold spray and held it there until it was clean and stepped out with it. Lifted the right foot. Watched the water drip from it. Set that foot on the bathroom floor. He shut the shower door. Let the water keep running. Keep sending the red down the drain.

Pounding with his fist again. "Sweet! What the hell is going on in there! This is my house! I want to know!"

He stood naked in the middle of the bathroom, dripping water onto the floor. He was so tired he couldn't think. He needed a good lie and he couldn't come up with one. Not even the kernel of one. The same sensation as reaching into a cereal box, feeling around, finding it empty. Not one nugget. Not even crumbs. He peered in the medicine cabinet mirror for inspiration. All he saw was an exhausted man with thinning hair matted to his head. He grabbed a towel off the bar and rubbed his scalp. Lifted it off his head. Hair all over the towel. He wrapped the towel around his waist and went to the door. Put his hand on the lock.

More knocking with the cane. "Justice! Open this fucking door right now before I break it down!"

He twisted the lock and opened the door. Stood silently in front of his pa.

"Sweet?" His pa's face didn't show concern as much as curiosity, and Trip found that unsettling. Minutes earlier, a woman had been screaming in their bathroom.

"She's d... dead, Pa."

"What? Who?"

"Keri. She c... cut herself real b... bad with the straight-edge."

"Killed herself? In our can?"

Trip jumped on the suggestion. "Yeah. Suicide. Yeah. She's been real d... d... depressed lately. About her weight and s... stuff. I walked in on her and . . ."

His father shoved him aside with his left arm and thumped over to the shower with his cane. He pushed open the shower door. The bottom of the door bumped against her body. Frank looked down. Squinted. Even with his poor eyesight he could make out the wound across her

190

throat. Deep, red, raw, oozing blood as water splattered it. The straight-edge razor on the shower floor. Pieces of something scattered all over the stall. Bent over to get a better look. The shower radio, busted in a bunch of pieces. Leaned closer. Saw the shampoo bottle propped under her body, letting the blood flow down the drain. He stood straight, turned, looked in his son's face. Trip thought he saw the corners of his pa's mouth curl up for an instant. Stifling a smirk. "Suicide my ass! You did the bitch!"

Trip took a step back from him and raised both palms defensively. "Pa. No. I didn't."

"Who in the hell kills themselves by slitting their own throat?" The old man closed the shower door. "Why'd you do it, Sweet? Why?"

It came to him; a noble reason with the added bonus of being partially true. "She was trying to k... k... kill you, Pa. She d... doped you up."

It worked. The old man's jaw dropped. Then: "What the hell? Why she wanna do that?"

Trip blurted out the first word that came to mind: "Money."

"What money? I don't got a pot to piss in, and neither do you."

"Your Social Security checks. She was gonna hide your body and make me cash the checks."

Frank's eyes narrowed. Suddenly his son was part of the plot. "How she gonna make you do that?"

"Blackmail." Trip regretted that word as soon as it left his lips, tried to switch gears before his pa asked the next obvious question. "Didn't you think it was weird the way you g... got all sleepy all of a sudden? She slipped you a sleeping p... p... pill. How do you suppose she gave it to you, P... Pa? Hid it in your food? Your beer?"

Frank thought about it. "She did give me a new pill

today, right before you got to the house. I knew it wasn't time for my usual meds. Vitamin. That's what she said it was." He shook his cane at the shower door. "Vitamin my ass. Murdering witch. Glad you did her, Sweet. I thank you for protecting your pa."

Trip was stunned at how easily his pa accepted murder. Even if it was murder with a palatable motive. He studied the old man. Saw more than acceptance in his expression. Satisfaction.

His pa pushed the shower door open again and looked down at the body. Said in a low voice, "Shows what goes around comes around."

"Pa?"

His voice sounded distant. Removed from the moment. "Reminds me is all."

"Reminds you of what, Pa?"

"Nothing, son." He pointed up at the showerhead with his cane. "Shut that off before we get a triple-digit water bill."

"What about the b... blood?"

"What about it? We'll rinse it all down the drain at once, when she's done bleeding like a butchered hog."

Trip stepped around him, leaned into the stall, shut off the water. "What do we d... do with her, Pa?" He started to shut the shower door. Didn't seem right to discuss it with her body bleeding right under their noses.

"Wait." His pa reached into his left pants pocket and handed Trip two coins. "Close her eyes and put these on them. Bad luck letting the dead watch you."

Trip fingered the money. "Thought you're supposed to use pennies."

"What did I give you?"

"Dime and a nickel."

"That penny stuff's an old wives' tale. Any coin should

do it. Except quarters maybe. Quarters are too big; probably wouldn't sit right on the eyeball. Besides, that's all I got on me except for some folding money. That sure as shit ain't gonna work."

Trip stood with the nickel and dime in his right palm. Remembered something about quarters and the dead. An echo from his childhood. What was it? He had goose bumps on his arms. Whatever it was, it was something bad.

His pa touched his shoulder. "Son. Wake up. Put them on her."

Trip kneeled on the shower stall lip, shut her right lid with his left index finger and held it down while he set the dime on it. Shut her left lid, put the nickel on it. He stood up and surveyed his handiwork. Silver on her lids was spooky. Made it seem as if her eyes were wide open and lit up from the inside out. A flashlight shining inside a jack-o'-lantern. "Pennies would have been b... better. More natural."

"Shut up about the stupid pennies. Close the shower if you don't like how it looks."

Trip pulled the door closed. "What are we gonna do with her?" He tightened the towel around his waist. Paced back and forth the length of the bathroom. Planted a hand on each side of his head, trying to press out an idea. Took his hands down. Black strands on his palms. Shook them off. "Could stick her in her car trunk and drive it a ways away. Leave it somewhere."

"She walked here. Her beater's parked in front of her trailer."

"Her trailer. What if we carried her back to her own trailer, dumped her in her own shower? I got a key."

"She'd be a big load to haul outta here. Wheelbarrow might work. We'd have to do it in the middle of the night. Nosy neighbors. Gotta watch for them. She's got that old bat living next door; never sleeps. No. Too risky taking her back to her place. Too many eyes around here."

"Gotta b... b... bury her or something."

"Need to dig a big fucking hole. Bobcat would come in handy." Frank chuckled. Thought that was funny. "Where the hell would we bury her? We ain't got no land."

"We c... can't leave her here."

His old man nodded. "She'd rot and stink up the place. Someone might smell her. Call the cops."

"The cops," said Trip. "Who knows she was here? Her b... b... boss?"

"Nah. I heard her on the phone. Told them some bullshit about visiting some boyfriend outta town. She sure as shit couldn't tell them she was fucking her client. I mean her client's son."

Good catch, Pa, Trip thought.

Frank scratched his chin. "So what do you do with a dead cow?" His eyes widened; he thumped his cane on the floor. "You cut it up and store it in the freezer." He thumped his cane again. "Yes sir. We got that great big chest freezer in the spare bedroom. There's a plan if I ever heard one."

The color drained from Trip's cheeks. Not only was the idea repulsive, but the enthusiasm his pa showed for it was sickening. This was wrong. All of it. From the minute he opened the bathroom door and saw his pa's face, it felt wrong. This man smirking over a dead woman, talking about cutting her up like a side of beef, this wasn't his pa. Not the one he knew. The bit with the coins. How did he know what did and didn't work? He'd done this sort of thing before. Covered his tracks after murdering someone. "Pa. I d... don't know."

Frank detected the horrified reaction in his son's voice. "I'm only trying to help, Sweet. What you've done here, it's

194

a sin." He nodded toward the shower stall. "But what she was planning was worse. A bigger sin. And you're my flesh and blood. Flesh and blood comes first. I got to help you."

Unconvincing speech. Still, he didn't know what to say. How to confront the old man. He was in no position to judge anyone.

"Okay. What do we d... do first? Maybe we don't n... need to cut her. She c... could fit as is."

His pa nodded. "Let's give it a try."

"How do we c... carry her down the hall without m... messing up the carpet?"

"That blue tarp in the shed. Should be plenty big and strong. Don't even have to lift her. Grab the corners of the thing and drag her."

Trip dropped his eyes. The blue tarp. He'd buried the bridesmaid in it. "I threw it away, Pa. Had a b... big hole in it. How about an old b... bedsheet?"

Frank shook his head. "Blood might drip through."

"We'll wrap her neck in a garbage bag. Seal it with d... duct tape. Got a couple of rolls in the kitchen, g... good and wide."

"Now you're talking. You get the tape and bag and I'll get the sheet."

Trip watched his pa thump out of the bathroom and head down the hall. He couldn't remember the last time he'd moved so quickly and with such purpose. His old man was having fun. He'd done this before, or something close to this. Would he be shocked to learn about the brides-maid? The ranger? Maybe not. What about the others Trip had flattened over the years? What about what happened in high school? Would it horrify his pa or make him proud? He brushed the thoughts aside. One thing at a time. He dropped the towel on the floor. Went into the hallway. Retrieved the clothes he'd left outside the bathroom door and slipped them on. While he dressed he watched his pa digging around the hall closet for an old sheet. He was humming to himself. One of Elvis's religious songs. "How Great Thou Art." He used to hum that song when he did household chores. When he had the strength to vacuum and sweep. As unbelievable as it seemed, this task of getting rid of a body had actually reinvigorated his old man.

Trip walked through the front room into the kitchen and pulled open a drawer to the right of the sink. The designated junk drawer. Stuck. Always stuck, crammed as it was with tools, glue bottles, rolls of tape, scissors, rubber bands, bottle caps. He yanked hard and it popped open. He reached into the back of the drawer and pulled out a roll of masking tape. The wrong stuff. He set it on top of the counter. Took out the claw hammer and pliers and screwdriver. Put those on top of the counter. Reached way back. Felt it with his fingertips. Slid it to the front of the drawer. There it was. A roll of silver-colored duct tape. He shoved the other junk back in the drawer and forced it shut. He opened the cabinet door under the sink and took out the roll of kitchen garbage bags. Ripped two bags off the roll. Held them up. They were a flimsy generic brand. Usually leaked. He pulled two more off the roll. That should do it, he thought. Shut the door. He went back to the bathroom. His pa was standing next to the shower stall with the door open. Staring at her body. An old sheet was draped over his left arm. Had cowboys on it. Trip never figured his old man would give up a set of cowboy sheets. Maybe that's all they had left in the closet. Maybe he couldn't see what he'd given Trip.

"Got the t... tape and garbage bags," Trip said, holding the tape in his left hand and the bags in his right. His pa didn't answer. Kept looking down at the body. "Pa? Having second thoughts about the p... p... plan?"

"No, no." That faraway voice again. "She reminds me of someone is all. Not her looks. Her position. How she's on her back, with her knees up. Any minute you expect she's gonna pluck those coins off her eyeballs, get right up, dust herself off, walk away. Like nothing happened."

His pa was acting weirder and weirder. Trip tried to dismiss it. Time to get down to business. Trip stepped in front of him and reached for the cold water handle to turn on the shower, rinse off the rest of the blood. His pa touched his arm. "Don't bother," he said. "Getting it wet again will make a bigger mess. We'll wrap her neck up real good as is. Clean up the stall later."

Trip stood still for a moment, not sure how to proceed.

"Go ahead, son. She won't bite. Not no more." His pa laughed.

Trip kneeled on the lip of the shower. He set the garbage bags and roll of tape on the floor. He studied her neck for a minute. Her throat was still bloody, although the oozing seemed to have slowed. The shower floor remained wet with water and blood. The plastic and duct tape would work regardless. He grabbed each end of a garbage bag and slid it under her neck. He wrapped it around a couple of times and tied the ends in a knot under her chin. He picked up another bag, wrapped it around, knotted it on the side of her neck closest to him. "I d... don't think she n... needs the other two."

"Good," said Frank. "Damn bags are expensive."

His pa hovered over his shoulder while he continued. Trip wasn't sure what he could and couldn't see. He unraveled two feet of tape from the roll and ripped it off with his teeth. He stuck one end of the tape on the far side of her neck facing the shower wall. Working toward himself, he slowly wrapped the tape around the bags, flattening it against the plastic as he went. He lifted her

197

head up by the hair on top of her head with his left hand and with his right, brought the tape around the back of her neck. He sealed the end, set the tape back down on the floor, sat back on his heels to admire his handiwork. Trip thought she resembled someone who'd been in a car accident and was wearing a whiplash brace.

Frank patted him on the back. "Good job. Couldn't have done better myself and that's a fact." He handed Trip the bedsheet. "I'll get out of here. Give you more elbow room." He went into the hall and stood in the doorway to supervise. He pointed to the floor with his cane. "Spread it out and drag her onto it. Don't lift her. You'll throw out your back. One cripple in the family's enough."

Trip nodded. He spread the sheet out as much as possible in the cramped space. He stepped into the shower, bent over the body, hooked the inside of his elbows under her armpits and lifted her a few inches off the ground. He stepped out of the stall with his left foot and then his right, dragging her over the shower lip. Her buttocks hit the floor with a soft thud. Trip slipped his arms out of her pits and let her head drop. Another thud. The coins popped off. He picked them up and put them back on her lids. Her legs were still in the shower, knees bent at the stall lip. He stood up straight; his back was aching from all the bending. He noticed the inside of his arms. Streaks of shave cream on his sweatshirt, from her pits. It repulsed him. He yanked off the shirt and threw it in the sink.

Frank: "What's wrong?"

"Nothing," Trip mumbled. He didn't want to touch her anymore, especially with his chest bare. Didn't want to feel a dead woman's skin against his. He bent over and picked up the corners of the sheet. Pulled straight out until her legs made it over the hump. Then he pivoted a bit and backed out toward the door. He scrutinized the bathroom floor as he went. Was relieved to see no blood. His pa stepped out of the way as he dragged her into the hallway. Another pivot and he walked backward toward the spare bedroom. The sheet was a little more difficult to pull across the carpet than the bathroom tile. "Pa!" he yelled.

"What?" His old man was behind him, walking toward the bedroom.

"The freezer empty?"

"Shit. Didn't think of that. Keep going. I'll give it a look-see."

"And make sure the blinds are shut in there."

He heard his pa thump toward the bedroom at the end of the hall. Again, he was amazed at how quickly he was moving. A man with a mission. Trip looked over his shoulder as he walked backward. Saw his pa open the door for him at the end of the hall. Trip pulled her through the doorway and into the bedroom. He let go of the sheet and wiped his forehead with his right hand; he'd worked up a good sweat. He leaned his back against the wall.

The window blinds were shut. The top to the chest freezer was open and his old man was feeling around with one hand. "Ice cream. Peas. Chicken patties. Couple tuna pot pies. Tater Tots. Something wrapped in aluminum foil."

"Guess what we're having for d... dinner?"

His old man laughed and started taking things out of the freezer. Trip helped. They piled the frozen food onto a card table sitting next to the freezer. Trip had traded the freezer for some work on somebody's truck engine. Frank held up one of the ice cream cartons and squinted. "What flavor?"

"Spumoni."

"When the hell did we buy that? Hate that shit. Dried fruit and nuts and such."

Trip smiled sadly. "Keri b... brought that for Italian night. Remember, a few weeks ago?"

His pa kept pulling stuff out of the chest and setting it on the table. "Yeah. I remember. Frozen pizza and spaghetti made with sauce from a jar." His old man stopped taking stuff out. Pointed to a sticker on the inside of the freezer door that was big enough for even him to see. "Which one is she?" The sticker was in the shape of a triangle. The top of the triangle showed which items could be kept frozen for three months: fish, ice cream, pork. Below that was six months: bread, duck, lamb. Nine months: beef and deer. At the bottom of the pyramid, what could stay frozen for a year: chicken, corn, peas.

His old man was laughing so hard he was bent in half. "Since she's a cow, I guess we can keep her in here nine months. What do you think, Sweet? We could cook her up next Fourth of July."

Trip didn't think it was funny. "What the hell is wrong with you? You b... been acting like a c... crazy old b... bastard."

His pa stopped laughing and straightened up. "I wouldn't talk, boy. Who sliced up a woman in the shower? Huh? Wasn't me." Trip didn't answer. He looked down at her body and then at the freezer. His pa read his mind. "You're right, Sweet. She'll fit without alterations. Good thing, too. That'd be a mess and a half to clean up. How we gonna lift her in, though? She's gotta weigh in at two bills."

More than the bridesmaid, Trip thought. "Let's g... get her right against the chest. I'll s... slide her up and hike her in." He pulled the sheet closer to the chest. Stood over her, a foot on each side of her. He adjusted his grip on the corners of the sheet and pulled her through his legs. Kept tugging and lifting until her head touched the chest. He stepped back and grabbed the bottom of the sheet and pivoted her body so she was resting against the chest, parallel with it. The coins fell out of her eyes, rolled onto the sheet. Trip bent over and picked them up.

His pa held out his right hand. "We'll put them back on after she's all tucked in." Trip gave them to his old man and he dropped them in his pants pocket. Frank looked down at her body. "I hate to say it, but you're gonna have to get under that fat ass of hers."

The idea made Trip shudder. He ran his eyes around the bedroom. The freezer was huge and took up most of the space. Besides the chest and the card table next to it, the room contained a set of folding chairs leaning against a wall. Car battery with a charger next to it, both sitting on a hunk of cardboard on the floor. A case of beer next to that. Two sets of busted stereo speakers stacked on top of each other. The closet door was open. Inside, down coats and jackets hanging from a rod. Snow boots and old shoes on the floor. Trip walked to the closet and pulled a winter coat off a hanger. Slipped it on over his bare chest, zipped it up. Pulled on the hood, tightened it around his head with the drawstring. Found some gloves in the pockets and slipped them on. "Now I'm r... ready."

He went back to the body. Kneeled at her side. Bent over like a man kissing the ground. Rammed his shoulder under her lower back. He slipped his right arm under her thighs and his left under her shoulders. He slowly stood up while sliding her against the chest. He felt her roll into the freezer. Heard a thud. Was never more grateful to hear a sound. Stood up straight and looked into the freezer while he pulled off the gloves and stuffed them back in the jacket pockets. Perfect landing. Right on her back. Her left arm was jammed against the side of the freezer and the right one was flopped over her chest, covering her breasts. A modesty in death she never had in life, Trip thought. Her left leg was bent at the knee but her right leg was sticking up over the top of the freezer. His pa grabbed her ankle, bent the leg

201

at the knee and tucked it down. Then the old man walked around to her head. Took the coins out of his pocket. Handed them to his son. He reached down and set one each on her eyes.

Trip glanced at the floor. "No spills. Sheet's c... clean."

"I think we can wash it up and use it again," said his pa. Trip shuddered at the thought of having the sheet on his bed but didn't say anything. His pa patted him on the arm. "Good job, Sweet. Let's find any personal shit she left around the house. Clothes. Whatever. Throw it all in with her."

"What are we gonna do with her d... down the road? Can't keep her in the d... deep freeze forever."

"I'll give it some thought. Got some friends in the foundry business." Frank gave her one last look. "That is one big freezer. Swear to God we could still fit another body in if we had to."

"We w... won't have to," Trip muttered.

"Good," said his pa. He reached down and pressed the coins flat to make sure they'd stay. He withdrew his hands, reached up for the lid. "Night, bitch. Sleep tight." He slammed it shut.

23

She woke up Wednesday morning with the taste of her mother's garlic sauce still coating the inside of her mouth. Garlic hangover, her brothers called it. She loved the stuff but as a rule, she avoided eating it during the workweek. It usually took at least two days to get rid of the bad breath. She slid off the couch and went into the guest bathroom to gargle with Listerine.

Erik sat up and yelled after her. "Hey, garlic breath! Where you going so fast?"

She spit into the sink. "Thought I'd spare you." She took another swig right out of the bottle, swished it around her mouth until it burned.

"Too late," he said. "I smelled it all night. Next time bring some home for me so we can make each other suffer. Or maybe you should have your folks invite me to dinner."

She spit into the sink again. "I don't think I'm ready for that scene quite yet, and neither are you. Trust me on this." She looked into the bathroom mirror. Ran her fingers through her hair to work out the tangles. She took a brush off the counter and gave her mane a few strokes. She'd left her parents' house Tuesday night after a tense meal punctuated by shouting matches between herself and her mother. It would have been worse without her brothers' mediating commentary: *She hasn't been happy for a long time, Ma. They can't even agree on whether to have kids. She needs to find someone else.* Her father concentrated on eating, but occasionally came up for air long enough to throw gas on the fire: *Remember what happened to that divorced cousin of yours in Lebanon? Remind her she can't remarry in the Catholic Church unless she gets an annulment.* She got home and Erik called, begged to come over. He brought a bottle of wine. They sat on her couch talking and drinking wine until well past midnight. She started crying when she talked about Jack leaving. Erik held her until her shoulders stopped shaking. They fell asleep, both dressed in their sweats. Arms around each other. Didn't even make love. That was fine with her; she wasn't ready to sleep with him again. She needed a friend more than a lover.

She set down the brush, walked back into the front room. She leaned over and puffed a breath of air into his face. "Is that better?"

"Oh yeah." He pulled her down onto the couch. Kissed her hard. His tongue darted into her mouth, scraping past her teeth. He pulled it out. Lifted his mouth off of hers. "I didn't know Listerine made a garlic-flavored mouthwash."

She gently pushed him off of her and stood up. "Let me get the coffee going."

He grabbed her left wrist with his right hand. "It's early. We could still go upstairs." He smiled. "Get a little more sleep. Or no sleep."

Ringing from a cell phone on the kitchen counter.

She tried to pull her hand away but he wouldn't let go. "Erik."

"Ignore it," he said. More ringing.

204

"No problem," she said. "It's your phone."

"Shit."

She pulled her wrist out of his hand and went to the counter. Picked up his cell phone and tossed it to him. He caught it and flipped it open. Put his stocking feet on her coffee table. She turned around and started filling the coffeepot with water. Poured the water into the coffeemaker. Pulled a filter down from the cupboard, set it into the basket and scooped some coffee into it. Set the pot under the filter and turned on the coffeemaker. The smell alone made her feel more awake. She leaned her back against the counter and listened to Erik's end of the phone conversation. It sounded like work.

"Yeah." A pause. "Really? Where exactly?"

She turned around and took two coffee mugs down from the cupboard. Ringing from the other cell phone on the counter. She set down the mugs, picked up the phone and walked across the front room. Opened the sliding glass doors and stepped out onto the deck in her stocking feet. Closed the door behind her, in case it was Jack. She inhaled the cold river air before answering. "Murphy."

Duncan: "You sound chipper for a change."

She walked across the deck. Held the phone with her right hand and with her left, leaned against the railing. A flock of geese honked overhead. "What's up?"

"They found Bunny Pederson."

She took her hand off the railing and stood straight. "In the park?"

"In some woods near the campground. Wrapped in a tarp and buried in a shallow grave. Real half-assed effort at hiding her."

"An obvious cause of death?" Erik was probably doing the autopsy. She guessed he was on the phone at that moment talking about getting the body down to St. Paul.

"Wasn't gunfire. Winter says some kind of massive trauma. Ramsey County ME is doing the workup."

"Sexual assault?"

"Nope. She was fully clothed and all that."

"Except for the shoe they found on the ranger," Murphy reminded him.

"Except for both shoes."

"The other is missing?"

"Yup. Purse, too. Robbery gone bad maybe. Who knows?"

Through the patio door, she saw Erik grab the remote and turn on the television. She asked Duncan, "On the news yet?"

"That's how I knew."

She walked back to the patio door, slid it open with her left hand, stepped inside and shut it behind her. In the front room, Erik was pacing while talking on the phone and channel surfing with the remote. The sound was off. She didn't see any images from the woods, only a weatherman standing in front of a map. "So Winter didn't call you?"

"Hell no. I called him," Duncan said. "Bastard didn't give me anything more than he gave the media. Told me since we don't have a piece of the case anymore, we'll have to read the papers along with the rest of the world. Fuck him."

She switched the phone to her left hand, walked to the galley, picked up the pot and poured coffee into the two mugs. "Actually, we might have an interest after all." She set down the pot.

That intrigued him. "Your wild idea? Let's hear it."

She went to her refrigerator. Under a magnet was the invitation for the all-class reunion Saturday. "Let me pull myself together and come in with it." She heard Erik tell his office he'd be there in an hour and she followed his lead. "Give me an hour."

"I can hardly wait." A pause. Then: "Hey. Who's there with you? That good ol' Jack I hear?"

She wondered how the hell Duncan could be so nosy. "See you in a bit," she said, and set the phone on the counter. Erik had already hung up his phone and was in the bathroom; she heard him peeing. She set his coffee mug on the kitchen table. "Coffee's ready," she yelled to the bathroom door. "I'm running upstairs to shower."

Her eyes were closed and her face was turned into the spray when she heard him push back the curtain. "Hey," she said. "I don't remember inviting you."

"I'm not going to do anything. Just want to share the shower." He stood behind her and squirted shampoo in her hair. Massaged her scalp while working it into a lather. He took a step closer so she could feel his erection.

"Erik. I'm not—"

"I know, I know. You're not ready for this. I just wanted you to know I am." He backed away and squeezed the soap out of her hair. Suddenly the water turned cold. He laughed. "That's one way to get rid of me." He stepped out, grabbed a towel and left the bathroom to get dressed. She silently thanked the defective hot water heater and quickly finished rinsing off in the icy spray.

Erik stood behind her while she locked up the houseboat. He had a travel mug of coffee in his right hand; she'd set her cup down on the dock while she fiddled with her keys. In the background, the sound of Tripod barking. "When will he get used to seeing me?"

"He still barks at Jack." She bent over, picked up her coffee cup, stood up. Took a sip; it was already cold. She jiggled her keys, remembered her spare. "Where's the key I gave you?" He patted his pockets. "Don't tell me you lost it."

"No. Left it at home."

"I want it back."

"Will I ever get a set of my own?"

Murphy studied his face. Wondered if the wounded puppy was about to make another appearance. "Don't push it, okay?"

He didn't say anything. They walked down the dock together and to the parking lot. Their cars were next to each other; she thought her red Jeep seemed dumpy sitting next to his sapphire Jag. They stood behind the two cars, each with car keys in hand. The sky was gray and it was cold enough for gloves. Murphy scanned the clouds and wondered if they'd get their first snowfall in October.

"Will I see you tonight?" he asked, zipping his jacket up to his neck. "How about eating at my place? Let me do the slicing and dicing for a change."

"Sure you won't be running late with this Pederson workup on top of the ranger autopsy? I could grab some stuff after work and get dinner going." She felt safer on her own turf, although the shower visit showed her that even there, she had to work to keep him at bay.

"I'll let you know." He bent down and kissed her on the mouth. "Whoever does the cooking, no garlic. Deal?"

"Don't know if it's possible for me to come up with a garlic-free menu."

"Then for sure leave the cooking to me." He kissed her again and walked to his car door. Opened it. Turned and smiled. "I love you," he said. He didn't wait for a response. He got behind the wheel and shut the door. She stood still for a few seconds, feeling guilty she didn't say it back. She wasn't ready. Couldn't force the words out of her mouth until she was.

She turned and walked to her car while digging in her purse for a pack of gum. She couldn't find any. The guys at the cop shop were not going to appreciate her breath. She opened her car door, threw her purse inside, got in, shut the door. In her rearview mirror, she watched Erik pull away. She reached over and opened the glove compartment. Rummaged around. Felt something promising. Pulled out a roll of Tums. Better than nothing, she thought, and popped a couple into her mouth. She started the Jeep, pulled out of the lot while sucking on the antacid tablet.

She walked into Homicide, hung her jacket on the back of her chair. She'd tucked the reunion invitation into her purse before she left home. She wanted to show it to Duncan. She pulled it out of her purse and tossed it on her desk. Threw her purse in her desk drawer. Dubrowski and Castro were out on a call. She saw Duncan in his office with his feet up. His customary working position. He was on the phone. Evans Bergen, the night guy, was hunkered over his desk with a pile of paperwork in front of him. Short. Thinning blond hair. The youngest detective in Homicide and the biggest whiner. He looked up and nodded a greeting. Put his head down again. Murphy checked her watch. Amazing. His shift was over and he was still at the shop, finishing paperwork. Duncan must have gotten on his lazy ass.

She saw Sandeen at the watercooler. Tall. In his early fifties. Thick head of white hair. Longtime union activist. He'd guided her through the internal affairs investigation that followed the surgeon's suicide. He was wearing a Homicide sweatshirt. She walked over to ask him if he could spare one for the deputy she'd met at the state park. He finished his drink, crumpled the paper cup, threw it in the wastebasket. "How ya doing, Murphy?" She knew it wasn't a casual question. He was still concerned about her emotional state, especially since Gabriel Nash, the detective who'd worked with her on the surgeon's case, retired early over the summer. He'd been her mentor and on occasion, her partner.

She resisted the urge to brush her bangs and make sure they were covering her scar. "Fine. I'm fine."

He nodded. "How was Moose Lake? See any moose?"

"Moose head in the hotel lobby." She pulled a cup from the dispenser and poured herself a drink. "Hey. Got any more of those sweatshirts?"

He smiled. "Step into my office."

She followed him to his desk. "Met this deputy up in Moose Lake. Sean Mahoney. Real nice guy. Broken up about the ranger's murder. He liked the shirt. Told him I'd send him one."

Sandeen sat down and started opening and closing his desk drawers. "You wore the shirt on a case?"

She took a sip from the cup. "Sure."

"Great. Good PR for us." He pulled a sweatshirt from the bottom of a file drawer and handed it to her. "Extra large is all we got left."

She tossed the empty cup in a wastebasket and took the shirt. Held it up. "It'll work. Thanks."

"Hear anything from Gabe these days? He still seeing that nurse?"

She draped the shirt over her arm and sat on the edge of Sandeen's desk. "They've been spending a lot of time up at the cabin."

"Cabin? You mean that fishing shack of his in Hayward? That ain't no cabin."

"She made him put curtains on the windows."

"You shittin' me?"

"I shit you not."

Sandeen suddenly wrinkled his nose and looked around the room. "Hey, Bergen. You eating those damn garlic bagel chips again?" Murphy covered her mouth, hiding a grin and bad breath behind her hand. Bergen didn't even bother looking up from his paperwork. Flipped Sandeen the bird.

She noticed Duncan was off the phone. She stood up. "Gotta go talk to Yo-Yo. Uh. I mean Duncan." She was trying to stop herself from using the nickname; he'd been pretty decent to her lately. Murphy walked over to her desk. Picked up the invitation, shoved it in her pocket. Went over to his office, knocked once on the open door. He waved her in. Murphy noticed the pile of papers on his desk was getting lower; maybe he was actually getting organized.

"Our agent from the north bureau. Have a seat." He tossed a balled-up piece of paper toward the wastebasket in the corner and made it in. He was getting better at it. She sat down on the chair across from his desk, the sweatshirt still over her arm. "What's that?" he asked. She held it up. "Cool. Where can I get one?"

She was surprised Sandeen hadn't given one to him. She threw it across the desk and he caught it. "This one's yours."

He ran his fingers over the embroidered badge and logo. "Who made these up?"

"Sandeen," she said. He set the shirt down on a pile of file folders, stood up and started unbuttoning his oxford. Her eyes widened. "You don't have to put it on right now."

He pulled off the dress shirt and threw it over the back of his chair. He had a white tank undershirt. She noticed the bulge of his upper arms, the muscles of his chest. His gut was flat and hard and his waist was trim. Duncan's disheveled wardrobe masked an athletic physique. He saw her studying his body. Their eyes met. She quickly looked down and felt her face redden. She didn't see the corners of his mouth curl into a satisfied smile. He pulled the sweatshirt on over his head. Smoothed the front of it with his hands. "Thanks, Paris."

The first time she'd ever heard him say her first name. Hearing it out of his mouth jolted her—and pleased her. She didn't know why. She shook it off. "Want to hear this theory or what?"

He sat down again and put his feet up on the desk. Knocked some papers to the floor. "Hit me with it," he said, leaning back in his chair and putting his hands behind his head.

She started at the beginning, told him about her earliest suspicions when she saw Justice Trip plastered all over the newspapers and television, weaving a sanitized story of his life. When she told him about the dinner she and Trip had shared and her fear that he'd doctored her drink, Duncan took his feet off the desk and sat forward. Interrupted her narration. "I would have decked the bastard then and there. Sent his sorry ass straight to the county jail."

"I thought of that," she said. "Even if the wine tested positive for drugs, I didn't see him do it. He could have argued that in a public place like that, a bar, anyone could have dropped something into the glass."

Duncan shook his head. "Trying to kill a cop. The dumb fuck."

"He didn't know I was a cop. Didn't tell him that night. Saved the surprise for the next day." She recounted their uncomfortable meeting outside the park, Trip's lame excuse as to why he was there and his reaction when he realized she was a homicide cop.

212

Duncan patted his chest. "You were wearing a sweatshirt like this one?" She nodded. He laughed. "That's rich. Good job, Paris."

When she got to the part about Elvis, Duncan held up his right hand. "Wait a minute. Let me get this straight. No one knew about the lyrics in her purse except the Moose Lake authorities?"

"And a couple of people from the wedding party."

"And I assume they were told to shut up about it."

She nodded. "Correct."

"Nowhere else—on television or in the newspapers—did anyone say Bunny Pederson had a thing for Elvis."

"The only person who mentioned Elvis was Sweet."

Duncan frowned. "Sweet?"

"Justice Trip's nickname in high school."

"Yuck."

"Yeah," she said. "And get this. Erik Mason says the finger Trip 'found' was in such good shape, it didn't make sense. No animal bites or insects or anything. Wasn't chewed off. It was cut off."

Duncan picked up a pencil with his right hand and thumped the eraser end on his desk like he was tapping a drum with a stick. "Okay. Okay. Here's what we got. Stop me if I get it wrong. This weirdo salesman cruises into a small town, spots this bridesmaid stumbling home Friday night, kills her, cuts off her pinkie. Then he joins up with the search party Sunday and makes like he found the finger."

"Yup. Then late Monday night or early Tuesday, Sweet drops the shoe while carrying the body into the woods. Ranger finds the shoe."

"Mr. Sweetie finds Mr. Ranger and nails him. I'm on board with that. But what did your high school pal do with the body between Friday night and Monday night?" Duncan dropped the pencil on his desk, pushed his chair back and stood up. Paced back and forth between his chair and the desk. "Do you think he held her somewhere and didn't kill her until Monday night?"

"Doubt it. Where could he have safely held a live person while still bopping around town and doing interviews? Scenario A says she was killed Friday night and he temporarily stashed the body until he found a spot he liked for burial. Under Scenario B, she was buried in that park since Friday night and he returned Monday night—after our dinner together—for some goofy reason. Maybe to bury the shoes with her."

Duncan stopped pacing and stood behind his desk.

"I don't like Plan B. Winter told me his people searched those woods thoroughly over the weekend. Dogs and everything."

"Scenario A wins the prize," she said. "Of course, the autopsies Erik is doing today on both bodies could flush both theories down the toilet."

"Another question." Duncan sat back down, drummed his hands on top of his desk. "Motive? Does this motive fly? Pretty extreme to go out and kill someone to generate some ink for yourself."

In a low voice, as if talking to herself: "He wouldn't find it extreme if he's killed before. Then it's taking it just one step further."

Duncan leaned forward. "Shit. You think this isn't the first time?"

Murphy thought about it. Eighteen years later, Trip still resented her for the role she played in his beating. It took a lot of pent-up anger to hold a grudge that long. "Tell you what. Let's see what the cause of death is on the bridesmaid. See if we've had other unsolved murders with the same MO, either in the Twin Cities or small towns. He's a salesman so he travels all over the state."

Duncan was all grins. A kid digging into a trick–or–treat bag. She threw another piece of candy into the sack: "I've got a high school reunion Saturday night." She pulled the invitation out of her pocket and threw it across the desk. Duncan picked it up. "Guess who else is going?" she said.

"Mr. Sweetie." He looked ready to jump out of his chair. "Need a date?" He handed the invitation back.

Murphy was going to ask Erik, but another homicide cop might be a better idea. "Sure," she said. "A well–armed date."

24

Blood and spumoni ice cream swirled around Trip's mind while he slept. A monstrous concoction. Pistachio green and cherry pink and vanilla topped by a red stream. All of it sprinkled with coins. Dimes and nickels and quarters and pennies. He could smell the pennies. Coppery. Or was that the blood? He woke at dawn Wednesday. Expected the odor of pennies and instead smelled bacon. Threw his legs over the side of the bed, sat on the edge of the mattress. Rested his elbows on his knees and his head in his hands. Realized he was naked. Why was he naked? He always slept in his underwear. His pa's cowboy bathrobe was on the floor next to his bed. Silhouettes of black longhorn cattle against red flannel. Why was his father's robe in his room? He struggled to sort the dream from the truth. Had he slit a woman's throat in the shower? Had his pa helped hide her in the freezer? Had they calmly collected her clothes and shoes and tossed them in the freezer with her, and then dined on chicken patties and peas? He couldn't accept it. Blamed it on the pills. He remembered he'd taken some pills to help him fall asleep. Felt groggy from them. He stood up. His legs were weak and his head felt muffled.

Stuffed with cotton balls. He feared what he would find, but he had to look. He stumbled down the hall to the back bedroom. His jeans and boxers were on the floor next to the freezer. Why? He put his hand on the freezer door. Opened it a crack. Felt a rush of cold air.

"Ask her if she wants some breakfast." Trip turned and saw his pa standing in the doorway, his cane in his right hand and a coffee cup in his left. His old man took a sip. "Go on," he said with a smirk. "Ask her."

Trip slammed the freezer lid. Ran past his pa, down the hall, to the bathroom. Fell to his knees in front of the toilet and vomited. Something yellow and stringy and bitter. The room reeked of bleach. Now he remembered. After dumping her in the freezer, Trip had stripped naked so he wouldn't ruin his clothes. Returned to the bathroom. Picked up the broken radio pieces. Opened a bottle of bleach and splashed it around the stall. Poured some on the straight-edge sitting in one corner of the shower. Turned the water on and let it run. Poured bleach on the bathroom tiles, pushed a towel around the floor with his bare foot. The towel was still in the bathroom; he saw it balled up in a corner, soaking wet. In the sink was his sweatshirt. He'd taken it off because it had her shave cream on it. The smell of the bleach and the sight of the sweatshirt made his head spin. He vomited again. Clawed some sheets of toilet paper off the roll. Blew his nose. Tossed the wad in the toilet. More of the night before came back to him. After cleaning up, he'd grabbed his pa's bathrobe from the door hook. Slipped it on. Retrieved the straight-edge from the shower stall, dried it off, took it back to his room and tucked it away in its box. Joined his old man in the kitchen. They ate everything they'd taken out of the freezer. Chicken patties. Peas. Tater Tots. Tuna pot pies. Even the spumoni ice cream. A gross feast, all washed down with shots of tequila.

He remembered sitting at the dinner table, getting drunk and spilling booze on the robe. They'd capped off their evening by pawing through Keri's purse and the stuff they'd emptied from her pants pockets. That's when Trip found the pills. The same ones she'd given his old man. The pills and tequila together were a mistake. He puked again. Hung his head in the bowl.

His old man had followed him into the bathroom after exchanging the coffee cup for the bottle of tequila. He walked over to his son, screwed off the cap. Held the bottle in front of Trip's face. "Take a swallow. It'll settle your gut."

"God, no." Trip rested his forehead on the toilet rim.

"You weren't shy about drinking it last night. Take it."

Trip took the bottle by the neck, put it to his lips, tipped it upside down. One. Two. Three gulps. Set it down on the floor. Sat back on his heels.

"Get up." His pa jabbed him in the side with his cane. "Damn bleach is what's making you sick. Come on. Get up and dressed. While you been snoring, I been cleaning this pigpen. Making you breakfast." More jabbing.

Trip wrapped his fist around the end of the cane. "Stop p... poking me with that damn thing!" Yanked it out of his old man's hand. It clattered to the floor, knocking over the tequila.

Frank held onto the towel bar for support. His eyes narrowed and went from his cane to his son to the tequila bottle. "Pick it up, boy," he said lowly. Trip reached for the cane. "No. The fucking bottle. It's the last of the booze." Trip righted the tequila. A puddle of it was on the bathroom floor. He picked up the cane and handed it up to his pa without looking at him. "Sorry," he mumbled into the toilet bowl.

His old man jerked the cane out of Trip's hand. "Get your ass up and out of here. I got eggs and oatmeal waiting for you on the table. Probably rubber by now." He pointed to the bottle. "Give it here before you spill the rest." Trip handed it to him. "Put some clothes on. I seen enough of your hairy backside to last two lifetimes." He stomped out of the bathroom, cane in his right hand and tequila in his left. Trip watched him go. For a second, wished it was his old man folded up in the freezer—cane and all—instead of Keri. He held onto the toilet rim with both hands and struggled to his feet. Swayed. Feared he was going to pass out. Gripped the edge of the sink. Hobbled to the back bedroom to retrieve his clothes. Stepped into his boxers and jeans with his back turned to the freezer. He kept wondering what she looked like all frozen, with coins on her eyes. He walked out of the room. Figured it would take a lot more liquor before he'd have the courage to open the lid and check it out. He went down the hall to his bedroom, opened his dresser drawer, took out his last clean sweatshirt. While he was pulling it over his head he noticed his suitcase empty and sitting on the floor next to the dresser. His dirty travel clothes were piled in the hamper. He didn't remember emptying the suitcase. Where was the peach purse?

His pa yelled from the kitchen: "Get your butt in here, boy!"

Trip ran his eyes around the room. No purse. Had to be with the dirty clothes. He went to the hamper, started throwing socks and shirts and boxers over his shoulders. Then he picked the basket up and tipped it upside down. Shook the clothes out. No purse. A shiver rippled through Trip's body. His pa had emptied the suitcase into the hamper while he was sleeping. Had he discovered the purse? He told himself to stay calm. The thing was probably in the pile of clothes. Needed to dig through it better.

His pa again: "What the hell you doing in there?"

Trip left the dirty clothes on the floor and headed for the kitchen. Walked in. His pa was sitting at the table. A plate of food in front of him and an ashtray with a smoking cigarette to his right. To the right of that, a syringe and needle. Every time she visited, Keri filled a bunch of syringes for his old man. She said he didn't see well enough to do it himself. Trip wondered how many prepared injections were left. When they were gone, he'd have to fill the syringes for his old man. Another nursemaid task Trip anticipated with trepidation. "After breakfast you better make a trip to the laundry," his pa said. He used a wedge of toast to shovel the last of his scrambled eggs into his mouth. Chewed and swallowed. Picked up the Lucky Strike. Took a long drag. Tapped some ash into the ashtray. "That mountain in your room is starting to smell as bad as your feet. Take that bleach rag in the bathroom with you. Throw it in with the whites."

Trip sat down. Touched his plate of eggs and bowl of oatmeal with his fingertips. Both cold and hard as marble. He stood up, took the plate to the microwave, set the dish inside, put the timer on thirty seconds. Leaned against the counter while his breakfast warmed. Saw the kitchen was cleaner. The dishes he had soaking in the sink last night were washed and put away. Counter was cleared of most of the junk. Floor was still sticky, but swept. His old man was wearing jeans and a flannel shirt for a change. Not pajamas. No baseball cap. Even with his cane and crappy eyesight, he'd been able to accomplish quite a bit. "You been b... busy, Pa."

His old man took a sip of coffee and nodded. "Yup." Took another pull off his cigarette.

The microwave beeped. Trip took out the plate and set it on the table. Looked down at the bowl of oatmeal. The instant cereal was gray and congealed. Decided to skip it.

Sat down. Six slices of bacon were draining on a paper towel in the middle of the table. Trip took a slice, shoved it into his mouth, chewed twice, swallowed. "You're c... cooking like your old self, too." Took another piece. Tried to make peace with his old man by cracking a joke. "If I d... d... didn't know better, I'd say stuffing f... folks into f... freezers agrees with you." Slid the second slice of bacon into his mouth.

Frank set his coffee mug down. Took one last puff off the Lucky Strike and crushed the stub into the ashtray. Took something from his lap and set it in the middle of the table. "And if I didn't know better, I'd say you killed that bridesmaid." The peach purse, with grease stains dotting the satin. His old man had found the bag, rifled through it while eating breakfast.

Trip's mouth hung open with the bacon inside it.

"Shut your mouth, boy. Keep chewing. I'll do the talking."

Trip chewed twice and swallowed. Coughed. Stared at the purse and started to say something: "I think—"

"You think! You think!" Frank slammed his right palm on the table, rattling the dishes and silverware. He picked up the purse, bunched it in his right fist, shook it at his son. "You ain't been thinking! That's the problem! You been fucking up left and right. Gonna land us both in the slammer. You slice that blond bitch open under your pa's roof and feed me that crap about Keri trying to kill me. Then I find this." He threw the purse down on the table. It knocked over an empty glass. Trip opened his mouth. His old man pointed a finger at him. "Shut the fuck up!" Trip closed his mouth and lowered his eyes. His pa sighed and his tone softened. "I know a man's got appetites, Sweet. Believe me I know. But you can't let your dick head lead you around."

His pa thought he'd raped the women, or that something sexual had happened. By the sound of his old man's voice, that made the murders more acceptable. Trip decided not to correct him. Not until he saw where this was going.

"Are you listening, boy?"

Trip kept his eyes down. "Yeah."

"Good. You better listen 'cause your pa knows more about this stuff than you think."

More cryptic words from his pa. Trip looked up. Locked his eyes on his old man's face. "Tell me. Tell me what you d... done and I'll tell you what I d... done." His old man averted his gaze. Stared out the window over the sink. Outside, the wind blew a bunch of leaves off the scrawny tree planted next to their trailer. Could his pa even see the tree? Maybe he could see a lot more than Trip knew. A long silence. The only sounds were the drip of the leaky sink faucet and the distant clang of a neighbor's wind chimes. "Pa?"

His pa continued staring out the window. Picked up a steak knife smeared with butter and dotted with toast crumbs. Tapped the flat side of the blade against the edge of his plate. The clink of the knife alternated with the drip of the faucet. *Clink. Drip. Clink. Drip. Clink. Drip. Clink. Drip.* The clinking stopped. His pa's faraway voice again: "You ain't ready to hear what I got to say. No sir." He pulled his eyes from the window. Trip studied the downturned corners of his pa's mouth; he'd seen that expression once before.

"It's g... got something to d... do with what happened to Snow White." His old man's brows wrinkled with confusion; he didn't know Trip called her that. "What happened to Cammie."

Frank's eyes widened for an instant, as if he'd touched a hot pan. The corners of his mouth curled back up into their usual hard, straight line. "Maybe it does and maybe it

222

doesn't. Ain't your concern. Your concern is saving your own ass. That's my concern, too. Your ass is in jail, mine is in a nursing home. Eating baby food and smelling other people's piss." He picked up the steak knife again and pointed the tip at Trip. In a conspiring voice: "What'd you do, Sweet? Tell your pa so he can help you."

Trip's turn to look out the kitchen window. "You know what I d... did. Killed Keri. That's it."

"Bullshit!" His pa reached across the table, picked up the purse, threw it at him. It startled Trip. He caught it, juggled it like a hot coal, dropped it on the floor. He bent over and picked it up, set it in front of him. "How'd you do her?" asked his pa. "Why'd you do her?"

Trip's mind was swirling like the ice cream and blood from his nightmare. He needed a story that involved rape, or at least some sex. His pa found it a reason to kill. "I f... followed her out of the bar, fucked her in the p... parking lot. She got p... pissed about something. Maybe I wasn't m... man enough . . ."

That was good. His pa's mouth hardened; no one challenged his offspring's sexual talents.

"She s... started to walk home. I followed her in the t... t... truck. Tried to give her a ride. She flipped me off. Told me to g... get lost. Said she was gonna call the cops. Tell them it was rape. I g... got scared. Stepped on the gas. Ran her over. Kept her in the t... truck a couple of days, until I could figure out where to p... p... put her."

His pa nodded; it was making sense so far. "What was that business with the finger?"

He paused, wondering if this part would sabotage the sex motive. Then decided it wouldn't. "I cut it off and d... dropped it during the search."

"To feel important again, like the time with the little girl and her necklace?"

Trip dropped his eyes and didn't answer. Didn't want to admit why he'd done it.

His pa continued. "Why Keri?"

"She found the p... purse. Was planning to t... t... turn me in."

Then a hard question: "Any others?"

Trip looked down at the purse, stroked the satin. More slippery than he remembered.

"Sweet? How many others?"

Trip pushed aside the purse. Picked up a coffee cup, took a sip. Cold. Set it down. His pa slid the tequila bottle across the table. Trip took off the cap, filled a juice glass. Drank until the glass was empty. Poured another full measure, drank half of it. Held the glass between his palms as it sat on the table. The room was rocking, like the trailer was bobbing in the water. Couldn't tell if it was the booze or his pa's question.

"Sweet? How many?"

In a voice so low it was nearly lost in the wind chimes: "Lost c... count."

"Dear Lord." His pa rested his elbows on the table and buried his face in his hands. Trip wished he could see through the wrinkled skin. Was he mad or sad or shocked? He lowered his hands and folded them in front of him. Trip saw something he'd never seen before. Fear. The fun had gone out of murder for his old man. The father-son scheme was really the son's dark project. "All run over?" his pa asked.

Trip made a quick decision. He wouldn't tell his old man about the ranger. His pa had a respect for any man in any uniform. Saw them all in the same light as the sheriffs and marshals in his westerns. "Yeah. All r... run over."

"All raped?"

Trip was insulted. "No. Most was w... willing at first and

224

then changed their t... tune. Tried to run off and tell t... t... tales like that bridesmaid gal."

His old man nodded wisely. "Women do that. Yes, they do indeed."

"They d... do," Trip added. "The b... b... bitches."

"Since when? How long this been going on? How long you been keeping me in the dark?" He sounded angry and jealous of the news, like he'd found out he'd been excluded from a party held weeks earlier. Underlying both emotions was that fear again.

Trip finished the glass of tequila. Tried to pour more into the juice glass. Empty. Set the bottle down but kept his right hand wrapped around the neck and his left around the glass. They were something solid he could hang onto and hold. Everything else seemed to be bobbing and rocking. Maybe the trailer would sink and they'd both go down with it. Drowning might not be so bad after all. Not in cold water, though. Not the way those mean boys in high school had drowned. He wanted to die in warm water. Bathwater. Should he tell his pa about those boys? Another instant decision. "Started w... with high school."

A quick intake of air by his pa. "You killed a girl in high school? Your high school? I don't remember any girl..." His old man's voice trailed off. A revelation that topped the earlier revelations. In an amazed voice: "You? All four of them?"

That tone angered Trip. His pa didn't have trouble believing he'd run over women, but he doubted he could kill men. After everything he'd learned about his son, Frank still thought his boy was weak. Trip lifted the tequila bottle up and slammed it against the table, scattering glass around the kitchen and leaving a broken neck in his hand. His pa leaned back in his chair, both hands clutching the edge of the table. Trip waved the jagged neck at him. "I k... killed

225

that p... park ranger, too. Fucking s... smashed his head in with a shovel. Is that m... man enough for you?" His pa opened his mouth; now it was Trip's turn. "Shut the f... fuck up!" Trip bolted up from the table, knocking his chair over. He hurled the bottle neck at the window and missed. It hit the backsplash and fell into the sink. He felt his bare feet stepping on broken glass and he didn't care. "I'm n... never good enough for you. Nothing I d... do is right. I can't even k... kill to your liking."

Frank raised both palms in the air as if he were surrendering to an armed man. "Son. Son. Sit. Calm down. Jesus Christ." In an accommodating, condescending voice: "Of course I believe you. I'm glad you did those bastards in high school. Thought it was an accident is all. The cops said it was an accident. Slippery road and such."

Trip smiled and folded his arms across his chest. "No sir. Was n... no accident. Fucked with their s... steering."

A nervous smile stretched across his pa's face. "Clever son of a bitch. That's what you are. Did you know it would kill them? Was that the plan?"

Trip shook his head. "Wanted to m... mess them up good. Them dying was a nice added b... bonus."

"Damn straight. They were mean shits. Good for you." That sounded sincere to Trip's ears. "But why the ranger, son?"

"He f... found her shoe in my t... truck while I was burying her in the woods. Couldn't let him t... tell."

His pa understood that, or at least pretended to. Nodded grimly. "Self-preservation. Man's gotta do what he's gotta do."

Trip liked that, his pa calling him a man. He puffed out his chest. Suddenly he felt the pain from the broken glass. He hung onto the counter with his right hand and picked up his left foot. Checked the bottom. Big sliver. Pulled it out. Dripped blood on the floor. "D... damn."

"What'd you do?"

"Cut myself."

His pa stood up. "One minute, you fool. I'll get something for that. Got a temper worse than your pa's."

Frank left the kitchen. Trip kept his foot up. Watched the blood drip in neat, round dots onto the floor. The trailer wasn't rocking and bobbing anymore, but he didn't like seeing his own blood. He looked up. Watched the wind bend the tree outside. Listened to the chimes. Wondered if his old man was getting bandages or calling the police. His pa returned with a box of Band-Aids and Trip's loafers tucked under his left arm. He walked over to his son, stepping over the glass and crunching it with the tip of his cane. "Careful, P... Pa."

"I got shoes on. Got sense. Not like others in this family." He bent down and dropped the shoes at Trip's feet. "Wipe your soles off first, make sure there's no more glass on them." He stood straight, pulled a Band-Aid out of the box and started tearing the wrapper.

Trip held onto the counter, brushed the injured foot with his hand. Clean. His pa handed him a Band-Aid. Trip slapped it over the cut. Slipped his left foot into the shoe with a grimace. Lifted his right foot. Dusted it off. One shard fell to the floor. Stepped into the other loafer. He looked at the mess he'd made on the kitchen floor. Broken glass and blood. "I'll c... clean it up, Pa."

His pa stood next to the kitchen table. Absentmindedly picked a large triangle of glass off the plate of bacon. "What about work?"

Trip righted the tipped chair. Crouched down. Picked some glass off the floor and wiped his own blood off the linoleum with his hand. "Got p... plenty to keep me b...

busy right here. Got to c... clean up this mess. Empty out the b... back of the truck." He wanted to keep his eyes on his old man, in case he turned on him and called the cops. "I'll go in t... t... tomorrow. They won't care."

His old man sat back down at the table. Picked up another piece of glass. A round piece that came from the bottom of the bottle. Looked at his son. "All these people you got rid of. I'm worried."

Trip stood up. "Don't be. I'm not n... nuts, Pa. Stuff happened. Won't happen no more. I p... promise."

"That ain't what I'm worried about." He set the round of glass in his left palm and held it there, as if weighing it. "How careful you been? How you been getting away with it? I can see getting away with it once, maybe twice. But to lose count. How?" His old man didn't sound worried or horrified as much as curious. Maybe he wouldn't turn his own son over.

"All the accidents..." Trip stopped at the word *accidents*. He'd never before given a formal name to his acts. Decided he liked that label. "All the accidents were at n... night on empty roads. Used the t... t... truck. Never had much d... damage to speak of. Couple of c... cracked windshields. Dinged hood. Easy enough to fix."

His old man scratched his chin. "I remember you coming home with those. So the *accidents* were all out of town, during your sales calls."

"Mostly."

"And with the exception of those boys, you didn't know them."

"They were all s... strangers to me. Gals I'd just m... met."

His pa's eyes narrowed. "Met where?"

Trip had never met any of the people he'd run over. They were less than strangers to him; they were targets.

228

They weren't all women, either. Still, he had to come up with something. He could feel his pa's eyes on him. Blurted the first place that came to his mind: "Bars." As an after-thought, to make himself sound careful: "I made sure n... no one saw me l... l... leave with any of them."

His pa sat for a moment, digesting this. "Smart," he finally said. He tossed the round of glass on his breakfast plate. "You played it smart." He pushed the plate away and got up from the table. Picked up his pack of cigarettes. "Too much excitement this morning. Gonna plop down on the couch. Catch some *Gunsmoke*."

He watched him thump out of the kitchen with his cane and his smokes. His pa was trying to play it cool, but he was scared. Was he afraid of ending up in a nursing home or ending up dead? Trip couldn't tell. Didn't care. All he knew for sure was he had to find out what his old man was hiding so he could use it against him if he threatened to call the cops.

25

Trip didn't know a cop was already planning a visit to his house.

Murphy wanted to make sure Trip went to the reunion. Wednesday afternoon, she decided to personally deliver the party invitation. She knew from reading the newspaper stories about him that he worked out of his house when he wasn't on the road. She figured she'd catch him at home. She was just as interested in finding his truck home. She wanted to get a copy of the treads to compare to the cast from the Moose Lake campground. She also hoped she could talk her way into Trip's place. Get a look around. In high school, it was well known that Trip lived in a trailer court. He was the only kid who did. She flipped through the phone book at her desk and found him still residing there. His name was under his father's. *Frank Trip. Justice Trip.* Each had the same phone number and address. Probably made Sweet feel better to have his own listing. At his age, he had to be uncomfortable living at home with a parent. She remembered his father well. Frank was even creepier than his son. Always staring at the female students, especially the youngest ones. Spending a lot of time cleaning the girls' bathrooms and locker room. She closed the white pages.

Now she needed a camera to get a picture of the treads. Castro and Dubrowski, the gadget kings, had to have one. Surveillance was their specialty. Both were on the phone. She stood up and walked over to Castro's desk. Eyeballed the mess on top of it. Didn't see anything under the greasy lunch sacks, foam cups, newspapers and reports. He hung up.

"What do you need?"

"A camera."

He pushed his chair away from his desk. "For what? Different cameras serve different purposes." He bent over and pulled out his bottom desk drawer.

Murphy stepped closer and peered inside. A pile of cameras. Nikon. Panasonic. Minolta. Pentax. Polaroid. Saw a lens nearly as long as her forearm. Binoculars. Something that resembled a ballpoint pen. She pointed at it. "How about that one?"

"Not unless you're going deep undercover. Are you going deep undercover?"

"No. Need something small and easy to use. Want to take a couple of quick ones and shove it in my purse. Get the image back ASAP."

He fished around inside the drawer and pulled out a silver Nikon a little bigger than a deck of cards. "Digital."

It looked complicated. "How do I use it?"

"These little babies are really sweet and easy. A no-brainer. Turn it on, point and click. No little hole to squint through." He pushed the On button and tipped the camera so Murphy could examine the back of it. She saw what looked like a tiny television screen. "What you see on the screen is what you get. Don't even need to focus it yourself. Does it for you."

"Dummy proof," she said.

"Exactly." Castro held it up so Dubrowski was in the frame. "Here's how you zoom in for those intimate shots." He pushed a button marked with a T for telephoto and the small screen went in for a close-up. Dubrowski hung up his phone and looked over at them. "Smile, you ugly bastard," Castro said. Dubrowski gave him the finger and Castro snapped a picture. "Captured for all eternity, or until you erase him from the camera's memory."

"Got it," she said.

Castro pressed a button marked with a W and the image on the small screen seemed to back up, capturing Dubrowski and the empty desks around him. "Wide angle. Good for those crowd scenes. That special riot you want to remember."

"Seems simple enough."

He nodded toward his partner, who was back on the phone. "Even numb nuts over there could handle a camera like this."

He handed it to her. She studied it for a few seconds, backed up, aimed it at Castro. Pushed the T for a tighter shot. The screen framed his face. She snapped a picture. "Works great," she said. "How do you develop the pictures?"

"No film to be developed. Download to the PC."

She frowned. "And how do I do that?"

"Tell you what. I'll handle that part. After you take some shots, bring it back to the office. I'll download the photos. From there I can crop it, cut it, paste it, make a print of it, send it to someone in an e-mail. Whatever you want."

"Thanks." She shut it off, went back to her desk, took her purse out of her desk drawer and tucked the camera inside. It fit easily. She took her jacket off her chair and slipped it on. Threw her purse strap over her shoulder. Headed for the door.

"Last thing," Castro said after her. "Don't forget to turn the damn thing off and save my batteries."

She gave him the thumbs-up and walked out.

Trip had seen her red Jeep in Moose Lake. She didn't want him to notice her driving down his block, give him time to close the shades and hide. Murphy took an unmarked car from the department fleet. A silver Ford Crown Victoria. She rolled out of the cop shop parking lot and steered the car onto the freeway, heading to the north side of the city. She saw the entrance to the trailer park from the highway. She took the exit ramp. Pulled into the neighborhood of narrow houses, narrow streets, narrow yards. Studied the street signs. Found the Trips' street. Pulled over at the beginning of the block and shut off the car.

Their trailer was at the other end; she could see Trip's red truck parked in front. A fire engine. She dropped her keys in her purse. Checked her bag to make sure she had the invitation. There it was, ready to hand to him. Checked her Glock. Ready to go, in case. She pulled the camera out and put it in her jacket pocket. She slid out of the car, slammed the door shut, hiked her purse strap over her shoulder and started walking toward the Trips' trailer. The wind was in her face. She zipped her jacket up to her throat and buried her hands in her pockets. Heard wind chimes tinkling but couldn't see where they were hanging. While she walked she rehearsed in her mind. If his father came to the door: *Hey, Mr. Trip. Remember me? Went to high school with Sweet. Got this reunion invitation for him. Is that coffee I smell?* If Trip answered: *Here's that invitation. Hope you can make it. Sure had a nice time having dinner with you in Moose Lake. Is that coffee I smell?* Once inside, she'd keep the conversation friendly. Avoid talking about Moose Lake. She didn't want to scare Trip away from Saturday night's gathering or make his father suspicious. She figured if Trip was hiding something, his father was helping him.

She got to the front of their house. Their blinds were down and the slats closed tight. She took the Nikon out of her purse, turned it on, knelt down on the street in front of the truck, aimed the camera at the driver's-side front tire. The image on the screen was sharp enough to clearly distinguish the tread pattern. She snapped the picture. Went in for a closer shot. Snapped again. Aimed at the front passenger tire and took a photo of that. Crouching down in the street, she went around to the back of the truck. Took pictures of both back tires. She kept glancing at the windows of the trailer and looking up and down the street to make sure no one was watching.

While Murphy was taking photos, Trip was frying his pa sliced hot dogs and diced potatoes for a late lunch. He spiced it up with some chopped onions, salt and a dash of Tabasco sauce. Exactly the way his pa liked it. Trip was frantically waiting on his old man. Keeping him happy. Keeping an eye on him so he wouldn't pick up the phone. He'd even promised to clip the old bastard's toenails. To soften them, he had his pa's feet soaking in warm water and Dreft detergent. Trip sensed his pa picked up on the urgency in his son's attentions. It seemed to convert the old man's fear to contempt. Trip thought his pa was even enjoying it, taking advantage of the situation. He had Trip darting around the house for him like a pinball. Trip hadn't even had time to clear the breakfast plates off the table.

The potatoes were sticking. Trip scraped the bottom of the frying pan with a wooden spoon. "Better not be burning those taters," his old man yelled from the front room. In the background, John Wayne's voice boomed from the television set in *Fort Apache*.

"Nothing's b... b... burning," Trip yelled back. Then in a low voice to himself: "Hope y... you choke on it." He decided he preferred a fearful father to a contemptuous, bossy one. He shut off the range and dumped the potatoes and hot dogs onto a plate. Walked into the front room with it and set it on the TV tray in front of his old man.

His pa took a pull off his cigarette. "Want me to eat with my fingers?" Trip went back to the kitchen and returned with a fork. Handed it to his pa. His old man jabbed a hunk of hot dog with it. "Foot soak's getting cold." He popped the hot dog into his mouth and chewed.

Trip bent over and dipped his right hand in the tub, the square plastic one he usually used in the sink for dishes. "Water's s... still warm."

His pa lifted a forkful of potatoes to his lips. "No it ain't. Cold as ice." He shoveled the food into his mouth. Stared at the television while he chewed. Grabbed the remote with his free hand and turned up the volume.

Trip sighed. "Pick up your f... feet then." His pa lifted his feet and Trip slid the plastic tub from under him. Stood up and carried the tub into the kitchen. Dumped the water into the sink. Set the bucket on the counter. Turned on the tap and felt it. He'd love to scald his old man. Boil some water and dump it in. Set his feet in it. Hold them in. *Hot enough for you, you old bastard?* He looked at the stove. The teakettle was on top; they used it to boil water for instant coffee and instant oatmeal and instant anything else they could find on store shelves. All he had to do was walk over, turn the burner to high. Wait for it to whistle. Dump it in the tub with some Dreft.

235

Slide it under his old man's feet and leave the room. Apologize when the old bastard burned himself. *Sorry, Pa. Should have tested the water. I feel terrible.* He'd heard diabetics could start losing sensation in their feet. Maybe his old man wouldn't realize the water was burning him until it was too late. Until the damage was done. Would it be enough to send him to the hospital and get him out of Trip's way? Would it push his pa over the edge, make him call the cops? He couldn't call if he was in a hospital bed, doped up. Trip shut off the faucet and walked over to the stove. Reached for the range knobs. Turned the one for the teakettle to high. Willed the electric coils to turn bright red instantly.

A knock at the door. "Shit," Trip said. "Who in the h... hell is that?"

"Door!" his pa yelled from the front room.

Trip tried to ignore it. Maybe they'd go away.

His old man again: "Door!"

Trip left the kitchen.

"Door!"

Trip walked past his old man to answer it. "I heard you the first two t... times. Ain't d... deaf."

"Could've fooled me," said his pa. He picked up the remote and lowered the volume. Squinted to see who was at the door while sliding his feet into his slippers.

Trip put his hand on the knob. What if it was a neighbor? Worse, the cops? He jerked his hand off the knob like it was a hot coal. Another knock. He turned on his heel and darted to his bedroom. Behind him, his father yelling: "What's wrong with you? Answer it!"

Hovering over his dresser, Trip inventoried the top. Picked out his sharpest yet easiest to conceal weapon. The switchblade. He slipped it in his right pants pocket and ran back out, shutting his bedroom door behind him. By the time he got to the front room, Paris Murphy was inside, talking to his pa. His old man was standing by the open door, leaning on his cane and laughing. He turned and glanced at his son. "Look who stopped by."

26

Trip stood next to the couch. Put his right hand out and clutched the back of it for support. A homicide cop was standing in his trailer. In his front room. Steps away from a room with a freezer. Inside the freezer, a naked dead woman. His hand left the couch and reached down, felt the bulge in his pants pocket. He slipped his right hand inside and with the tips of his fingers, touched the edge of the folded knife. Her eyes met his and then fell to his right arm. Whistling, in the kitchen. He started and drew his hand out of his pocket.

"Is that tea?" she asked, her eyes leaving his empty hand to take in his face.

"Paris," he said, his eyes meeting her gaze and then dropping. "What d... do you want?"

She smiled. Took a couple of steps into the front room. Raised her right arm and extended a piece of paper to him. "I brought it by in case you couldn't find yours."

He frowned. "My what?" In the kitchen, the whistling from the teakettle seemed to grow sharper and louder.

"Reunion invitation."

The reunion Saturday. He'd forgotten about it. "Thanks,"

he said, and stepped forward to take the paper out of her hand. He wanted to get rid of her, chase her back outside.

She lowered her arm before he could grab the invitation. "Is that the teakettle I hear? I'd love some tea."

He looked down at the paper and then at her face. Was she up to something?

"Don't stand there, Justice," said his pa. "Get the lady some tea." Trip's eyes went to his old man's face. Frank cracked a small smile and shut the front door. Tipped his head toward the couch. "Sit, Paris. Sit a spell while Justice gets us some tea." He thumped over to the couch, sat down. Took the remote off the TV tray and turned off the television. He patted the seat cushion next to him with his right hand. "Sit. Tell us what you been doing all these many years."

Trip watched his father and thought: *He doesn't know she's a cop. If he knew, he wouldn't invite her to stay.*

Frank looked at his son. That small smile again. "Paris is a policeman. A pretty lady like this a policeman. Isn't that something, Justice?"

Paris Murphy isn't the sneaky one, thought Trip. His pa was the person trying to pull something.

"Tea sounds wonderful," Murphy said. She walked over to the couch, unzipped her jacket and sat down with her purse in her lap. Her eyes went from the son to the father and back to the son. The whistling in the kitchen continued, but Trip wasn't budging from his spot. Stood in the middle of the front room. A tall, pale statue. "Why don't I make the tea?" she said. "I'm pretty handy in the kitchen."

She started to stand up and Frank grabbed her jacket sleeve. Pulled her back down to the couch. "Justice can wait on us, pretty lady." He glared at his son. "Did you forget where the kitchen is all of a sudden?"

Trip started to cross the front room to head for the kitchen.

"Wait," said his pa. He lifted his plate of potatoes and hot dogs. "Take this slop with you." He leaned into Murphy's left ear and said in a low, conspiring voice, "Justice ain't much of a cook. Some days, I swear he's trying to kill me."

Trip yanked the plate out of his old man's hand and went into the kitchen. Slammed the plate on the counter. A few minutes ago his pa didn't think it was slop. A few minutes ago, the bastard was inhaling the stuff. His old man was putting on a show for Paris Murphy and Trip wasn't sure why. That crack about his son trying to kill him. Was his old man trying to plant that idea in her head—that Trip could murder his own pa?

The kettle was still whistling, the noise drilling a hole in his head. Giving him a headache. Trip went over to the stove and turned it off. He picked up the kettle and moved it to the counter. Opened the cupboards over the counter. All their usual coffee cups were dirty. He reached in back and pulled out three dusty mugs they hadn't used in a while. Two with *Far Side* cartoons on them. A third with some other cartoon on the outside and a dead fly on the inside. He tipped the bug into the sink. He scanned the food shelves. Pushed around some canned goods. Found an ancient box of Lipton tea bags still sealed in cellophane. He set it on the counter, clawed off the wrapper, tore off the cover, took out three tea bags. He dropped a bag in each of the cups and poured hot water over them. He stared at the steam rising from the mugs. Thought about how he'd almost poisoned her with those pills. Should he give it another try? No. Not here. Too chancy. They weren't in a restaurant this time. She'd know to blame the tea if she got sick. What if he put enough pills in so she died? Bad idea. She'd probably told the other cops at the police station where she was going. No. No poison. At least not now. That reunion offered plenty of possibilities, however. All those people. Old classmates. Old grudges. Jealous of each other's success. Still trying to get an old girlfriend or former flame in bed. Any one of them could be suspects.

He was glad she came by with the invitation. Another opportunity to get back at her. Plus like she had said earlier, the reunion would give him a chance to show off his hero status. How had she put it? *Wave it in their faces.* That's what he'd do. Wave it in their faces.

In the front room, Murphy sat on the couch next to Trip's father. She breathed through her mouth as much as possible to avoid smelling the booze and cigarettes. Another smell, too. Urine? She wished she could plug her ears as well as her nose so she wouldn't have to listen to Frank Trip's lame ramblings as he tried flattering her and flirting with her. "I always thought you were the nicest out of that whole crowd . . . You weren't homecoming queen? I'd have sworn you were . . . Your folks must be so proud of you . . . Bet you're the prettiest police officer on the force . . . What color are your eyes? They're Liz Taylor eyes."

He'd wave his hands around when he talked and then bump her left thigh with his hand when he set his arms down. As if it was an accident. It reminded her of the crap he pulled when he was a janitor at her school. He'd yell a warning and then roll his bucket and mop into the girls' bathroom. Feigned embarrassment when he caught someone still sitting on the toilet or standing in front of the mirror. It got to be a joke among the girls. When they heard him coming, one of them would lean against the door so he couldn't open it. Whisper a warning to the others. *Hurry up, the perve is here!* No one ever wanted to use the bathroom alone.

She was actually relieved when Trip walked into the front room. He balanced the mugs of tea on an old cookie sheet. He held the tray under his father's nose. "Justice," said Frank. "Serve our guest first."

"Oh, s... sorry." He held the tray in front of Murphy, his eyes down.

She picked up a mug. "Thank you." She looked at what was painted on the side and inhaled sharply. Struggled to hide her shock. She felt as if all the blood were draining from her body, being replaced with ice water. A *Flintstones* cartoon showing Betty and Barney standing in front of a cave. She felt under the mug. The one she'd given Denny had a chip on the bottom from bouncing around the car. She held the mug by the handle with her right hand and ran her left index finger in a circle around the bottom. She found the chip. The only way Trip could have that mug was if he took it from Denny's car. He'd been inside Denny's car. Why? To steal a mug full of coins? When had he taken it? She had seen it in the car days before the accident. Another cold wave washed over her. Trip had tampered with the car. Caused the crash.

She didn't want to give away her horror and anger. She tried to put on a calm face and voice. She blew on the hot tea and pretended to sip. No way would she ever drink anything Trip gave her. She studied her own hands. Felt reassured they weren't shaking. She tried to think of something to say. She glanced around the front room. "You keep it pretty neat for a couple of bachelors."

Trip's father picked up a mug. Trip took the last one. Set the cookie sheet down on the floor. Eased his tall frame into a recliner across from the couch. "I g... guess so." He held the hot mug between his hands.

She imagined herself taking out her gun and shooting Trip in the forehead. A clean, wide target. She could see the hole as she watched him. She blinked and turned to his father. "This reminds me of the layout of my houseboat."

Frank set his mug on the TV tray, picked up his cigarette, put it to his lips. "You live on a houseboat, do you? How big?" He took a drag and exhaled.

"Smaller than this. At least I think it is. I'd have to see the rest of your place to judge. How many bedrooms you got?" She took another pretend sip. Stifled a cough from the cigarette smoke.

Frank set his cigarette in the ashtray. Stood up. Leaned his left hand on his cane and bent his right arm at the elbow like a wing. Smiled down at her and winked. "Take my arm, pretty miss, and I'll give you a walking tour of our Graceland. Free of charge."

Murphy stood up, reluctantly set her mug on his tray. She wanted to take it home with her, but it could be evidence. She threw her purse strap over her shoulder. Looked across the room at Trip. His hands were locked motionless around his cup and his mouth was hanging open. Eyes as big as saucers. His father's suggestion of a tour obviously horrified him. Trip was hiding something. She looped her left arm around his father's right elbow and grinned. "Do you have a jungle room, too?"

Frank threw his head back and laughed. "Closest we got is Sweet's room. You could call that a jungle."

Trip bolted out of his chair, spilling tea all over the front of his legs. "Godd...dammit to h... hell."

"Son. Watch your language in front of a lady."

Trip ignored him. Ran into the kitchen with the mug, set it on the counter and grabbed a towel. Returned to the front room with it. Wiped his pants legs while he talked.

243

"Pa. Wait. This ain't such a g... good idea. Bedrooms are a m... mess. A regular d... d... disaster area."

"Speak for yourself, son. My room is fit for a lady." Frank paused and smiled suggestively at Murphy. "I mean fit for a lady's eyes."

Murphy wished she could knock his cane out from under him. She grinned at Trip. Thought her face would crack from the effort. "You should see my place. Regular pit, and I live by myself."

"Not married?" asked Frank.

"Separated," she said. "Getting divorced."

Frank started to cross the front room floor and headed to the kitchen with Murphy on his arm. "So you're available."

Trip suddenly remembered the mess on the kitchen table, and in the middle of it, the peach purse. He dashed ahead of Murphy and his pa, plucked the purse off the table. He opened the cupboard under the sink and pulled out the wastebasket. Tossed the purse into it. He looked up. Murphy and his father were stepping into the kitchen. He snatched a dirty plate off the table and scraped the leftover bacon and eggs into the trash and set the plate in the sink. He needed more garbage to hide the purse. He saw the bowl of congealed oatmeal on the table. Picked it up. Tipped the gluey mess into the trash and tossed the dirty bowl in the sink. Looked into the wastebasket. Still saw edges of peach material. The hot dogs and potatoes. He took that plate off the counter and tipped the scraps into the garbage. He looked down again. Perfect. No peach peeking out. He kept scraping food scraps into the trash and setting the dishes in the sink. Picked up the remains of glass from the broken booze bottle and chucked those into the wastebasket.

"Justice. Take it easy," said his pa. He and Murphy had stopped in the middle of the kitchen and were both gawking at his frantic cleaning efforts as he bent over the garbage can.

"Told you, P... Pa. It's a d... disaster." Trip stood straight and glanced at the two of them—his old man and a cop— arm in arm. Like best friends, and it made Trip furious.

"Son. Paris is available. Maybe you should ask her to this reunion thing."

Trip glared at his old man and his pa stared back. A long silence. Murphy cleared her throat. Decided to lay some groundwork for Saturday night. "Actually, I'm seeing someone. I'm going with him."

"A policeman?" Frank asked.

"Yes," she said. Murphy gently disengaged her arm from Frank's and stepped farther into the kitchen. She could feel her shoes sticking to the linoleum. She noticed the room smelled like alcohol.

"This here's where Justice works his culinary magic," said the elder Trip.

Murphy didn't see anything suspicious on the counters or table. She walked around the kitchen table and went over to the cupboards. Trip was on her heels. "You've got more shelf space than I do." She reached up and pulled open a cupboard while keeping an eye on him. Wanted to observe his reaction. He didn't flinch. Nothing in the cupboards he cared about. She scanned the shelves and shut the door. She saw the wastebasket between the kitchen table and the sink. Trip's eyes darted down to it and then away. She glanced inside it. Saw a broken liquor bottle. Was that what he was hiding?

"Excuse the m... mess," Trip said. He opened the cupboard under the sink, set the wastebasket inside and shut the door.

With the tip of his cane, Frank pointed to a doorway on one side of the kitchen. "My digs are on this end."

She eyed Sweet. He was glancing out the kitchen window; this part of the tour didn't worry him. She walked past Frank and poked her head through the door. The full-size bed was made. A set of longhorns mounted on the wall over the headboard. Western print on the spread. Matching curtains on the windows. Nightstand. Dresser. Lamp on the dresser that looked like a miniature covered wagon. Elvis clock with swinging hips hanging on the wall above the dresser. "Nice," she said.

"You've already seen our great room," said Frank. She walked through the kitchen and ahead of him into the front room. Sweet was a step behind her. "Guess it's not too great. Let's call it our 'okay room.'" He laughed at his own joke and followed her.

She pointed down the hall on the other end of the front room. "The jungle room this way?"

Sweet stepped in front of her and barred her way, planting a hand on each side of the doorway. "No, Paris. Really. It's t... too m... m... messy."

She read his face. *Fear.* In one of the rooms or closets down this hall, Sweet Justice Trip was hiding a terrible secret.

Frank slipped between the two of them. Leaning his right hand on his cane, he faced his son. Said in a voice that was low and loaded with threat, "Out of the way, Justice. Let me finish the tour. I want her to see the rest of the place. *All of it.*" Sweet didn't move. Kept both arms up. His father lifted his cane and with the hooked handle, pulled down his son's left arm. In a guttural voice, the older man said, "Get the fuck out of my way. Now." Murphy took a step backward. She thought the two men were going to start swinging at each other. Instead, Trip stepped aside and let his father pass. "This way, Paris," Frank said over his shoulder.

Murphy didn't look at Trip. She followed his father down the hall.

Standing and watching the two figures' backs, Trip reached into his right pocket and grabbed the switchblade. He paused. Plenty of time to pull it out, he thought. He let go of the knife and took his hand out of his pocket. Followed his pa and Murphy.

Frank pushed open his son's bedroom door, flipped on a light switch and thumped into the middle of the room. Turned around to face Murphy. She took a couple of steps into the room and stifled a gasp. A medieval arsenal. Knives and swords and daggers mounted on the walls and displayed on the dresser. Was this what Sweet didn't want her to see? She heard him behind her and turned around. He was standing with both hands in his pockets, surveying the room with pride. No. His room and its contents weren't the big secret. In fact, she sensed Sweet wanted her to say something complimentary. "Impressive collection," she said.

He blushed and averted his eyes. "Thank you."

"Bunch of expensive junk if you ask me," said his father.

She noticed a street sign on the one spot on the wall not covered with weaponry. It said ELVIS PRESLEY BOULEVARD. She pointed to it. "That from your souvenir shop back home?"

"Yup," Frank said. "Worst thing we ever did was sell that place. It'd be a gold mine now." Frank walked out and Murphy turned and followed. Trip was on her heels.

They went past the bathroom. The door was open. Frank pointed inside with the tip of his cane. "It's a small can, but it's all we need. No bathtub. Wish we had one. Got a shower though." He looked over Murphy's head at his son. Said slowly and deliberately, "That shower gets more than its share of use."

247

Murphy turned and glanced at Trip's face. Saw only anger directed at his father. She didn't like standing between the two men. Might as well stand between two snarling dogs. She stepped inside the bathroom. "Mind if I wash my hands?"

"Go right ahead," said Frank, his eyes still locked on his son's face.

She went to the sink, turned on the faucet and put her hands under it. She heard whispering and gave a sideways glance. Frank was standing in the hall at the entrance to the bathroom, resting both hands on his cane. Sweet was leaning his back against the wall and looking at his father, shaking his head. The elder man noticed her staring at them. She had to say something. "Any hand soap?" she asked.

"Above the sink," said Frank. "Help yourself."

That's what she wanted to hear. Permission to snoop. She pulled open the medicine cabinet. Quickly surveyed its contents. Saw only a disposable razor and shave cream. Bottle of Tylenol. Bottle of aspirin. Cold medicine. Bar of Lava hand soap. She took down the soap, shut the cabinet. Tore off the paper wrapper and looked for a wastebasket. Saw it next to the toilet. Tried to peer inside it without being obvious. Saw it was empty. She dropped the wrapper into the basket. She held the bar under the water and rubbed it into a lather with her hands. She set the bar on the edge of the sink. Rinsed. Didn't see a towel. Wiped her hands on her pants legs.

"Sorry," said Frank. "My boy needs to get to the Laundromat pronto."

"That's okay," she muttered, and stepped out of the bathroom. She glanced at the last door down the hall. "That the guest room?"

"Let me finish the tour," said Frank. He thumped toward

248

the door and put his hand on the knob. Turned and pushed it open. Went inside. Murphy followed.

"A freezer," she said. "Good idea. I've been thinking of getting myself a small one." Murphy walked over to the chest and put her right hand on the lid.

Standing in the doorway, Trip watched her back in case she turned suddenly. He reached into his pants pocket and wrapped his right hand around the switchblade. He pulled the knife out. Put it behind his back. As he opened it, he coughed to cover up the click it made when the blade locked. In his mind, she was already sprawled out on her back in front of the freezer. He could see her bleeding from a gash across her throat. Struggling for breath. Dying. Dying. Dead.

Murphy turned her head and looked into the hall. Sweet was hunched in the doorway. His left hand planted on the door frame. His right behind his back. A pained expression on his face. A trickle of sweat snaking down the middle of his forehead. He could have been a man getting ready for his own crucifixion. She directed a question at Trip to hear his voice. Listen for the fear. "How much does it hold?"

Trip seemed startled. Surprised she'd asked him a question. "What?"

"How much does the freezer hold?"

Sweet's mouth opened but nothing more came out. His father answered. "More than you'd think." Frank rested his right hand on top of hers. "Would you like a dish of ice cream? I think we got some spumoni." He rubbed his sandpaper palm over her fingers.

She slipped her hand out from under his. "No. Thanks." Something was in this room, maybe even in the freezer. Drugs were a good bet. Money possibly. Regardless, Murphy's instincts told her to get the hell out of there. Get away from Sweet. The murdering bastard. His creepy father and his creepy house filled with knives and swords. She could always come back with a search warrant after the reunion Saturday. She backed away from the freezer, opened her purse and pulled out the party invitation. Turned around and headed for the door. Sweet took his hand off the door frame and stepped out of her way. "Thanks for the tea and tour," she said, and handed him the invitation as she passed.

Sweet took the piece of paper with his left hand and nodded. Stuffed it in his left pants pocket. "I'll w... walk you out." She went ahead of him down the hall. Trip exhaled with relief. His right hand still behind him, he closed the switchblade, slipped the knife back in his right pocket. He followed her down the hall. Wiped both palms on his pants as he went; they were wet with sweat.

Leaning against his cane and standing in front of the freezer, Frank watched them go. He was disappointed. He'd hoped his son would take her in front of him; he would have found that exciting. Satisfying. Still, he'd had fun tormenting Sweet. He yelled after them: "Nobody wants ice cream?" He lifted the freezer lid a crack. His lips stretched into a smile as a frosty mist rolled out.

27

Two corpses left Erik no time for cooking. As Murphy expected, he was too immersed in autopsies to make dinner. She didn't mind; she wanted a break from him. "Give it up," she told him when he called her at the cop shop Wednesday night to suggest a midnight meal. "You sound tired. I've got stuff to do."

"Stuff?"

"Grocery shopping."

"Exciting. Sure you don't want my company?"

"I'll take a rain check," she said, and hung up. She was tired and hungry by the time she left the station and went to the grocery store straight from work. Her visit with the Trips had rattled the hell out of her and mystified her at the same time. She couldn't believe Trip had handed her the mug he'd taken from Denny's car. She wanted to put it out of her mind for a while. Seeing it had been a shock, and it sent her emotions through the ceiling. Maybe she was reading too much into a stolen mug. She had to admit Erik would be good at helping her sift through a pile of wild ideas to come up with a solid theory. This wasn't one for over the phone, though. She'd wait until they got together again, whenever that would be. After that surprise in the shower, a part of her wasn't in that big of a hurry to be alone with him. Maybe they could meet in a restaurant and talk on Thursday.

She steered the Jeep onto Grand Avenue, a tree-lined two-mile meander of trendy shops, restaurants and old homes that started at the western edge of downtown and ended at the Mississippi River. About a mile down Grand she hung a right into the parking lot of Kowalski's Market, a family-run grocery store loaded with imported cheeses, organically grown produce, cut flowers, fresh seafood, meats. Inside, she piled the cart with some basics. Steaks, chops, a roast, a chicken, oranges, celery, milk, butter, bread. A carton of eggs. She'd hit the farmers' market later in the week for more produce. Saw pumpkins for sale, but decided it was still too long before Halloween to buy one. The Greek olives looked good and so did the ready-made wild rice salad, but the line in front of the deli case was deep and her stomach was growling. She couldn't decide between Gouda and cheddar. Tossed both into the cart. She ate a Hershey's bar while standing in the checkout line and felt embarrassed when she handed the woman an empty wrapper to scan. Gnawed on a hard-crust roll in the car while driving back to the houseboat, brushing crumbs off her lap at every stoplight. While cramming food into the refrigerator, she ate some cheddar. Didn't bother slicing it. Peeled off half the wrapper and nibbled on the block. She wanted to wash it down with a glass of wine, but all she had left in the rack was a bottle of champagne. She thought about a liquor store run, but instead fell asleep on the couch watching television, the half-eaten cheese in her hand.

She woke early in the morning still fully dressed. Even her jacket and shoes. The television was on. Her back was sore from another night on the couch. She shut off the television, stood up and stretched. Felt something under her foot. She looked down. She was standing on the block of cheese. "I'm pathetic," she muttered, and bent over to pick it up. She brushed it off. Figured the five-second rule was long past, but put it in the refrigerator anyway. Tripod loved cheese. Threw her jacket over a kitchen chair. Falling asleep on the couch with her clothes on and a block of cheese in her hand. Slob behavior, she thought. Nothing repressed the slob in her like a good run. She went upstairs, pulled on some sweats and a stocking cap. Opened the bedroom patio doors and stepped out onto the deck. Cold and cloudy. She scanned the activity on the river and saw some rowers from the Minnesota Boat Club skimming the brown water in their shell. They'd just pulled away from their stucco boathouse on Raspberry Island, a wedge of land downstream from Murphy's houseboat. She'd tried rowing that past summer and tipped the boat. She wondered what it would feel like to tumble into the water on a chilly fall day. She shivered and went back inside, slid the door shut and dug around in her closet for a windbreaker and gloves. Found them on the floor. Shook off the dust bunnies. Put them on. Pulled on her shoes. Checked the treads. Worn down. She'd have to get to the mall sometime soon. She thumped downstairs and out the door. Locked up and tucked the key in her windbreaker pocket. Did some quick stretching on the dock while a V-shaped flock of Canada geese honked in the slate sky overhead.

Instead of her usual route along Wabasha, she headed for Lilydale, a road that followed the river and sliced through a thickly wooded regional park. As she pounded along the tar running path, she had trees and the Mississippi to her right, the street and steep bluffs to her left. Even on a gray day, the colors of the fall leaves seemed fluorescent. She saw another runner yards ahead of her and a bicyclist glided past her. Otherwise the trail was quiet. It would grow quieter as it got closer to winter until only a hardy handful braved the cold to use the path; she would be one of them. She tried to use the run to clear clutter from her head. She was successful at pushing the Trips from her mind, but her thoughts about Jack were tougher to put aside. Jack. His back to her, growing rigid with the news that Erik was her lover. His questions. *In the same bed where we made love? On the same sheets?* She hadn't heard from him since he walked out. She wondered if she should call him, but didn't have a clue what she'd tell him other than what she'd already said. *I'm sorry.* When it came to responding to Erik's declarations of love, she was equally incapable of finding the words. Lately, responding to his touch had also been hard. Jack dumping her had shifted her emotions. Unsettled them.

After twenty minutes she turned around and took the same path back to the boat. At the parking lot, she slowed to a walk. Wiped her forehead with the hem of her jacket. Saw Erik's car in the lot. What was he doing there so early in the morning? She'd have to get that spare key back from him; she didn't mean for him to start using it so freely. When she set her feet on the dock, she looked for her copy of the *Pioneer Press*. Didn't see it. Looked over the edge into the water. Dead carp. Oily log. No floating newsprint. She made a mental note to call the paper and bitch. Maybe she'd complain to Cody, to aggravate him. Reporters hated when people called them with delivery gripes. She pushed open her houseboat door.

Erik was in the galley, standing at the counter, wearing her "Kiss the Cook" barbecue apron over his slacks and dress shirt. His sleeves were rolled up. His tie, blazer and jacket were thrown over the back of a kitchen chair. He must have pulled an all-nighter and come right from work. He was cracking eggs into a bowl with one hand—a skill she could never master. He turned and looked at her, egg in hand. "Figured you were running. Made myself at home in the kitchen. Thought if I couldn't make you dinner, I'd make you breakfast."

"Thanks." She pulled off her sweaty stocking cap and gloves and stuffed them in the pocket of the windbreaker.

"What's with the cheese?" He held up the dirty block of cheddar with teeth marks on it.

She took it out of his hands, opened the refrigerator, set it inside. Took out a bottle of spring water. "You weren't going to use that in the omelet?"

He started whipping the eggs with a wire whisk. "No."

"Good," she said, shutting the refrigerator door. "It's dog cheese. For Tripod."

He stopped whipping and frowned. "Dog cheese? Never heard of such a thing. Where do you buy it? Petco?"

She opened the bottle of water and took a gulp. Wiped her mouth with the back of her hand. "Yeah. Petco." Took another drink.

"Still thinking about a dog?" He set an omelet pan on a burner, turned the heat to medium, tossed a small chunk of butter into the skillet.

She leaned back against the counter. "Jack thought it was a bad idea, me being gone so much and all. He's probably right." She started chugging the rest of the water.

He moved the butter around the pan with a fork. "I could keep the pooch whenever you're out of town. I could come here and watch him. Or I could move in." She choked on the water. Coughed and covered her mouth. "Is that a yes or a no?" he asked with a grin.

She gave him a sidelong glance, tossed the bottle in the wastebasket and headed for the stairs. "I'll shower real quick." She sniffed and pointed to the toaster. "Toast is burning."

She ran upstairs, yanked off her damp clothes, turned on the water and stepped into the shower. Tried to process what Erik had suggested. He said it so casually. Was he kidding? He had to be. In the span of a few days, she couldn't split from her husband and allow another guy to move in. She needed more time. No, she thought. He had to be kidding. She pushed her worries aside. Squirted some shampoo in her hair and scrubbed. The shower was lukewarm; she feared her hot water heater was quitting on her for good. She stayed under long enough to rinse the soap out of her hair and by the time she was finished, the spray was cold. While she was toweling off, her cell phone rang. She dropped the towel, took her bathrobe off the door hook, pulled it on and went into the bedroom. The ringing stopped. "You suck," she said to the phone. She turned to go back to the bathroom and it started up again. She ran to the nightstand and picked it up.

Duncan: "So what should I wear to this deal?"

"What? What deal?"

"This reunion deal. I'm going through my closet here and I don't know if I have anything. Been a long time since I been out anywhere fancy."

Murphy sat on the edge of her bed and checked the clock on her nightstand. Still early. "Where are you?"

"Home."

She switched the phone to her left hand and with her right ran her fingers through her damp hair to work out the biggest knots. Stood up, walked across the bedroom, took a comb off the dresser and started dragging it through her hair. "Can we talk about it when I get to the shop?" She heard Erik coming up the stairs. "I just got out of the shower."

256

Erik reached the top of the bedroom stairs and yelled, "Come on! Omelet's getting cold, lover."

Murphy set down the comb and covered her face with her right hand. Waited. Knew it was coming.

Duncan: "That sure as shit ain't Jack."

"No," said Murphy. "It sure as shit ain't." Erik walked over to Murphy. Raised his brows and pointed at the phone. She put her hand over the mouthpiece and said in a low voice, "Work." He nodded, turned, trotted back downstairs.

Duncan was speechless on the other end and Murphy didn't want to help him out. Wished she could see him squirming. Finally he blurted, "Shit. Sorry. Didn't know. Since when?"

She was going to rip into him for being nosy, then decided he'd find out eventually. "We'll talk about it when I get in."

"I'm here for you, Paris."

"Appreciate it." She couldn't imagine leaning on Duncan, but knew he meant well.

"If you need some time off or something . . ."

"No," she said quickly. "Really. I'm fine. It's all fine."

"I like Jack. Really do. Hope it wasn't the job. Can be hell on a marriage. Ruined mine."

She opened her mouth to say it wasn't the job, but stopped herself. The job was part of the problem, and she had to give Duncan points for recognizing it. Every cop knew their work strained their marriage, but few admitted it out loud. "It was a lot of things," she said.

Erik poked his head upstairs again. Murphy nodded. "I gotta go," she said. "We'll discuss your wardrobe for the reunion when I get there."

"Do I need a tux? Should I rent a tux?"

"God no. Don't rent or buy anything. Wait till we talk."

"When?"

"An hour. Give me an hour." She threw the phone on the end of the bed, tightened the belt around her bathrobe.

Erik was standing at the top of the stairs with his arms folded across his chest and a spatula in one hand. "Who the fuck was that?"

"Duncan." She walked past him and headed down to the galley.

He followed her. "Why in the hell is he calling so early? What's this reunion thing?"

The kitchen table was set. The flowers he'd given her earlier in the week were sitting in the middle. The flowers that had helped end her marriage. She picked up the vase, set it on the counter, pulled out the flowers, tossed them in the trash. She turned and saw Erik watching her. He looked hurt. "They were dying," she mumbled, and took a seat at the table. She lowered her eyes, put a forkful of egg into her mouth. Chewed and swallowed. "Really good. Is that mint?"

"Mint and cumin." He took off the apron, threw it on the counter, sat down. Didn't touch his omelet. "The reunion?"

She took a sip of juice, wiped her mouth with the napkin. "My high school is having an all-class reunion Saturday night."

"Why are you taking Yo-Yo? What the hell is that about? Thought about taking me?"

He was jealous of Duncan, and that made her smile. "I don't know if you'd be much use to me. How good of a shot are you?"

"What?"

She picked up a triangle of toast and set it down again. Cold. "This is a work-related outing. Justice Trip is going to be there."

258

"Oh." He started cutting into his omelet with his fork. "Sorry I lost it. What's the plan?" He lifted a forkful of food into his mouth and chewed.

"Duncan and I are going to mingle. Maybe Sweet will take me for a turn around the dance floor."

"Be careful." He picked up a piece of toast, bit off a corner.

"I dropped in on him yesterday, at the trailer park."

"You went by yourself?"

"Me and my Glock," she said. "His father was there, too. He lives with his father."

"His pop as creepy as he is?"

"No, but he thinks he's hot shit. Kept getting touchy-feely with me."

He threw his toast down on his plate. "Great. That's great. You're by yourself in this trailer park with these two creeps and one of them is a killer and the other is trying to cop a feel."

"Don't pull a Jack on me, okay?"

His eyes narrowed; he didn't like the sound of that. "What is that? 'Pull a Jack'?"

"That's where you freak out whenever I tell you about my day. Don't do that to me. I'll stop telling you stuff, and I don't want to do that. I like that we talk. Jack and I couldn't talk."

He picked up his fork. "Then you promise me you won't compare me to Jack every time you turn around. I am not Jack. Deal?"

"Deal," she said. She took another sip of juice. Decided after his reaction to hold off on telling him about the *Flintstones* coffee mug. "What's the latest on the dead folks?"

"So far looks like the ranger got his head bashed in. My guess is the weapon of choice was a BFS."

"Come again?"

"Big fucking shovel."

Murphy nodded, picked up her fork. "He buries Pederson. Comes across the ranger. Kills him with the same shovel he used to dig the hole."

"Yup."

"Cause of death on Pederson?"

Erik took another bite of omelet, chewed, swallowed. "I'm gonna go out on a limb here and say BFT."

"Big fucking something."

"Truck. Big fucking truck. You pick up on that medical terminology real fast, woman. Want a job at the ME's office?" He pointed his fork at her. "I got a pair of gloves with your name on them."

"She was run over? That's it? Sexually assaulted first? Beaten? Any physical indications she'd done something to really piss someone off before she got nailed?"

"Nope. In fact, I'm thinking she was passed out on the road when she was run over."

"Tire marks on her? Any good?"

"Not as good as the cast from the park—and that was a partial."

She set her fork down and frowned. Killing four boys in high school out of anger and then running a woman over years later for no apparent reason. No pattern there. Was she wrong about Trip? Maybe he had nothing to do with the earlier crash and maybe he hit Bunny Pederson by accident, and then took advantage of the situation to play hero. The ranger got in the way. Could it be there were no others? No. Her gut told her there was more to it.

Erik studied her face. "Disappointed?"

She picked up her fork. "I was hoping for an MO that might point to other murders. Signs of pent-up anger let loose. A simple hit-and-run, though. I don't know. Wish there'd been more out of the autopsy."

"If Justice Trip did it, and then hid her body and planted her finger. Well. Shit. I'd hardly call that *simple*." He rifled the rest of his toast in his mouth.

"What else?" She took another bite of egg.

He chewed, swallowed, took a sip of juice. "They found a knife near the grave."

"Prints?"

"On the handle."

"Match the one off the shoe?"

He nodded.

"What kind of knife? Hunting?"

"No. Not what you'd expect. Stiletto. Odd."

"I'll show you odd." She got up from the table and ran upstairs. She came back down with a slender volume in her hands. She sat down at the table, opened it and slid it over to Erik. "Check this out," she said, pointing to a photo.

He looked at where she was pointing. A yearbook picture of a kid with black hair and dark eyes. Under the mug shot: *Justice Franklin Trip. "Sweet." "Trippy." Ambition: to move back to Memphis. Likes heavy metal . . . working on trucks . . . collecting knives. Remembered for blushing a lot, being the tallest kid in school.*

"Collects knives," said Erik. "Shit."

"Yeah. I got a gander at that knife collection yesterday. His bedroom is a sword museum or something. And the way he behaved. His dad gave me a tour of their trailer and Sweet was on edge the whole time. He's hiding something in that mobile home. I'm sure of it." She closed the yearbook. "That tire tread from the park and the finger-prints. Can you get me copies real quick?"

Erik cut off another wedge of omelet and jabbed it with his fork. "On the sly maybe. Winter is being a prick about releasing info, even to other agencies. Yo-Yo really pissed him off." He popped the egg into his mouth, chewed.

"Yeah. Duncan." She wiped her mouth with the napkin, stood up and took her plate over to the sink. "I better get to the cop shop before he does something goofy, like buys a tux for this reunion thing."

Erik stood up with his plate. "I'll say it again. Be careful."

She scraped the scraps into the trash. "I can handle Sweet."

Erik opened the dishwasher. "I'm talking about Yo-Yo."

She stopped scraping. Set the plate on the counter. "Give me a break."

"You think I'm kidding?" Erik started loading the dishwasher.

She walked to the table to retrieve the dirty glasses and silverware. "Duncan's goofy; I'll give you that. But he's got an honest heart. I really believe that."

Erik pulled the box of soap from under the sink and filled the dispenser in the dishwasher. "The guy's legendary. He lived on the street for years. The junkies were afraid of him. He's a fucking wild man."

She stopped in the middle of the kitchen with a fistful of silverware. "Then why did they put him in charge of Homicide? Why's he a commander?"

Erik pulled the silverware out of her hands and dropped them in the dishwasher basket. "You got me. Maybe Christianson doesn't give a shit anymore because he's on his way out. Maybe he needed to rein in the wacko before he turned into a real PR nightmare. I hear by the time they took him off the streets, he was shooting up. Mainlining serious shit."

Murphy handed him a couple of dirty glasses. Recalled Duncan pulling off his shirt. She would have noticed needle tracks. All she saw was an athletic body. No. She didn't believe it. "You're full of shit," she said.

Erik set the glasses in the dishwasher, shut the door, and glared at her. "I don't like how you're Yo-Yo's big defender all of a sudden. What's up with that? You don't even call him Yo-Yo anymore. It's 'Duncan this' and 'Duncan that,' and frankly I don't like it."

She smiled wickedly. "He is hot. I especially like the way he dresses. That 'slept-in' look really turns my crank."

"Fine. Make fun. Don't blame me when Yo-Yo gets the both of you tangled in some big fucking mess."

28

No way. Can't be true, she thought. While driving to work later that morning, she mulled over what Erik had said and wanted to dismiss it as jealousy. Duncan was odd, but he was also a good cop. She'd worked with him a couple of times back when she was in Vice. He'd received more medals and commendations than anyone else on the force. Taken more dealers off the street than anyone else. She turned into the cop shop parking lot, shut off the Jeep and dropped the keys in her purse. Glanced at the Glock in her bag. Thought about Saturday night. Duncan also had more kills than anyone else on the force, but not all of them were clean. A few years back, Duncan had had a midnight meeting with a dealer in a downtown apartment. The guy smelled a bust and fled the building before Duncan came up. Duncan saw him running down the sidewalk and shot him. He said the dealer had pulled a gun on him. No weapon was found. Only a lighter, and it was still in the guy's pocket. Duncan concocted some bullshit story that the piece had tumbled down the sewer. Internal affairs and the police-civilian review panel bought it and nobody questioned their findings. Nobody cared. The lone ranger had blown away another bad guy. Murphy closed her purse, stepped out of the Jeep, slammed the door and walked to the shop. Decided she'd have to go over Saturday night's plan in detail with Duncan. She was worried about more than his wardrobe.

She didn't bother tossing her purse and jacket on her desk. She walked through Homicide and into Duncan's office. He was getting in himself. Draping his suit coat over the back of his chair. Underneath, his usual rumpled shirt and crooked tie. The tie was out of season; it was decorated with Christmas trees and holly leaves. At least he'd stopped throwing his blazer on the floor.

"Hey, Murphy." He pulled at the tie like it was choking him, loosened it and then took it off. Curled his upper lip and dropped the tie on top of his desk in disgust, like it was a moldy sandwich. He pointed to the chair across from his desk. "Take a load off." He noticed her hands were empty. "Coffee?" He jogged out of his office before she could answer and returned with two foam cups. Set one down on his desk and handed her one. "Black okay?"

She took it. "Thanks." She set hers down on the edge of his desk. "Let's talk," she said. He watched her while she turned and closed his office door. Even though there were no other detectives in yet, they could be walking in any minute and she didn't want them to overhear her concerns about working with Duncan. He was having enough problems with his credibility in Homicide. She pulled off her jacket and hung it over the back of the chair. Set her purse down on the floor and sat down. Picked up the coffee cup and sipped.

He lowered himself into his chair and clasped his hands together, resting them on top of his desk. His face took on a serious expression. Furrowed brows and down-turned mouth. He spoke in a low voice. A priest offering counseling to a penitent. "I'm glad you feel comfortable coming to me, Paris. Like I said, I know the stress this job can place on a marriage. Have you talked to a shrink? I'm pretty sure our medical covers it. Nothing to be ashamed of. They tried to set me up with one once or twice. I didn't go, but that doesn't mean you shouldn't."

She set the cup down. Held up both palms defensively. "Stop. That is not what this is about. I appreciate it, but I can handle everything on the home front."

He smiled grimly and nodded. "That's what *I* thought. Then I come home one night and all the furniture is gone and so is the wife." He picked up his cup and sipped.

"Saturday night," she said.

His eyes lit up. The priest was elbowed aside by the excited boy. "Yeah. Saturday." He leaned forward. "Sure this Trip is going to be there?"

"Took an invitation to him yesterday afternoon. Visited him at the family estate. Lives in a trailer park on the north side of town with his dad."

"How'd that go? What'd you see? Anything sound an alarm?"

"Sweet was nervous as hell. All he wanted to do was get me out of there. Meantime, his creepy dad is giving me the grand tour of the place and hitting on me at the same time."

"Yeah?"

"Yeah. Sweet's bedroom took the prize. Enough knives and daggers and swords to outfit an army."

"This dude's gotta be the killer."

"He's been a killer going back to high school."

He frowned. "What do you mean?"

She took a breath. She didn't know it would be so hard to talk about it. "He served me tea from this coffee mug.

266

When I was in high school, I gave the mug to this kid. My boyfriend. Denny." She took another breath. "Denny and three of his buddies died in a car wreck. Lost control and flew into a lake. The only way Trip could have the mug is if he stole it from the car right before the accident."

Duncan's eyes widened. "Am I understanding you right?"

"I'm thinking the accident wasn't an accident. Sweet messed with the car so it would crash. Fucked up the brakes or the steering or something."

"Why would Sweetie take the mug? A sick souvenir?"

"Maybe. More likely he stole the mug because it was filled with change." She sipped her coffee. "One thing I don't get. Why was he stupid enough to serve me tea in the mug?"

"Did he know you gave your boyfriend the mug?"

"No."

"Then he didn't know it was a big deal. Plus he probably had it sitting around his house so long, he forgot where he got it from."

"Sweet remembered Denny liked cartoons. He made a crack about it in Moose Lake."

"Just because a guy remembers a goofy fact doesn't mean he remembers *how* he acquired that fact in the first place. Hell. I'm a fount of useless information. I have no idea why I know certain shit."

She took another sip of coffee and nodded. "Yeah. I buy that."

"And you know, it is possible he stole the mug and didn't mess with the car. Could be the timing of the accident was a coincidence."

"No," she said. "I'm sure he did it."

"Why are you sure?"

She thought about it. Her intuition and instincts had

always served her well in navigating cases. The times she'd ignored them had led to disaster. "I just am."

Duncan nodded. "Okay. We'll get something out of him at the reunion." He took a gulp of coffee. "Saturday night. What do I wear?"

"What you've got on is fine," she said. She pointed to the heap of silk on the desk. "Except a different tie."

He took another sip of coffee, held the cup between both hands. "What are you wearing?"

"A dress."

"A fancy one?"

"God no. We're not going to the opera. A cocktail dress."

"Then I should wear a suit." He slurped his coffee. "Gotta get a suit. A suit coat would hide my piece."

"Duncan." She paused. Clearly he was looking for an excuse to get dressed up. "Okay. Get a suit. But save the receipt."

"Good idea." He polished off the coffee and tossed the cup toward the wastebasket. It hit the wall and bounced in.

"Now let's talk strategy," she said.

"Strategy," he repeated. He leaned back in his chair and put his feet up on his desk. The running shoes were still part of his uniform.

"Wait," she said. She pointed to his feet. "Lose those, okay? I hate jokers who wear sneakers with suits. They think it's cute and it's not. Dress shoes, okay?"

He gave her the thumbs-up signal with his right hand. "Got it, Chief. Next?"

" 'Chief' is the operative word here. I'm in charge of this operation." She took another sip of coffee and set the cup back down on the edge of his desk. "No cowboy stuff." She braced herself for an angry comeback but he only nodded. She kept talking. "I'm getting a copy of the cast from the tire treads. Before I knocked on Sweet's door, I took some photos of his truck tires. We'll use those to compare. If we're still not sure we'll take the cast copy to the reunion and compare it to the actual treads on Sweet's truck. As far as getting Sweet's fingerprints, we'll have to be sneaky about it. Maybe give him a clean wineglass and take it back after he handles it."

"So we can compare it to the print off the shoe?"

"And the stiletto," she said.

He held up his hand to stop her. "Stiletto?"

She felt bad for Duncan; that bastard Winter was doing a good job of keeping him in the dark. "They found a stiletto near Pederson's body."

"Part of Sweetie's knife collection?"

She nodded. "Got prints off the handle." Then, so Duncan would know she wasn't talking to Winter behind his back: "Erik Mason told me."

He snapped his fingers. "Mason. That's who I heard when I called you this morning. Knew I recognized the voice. You two move in together or what?"

"No," she said, lowering her eyes. "I'm not ready to have anyone move in." She looked up, could feel her face growing hot. "Can we talk about my personal life some other time?"

"Sorry," he mumbled. "Been saying that to you a lot lately." He took his feet off the desk and stood up. Unbuttoned his left shirt cuff and started rolling up the sleeve while he talked. "I take it Mason is the one slipping us the copies of the treads and prints."

She stared at his left arm. No tracks. "Yeah. Erik," she said distractedly. "Keep it under your hat. If Winter found out, he'd be pissed."

"What time should I pick you up?" He unbuttoned his right shirt cuff.

"Seven," she said. "Cocktails and appetizers at seven, dancing at eight."

"Dancing, huh? I better warn you. I'm a damn good dancer. Better keep up." He rolled up his right shirt cuff. "Where's it at?"

She studied his right arm. Again, no tracks. "Reception hall on Summit Avenue."

"The one with the wrought-iron fence, right? I know the place. Nice joint." He sat back down, rested his arms on the desk and caught her studying them. A tight smile stretched across his face. "You heard that bullshit story, too." Her mouth fell open; she didn't know how to respond. "I'm surprised you swallowed it. A smart cop like you. How long would I have lasted on the streets if I was doing that shit? Who fed you that crap? Your new boyfriend? Tell Mason he can kiss my ass."

She stood up. The cordial meeting had turned ugly. "My turn to say it. I'm sorry." She picked up her purse, threw the strap over her shoulder and turned to walk out. She put her right hand on the knob, pulled the door open a crack.

He bolted out of his chair and was right behind her. Pushed the door shut with his right hand. "Not so fast," he said in a low voice. "That hurts, Paris. That really fucking hurts. We worked together."

She kept her back turned to him. She wondered how he'd guessed Erik was the one who told her; they must have crossed paths before. It didn't matter. Erik was the one who told her, but she was the one who believed it, even if for an instant. She said again in a low voice, "I'm sorry."

He planted his left hand on the other side of her. "Well 'I'm sorry' ain't gonna fix it."

They were standing too close. She felt trapped. Wished there was someone else in the office. At the same time she noticed he smelled good. Irish Spring soap and a cologne she recognized but couldn't place.

"Listen," he said. "I'm only gonna give you this speech once. I'm fucking sick of defending my undercover work. Sure I dressed like a dope fiend. Hung out with them. Acted like a dope fiend. But that's all it was. A fucking act, and a good one at that."

She turned and looked at him. He was genuinely hurt, and she felt bad. For the first time she noticed he had blue eyes. Not dark blue like hers. Light blue. Then she silently berated herself for noticing his eyes. Noticing his scent.

With her facing him, he suddenly realized how close they were and it seemed to embarrass him. He quickly took his hands off the door and lowered his arms. Took a step back from her. Folded his arms across his chest. "My record speaks for itself."

She didn't know what to say. Had no good excuse. "I'm sorry. I really am. I told Erik he was full of shit."

"But you had to see for yourself. Didn't you? Had to check out the junkie's arms. Look for the lines." He took a step toward her, turned both his arms and raised them so she could see the inside of his forearms. "Here. Take a closer peek. Push the sleeves up more if you want." She lowered her eyes and shook her head. He stepped closer. Raised his arms higher. "Really. I insist."

She grabbed each of his wrists with her hands and pushed his arms down. "Duncan. Stop."

He pulled his arms away from her and paced the width of the room once. "Jesus Christ. How about a little common sense? Would that tight-ass Christianson have put an addict in charge of Homicide?" He stopped walking and stood in front of her, even closer than before.

"No," she said. She couldn't keep from looking in his eyes. Bloodshot. Angry. Incredibly blue. If Jack was young

271

James Caan and Erik was old James Dean, Duncan was Robert Redford after a rough weekend.

"*No*. Fucking right *no*. Why do you think people spread that kind of manure? Hmm? Think that new boyfriend feels threatened?"

Her eyes narrowed. "What do you mean?"

He leaned into her left ear and whispered, "A smart cop like you, you know exactly what I mean."

"No I don't," she snapped.

He turned and walked to his desk, sat on the edge of it. Picked up her coffee cup and took a sip. Set it down. "You know, I'm the one who should be worried about who I'm partnering with. I hear that crazy doc not only blew his brains out in his own house with *your* gun, but did it with *your* encouragement. That right, Murphy? Did you egg him on? The poor, crazy fuck."

She gasped. How did Duncan find out? Only one other cop knew what had happened that night. Gabe had heard the words she and the surgeon exchanged before the gunshot, and he kept it out of the report. Did Gabe share her secret with Duncan?

As if he'd read her mind: "Did I ever tell you who my first partner was?"

"You bastard," she said.

"Yeah. Nash and me, we were like this." He held up his right hand, with his middle and index fingers twined together. "Every once in a while, when something is bugging the shit out of him and he can't dump on anyone else, he calls me."

"Why? 'Cause you're so good at keeping your mouth shut?"

"I *have* kept my mouth shut, against my better judgment." He stood up and walked toward her. "I told Nash he should've turned you in. It's one thing to take out a

272

dealer in a good, honest shoot-out. But to talk someone into suicide." He stepped in front of her, stood inches away. Pointed his right index finger in her face. "That is fucking nuts."

She turned, put her hand on the knob, pulled open the door. Felt relieved to walk out. Felt even more relieved to see Castro and Dubrowski and Sandeen sitting at their desks. Duncan stood behind her, a hand on each side of the open doorway. Said loud enough for the entire office to hear, "Know what else is nuts? Dumping a decent guy like Jack for a puke like Mason. If you ask me, Paris, you traded down."

She froze in her tracks. Saw the three detectives look at her and then Duncan and then her again. Her colleagues were waiting for her to return the volley. She spun on her heel to blast Duncan but before she could say a word, he threw her jacket at her. She caught it, and he delivered one last jab: "I'll pick you up at seven Saturday. I know where you live. Wear something hot for a change." He went back inside his office, slammed the door so hard he rattled pictures on the wall.

29

"Fired!" The word kept repeating itself. Over and over. Each time getting louder. *"Fired!"* At a stoplight, he covered his ears with his hands but it didn't do any good. The word was inside his head, not inside his truck. He grabbed a Manowar disc, *Louder Than Hell*, to drive out the loud word. His hands were shaking so much he dropped the CD on the seat. He picked it up again. Shoved it into the player. Cranked up the volume. Even the thumping of the bass guitar failed to drive the word out of his head. *"Fired!"* The light changed and he stepped on the gas. Squealed through the intersection.

Thursday had started badly and gone downhill, bottoming out with that word. "Fired." He'd tossed and turned and gotten tangled in his sheets Wednesday night. He couldn't sleep. He was worried about the visit Paris Murphy had paid to their trailer. Why had his old man invited her in? He feared his pa was going to turn him in to the cops. The pills he'd taken—some Tylenol with codeine he'd found in Keri's purse—didn't knock him out as he'd hoped. They only made him dizzy and tired and sick to his stomach. He'd gotten up in the middle of the night and taken two more. A few hours later, two more. Still no sleep. Only the room spinning and his stomach churning. When he rolled out of bed Thursday morning, he felt like he hadn't slept for days and was constipated on top of it. He sat on the pot reading the warning labels plastered all over the bottle. One was yellow and had a drawing of a sleepy eye with the lid half-open. "May cause drowsiness," it read. "Alcohol could intensify this effect." He knew he should have taken it with a shot of booze, but there wasn't any left in the house. Another label, also yellow: "Use caution when operating a car or dangerous machinery." The white label next to it had a drawing of a loaf of bread: "If medication upsets your stomach, take with a modest meal, crackers or bread." Wished he'd read that label the night before. He'd skipped dinner Wednesday; he was too busy cooking for his old man. Waiting on him. Listening to his lies about why he'd invited a cop into their house. *I didn't mean anything by it, son. Just being a gentleman. Fine-looking women get the best of me.* The final label on the pill bottle, another white one, made Trip laugh: "Caution. Federal law prohibits the transfer of this drug to any person other than the patient for whom it was prescribed." Out of curiosity, he checked the prescribed dosage and patient name on the bottle. "Take two tablets by mouth every four hours as needed. Dunkling, Mildred R." Poor old Mildred R. Dunkling was missing some pain pills, courtesy of Keri Ingmar. Trip set the bottle on the edge of the sink, stood up, pulled up his boxers. Constipated or not, he had to get his ass in to work. He should've checked in with Murray Wednesday but didn't. For sure he had to show up today.

He stood in front of the bathroom mirror. Looked even

worse than he felt. Turned on the faucet and let it run until it got hot. Opened the medicine cabinet and took down the shave cream and a disposable razor. The same shave cream and razor Keri had used. He wanted to throw away the razor, but it was the last one on the shelf. Dried cream on the handle. Dried hairs on the blade. Keri's hair from her pits or crotch. He shuddered and held the blades under the hot tap water. Whacked it against the side of the sink. Watched the tiny blond hairs disappear down the drain. Rinsed the handle. He bent over, cupped his hands under the faucet and splashed scalding water on his face. The burn felt good. Jarred him awake. He stood up, squirted a mound of foam into his hand and lathered his face. He dragged the razor across his skin. Cut himself a couple of times. The blade was dull after servicing Keri. He rinsed off the cream, turned off the tap and stood up. Studied the shadowy face in the mirror. A little more human.

He turned and looked at the closed shower door. He'd have to use it eventually. Might as well get it over with. He pushed open the door and reached inside. Turned on the shower. Stepped out of his boxers and into the stall. He faced the shower and ducked his head under. Bent his neck down so the spray kneaded the back of his head. Reached for the shampoo. Squirted a dab in his hair and put it back. While he worked it into a lather, he remembered the shit Keri had given him for using baby shampoo. *Ain't you old enough to use big-boy suds?* He squeezed the soap from his hair. She'd said there was nothing he could do to save his hair and that he'd have to get a rug. He looked at his wet, soapy fingers. More strands of black hair tangled around them. He pulled them off and dropped them on the shower floor. The bitch was probably right. Still, better bald than dead. He wondered when someone would notice she was missing. She didn't have any family in town. His pa was right about the neighbors; they were nosy, especially that old lady next door to Keri. How many of them saw Keri walk to their trailer Tuesday? Her job would probably be the first to sound an alarm, however. When was she scheduled to work next? She'd said she had the rest of the week off. Did she say that included the weekend? Even if the cops came by her place, they wouldn't find anything unusual. Her car would be parked in front of her house. The trailer would be locked up. Everything would be in order, as if she'd left town with someone. His pa had said she concocted some story for work about visiting a boyfriend. Maybe he and his old man could add to the tale. Come up with a description. Send the cops after this phantom fella of hers. Yeah. Good idea, he thought. Only problem was it required his pa's cooperation and he didn't know if he could count on it. Didn't know if he could count on his old man for much of anything anymore. Kill a few folks and that family loyalty goes right down the crapper.

He heard his old man thump into the bathroom. He banged on the shower door with his cane. Trip hated the way his old man used it as a weapon. "What?" Trip yelled from the shower.

"Going into the office?"

"Yeah."

"I bagged up the dirty clothes. Make a run to the Laundromat when you get a chance."

Trip was going to do the wash Wednesday night, but he was too nervous to leave his old man alone. He was still nervous, but he had to leave the house sometime. His pa banged on the shower door again. "Yeah," Trip yelled. "I heard you. Laundry. I'll d... do it. Can't a g... guy wash his d... dick in peace?"

He heard his old man lift up the toilet lid, take a pee. Sure enough, he was hitting the wastebasket. Trip could tell from the sharpness of the tinkle. He opened his mouth to yell something and closed it again. Better leave the old coot be. Let him piss where he wants, like a mean, old, blind dog. His old man flushed. He knew not to flush. Suddenly the shower turned scalding. Trip backed away from it. "Pa!" he yelled. "Why the fuck you d... do that?"

He heard his old man laugh. "Wash your pecker with that." He thumped out of the bathroom.

Things sure as hell had changed between him and his old man. He'd have to find out what he was hiding; Trip needed some collateral. In the meantime he'd have to get to the office. For a change, work didn't seem like such a bad place to be. He assumed Wade Murray had some lingering respect for him. Not like his old man.

Trip's assumption was blown out of the water at nine-fifteen that morning, when he poked his head into Murray's office.

"When's the s... sales meeting?" Trip asked.

Murray glanced up from a stack of papers and frowned. "Come in. Shut the door."

Trip raised his brows. Ducked through the door, shut it behind him. Looked at Murray. He was a short, fat man with a washboard forehead. He always had sweat above his upper lip. He had short, black hair on the sides of his head, but the top was pink and shiny. So shiny, Trip wondered if Murray waxed it. Trip figured he'd better take notes; he'd be joining that club soon enough.

"Sit," Murray said, pointing to the metal folding chair on the other side of his desk. Pinecone Clothing Distributors had had an address at Riverview Industrial Park south of downtown St. Paul for years, but the offices—a small room, a larger conference room and a greasy rest room—were furnished as if the company had recently moved in or was in the process of moving out. Folding chairs. Card tables. Empty boxes piled in corners. Murray and his sales force worked out of their homes and cars, and used the industrial park space mostly for meetings and to pick up samples. No warehouse; the shirts went directly from the manufacturer to the clothing store. Murray sat at a metal desk in the small room. The walls were bare except for a map of Italy. The edges were ripped and curling. Murray was always talking about a vacation in Italy. Trip figured it would never happen because it would require Murray to take a break from work, and he never stopped working.

Trip started to take off his jacket before he sat down.

"Don't bother," Murray said. "This won't take long." Trip lowered himself into the chair. Murray glared at him. "Where in the hell have you been?"

"On the road. Just got back to t... town."

"Why haven't you been answering your phone?"

Trip had left his cell phone in the truck all day Wednesday. "Must have b... been out of range."

"That's a load of crap." He looked at the top of Trip's head and frowned. "I suppose you've been wearing that on your calls."

Trip reached up and pulled off his *E.P.* baseball cap. Held it in his hands. "The sales meeting . . ."

"Was two hours ago. You blew it, pal. I've had it with your bullshit. You're fired. Turn in your orders—if you have any orders—and we'll mail you your last check."

Trip felt like someone had kicked him in the chest. "Fired? I'm fired? Why am I f... fired?"

Murray bunched a stack of papers in his right fist and shook them at Trip. "Because you ain't been bringing in

279

enough of these. Know what these are? Orders." He dropped the papers on his desk. "We are in the business of selling shirts. You want to save the world, get your face on television, in the newspapers? Fine. But if you can't bring in orders, we don't want you."

"I got orders," Trip said.

"How many? Where are they? Who are they from?"

Trip's jaw dropped. He studied the hat in his hands, hoping an answer would materialize on the brim. He couldn't think of a believable number. He couldn't produce any paperwork. Couldn't even make up the name of a customer. The only thing in his head was that word. "Fired!"

Murray folded his hands together on top of the desk. Stared at Trip. Waited for an answer. After several seconds of silence: "Yeah," Murray said, straightening the stack of papers. "That's what I figured."

"Can I g... get my money b... back from the unopened samples?"

"You gotta be kidding me." Murray pointed to the door. "Hit the bricks."

Trip stood up and pulled the cap back on his head. Went to the door. Put his right hand on the knob. He was exhausted. Could hardly move his arms and legs; something was dragging them down. Like swimming through a weedy lake. He opened the door. Turned to ask a question that was addressed more to himself than to Murray. "What am I gonna do with all those d... damn shirts?"

Murray was paging through the paperwork again. Didn't bother looking up at Trip when he answered. "You'll be the best dressed chump standing in the unemployment line." Trip started to walk through the door. "Hey," said Murray.

Trip took a step back into the room. Maybe Murray had reconsidered. "Yeah?"

Murray pointed up at the hat. "Always wondered. What's that E.P. stand for?"

"Elvis Presley," Trip muttered, and walked out.

30

Trip drove north through downtown and instead of steering onto the freeway, took meandering side streets toward home. He needed time to empty his head of the word. "Fired!" If the Manowar CD didn't do it, maybe a couple of the right pills would. He pulled into a liquor store parking lot and put the truck in park but kept the engine running. He pulled a bottle of pills out of his jacket pocket. Another find from Keri's purse. He hadn't even checked the label yet. Prayed they were something potent and wonderful. Amphetamines would be good, but he knew that was asking too much. Keri had warned him they were getting harder to come by. She'd said she had one patient on them—a guy with narcolepsy—and he was wising up to her pilfering. Trip needed something to lift him up. Take him someplace. Any place was better than where he was now. Listening to that word rattling around inside his head. He read the label. "Fuck," he muttered. They weren't even part of Keri's stolen stash. Her name was on the bottle. "Ingmar, Keri M." Below that: "Take 1 capsule by mouth every day. Prilosec 20mg capsules." He unscrewed the top and dumped the contents of the bottle into his hand to make sure she hadn't filled the container with something else. He recognized the purple capsules. He'd watched her pop them into her mouth when her stomach was bothering her. She told him they neutralized the acid in her gut. He was poised to toss them on the floor of the car, but stopped. Poured the capsules back, screwed the cap back on, returned the bottle to his pocket. The way his life was going, he'd probably need the pills. He shut off the engine and shoved the keys in his pocket. Hopped out of the truck and slammed the door shut. Headed for the liquor store. If he couldn't get stoned before he got home, might as well get drunk. He walked inside, headed for the whiskey section of the store. Spotted his old man's favorite. Reached for the Jim Beam. Some liquor might soften the blow. *Got fired, Pa. Let's do shots.* Trip scanned the shelves for his own numbing agent. Vodka? Gin? Tequila? Tequila would work. He took it down. Wished he could twist off the cap and chug it right there in the middle of the aisle. He walked over to the counter and set both bottles down. Saw some beef sticks on a rack in front of him and threw a fistful on the counter.

"That it?" The clerk was an old woman with greasy gray hair and crooked teeth.

Trip scanned the rack for more snacks. Grabbed two bags of salted-in-the-shell peanuts. A can of cheese balls. Set them with the other stuff.

"Breakfast?" the clerk asked with a chuckle.

Trip didn't answer. Tossed some bills on the counter. He remembered the laundry. Pulled a few more bills out of his pocket. "Give me s... some quarters."

He pulled in front of the Laundromat. Turned off the truck and slipped the keys in his pocket. He sat behind the wheel. Stared through the storefront windows. Only a couple of folks inside. He grabbed the bag of munchies off the passenger's seat and eyed the other two bags—the liquor—with longing. He looked in his rearview mirror and scanned the sidewalk. No one close. He pulled the tequila out of its sack and picked at the paper seal. He needed a knife. He reached over and popped open the glove compartment. Took out a jackknife. He stared at his one-hitter kit. A toke would be so good right now. Exactly what he needed. Still, he'd better save it for later. With Keri dead, his pills dwindling and his job gone, he'd have to conserve any and all mood-altering materials. He opened the jackknife and cut around the paper seal of the tequila bottle. Closed the knife and tossed it back in the glove compartment. Stared at the one-hitter kit again. Told himself to be strong. He shut the glove compartment. Screwed the cap off the tequila. Looked up and down the sidewalk again and then put the bottle to his lips. Took a long drink. So good going down. He took a longer drink. Put the cap back on. Slipped the bottle back in the bag and set it on the floor on the passenger's side. He opened the driver's-side door and slid out, taking the bag of snacks with him. He shut the door and went to the back of the truck. Opened the gate. His stomach churned. Behind the garbage bag of clothes were all the shirts. He knew exactly how many he had because, like the other salesmen, he'd paid for all his own samples. Five sealed boxes. Twenty-four shirts in each. Two opened boxes. Twenty shirts in each. Twenty-three loose shirts. Each boxed and loose shirt was individually polybagged and ready for sale. Plastic inside the collar. Cardboard on the back. Stickpins here and there. Then there was the one dirty shirt rolled up in a ball way back in the corner. He'd used that to dry the truck at the car wash. That made 184 shirts. What was he going to do with all those fucking shirts? He grabbed the garbage bag with the dirty laundry and pulled it out of the truck. Slammed the back gate shut and crossed the sidewalk to the Laundromat. Bag of clothes in his right hand and bag of snacks in his left.

Trip sat on a chair in front of the dryers, stared through the round windows at the clothes rolling around and gnawed on a beef stick. The last of his snacks. In the chair to his right were his jacket and a pile of food wrappers and peanut shells. He rifled the last inch of beef stick into his mouth, chewed three times, swallowed. He leaned back in the chair and stretched his legs out in front of him. Folded his hands together and rested them on his stomach. His belly was full and his head was light. During the rinse cycle, he'd gone back out to the truck and chugged more tequila. He decided the Laundromat wasn't such a bad place to be drunk. Outside was gray and cloudy. Through the storefront windows, he could see crumpled paper and leaves being chased down the street by the wind. Inside, it was warm. It smelled clean from the dryer sheets and detergent and bleach. Not like the trailer, with its stink of his old man's cigarette smoke and urine and whiskey. The two other people doing laundry—an old guy in baggy khakis and a young woman in tight jeans—had finished their loads and were gone. He had the place to himself. Nice and quiet. The only sounds were the hum of the dryers and the muffled thump of the damp clothes inside them. Not like home, with his father barking orders and waving his cane around. Television cranked loud with the noise of gunplay from yet another western show. Didn't that channel ever run out of cowboys?

The first dryer stopped. Trip stood up. Swayed. Dug his hands into his pockets. Even if the clothes were dry he'd be willing to keep plugging the machine with quarters to listen to the drone. No change in his pants. He picked up his jacket and checked. No change there, either. Only his car keys and Keri's stomach pills. His gut was starting to ache from all the junk he'd eaten. He took the bottle out, removed the cap and fished out a capsule. Swallowed it dry. Put the cap back on and shoved the bottle back in his jacket.

The second dryer stopped. Fuck it, he thought. Time to go home. Where did he put that garbage bag? Had he tossed it by mistake? No. Here it was, under his chair. He took it over to the first dryer, opened the window, bent over. Started filling the bag with warm, clean clothes. The room began spinning. He dropped the bag and ran to the bathroom in back of the Laundromat. Fell to his knees in front of the toilet and vomited. Tequila and beef sticks and peanuts and cheese balls. He figured the purple capsule was in there somewhere, too. He blew his nose on some toilet paper. Stood up. Hobbled back to the dryer and finished emptying it. Went to the second dryer next to it and started digging out clothes. He wished he could crawl inside with the warm fabric. He shut the dryer and stood up. Started for the door and stopped halfway there. He'd forgotten something. What? His jacket. He dropped the bag on the floor, went back to the chair, picked up his jacket, slipped it on. The room was spinning again. His right hand darted out and held on to the dryer. Shut his eyes for a moment and opened them again. The spinning had stopped. He picked up the bag and went out to the truck.

He walked through the trailer door with the bags of liquor cradled in the crook of his right arm and the garbage bag of clothes in his left hand. He dropped the garbage bag on the floor. Saw his pa sitting on the couch, asleep. The TV tray in front of him. Loaded with chips, dip and other junk. Ashtray with a smoking cigarette. A spent insulin syringe and needle. The television was blaring. The theme from *Bonanza*. Was it that late? Almost dinnertime. Trip picked up the bag and walked to his bedroom. Threw the bag in a corner. Set the booze on his dresser. Took off his jacket and threw it on the bed. Wanted to collapse on top of the sheets and take a nap. His head was still spinning from the booze, but not as bad as before. He was sobering up. Maybe he should reverse the trend, he thought. Best to break the news to his old man while he was drunk. While they were both drunk. He went back to his dresser and took the Jim Beam out of the bag. He'd save that for his old man. No good mixing tequila and whiskey. He took a knife off his dresser and cut around the whiskey bottle's seal. Set the knife and whiskey bottle down. Slipped the tequila out of its bag, screwed the cap off and took a long drink. Burped. His mouth tasted like tequila and cheese balls and vomit. He took another drink, swished it around in his mouth and swallowed. He set the bottle on the dresser and went to his bed. Sat on the edge and pulled off his dress shoes and socks.

His pa bellowed from the front room. "Where in the hell you been all day? Thought that meeting was just the morning. I'm hungry. Been eating crap all day."

Trip got up from the bed, grabbed both bottles and walked into the front room. Sat down on the couch next to his pa. Took the cap off the Jim Beam. "Why d... d... didn't you make yourself something? You ain't helpless. You been making me b... breakfast." He handed his old man the whiskey bottle.

"Nothing in the fridge." His pa took a coffee cup off the

TV tray, tipped it in his mouth to finish off the coffee and poured himself a drink. Set the bottle between his legs. "We need groceries." He guzzled the whiskey like it was water. "You left me here to starve."

"I'll g... get some groceries. Meantime, let's order a p... pizza."

"You drunk?"

"Getting there."

"When did you start?"

Trip didn't answer. He took a juice glass off his pa's tray. Looked inside it. A layer of something orange on the bottom. Probably orange juice from the morning. Trip filled the glass halfway with tequila. Set the bottle on the floor at his feet.

"Maybe you didn't hear me, boy." He set the cup down, picked up his cigarette. Took a pull and set it down again. "When did you start drinking? Middle of the day?"

Trip threw his head back and bumped off the tequila without tasting it. Shuddered. "Hell n... n... no. I was already good and d... drunk by the middle of the d... day. This here is my s... second wind."

"Why you drinking like this? Did you make it in to work?"

Trip filled the juice glass. "I m... m... made it in all right. In and out."

His old man picked up his cup, took another drink of whiskey. Set the cup down on the tray. Stared at his son. "You been fired."

Trip nodded. Sipped from the juice glass. He'd filled it too high and spilled some of it on his shirt. "Shit," he muttered.

"Shit is right," said his pa. "We in a world of shit now."

Trip set his glass on the TV tray. "What d... do you mean?"

"Expenses. Our lot rent for starters. How we gonna pay? That's three hundred a month right there. Electricity. Groceries. My cigs. My meds. Jesus. How we gonna pay for my shots and pills and such?"

Trip had stopped listening. He stood up. Swayed. Started to unbutton the shirt and stopped after the top button. "Who g... gives a shit? There's more where this c... c... came from." He loosened his necktie, yanked it over his head and threw it on the floor. Ripped the shirt open with both hands, popping the buttons off.

"What the hell you doing? You nuts?"

Trip pulled off the shirt, held it up in front of him and ripped it down the middle as if he were tearing a sheet of paper in half. "Fucking shirts. I h... hate these shitty shirts."

His pa frowned. Softened his tone while watching his son's erratic behavior. "Now don't be wasting stuff like that, son. We got to be frugal now that you're . . ."

"Now that I'm what? Fired? Fucking f... f... fired?"

"You ruined a good shirt is all."

Trip threw the shredded shirt at his pa. "We g... g... got shirts up the ass." Barefoot and dressed in his tee shirt and dress slacks, Trip stumbled out the door, went to the back of his truck, opened the gate and pulled out both of the opened boxes of dress shirts. He went back inside. Dropped the boxes on the front room floor.

"What you got there, son?"

Trip didn't answer. Ran back outside and grabbed two of the sealed boxes and brought them inside the trailer. After three more runs to the truck, his entire supply of shirts was on the front room floor. He looked at the sealed boxes. He needed a knife to open them. He ran to his bedroom and grabbed the first knife he saw on his dresser—the straight-edge he'd used on Keri. Sitting folded in its box on his dresser, waiting to get sharpened. He took it out, shoved it in his pants pocket and ran back to the front room. Stood in the middle of the pile of boxes and shirts. Scanned the room. Saw what he needed. He headed for the couch. Fell over a box on his way there. Crawled to his feet. Picked up the tequila bottle. Put it to his lips and chugged. Wiped his mouth with the back of his left hand. He carried the bottle over to the pile of boxes and shirts. He shifted the tequila to his left hand, bent over, and with his right took a packaged shirt out of one of the opened boxes. He stood up with a pink men's long-sleeve in his right hand and the booze in his left. "Wrinkle f... free. Athletic fit. Size s... seventeen." He drew his arm back and whipped the package at his old man like a Frisbee.

Frank caught it with both hands. Set it on the couch. "Son. Why don't you settle down? Take a nap. I'll order that pizza."

Trip took another drink of tequila and pulled a blue-and-white-striped shirt out of the box. "Size s... s... sixteen. Cotton-poly b... blend." Tossed it at his pa. The package hit him flat in the face.

"Stop!" the old man yelled, throwing the shirt to the floor.

Trip set down the tequila. Took out the straight-edge, opened it. Saw his pa's eyes widen.

"Afraid I'm gonna c... cut you, old man?" He laughed and bent over. Cut the tape on one of the sealed boxes. Closed the knife and shoved it back in his right pants pocket. Pulled open the cardboard flaps and took out a white shirt. Held it up. "Size fifteen. French c... cuffs. Perfect for a n... night on the t... t... town. A favorite with the ladies." He threw it as hard as he could. The corner of the package caught Frank above the left brow. The shirt ricocheted off the old man's head, knocked the coffee cup off the TV tray and landed on the floor. Frank felt something warm trickling down his face but was afraid to get up. Afraid what his son would do if he tried to leave the room. Hands shaking, he wrapped his right fist around the neck of the Jim Beam and raised the bottle to his mouth. He took a drink and set it down between his legs.

By the time he was finished, Sweet Justice Trip had hurled 183 polybagged dress shirts at his pa. They were all over the couch and on the floor at the old man's feet. Frank sat motionless on the couch. Blood on his face, fear in his eyes, a polybagged size seventeen blue oxford shirt in his lap.

31

Duncan finally got his big, dramatic scene in the office, and it was at her expense. Sandeen pulled Murphy aside Thursday afternoon. Told her she had grounds to file a complaint. "That personal shit is way out of line." They stood whispering by the watercooler. Duncan had kept his office door closed all morning, but opened it after lunch. Every so often he looked out the door.

"Want to forget about it. If I filed, we'd have a tough time working together." Her real fear was that Duncan would tell their superiors about her role in the doctor's suicide. "I hate to say it, but I want him with me Saturday night."

Sandeen pulled a paper cup out of the dispenser and filled it with water. "I could do it." He took a sip. With his other hand, he ran his fingers through his white hair. Smiled. "You could tell your old high school pals you like older men."

She laughed. "Appreciate it, but he's up to speed on this case. I'm not gonna let his big mouth blow it."

"Fine." He downed the water and tossed the cup in the wastebasket. "But if that asshole gives you any more grief, I want to know about it."

"You will," she said.

"Now I hope I'm not out of line here." He touched her left arm with his right hand. "I'm sorry about you and Jack."

"Thanks. I'm sorry you had to hear about it the way you did. And for the record, Jack did the dumping." She looked across the room and saw Duncan watching her through his office door. She turned her back to him and continued talking to Sandeen.

Later that afternoon, she sat down at a computer and did a Google search using Justice Trip's name, to see what would come up. She found some online newspaper articles she hadn't read before, including stuff from the Eau Claire *Leader-Telegram*. The story was a rehash of Trip's brush with fame in that community, recalling how his volunteer efforts helped police find a missing girl. She got to the end of the piece and was ready to exit out of the site when she noticed the newspaper's seven-day archives at the bottom of the page. She scanned the list of headlines to see if there was anything else on Trip. A headline about an old hit-and-run case caught her eye. She called up the story, a short piece about how the Eau Claire County Sheriff's Office was still trying to solve the crime. A father of four was struck and killed on a dark country road. He was walking home from a local bar. Like Bunny Pederson, thought Murphy. No witnesses. No vehicle description. No suspects. From the magnitude of injuries, the cops thought it was a truck. Again, like Pederson. Murphy noted the date of the accident and went back to the story on Trip. Checked when Trip found the girl's necklace in the cornfield. Went back to the article on the old hit-and-run case, to make sure she was reading it correctly. Yes. Trip was in the area at the time of the fatal accident. Maybe *accident* wasn't the right word, she thought. Was the father of four another one of Trip's victims? At the bottom of the story was a link to the Eau Claire County Sheriff's Office. She clicked on it and saw a summary of the case under the heading *Detective News*. At the end of the summary: *If you have any information, even if you think it may be insignificant, please call Sgt. Vern Gilbert.* She picked up the phone and punched in the number. Got Gilbert's voice mail. Left a message. Hung up. Put the cursor on the Print icon and clicked.

She went home from work with the printout of the Eau Claire website and the stack of tire tread pictures Castro had printed off the digital camera. She thought about calling Erik for copies of the tire tread cast and fingerprints, but she was afraid she'd start venting about Duncan. She didn't want to give Erik the satisfaction. Didn't want to admit he could have been right.

She resented that Duncan had dragged her and her home life into one of his door-slamming displays, but she figured it was just a play for attention. Public dramatics. She dismissed his criticism of Erik and his praise of Jack. He didn't know either one of them well enough to have meaningful insight. He had no idea what they were like off the job. She couldn't so easily write off Duncan's opinion of the doctor's suicide. Right after it happened that summer, she told herself it was self-defense. The murderer had her own gun trained on her. Told her he intended to rape and kill her. She had to do something. Talking him into suicide was the same as struggling over the weapon and winning. Shooting the bad guy before he shot her. As time went on, she had had doubts. Had she made a horrible mistake? Gabe had tried to reassure her she'd saved the taxpayers some money. If he really believed that, why had he confided in Duncan? She considered calling Gabe and then talked herself out of it. She was a big girl. She didn't need to keep leaning on someone else. But she wanted to know why he told Duncan. She fell asleep on her bed with the phone in her hand, still undecided.

Murphy didn't go into the cop shop Friday. She called Duncan's number in the morning and left a terse message on his voice mail: "I'm working the case at home today. Be here at seven tomorrow night." She hung up before she added what she really wanted to say: "Go fuck yourself."

She checked the clock on her nightstand. Too early to call Martin Porter, her buddy at Public Safety. She'd left a message for him Thursday. Wanted to run some questions by him about pedestrian traffic deaths.

She got out of bed, walked to the bathroom, reached inside the stall and turned on the water. Ice cold. She waited. Put her hand under again. A little warmer. She dropped her nightgown on the floor and stepped into the shower. Shivered in the lukewarm spray. Could it be she needed to turn up the temp on the water heater? No, she thought. Too easy. With her luck, the thing needed to be replaced. In between calls on the case she'd search the Yellow Pages. Did Erik know anything about plumbing? Doubtful. Like Jack, he probably preferred paying someone else to do it. She squirted some shampoo on top of her head and worked her hair into a lather. In the middle of rinsing, the water turned icy. She held her head under it as long as she could and frantically scrubbed to get all the soap out. Teeth chattering, she shut off the water. Stepped out. She had a cold headache. She pulled a towel off the bar and wrapped it around her shaking body. Grabbed another towel and rubbed her head. Thought she heard ringing. Was it in her frozen head? She stopped rubbing. More ringing; it was real. She dropped the towel wrapped around her body, yanked the bathrobe off the door hook and pulled it on. She wrapped the other towel around her head and twisted it into a turban. Ran into the bedroom while she tied her bathrobe belt. Where had she tossed the phone this time? Not on the nightstand. Not on the dresser. She pulled the bedspread back and found it under the sheets. She picked it up.

Porter: "Since when do you give a shit about pedestrians? They demoting you to traffic or what?"

"Marty, Marty, Marty. Why would sending me to traffic be a demotion? You have a serious self-esteem problem, my friend." Murphy liked teasing Porter. He was a cynical numbers guy in the Minnesota Department of Public Safety's Office of Traffic Safety. He wrote reports about accident prevention and continued to pilot his Harley at the speed of light, and without a helmet.

"You sound crabby. Am I getting you out of bed?" he asked. "I know how you homicide dicks keep bankers' hours while the rest of us are up early, doing real work. Want me to call back when you wake up, like at noon?"

She sat down on the edge of her bed. Pulled off the turban. Ran her fingers through her wet hair with one hand and held the phone with the other. "Shut up a minute. Let me do the talking. I want to run something by you, but first give me some answers to a couple of questions. Traffic-type questions."

"Traffic-type questions. I live for those. One second. Let me grab the latest edition of the Bible."

She got off the bed and went to her dresser for a comb. Went back to the bed and sat down again. "Which Bible is that?" She switched the phone to her left hand and with her right hand, started pulling the comb through her tangles.

"The only one in this office. *Minnesota Motor Vehicle*

Crash Facts." She heard paper shuffling. "Okay," he said. "Fire away."

"How many pedestrians are killed each year in Minnesota?"

"Way too easy. Don't even need the book for that. Last few years it's ranged from the low forties to the high fifties."

"We could say about fifty each year." She tossed the comb on her nightstand.

"Fifty. Yeah. That works."

"Who are these people? What can you tell me about them? Anything?"

"Actually, I can tell you quite a bit. People younger than twenty-five account for a big chunk of those killed. Guys are more likely to get flattened than gals. Am I boring you yet?"

"You never bore me, Marty." She switched the phone to her right hand. "Keep rolling."

"Fine. Let me know when you've had enough. While most of the fatalities are in urban areas, a decent percentage—better than a quarter—are in rural areas."

"Stop," she said. The newspaper stories about Trip said he worked as a traveling salesman servicing small towns in Minnesota and Wisconsin. "What do you mean by 'rural' exactly? That includes small towns, right?"

"We're talking small-town Minnesota. Communities with less than five thousand folks."

"Okay. How are most killed? What I mean is, what are they doing when they're nailed? Jogging along the side of the road? In a crosswalk pushing a baby stroller? Standing in the middle of the street?"

He sighed. "Ah. The myth of the blameless pedestrian. About a third of those killed were trying to cross a road where they *shouldn't* have been crossing."

"Meaning?"

"No signal. No crosswalk."

She sat back against the bed pillows, put her feet up and tucked her toes under the bed linen. "I suppose I shouldn't be surprised."

"No. But this next thing is moderately interesting. Of those killed who were tested for booze—and most are tested—more than a quarter had concentrations of alcohol over the legal driving limit."

Murphy thought about Bunny Pederson, drunk when she left the wedding reception. The father of four in Eau Claire had left a bar before he was hit. "Walking while intoxicated," she said.

"Probably more like stumbling while intoxicated," he said. "I heard a story about this one poor bastard. Driving drunk. Ran out of gas. Started walking. Passed out in the middle of the highway. He was wearing black clothes. A tuxedo, I think. So many cars ran over him, the State Patrol had trouble figuring out—"

"Enough," she said. "We're veering off course here."

"Trying to give you a little flavor is all. Is this what you want?"

"Yes and no."

"What are you looking for, Murphy? What's going on?"

"Let me ask you this, and it might be out of your area, so if you can't answer, that's cool."

"Want me to make up shit? I can make up shit if you want. I'm really good at it. Ask my wife."

"No. Don't make up shit. What happens when people, when drivers, hit pedestrians? Do they stop? Do they keep going? If they freak and keep going, are they usually caught later? Does someone usually see them? Get a license plate? How hard is it to get away with it?"

"I'm talking off the top of my head here. I don't have anything in front of me that supports this. But I think

298

people usually stop; it's damn stupid not to. If you flee, you can get in a hell of a lot more trouble. Do some dummies keep going? Sure. Are they always caught? No. Since time began, there have been cases of fatal hit-and-run accidents without suspects and without clues. Happens all over the state. Hell, all over the fucking world."

"What if it's not an accident. How hard would it be for someone to do it on purpose and get away with it?"

"On purpose? Depends. They hit someone they know?"

"No. A stranger. For the sake of argument, let's say he hits a stranger."

He paused. "Okay, this is more good stuff off the top of my brilliant noggin. We all know it's a lot easier to get away with murder if you kill someone you don't know. Could be even easier if you're in a car. You're already in your getaway vehicle."

"Yeah," she said. "You've saved a step right there."

"Yeah. But you still have to be clever about it. Pick the right road. Drive a big mother vehicle. Do it at night. Watch out for witnesses. It would help if you knew what you were doing, had some practice. A professional hit man." He paused and then started laughing. "Get it? Hit man?"

"He's clever," she said more to herself than to Porter. "And he's had lots of practice."

"What? Who are you talking about?"

She posed the question her mind had been dancing around: "What if one man was responsible for a number of these cases in Minnesota and Wisconsin over the last, I don't know, ten or fifteen or eighteen years? What if the reason there were no suspects or clues is because he's gotten really good at it? Really practiced?"

Murphy pressed the phone to her ear. Waited anxiously for an answer or a reaction. Wanted to know how nuts her theory sounded. Finally Porter asked, "What are you thinking? Some sort of serial hit-and-run killer? Jesus. Someone would have noticed the numbers jump, connected the dots."

"Not if the deaths were spread out over the years."

"You're scaring me here, lady. Have you got someone in mind? Some evidence?"

"I don't have spit yet. Just some wild ideas."

"You gonna pull those old cases? Look for a pattern?" He sounded excited.

"I'm not at that stage yet. I don't want to sound any alarms until I have more. Keep this call off the record, okay, Marty?"

"Sure thing. That is fucking scary, man. If it's true." He paused. Murphy expected him to say it couldn't possibly be true. Instead: "Let me know if you want some help going over those records."

She pulled on some jeans and a sweatshirt and a pair of wool socks. She always found the best part about working at home was wearing rags while sounding professional over the phone. She went down to the galley, put a filter and coffee in the coffeepot basket. Poured in some water. Turned on the pot. She opened the door to the dock and scanned the expanse of gray boards. No newspaper. She was about to shut the door when she noticed a neatly folded paper in front of the door, right under her nose.

"They finally hit the mark," she said. She bent over and picked it up. Took it inside and slapped it on the kitchen table. She went over to the pot and poured herself a cup of coffee. Sat down and unfolded the newspaper. The cell phone rang on the counter. She got up and retrieved it. Sat down and answered it. "Yeah."

"Detective Murphy? Sergeant Vern Gilbert. Eau Claire County Sheriff's Office." He sounded like an older officer.

"Great. Thanks for calling back." She pushed the kitchen chair away from the table and put her feet up on another chair.

"This your home number? Hope I didn't drag you out of bed."

"No. No. Sitting down with my coffee and the paper. Speaking of the newspaper, that's what inspired me to call you. I saw something online in the *Leader-Telegram* about this unsolved hit-and-run. Went to your website."

"Hard case. The wife still lives in the area. Supermarket cashier. It's been a struggle for her. She almost lost the house. He didn't have life insurance of course. She says the toughest part is not knowing who did it. Wondering if it was a neighbor. Makes her look twice at everybody going through the checkout line."

"Sounds like you guys have done a good job of staying in touch with her. That's something."

"Your heart goes out. You know how it is. Anyways, you've seen enough I'm sure."

"Yeah. Seen enough is right."

"Anyways, you got something for us?"

"Maybe," she said. She paused, not knowing how much to tell him. An older cop might not buy into it, might write her off as flakey.

He sensed her hesitation. "Didn't you pick up on that tone of desperation from our website? We'll take anything. The case is colder than shit."

She felt sorry for him, and for the widow. "Fine. I'm gonna spill my guts on this thing, but you've got to keep it quiet. It's this wild theory I'm playing with and maybe if I lay it all out for you, it'll shake something loose in your mind."

"Let 'er rip," he said. "Both barrels."

"Remember that Justice Trip? The one who found the little girl's necklace?" He didn't answer; only silence on his end of the phone. Murphy wondered if they'd been disconnected. "Hello? Sergeant? You still there?"

"Fuck," he said. "I knew it. That spooky son of a bitch."

She pulled her feet off the kitchen chair and sat straighter. Held the phone tighter. "You were looking at him for this?"

"Damn right I was. Nothing to base it on but my gut and a cracked windshield."

"That sounds more than a little intriguing. You show me yours and I'll show you mine."

He laughed. "I've fallen for that one before. I'm a sucker. Anyways, here goes. This tall, spooky goof rolls into town, gets dragged into a volunteer search party. And I mean dragged. Whines like a big baby the whole time. I remember it well. 'It's t... too h... hot. Corn's t... too high. There's t... t... too many b... b... bugs.' He stutters you know."

"I noticed," Murphy said. She took a sip of coffee.

"Anyways, he lucks out and finds the kid's jewelry while he's bending over to tie his shoelaces. The media makes a big deal out of it. Makes him into Superman, and he eats it up. Somebody even gives him a fucking trophy. Wish somebody would give me a fucking trophy. In the middle of the circus, we get this hit-and-run. Then I notice. The hero has got a crack in his windshield that wasn't there the day before. I ask him about it. One of his dumb-ass fans, one of our local do-gooders, says, 'Oh, no. That's been there all along.' Stands up for the joker. Gets some others to say the same thing. One even gives me some bullshit about spending most of the night with him, showing him the town. I know that's a lie. The goof is not a social butterfly."

"They all cover for him?" She bumped off her coffee and stood up to pour another cup.

"I don't even know if they realized what they were doing. They were all swept up in the excitement. The reporters and cameras bopping all over town. I think they didn't want anything to mess it up."

"Are you shittin' me?"

"I shit you not. Swear to God. You gotta love that citizen involvement. Anyways, I talk to the sheriff and he tells me to forget it. Says the big guy can't be our man if all these people saw the crack there before, and if he's got an alibi for that night. Plus he didn't have dick on his record. I let it go, but reluctantly. My gut says he was involved."

She stood at the counter and refilled her cup. Took it back to the table and sat down again. "I think your gut is right on."

"Anyways, your turn. Show me yours, and don't be shy about it."

She took a sip of coffee. "You been reading the papers on this Moose Lake deal?"

"Yeah. Noticed the big hero jumped in again. Found the gal's finger. Guess once you get a taste of fame, you gotta come back for more. Anyways, they find the rest of her yet? I haven't been keeping up with it."

"They found her body in the state park up there."

"Too bad. Cause of death?"

"Looks like she got hit by a truck."

A long pause, then: "The hero?"

"That's what I'm thinking." She downed her second cup of coffee and stood up. Went over to the counter with the cup and poured a third. She was wired and she didn't know if it was the caffeine or the conversation. Regardless, she didn't mind the feeling.

303

"Wait a minute here," he said. "Are you thinking he hit her and then fixed it so he'd find the finger? So he could be Superman all over again? Get another fifteen minutes?"

She leaned her back against the counter with the cup in her hand. "Yup." She knew he'd have the most trouble wrapping his mind around that part of it.

"On purpose? So you're thinking he hit her on purpose?"

"Yeah." She sipped. Set the cup down. Walked back and forth in front of the counter with the cell phone pressed to her ear.

"That is one hell of a theory. Man." He paused and then said, "If that's the case, it really makes me wonder . . ." His voice trailed off.

She stopped pacing and picked up the cup again. "Wonder if he did your victim on purpose?"

"Yeah." Another brief silence while the idea sunk in, and then anger. "Bastard. Sick son of a bitch. Are you looking at him for any others?"

"Possibly. I've got some ideas. A buddy at Public Safety is ready to help me sift through old cases."

"If there's anything I can do on the Wisconsin end, let me know. Pulling records. Making calls. Whatever. I want a piece of this. I'd love to hang that spooky Superman by his fucking cape."

32

Spooky Superman passed out facedown on the front room floor Thursday night and woke Friday morning with a hangover. He raised his head and saw all the boxes and shirts around him and briefly wondered why they were there. When it came back to him, he groaned and set his head back down on the rug with a thud. "Fuck," he muttered into the carpet. He smelled that urine smell again in the rug and rolled over onto his back. Stared up at the ceiling. Noticed some water stains. Something was in his right pants pocket, jabbing his leg. He reached down and slid his hand inside. His straight-edge razor. He'd used it to open the boxes. At least he'd remembered to close it before shoving it in his pants. He pulled his hand out and threw his forearm over his eyes. He heard his old man bumping around the kitchen with his cane. Heard him talking. Trip's body stiffened. Was there someone else in the trailer? Had Paris Murphy come back to arrest him? He held his breath and listened. No. His pa was on the phone. He rolled back onto his stomach, cocked his head toward the kitchen and strained to hear the words.

"No. I ain't seen her since she left our place Tuesday."

His pa stopped talking, apparently listening to someone on the other end. Then: "That's what she told us, too. Yeah. Yeah. That's right. Sorry. Don't know his name." Another pause. "Don't know that neither. My guess is he picked her up 'cause her car is still parked in front of her trailer." A break again and then something that, at least for the moment, restored Trip's faith in his pa's loyalty: "I seen him hanging around her place before. Short, round fellow. Big ears. Walks with a limp." He laughed. "That's a good one. I don't know what he sees in her neither." He stopped talking, listened again. Finally: "That's all I know. Sorry can't be more help. Guess you'll have to get by without her this weekend."

Trip heard his father hang up the phone. He crawled to his feet. His head was pounding. He lifted his right hand and pressed his palm against his forehead, as if that could stop the thumping. It didn't. He weaved around the obstacle course of boxes and packaged shirts. Walked into the kitchen. His old man was sitting at the kitchen table, a cup of coffee and an ashtray in front of him and a cigarette between his fingers. To his right was a spent insulin syringe and needle. Trip saw a Band-Aid on his pa's left brow. That's where a package had cut him; Trip was hoping that memory from the night before was part of a bad dream. His old man looked up at Trip. "That was a fucking close one." He tipped his head toward the phone on the kitchen wall. "Know who that was?" Trip shrugged his shoulders. "Take a fucking guess." He took a drag off his Lucky Strike.

"Keri's w... work?"

He exhaled. "Damn straight. They're short. They want her to pull some extra shifts this weekend. They know we were her last stop Tuesday, and they know we live down the street from her. Guess who saved your ass?" Trip opened his mouth to answer but his old man didn't give him a chance. "Your pa, that's who." He picked up his coffee and took a sip.

Trip crossed the kitchen floor, took a mug down from the cupboard. Recognized it as the one Paris Murphy had sipped tea from. He shuddered and put it back, took a different one. Poured himself a cup of coffee. Noticed the pot on the counter was already half empty. His old man had been up awhile. Would have had plenty of time to call the cops. What did they call it? *Senior abuse.* His old man could have reported him for *senior abuse.* Did he? Would the police be knocking before he finished his coffee? Trip took a sip and stared at his pa.

"Why you looking at me like that?" asked his old man. "You got no call to look at me like that. I saved your hairy backside."

Trip took another sip. The coffee was strong and bitter and burned. Tasted like it had been cooking on the warmer for hours. He dumped the rest of it down the drain and set the cup in the sink. "Like what? How am I l... looking at you?"

"Like a dog that's been kicked for doing nothing."

Trip leaned his back against the counter and crossed his arms over his chest. "I ain't l... looking at you any which way. You're n... nuts."

"Oh, *I'm* nuts. That's funny coming from you." His pa raised his left hand and touched the Band-Aid with his fingertips. "How's your throwing arm this morning? Huh, son?"

Trip lowered his eyes. "I'm s... sorry about that. Didn't m... mean to get all w... wild and drunk like that. Was b... bummed out over g... g... getting fired."

His old man tapped a tube of ash into the ashtray. "I'm bummed out, too." He put the cigarette to his lips and

307

inhaled. Exhaled as he continued. "Don't see me throwing stuff all over the house. Throwing shit at you. Speaking of which, why don't you clean up that mess you made during that fit of yours? Do something with those goddamn shirts."

Trip looked up. "We could divide them up. Each get half."

His pa took a long pull and blew smoke in his son's direction. "What am I gonna do with all those shirts? I don't hardly leave the house. Far as you're concerned, ninety-nine percent of them shirts don't fit your monkey arms."

Trip cracked a small smile. "How about a garage s... sale? Buy one, g... g... get one f... free?"

His old man crushed the stub of his cigarette in the ashtray. "Brilliant idea," he said dryly. "First off, how many folks in this trailer park have cause to wear dress shirts? Hmmm? How many of them got suit-and-tie jobs? Not too damn many. Otherwise they wouldn't be living in this dump."

"I l... live here and I got a s... suit-and-tie job."

"Past tense. You *had* a suit-and-tie job." His pa bumped off the remainder of his coffee. "Secondly, do you think it's a good thing to have folks coming by the trailer? Sneaking around and peeking around? You forget what we got in the back bedroom? We got to keep a low profile. Garage sale. Jesus H. Christ." His pa snickered. "How s... s... s... stupid can you g... g... get?"

Trip's jaw tightened. The echoes of school-yard taunts filled his head. He couldn't believe his own pa had made fun of his stutter. He'd never done that before, at least not to Trip's face. He'd always told him it didn't matter and that anybody who teased him was trash. They'd get theirs, he told Trip. *What goes around comes around.* How often had he heard that from his old man when he was growing up?

Didn't it mean anything anymore? Had it ever meant anything?

His pa got up from the table, turned his back on Trip and started to cross the kitchen floor. Trip took two steps toward him. "Don't t... turn your b... back on me, old man. Don't call me s... s... stupid neither."

His pa turned and glared at him.

Trip continued. "You g... got balls making fun of the way I talk. You c... could of g... got me help when I was a little k... kid and you didn't. The way I talk is your f... fault."

"So now it comes out. You blame me." He rested his left hand on the cane and with his right pointed a finger at Trip as if he were correcting a child. "I told you before. It runs in the family. Ain't my doing. Ain't nothing to be done about it."

"That's a l... lie. You're lying. Who s... s... stuttered in our family? Who?"

"Your sister." A grin stretched across his old man's face. "Of course, she did manage to fix it towards the end of her life. So maybe there is hope."

Trip's mouth dropped open. "End of her l... l... life?"

"As long as we're unloading, I might as well tell you. She's dead."

"My sister? My sister is d... dead? I never g... got to know her and she's dead?"

"You got to know her, all right. Know her and then some." His pa smiled a sick smile. "Like I got to know her."

Trip stepped backward until he felt the counter behind him. He needed to touch something solid because he sensed the rest of his world was dissolving. "What are you s... saying, old m... man?"

His pa's eyes narrowed. "You know damn well what I'm saying."

Trip's face whitened. "No." He pressed his back harder against the kitchen counter.

"Yeah, you do." His pa took a step toward him. "Like you, I have appetites. Only difference is I like to keep it in the family. That's why your bitch ma run off." Frank rested both hands on the handle of his cane. His posture and voice took on that of a kindly old storyteller, but the tale he recounted was horrific and real. "Your ma knew what was going on in your sister's bedroom, but she didn't say nothing. How could she? Shit. Mary was my daughter, too. I could do what I wanted. But when you were born, that was the last straw. Anna was praying for another girl and she got you. Said she didn't want to live under the same roof with another Trip male. Not even her own son. She couldn't stand the sight of you. She packed up Mary and took off. No loss. Wasn't much of a wife anyway. Couldn't cook worth a damn. Lousy in the sack." He smiled. "Not like Mary."

Trip's fists tightened at his sides. "You slept with your own d... daughter. My poor sister. How could you? Sick b... bastard."

"You're one to talk. Let me tell you something, boy. Anna only left because she was afraid you were going to hit on Mary, too." His pa paused to let that sink in. "As it turns out, she was right."

What was his old man saying? Suddenly it hit him like a punch in the gut. Trip realized who he'd slept with more than twenty years ago. He wrapped his arms around his stomach and folded onto the floor. Slowly. A giant melting down to a midget. "I d... didn't know. I wouldn't have d... done it if I knew." He wished he would lose his mind. Pass out. Black out. Anything to banish the image from his mind. His body tangled with hers.

His old man stepped closer. Jabbed him once in the side

with the tip of his cane. "That's right, boy. We're both sick bastards." Frank stood over him. The storyteller kept weaving his tale. "I didn't know what she was up to when she come back after all those years with that made-up name. Cammie Lammont. Stupid name. Those fancy clothes. Thought maybe she wanted to get a look at her little brother. Reconnect with family. She asked me to keep my mouth shut about the past and I told her I would. Figured I owed her that much."

Trip curled up into a ball on his side. Shielded his face with his arms. He didn't want to look at his pa anymore, but he continued listening to his old man's voice. The story wasn't over.

"Then one night we're working at the shop, the two of us. She's got Elvis cranked so loud on the tape player I can't hear myself think. 'Viva Las Vegas.' She's bopping and swaying those hips of hers. Teasing hips. I turn it down and tell her to knock it off. One last customer might come in. She stops dancing. Gives me this weird look. Goes to the door. Locks it. Walks back to the register where I'm going over the receipts. I'm in the middle of counting the quarters when she tells me. Says it ever so casual, like she's telling me we run out of snow globes and backscratchers and we have to reorder. She's sleeping with you. You. Her brother."

There. His pa said it out loud: Trip had slept with his sister. Hearing his old man say it jolted him. Forced him to uncurl his body. He wiped his eyes with his shaking hands and crawled to his feet. Turned his back on his father and clutched the edge of the kitchen sink, afraid he would fold again. He wished that he could puke. Wished that the single act of vomiting would somehow send the filth of his teenage sin down the kitchen drain. He heard the neighbor's wind chimes tinkling. He stared out the window. The scrawny tree was being buffeted by the breeze, losing the last of its leaves. He longed to be one of those leaves. A dead thing floating away on the wind. His pa kept talking.

"I can't look at her I'm so mad. I look at this handful of silver in my fist. She keeps jabbering. Says she's gonna walk home. Gonna tell you she's your sister. Then she's gonna grab her suitcase and leave. Mess up your life the way I messed up hers. She walks to the door, unlocks it and walks out."

Trip bent his head down. Stared into the sink. Stained and dirty. Like the ceiling. Like his life. "You d... did it? Those quarters they f... found next to her. Your quarters from the t... t... till."

"Bet your ass."

"All these years I h... had an idea in my h... head of who did it. The ones who r... ran her over, I thought they were mean t... teenagers. Mean kids from around t... t... town. Jealous k... kids."

"Jealousy killed her all right," his pa said. His voice was so low it was almost lost in the wind chimes. "Not the kind you imagined. Was your pa's jealousy."

Trip raised his eyes to the window. One leaf left on the scrawny tree. Another gust of wind and it was gone. He turned to face his old man. They stood a foot apart. He asked in a voice barely above a whisper: "You mean you didn't k... kill Cammie to p... p... protect me?"

His old man's brows went up. "What?" He paused for a moment, confused. Then he threw his head back and laughed. "Son. Son. You a piece of work. Protect you? Hell no. I was jealous. Mary finally come back and she's sleeping with you instead of me." Frank turned his back to his son and headed toward the front room.

Trip gasped. No honor left for him to cling to, not even

312

the idea that his father had killed to protect him. Nothing clean remaining in his life story. His pa was a pervert. His ma never wanted him. His sister was his first lover. He couldn't breathe. The sound of rushing water filled his head. He was drowning right there in the kitchen. Suffocating in a shitty trailer parked on the edge of a cold city. Over the din in his head and the tinkle of the wind chimes in his ears, Trip could make out his pa's voice floating from the front room.

"Clean up this junk before I fall and kill myself."

Kill. The only word Sweet Justice Trip understood. He reached into his right pants pocket and pulled out his straight-edge. Flipped it open and held it behind his back. Walked into the front room, crushing boxes and shirts beneath his bare feet as he went. His old man was standing in front of the TV, squinting to see which western was on the screen.

El Dorado. Sheriff Robert Mitchum is hunkered down in the jail with his deputies.

Frank took a step closer to the set. "Damn," he muttered. "It's almost over."

Bullets pound the jail.

Justice Trip crept behind his pa and wrapped his left arm around the old man's chest. Frank dropped his cane and reached up with both hands to pull his son's arm off him. He said in a calm, firm voice, the voice he used when he was giving orders to his son: "No, Sweet." Then frightened: "No!"

Injured John Wayne falls through the jailhouse door.

Trip whipped his right arm around, pressed the razor hard against his father's neck and pulled it across his throat in one left-to-right motion. The blood spurted out. Like water from a garden hose when there's a thumb over the nozzle. His pa jerked and made a gurgling noise. Trip backed up and let his old man fall to the floor in front of the television set.

Bad guy Ed Asner is released from his jail cell and steps around John Wayne's writhing figure to walk out the door, a free man.

33

For an instant, Trip felt as if the straight-edge burned in his hand. He dropped it on the rug. Expected to see it glowing red and setting fire to the rug. He looked down at the knife. Cold metal against the carpet. Nothing more. He checked his right palm. No blisters or burns. He'd imagined it. Stop imagining stuff, he told himself. Trip looked down at the body. "Pa?" Trip said in a low voice. The voice he used when he was trying to wake his old man and get him up off the couch for dinner. "Pa?" He waited. Expected his old man to sit up and tell him to clean up the mess. A third try: "Pa?" He went down on his knees next to the body. Bent his head. Covered his face with his hands. He stayed on his knees until they were numb. He kept his face covered and, behind his fingers, his eyes shut tight. He couldn't look at what he'd done. He was guilty. More than that, he was afraid of being left alone. He'd lived thirty-six years with this one human being. Frank Trip was cruel. Demanding. Abusive. A drunk. A molester and a murderer. He was all Trip ever had, and now he was gone. Slowly, Trip lowered his hands from his face. He breathed in and out twice and opened his eyes. Looked at his father's chest.

It wasn't moving. Why wasn't it moving? Trip fell forward and buried his face in his father's bloody flannel shirt and wept. He looked like a man prostrate in worship. The two-word prayer he uttered into his father's chest: "Pa, p... p... please."

By the time he was all cried out, Trip couldn't tell how much of the wetness on his face was from the tears, and how much was from the blood. He raised his head off his father's chest and sat back on his heels. Wiped the moisture from his cheeks with the hem of his tee shirt. Noticed blood on his tee shirt. He yanked it off and used it to wipe his face again. Dropped it in a ball at his father's side. The television was still on. Trip couldn't tell if the gun battle was from *El Dorado* or if he'd been crying so long another movie had started. He rose to his feet. Stepped around his pa and shut off the set. Saw there was blood on the screen and on the wall behind the set. It looked as if someone had taken a bucket of red paint and thrown it. Even tiny spatters on the window blinds to the left of the television. The windows! The slats on the blinds were open. His instincts kicked in; if nothing else, his father had taught him self-preservation came before everything. Trip stepped up to the window. Peeked through the blinds. The street in front of the house was empty. He lifted the blinds away from the wall and checked the window. No blood on the window. He set the blinds back against the window and closed the slats tight. Trip turned and looked down at the still body. Pool of blood collecting under his head and neck. More red paint. His pa had landed on his back with his knees up. The way Keri had fallen in the shower. "What goes around comes around," Trip muttered tiredly. He knelt down next to the body, this time not in prayer but out of curiosity. Was

316

his old man really gone? He picked up his pa's right wrist with his left hand and felt for a pulse with his right fingertips. Nothing. He dropped the wrist. It made a soft, heavy sound when it hit the rug. A dead bird hitting the ground. He studied his old man's face. So gray. Was it that gray before, or was death draining his cheeks? The eyes wide open. Surprised. Trip knew he didn't have any change in his own pockets. He carefully slipped his right hand into his old man's right pants pocket. Still warm in the pocket. Trip extracted a handful of coins. Dimes and nickels. He picked out one of each and set them on the rug next to the body and shoved the rest of the change in his own pants pocket. He reached up and pulled down his pa's right lid with his right forefinger. He picked up a dime with his left thumb and forefinger and set the coin on the lid. He pulled down the left lid and set the nickel on it. He stared at the silver for a few seconds. The coins seemed to be holding. He picked up the straight-edge and studied the blade. Not as much blood on it as he thought there'd be. He closed it and stood up. Shoved it back in his right pocket.

He didn't want to mop up the mess yet. Didn't want to touch the body until it had turned cool. All he wanted to do was get clean. He stumbled over the boxes and shirts and went into the bathroom. Peeled off his pants and boxers and kicked them into a corner. He grabbed the Lava from the edge of the sink. He pushed open the shower door, reached into the stall and turned on the water. Didn't bother feeling for the temperature. Stepped in and shut the door. Hot. He started with his head and worked his way down. Didn't care what the pumice did to his hair or his skin. Clean. He needed clean. He started crying again when he got to his knees, but he kept scrubbing his skin with the bar of soap. He stood on his left foot and ran the

317

Lava back and forth over the bottom of his right foot. Then he switched and stood on his right foot while he rubbed his left sole. He dropped the bar on the shower floor and stood up. Bent his head under the spray. His body felt hot and raw. He reached over and turned the shower all the way to cold. Shivered while the water soothed the burn. He'd finally stopped crying, this time for good. He shut off the water. Ran his hands over his scalp to squeeze out the water. He studied his hands. No black strands this time. He looked down. The shower floor was covered with black hair. His baldness would be his father's legacy to him. He wondered what sort of monster he and Cammie would have produced had he impregnated her. Horrible thought. He shook his head until he was dizzy. Wanted to put it out of his mind. He had to clean up the big fucking mess in the front room. Think about that, he told himself. He stepped out of the shower, pulled a towel off the bar, rubbed his head. The towel smelled of mildew. He remembered he had clean towels and clothes in the garbage bags in his bedroom. He wrapped the towel around his waist and then took it off. Dropped it on the floor. His old man was dead. No one to yell at him for being naked. He went to his bedroom, dug around in the garbage bag. It smelled like dryer sheets. He pulled out some boxers. Stepped into them. Decided not to wear anything else as it might get bloody. Then he pulled off the boxers and tossed them on the bed. Figured he might as well clean the house naked.

He went into his pa's bedroom. Yanked the cowboy spread and bronco top sheet off his pa's bed, bunched them up in his arms and carried them into the front room. He dropped them next to his old man's body. "Clean up this mess you made, Pa," Trip muttered. He crouched next to the body, held his pa's head up with his left hand. With his right hand, he twined the sheet around his old man's neck. The coins fell off but the eyes stayed closed. Trip set his pa's head down; his old man looked as if he'd fallen asleep on the carpet while wearing a winter scarf. Trip stood up. Laid the spread flat next to the body. Hooked his arms under his old man's armpits and dragged him onto the middle of the spread. His pa's knees were still up. Trip didn't want to try pressing them down; he was afraid of what would happen. Imagined them cracking or snapping back into the same position, and that would scare the shit out of him. Trip picked up one side of the spread and folded it over his old man and did the same with the other side, creating a lumpy ghost covered with cowboys.

He faced forward and towed the spread behind him, kicking boxes and shirts aside as he went. Dragged it down the hallway. He kneed open the door to the back bedroom and pulled the spread up against the freezer. His old man was a lot lighter than Keri. Skinnier. He figured they'd both fit. Trip dropped the spread, put his right hand on the freezer lid. He'd open it without looking inside. He said out loud, "One. Two. Three." He looked the other way and flipped it open. The lid hit the wall with a bang. Trip could feel the cold air pouring out. He bent down to pick up the cowboy ghost. Decided the spread would take up too much room. He unwrapped his old man. Didn't look at his face. Didn't want to know if the eyes had popped open again. Didn't want to touch his pa's skin or clothes, either. Looking off to the side again, he slipped his arms under the spread and stood up, rolled his pa into the freezer. The body made a strange noise when it landed inside. He'd heard that noise before, when he was throwing fresh meat into the freezer on top of frozen. Something soft hitting something hard. He stepped closer to the freezer, shut his eyes and reached up for the lid.

Pulled it down. "No," he said out loud. "Fuck n... no."
Trip opened his eyes a crack. The lid wouldn't close; there
was a six-inch gap. He could see the top of his pa's knees
poking up. He pressed down on the lid with both hands.
It closed a little more, but there was still a gap. He put his
back against the freezer and rested his hands on the lid, one
on each side of him. He hopped up; his bare butt landed
on the lid with a smack. He felt something give when the
lid came down; he didn't want to think about what might
have broken or cracked inside the chest freezer. He turned
and studied the lid. Closed tight. "Sorry, P... Pa," he said
to the freezer. He bent down, picked up the spread and
carried it out of the bedroom, shutting the door behind
him.

He went back to the front room. Dropped the spread on
the floor. The thing would have to be burned or washed;
there was blood on it. He ran his eyes around the room.
Didn't see any more blood besides what he'd already noted.
How would he ever get the stain out of the carpet and off
the wall? He still had the boxes and shirts to pick up. The
sight exhausted him. Was there anything left in the house
that could energize him? All the pills from Keri's purse
were downers. Stupid stomach pills wouldn't do him any
good. He needed to hang on to those Roofies. Maybe
some music. He walked over to his pa's TV tray for the
remote. He found it sitting next to the Jim Beam. He
picked up the bottle by the neck and raised it to eye level.
Still half full. He unscrewed the cap, put the bottle to his
lips and tipped it upside down. He put it down, took a
breath, brought it to his mouth again and took another
gulp. He set it back on the TV tray. Saw his pa's pack of
cigs. Picked them up. Reached inside. Pulled out a Lucky
Strike. He didn't like smoking, but he needed something in
his mouth. He threw the pack on the tray and put the

cigarette between his lips. Found the lighter. A keepsake from their souvenir shop.

He ran his thumb over the engraved image of Graceland. He missed Tennessee. Nothing keeping him in Minnesota. No job. No woman. No family. He could leave anytime. Tell the neighbors he and his pa were going back home. Hell, he didn't have to tell them anything. They wouldn't care. They didn't like his old man and they only liked him when he worked on their trucks. He'd mop up the trailer real good. He still had jugs of cleaner around from that janitor supplies job. Some of the stuff promised to neutralize blood. Then he'd pile his frozen pa and frozen Keri into the back of the truck. Pull out of town. Let the trailer park take back the mobile home. He could bury his old man and Keri somewhere between St. Paul and Memphis. No one would know. Keri's work would be looking for the phantom boyfriend. Back in Tennessee, there'd be no one keeping tabs on him or his old man. No family left to speak of; his pa had taken care of that. He'd leave from the reunion Saturday night. He still wanted to make it to that. Take care of Paris Murphy. *What goes around comes around.*

He flipped open the lighter, lit up the cigarette. Closed the lighter and tossed it on the tray. Picked up the remote. Held it in his right hand for a moment. He couldn't remember the last time his old man let him touch the thing. The edges were smooth, rounded. It felt comfortable in his hand the way a well-worn wrench or ratchet from his toolbox felt comfortable. Almost as familiar as an old knife handle, but not quite. He turned around, aimed the remote at the set and hit the power button. Another cowboy show. Another shoot-out. He'd never have to watch that crap again. He punched the channel changer until he came to MTV2. Through the blood-spattered

321

screen, he saw Marilyn Manson shrieking and convulsing. His pa would have hated it. He cranked up the volume and dropped the remote on the couch. Decided maybe it wouldn't be so bad without his old man after all.

34

Murphy stared at the photos. "Think there's a match?"

Erik frowned. "If there is, I can't see it."

They sat across from each other at Murphy's kitchen table Friday night. He was in his stocking feet, jeans and a sweater. She was dressed in a tee shirt, sweats and a pair of slippers. The photos were spread out in front of them. All the pictures were printed on computer paper. A dozen of the sheets were the photos Murphy had taken of Trip's truck tires from different angles. One was a photo of the tire track found at Moose Lake State Park. "I don't know," she said. She picked up the photo of the tire track and held it by the edges in her right hand. "It's hard to read this thing. That's the problem. You sure you can't weasel a copy of the cast?"

"I'm lucky I got what I got."

"Who e-mailed it to you?"

"Winter."

"No way," she said. "How'd you get him to cough it up?"

"Told him I needed it for the autopsy report, which I do."

"Sure you do," she said dryly. "What about the finger-prints?"

"I'm working on it," he said.

"Good." She picked up one of her photos with her left hand and held it next to Erik's photo.

He reached across the table and touched her left ring finger with his fingertips. "Why haven't you gotten rid of that thing?"

She dropped both pictures on the table. "*That thing?* My wedding band?" She gripped it instinctively with her right thumb and forefinger. Twisted it back and forth but didn't try to take it off.

"Yeah," he said. "It bothers me. Makes me feel like I'm chasing after a married woman."

"You are," she said. The oven beeped. She got up from the table, pulled an oven mitt off the counter and slipped it over her right hand. She went to the stove. Bent over and opened the oven door. She pulled the oven rack toward her with the mitt.

"Has Jack called since the blowup?"

"No," she said. "I would have told you."

"Then what's going on?"

She checked the thermometer on the roast. "Almost ready." She pushed the rack back in, shut the oven door and stood up. "Nothing's going on."

"Do you have a lawyer yet?"

She leaned her back against the counter and sighed. "Know what? I'm not up for this conversation right now."

"You're never up for it. Don't play with me, Paris." He paused and then said it again. The words she had trouble saying to him: "I love you."

She opened her mouth but had no idea what was going to come out. Not those three words. Something else. A knock at the door. Relieved, she pulled off the mitt, threw it on the counter, walked to the door. "That's gotta be the liquor store."

She pulled open the door and took a step back. "Jack!"

Erik dropped the photo, pushed his chair away from the table and stood up. Turned around. Saw Jack standing in the doorway. Jack looked at him and walked through the door into the kitchen. He didn't shut the door behind him and a wave of cold air followed him into the galley.

"Speak of the devil," said Erik.

Jack looked at his wife and at Erik and then back at his wife. "Figured you two would be together on a Friday night. Smells good. What's for dinner?"

"You're not invited," Erik said. He walked away from the table and stepped in front of Jack. The two men stood a yard apart, facing each other. She smelled alcohol on Jack's breath and saw his eyes were bloodshot. She was afraid for Erik. She was afraid for both men.

"This isn't your house," Jack said. He looked over Erik's shoulder at Murphy. "And that sure as hell isn't your wife."

Murphy slipped between them. Jack was at her left shoulder and Erik at her right. She raised a palm toward each of them. "Back off."

Erik looked past her at Jack. "She's not yours. Not anymore. You dumped her. That makes her a free woman."

"Bullshit." Jack wrapped his right hand around her left wrist and held it up. "What's this, asshole? Looks like a wedding band to me."

"We were talking about losing that," said Erik. He looked at Murphy. "Weren't we?"

Murphy pulled her wrist out of Jack's hand. Looked

from one man to the other. Each was red in the face. Ready to explode. She took a couple of steps back so she was at their sides but not between them anymore. She didn't want to get flattened if fists started flying. She used the calm, low voice she reserved for hysterical crime victims and pumped-up junkies. "This isn't going to happen. Not tonight in my kitchen."

"Tell him, Paris," Erik said. He addressed his words to her but kept glaring at Jack. "Tell him how we were talking about losing that ring and finding you a lawyer and making plans for the future. Tell him."

"I don't believe that," Jack said. "She doesn't give a shit about you. You don't have a future with her."

Erik reached into his right pants pocket and pulled out his key to Murphy's houseboat. Walked up to Jack and held the key in front of his face. An exorcist armed with a crucifix. "Oh yeah? Look into the future. We're moving in together."

Jack snatched the key out of Erik's hand and tossed it over his shoulder. It went through the open kitchen door and landed outside on the dock. "There's your future! Get out, you piece of shit!"

Erik charged toward Jack. Murphy grabbed his left arm to stop him but he pushed her hand off him. He shoved Jack backward through the kitchen door. Jack tripped over the threshold but regained his footing on the deck. Erik followed him outside, stepped up to him and cocked his right arm back. He went for Jack's face. Jack deflected Erik's fist away from him with his left arm and took a swing at Erik with his right. Jack's fist slammed into the left side of Erik's face. Erik went down on his back, sprawled in the middle of the deck. Jack stood over him, fists raised and ready for another punch.

Murphy ran outside. "Stop it!" She crouched down next

to Erik; he was up on one elbow. "Stay down," she said, pressing his chest down with both her hands.

He pushed her hands off him. "Bullshit." He stood up and went after Jack again. Took another right swing and nailed Jack in the left eye before Jack could block him. Jack stumbled backward but didn't go down. Their brawl was working its way to the end of the dock. Murphy stayed with them, fearful one of them would end up in the dark water. Tripod was barking next door. She was sure a neighbor was going to call the cops. Her own address would end up on a police report about a domestic call. Both men went down, rolling around close to the edge. Jack delivered another blow to Erik's face, hitting his nose.

A voice boomed out of the night air: "What the fuck is going on here?" Duncan was walking down the dock, straight for Jack and Erik. He could see the two men fighting, their tangled figures illuminated by the streetlights that dotted the shoreline and by the deck lights on the boats.

Murphy had no idea what he was doing there, but she was happy to see him. Another set of hands to break up the fight. "Duncan," she blurted. "They're going to kill each other."

"Not on my watch," Duncan said. Jack was on top of Erik and had his right arm pulled back to deliver another punch. Duncan bent over and grabbed Jack's right wrist. Erik's nose was bleeding. "Get off him, Jack. You've made your point." Jack tried to pull his arm out of Duncan's grip but Duncan was too strong, and that surprised Murphy. "No," Duncan said.

Jack looked down at Erik with contempt. "Fine," he said. Duncan let go of his wrist. Jack rolled off Erik and stood up. Duncan put his right hand on Jack's shoulder and started walking him off the dock and toward shore.

Erik crawled to his feet and wiped blood from his upper lip with the back of his right hand. Murphy was standing at Erik's side, but couldn't stop looking at Jack as Duncan led him away. A gust of wind made her shiver and wrap her arms around herself. "Let's go back inside," she said, and pulled Erik by the elbow toward the boat. "Get some ice on that nose."

Duncan and Jack stopped next to Jack's Beemer in the parking lot. Duncan folded his arms over his chest. "How drunk are you?"

Jack shoved his hands in his jacket pockets and stared at the ground. "Not drunk enough." He looked up at Duncan and smiled grimly. "A couple of shots after work."

"Doesn't take much when you're already wound up," Duncan said.

Jack leaned his back against the side of his car and stared across the river at the lights twinkling downtown. A view he and his wife had enjoyed while in her bed on the boat. It angered him that Erik had made love to her in the same bed. Taken in that same view of downtown. "I can't believe she slept with that jerk."

"You can fix it," said Duncan. "But fists ain't the way to do it."

"Too late to fix it. I already told her I wanted out. I don't even know why I came back."

Duncan realized he was wrong, that Jack had left her and not the other way around. It made him feel even worse about what he'd said to her. He stumbled to find words for Jack while wrestling with his own guilt. "You came back because you still want her."

"Maybe if that scumbag hadn't been here we could have talked it through. But seeing him with her pisses me off all over again."

"Cool off. Give it a few days and give her a call. Apologize. They love it when you apologize."

Jack sputtered. "Apologize? For what? I'm not the one who fucked around. I don't care if it was one time. Might as well be a hundred."

So Murphy had slipped once—probably in a weak moment when that asshole Mason was ready to leap on it—and now her husband was hanging her for it. Duncan thought Jack should give her another chance; he would if he was married to her. "Just think about it. Sleep on it."

"Sorry you got roped into this. It isn't your problem." Jack touched his left eye; he'd have a shiner. "What are you doing here?"

"I've got to talk to her about a case. Put a steak on that eye when you get home."

"Thanks, Doc."

"Want me to follow you home?"

Jack shook his head. "I'm sober." He dug his keys out of his jacket pocket. Started talking as much to himself as to Duncan. "She hasn't been the same since the summer. Since that maniac banged her up and then killed himself in front of her. It's like that scar on her forehead is more than skin deep."

"It is." Duncan suspected Jack didn't know the whole story and he wasn't going to be the one to tell him. "She's been through a lot. Probably still going through it. She needs you to help her."

"I don't know if I can," Jack said in a low voice. "I wish she'd quit that horseshit job. Who in the hell is nuts enough to like police work, especially homicide?" Jack stopped himself. Mumbled to Duncan, "Sorry. No offense."

"None taken. We're all a little crazy up there, but especially my corner of the asylum." He slapped Jack on the back. "Go home. No bar stops. Straight home."

Jack opened the driver's side of his car, slid inside, put his hand on the door. "Thanks." He slammed it shut.

Duncan watched him pull away and walked back toward the dock. He felt pity for Jack and disdain for Erik. He didn't want to think about what he felt for Murphy; it would complicate everything. Besides, he figured all she felt for him was dislike. Duncan padded down the dock. Saw a key on the boards in front of Murphy's boat. Figured it was hers. He picked it up and shoved it in his jacket pocket. The door was still wide open. Duncan walked through it and shut it behind him. He opened his mouth to announce his presence and heard voices upstairs. Heated talk between Murphy and Erik. He turned to leave but changed his mind. Erik could still be revved up from the fight and he wanted to make sure Murphy was okay. Duncan stood in the galley and waited for someone to come down.

Murphy: "And what was that crap with the key?"
Erik: "What do you mean?"
Murphy: "Waving it in his face like that. You could see he was already losing it."

Duncan slipped his right hand into his jacket pocket and pulled out the key. Studied it. Guessed it was the key they were talking about. He put it on the kitchen counter. Leaned his back against the counter and kept listening.

Erik: "You're taking Jack's side in this. He's the one who barged in."
Murphy: "You and Jack are both assholes. Duncan is the only hero in all this. He kept you idiots from rolling right into the fucking river."

*Erik: "Duncan again. Maybe you should dump me and invite
    him to move in."*

Duncan smiled to himself. Murphy didn't hate him; she
liked him.

*Murphy: "Shut up about Yo-Yo. Here. Lie back until the
    bleeding stops. Keep the ice on it."*

The smoke alarm in the kitchen went off.

Erik: "Something's burning."
Murphy: "Shit. The roast."

Duncan looked at the stove. Smoke was seeping out of
the oven. He saw the mitt on the counter. He slipped it
over his right hand, went over to the oven, opened it.
Smoke rolled out. He coughed and pulled the rack toward
him. Murphy materialized at his back.

"How's it look?" she asked. She picked up one of the tire
photos and started waving smoke away from the ceiling-
mounted alarm. It stopped buzzing.

"It looks like you should order a pizza." Duncan stood
up and ran his eyes around the galley. "Got another mitt?"
She set the picture back down on the table. Went to the
counter, opened a drawer, pulled another mitt out and
handed it to him. He slipped it over his left hand, bent over
and picked up the pan. He set it on top of the stove, shut
the oven door and turned on the vent over the range. He
pulled off the mitts and threw them on the counter.
"Sausage and pepperoni?"

She stepped closer to him and asked in a whisper, "Jack
okay to drive home?"

"He's fine."

"Good. What did he say?"

"Not much."

She paused and then it occurred to her that he might have heard something he shouldn't have. "When did you walk in?"

"In time to keep your boat from catching fire." He picked the key up off the counter and handed it to her. "Found this outside. Assume it belongs to you or one of your boxing buddies."

She snatched it from him. "It's mine." She shoved it in the pocket of her sweatpants. She picked up the oven mitts and slipped them on. She took the thermometer out of the black roast and set it in the sink. Picked up the pan. She nodded toward the door. "Open it, would you? I want the stink outside." He opened the door. She carried the pan outside, bent down and set it on the dock to the right of her door. Stood up and pulled off the mitts. "Tripod can have at it when it cools off." She stepped back inside and he shut the door behind her.

"Tripod?" he asked.

She tossed the mitts on the counter. "Three-legged dog. He was barking while the boys were punching the shit out of each other." She turned, took a breath and leaned against the counter. Stopped moving for the first time since he got there. Noticed he looked more pulled together in casual clothes than he usually did in his office wear. Black leather jacket over a black turtleneck and black jeans. She wondered what he thought of her sloppy clothes. She brushed her bangs to make sure her scar was covered.

Erik came down the stairs holding a washcloth stuffed with ice to his nose. "Duncan."

Duncan saluted him. "Erik."

Erik tossed the cloth and ice into the sink. Touched

under his nose and checked his fingers. No more blood. "How'd you happen to show up in time to referee?"

"My good luck. Actually I've got some stuff to talk to Murphy about. Stuff about the case."

Murphy picked up a jean jacket that was hanging from the back of a kitchen chair and handed it to Erik. "Before you launch into it, let me see Erik to the door."

Duncan looked at Erik and saw his mouth harden. Erik took the jacket from her and slipped it on. Duncan stifled a smirk; she was throwing her lover out. Erik stepped into his running shoes parked by the front door. She pulled the door open for him. As he was walking out, Erik bent toward her to kiss her and she leaned away from him. Duncan turned his back to them, pleased she was mad at Erik. Duncan pulled his cell phone out of his right jacket pocket, turned it on and used the voice dial. "Pizza." He heard the door shut. He turned around and Murphy walked toward him.

"That's sad," she said.

"What?" he asked.

"You have the pizza joint on voice dial."

He laughed and then said into the phone, "Yeah. For delivery. A large sausage and pepperoni. Houseboat parked at the St. Paul Yacht Club." He paused. "I don't know. I'll meet you on the dock. How long?" He hung up and shoved the phone back in his pocket. "I'm sorry."

"For?"

"The deal in my office."

She put her hands on her hips. "So this isn't about the case."

"It's more about my groveling."

"You made up for it tonight. If you hadn't showed up, I'd have two wet fools sitting at my table right now."

"And a charred kitchen. Don't forget that."

333

"And a charred kitchen."

"Not bad for a Yo-Yo."

Her mouth dropped open. He'd heard her call him that. Then she realized he'd listened to more upstairs than he let on. She didn't know if she should be embarrassed or angry. She wrote off both emotions. She pulled out a chair. Sat down. "Tell you what. You can pay for the pizza." He took off his jacket and draped it over a chair. Pulled the chair out and sat down next to her.

He eyed the photos on the kitchen table. "Your photos of Sweetie's truck tires?"

"Yeah."

"Turned out pretty good."

"Castro's digital."

He picked up the photo of the tread mark found in the park.

"Winter e-mailed it to Erik," she said.

He held the tread mark photo in his right hand. His eyes ran over the photos she'd taken. He pushed them around with his fingers and, from the bottom of the mess, picked up one from the table. Held it next to the one from the park. "I'd say we have a winner."

She stood up and went behind him. "Really? Erik and I couldn't see it." She looked over his shoulder at the two photos as he held them next to each other. Rested her right hand on his right shoulder and leaned over. "Son of a bitch. You're right. That is a match." She realized how close they were. She wasn't wearing a bra. Her right breast was pressed into his back. The only thing separating them was her tee shirt and his thin turtleneck. She suddenly straightened and took her hand off his shoulder.

He turned his head and looked at her. "What's wrong?"

"Nothing," she said. She went to the refrigerator.

Behind her back, he was grinning.

She pulled open the refrigerator. "How about a beer?"

"Sure. The tread marks and tires should match even better after a couple of beers." He reached across the table and collected all the photos. Stacked them into a pile. "Wish we had a copy of the cast itself. We could take it to the reunion and compare it to the genuine article."

She pulled out a six-pack of St. Pauli Girl and shut the door. "Let's just worry about getting those fingerprints off of him tomorrow night. Getting some information out of him. Bring up those boys who died in high school. See what that does." She plucked a magnetized bottle opener off the refrigerator.

"You never told me why Sweetie did those boys."

"They beat the shit out of him for asking me to homecoming." She set the opener and beer down on the table. Was going to take a chair across from Duncan and told herself that was stupid and paranoid. She sat down next to him. "Now I'm thinking he killed a lot more people in between those four in high school and those two in Moose Lake. They were the tip of a big fucking iceberg."

"Why do you think that?"

"I made some calls today. He was a suspect in at least one other hit-and-run. In Wisconsin. I've got a buddy in Public Safety ready to help me plow through old Minnesota cases."

Duncan sat for a few seconds, digesting what she'd said. He shook his head. "Scary."

"Scary. Good description of Sweet. Of both Trips."

"The scary Trips," Duncan muttered. He pulled a bottle out of the pack. "St. Pauli Girl. Good choice."

"I'd offer you wine but I'm out and the liquor delivery guy probably got lost. Your pizza guy will get lost, too. They can never find this place. I don't get it. The

Mississippi is such a big landmark. It's not like I tell them to take a right at the big rock or something."

"Liquor delivery? You call me pathetic."

"Shut up. I've been busy."

She tried to hand him the opener. "Don't need it," he said. He grabbed a second bottle out of the pack, tipped it upside down and used the cap to pry the top off the first bottle. He set the second bottle down and saw her staring. "What?"

"That's how my brothers open a beer bottle in a pinch."

He took a sip of beer. "Is that how you see me? A brother?"

"I don't know how I see you, Duncan. We really don't know each other."

"We're not in the office. How about using my first name?"

"Axel."

"I like hearing you say it." He took another sip and set the bottle down. "Well, Paris. What are you going to wear?"

She popped the cap off her bottle, dropped the opener on the table. "I've got my marching orders. I'm to *wear something hot for a change*. Isn't that how you put it?"

"How long do I have to live that down?" he asked. "I said I was sorry."

"You guys." She took a sip. "You think that's all it takes."

"What can I do to make it up to you?"

"Cover my back tomorrow night."

"I think we're going to make a good team." He held up his beer in tribute.

"We'll see," she said, and clicked her bottle against his.

He put the bottle to his mouth, took a drink. Stifled a burp. Put the bottle on the table. "Can you dance worth a shit?"

"Hell yeah." She took a bump off her beer. "Can you shoot worth a shit?"

"Fuck yes."

"Then we'll make a great team."

35

One hundred and eighty-two polybagged dress shirts. The entire knife collection packed away in an old steamer trunk. Stereo and CDs. Metal chest filled with car repair tools. Elvis Presley clock. "Elvis Presley Boulevard" street sign. E.P. hat. Box of Graceland cigarette lighters. Graceland snow globe. Bunny Pederson's peach purse. Keri Ingmar's purse and clothes. Two frozen bodies encased in cowboy bedsheets. Bloody towels.

On his way to the reunion Saturday night, Trip took a mental inventory of what he'd packed into the back of his truck late Friday and early Saturday while his neighbors slept. The last he'd loaded, and the worst, had been the bodies. He'd again donned the hooded parka and gloves so he wouldn't have to feel their hard skin when he fished them out of the freezer. His father wasn't frozen solid like Keri; he still had some bend. He'd dropped his old man in the middle of the sheet with the bloody towels from the cleanup. Gathered up the corners diagonally and tied them. A neat package. Dragged the bundle down the front steps and lifted it onto the gate without much trouble. Pushed it tight against the other stuff. Getting Keri out had been a bitch. Couldn't lift her out of the freezer for anything. Couldn't get a good enough grip. He'd been terrified something would snap off. A finger or an entire arm. He'd finally pushed the freezer over on its side and pulled her out. Rolled her onto the sheet like a boulder. Strangely, the coins had stayed stuck to her eyes. She'd looked frosty. A hunk of meat with freezer burn. He'd thrown her clothes and purse on top of her. Remembered the bridesmaid's purse in the garbage. Dug it out, tossed it on top of her. Gathered up the corners of the sheet and tied them and then twined nylon rope around the works. Used the rope like a handle to pull her down the steps. Lifting her onto the gate had nearly killed him. Wedged her next to his old man. Two bundles wrapped in cowboys.

Didn't go to bed. He'd sat on the couch and watched television, occasionally dozing off. Falling asleep with the remote in his hand. A privilege only his old man had enjoyed. Every so often he'd gotten up off the couch and peeked through the front room window to make sure no one was messing around near the truck.

Before he'd left for the reunion, he eyeballed the front room one last time. If anyone looked closely they could find evidence of blood, but he figured he'd given no one reason to scrutinize the place. His plan was to drive carefully and stay sober and straight while on the road. Give no state trooper reason to stop him. Bury the bodies, the towels, the women's purses and Keri's clothes at night. Somewhere between St. Paul and Memphis. The only thing he'd keep were the assortment of pills from Keri. He'd dumped the entire stash in with Keri's Prilosec prescription—including the Roofies.

As he steered the truck down Summit Avenue, he slipped his hand inside his right jacket pocket and touched the bottle. Safely tucked away. He withdrew his hand from the jacket and felt the bulge in his right pants pocket. The straight-edge. In case. His hand moved to the controls on the CD player. He turned up the volume on "Evil Element" by Taste of Insanity. The guitar squeals ripped through the cab. He pulled at the neck of his shirt. He'd sifted through all the shirts and picked out one of the few with sleeves long enough for his arms. A pale gray shirt. Athletic fit. Fifty cotton. Fifty poly. Button-down collar. Perfect with his cuffed slate-gray dress pants. No tie. After getting fired from his sales job, he never wanted to see another tie. Instead of a suit coat he wore his best jacket, the gray suede bomber. The black leather belt and black dress shoes were his old man's. His pa didn't need them anymore.

He stopped on the street in front of the reception hall, an old mansion like the other mansions that lined Summit Avenue. The three-story stone house was surrounded by wrought iron. The fence was draped in dried vines and white Christmas lights. The front yard was illuminated by a coach lamp mounted on a post, and by ceiling lights on the open front porch. Trip could see a few people milling about on the porch with their cigarettes and cigars. The rest had to be inside; it was cold and windy outside and an icy drizzle was starting to slice the air in diagonal lines. Trip wouldn't miss the Minnesota weather.

All the street parking in front of the hall was taken on both sides of Summit. He turned down the side street that ran alongside the mansion. Was frustrated parking wasn't allowed on one side. Found a space at the end of the block on the other side. He made a U-turn and pulled into the space. He shut off the truck. Shoved the keys in his left pants pocket. Hopped out. Slammed the driver's-side door and pulled on the handle to make sure it was locked. He glanced at the topper. Nothing suspicious. He sniffed. No stink. As long as the cold weather held, the bodies would keep. He buried his hands in his pockets as he walked down the sidewalk. The wind was in his face; the rain felt like needles on his skin. Ahead of him, a man and a woman were walking arm in arm under an umbrella. They were probably headed to the same place. He wondered if he knew them. Was the man a jock who'd shoved his face into a locker? Was the woman a bitch who'd whispered with her friends? Pointed at him? Laughed at him? The couple crossed under a streetlight. They had gray hair. Too old to be his former classmates. Since it was an all-class reunion, there'd be a lot of people he didn't know. He didn't care. As long as one person in particular showed up. He kept walking. Wondered what she'd be wearing. Who this fella was that she'd have on her arm. Trip had more than enough pills. Maybe he'd waste both of them.

Trip paid the cover charge at the door and walked in. Didn't bother standing at the table inside the front door to fill out a name tag. Ignored the other tables filled with St. Brice High memorabilia. Yearbooks. Homecoming buttons. Programs from school plays. Football trophies. Basketball trophies. Hockey trophies. None of that had ever been a part of his life. That was some other world he'd heard about but never experienced. He saw people carrying their jackets upstairs. He didn't want to leave his jacket in the coatroom. He wanted it handy so he could bolt when he wanted.

Most people were funneling into the largest room on the main floor, an area that originally must have been the mansion's front room and dining room. Trip followed the crowd. A fire crackled in the fireplace. Chandeliers hung overhead. At the front end of the room was a band setting up on a small stage. At the opposite end, against the back wall, was a cloth-covered banquet table filled with food. Trip thought it was typical Minnesota fare. Veggies and dip. Fruit. Cheese and crackers. Sliced meats and rolls. Meatballs simmering in barbecue sauce. He wondered whatever gave northerners the idea of polluting barbecue sauce with meatballs. In his mind, he was already home eating real southern cooking. Interstate Bar-B-Que would be his first stop. A slab of pork ribs with a side of beans.

People were coming upstairs from the basement with drinks in their hands. He went down. He told himself he needed a drink in his hand so he wouldn't look suspicious. So he had something to do besides sit. Everyone else went downstairs for their drink and took it back upstairs to the main floor. Trip stayed in the bar, a converted cellar with stone walls and a low ceiling. He sat at a table in a far corner with his back to the wall and his eyes trained on the floor. He raised his eyes whenever he heard a female voice at the bar; he didn't want to miss her. Though a parade of people passed through the basement, he didn't try talking to anyone and no one tried talking to him. His resolve to stay sober melted in the crowded reception house. For him it was filled with two kinds of people: those he didn't know, and those he knew and never liked. One pair of blondes in particular. He remembered them. Recognized them the instant they walked into the bar. Long, straight hair parted down the middle. They wore their hair the same way in high school. They weren't related but the pair's nickname was "The Twins." They did everything together. Both were cheerleaders. Shared their lunch bags with each other. Took the same classes. They stood behind him on the choir risers. They'd complain in voices too low for the teacher to hear but loud enough for his ears: "Can't even see with the f... f... freak in the way." "Wish the f... freak would move his f... fat f... fucking head." "The f... f... freak can't sing worth a shit." They were "The Twins" and he was "The Freak." He hated them. They were giggling as they left the bar with their glasses of wine. They didn't see him sitting there, but he was certain they were laughing at him.

He ditched the idea of trying to impress anyone with his heroic volunteer efforts. Nothing he could do would ever make them accept him, even after all these years. All he wanted to do was poison Paris Murphy and her boyfriend and leave town. He reached into the right pocket of his jacket and touched the pill bottle again.

36

She'd considered wearing something dumpy to piss off Duncan and then thought she'd show him up instead. Murphy stood in front of her bedroom dresser mirror and scrutinized her evening attire. A fuzzy three-quarter-sleeve black cashmere sweater with a high neckline and a low back. Fitted black satin skirt with a hemline that fell just above the knees. She wished she could dump the panty hose—they were too confining—but it was cold outside and the wrong season to go bare-legged. She turned sideways and examined her profile. Murphy hadn't worn the outfit in a while; the material hung a little looser on her than she remembered. She hadn't been watching the scales lately and suspected she'd lost some weight since the summer. She blamed it on the surgeon's case. The "stress diet" was always effective. She took a brush off her dresser top and gave her hair a few strokes. She brushed the bangs; she'd never get used to those things. Peering into the mirror, she studied her forehead to make sure the scar wasn't visible. She didn't want anyone seeing it and asking about it. Worse, someone staring at it while trying to act like they weren't.

She heard a knock at the door. She stepped into her black pumps and went downstairs. She pulled open the door and blinked. "Nice."

Duncan could have been a catalog model in the black wool crepe suit. Underneath the three-button jacket were a white shirt and a silver silk tie. Over his arm was draped a black trench coat. He stepped inside. "You like it? Went to the Mall of America this afternoon. Found the whole kit and caboodle on the clearance racks at Nordstrom's. Even the rain gear." He was grinning like a kid showing off his trophy fish. He reached into the pocket of the coat and pulled out some paper. "Saved the receipt and the tags. Like you said." He shoved the scraps back in the pocket.

"I think you should keep it," she said. He pushed back his blazer and showed her his gun hanging from a shoulder holster. "Keep that, too," she said.

He raised his brows. "Hey. You look great."

"Thanks." She eyed his coat. "Raining out?"

"Starting to."

"Let me get my black trench coat. Then we can match. Plus I need my purse."

"Why? Don't need to drag around any makeup or anything, do you?"

"I need to drag around my gun." She ran upstairs to her bedroom.

He watched her go and said in a low voice, "Hot. Hot. Hot."

She came back down, pulling the coat on as she went. "Did you say something?"

"Got to go." He slipped his coat on.

"We're okay. We've got time." She threw her purse strap over her shoulder. Fished a pair of leather gloves out of her coat pocket and pulled them on. Took her house keys out of her purse. "Don't want to be the first ones there."

He held the door open for her and motioned her outside with his hand. "I've got some fancy wheels to go with your fancy outfit." She stepped outside. He followed, shutting the door behind them. She locked up and dropped the keys in her purse.

"I thought I was going to drive," she said as they walked down the dock. She'd heard Duncan was a crazy man behind the wheel.

"Paris. Have you been listening to those naughty stories about me again?"

She was glad it was nighttime so he couldn't see her face redden. "No. No. I like my Jeep is all."

"I like my little ride. Come on. I'll keep the needle under a hundred."

The instant their feet touched shore the drizzle quickened. They pulled their coat collars up and dashed to his car. He opened the passenger's-side door for her. Even in the rain she had to step back and take in the car. "A black boat." She slid inside. Red leather seats and interior, like a bar lounge. He shut her door, went around, got into the driver's side. Slammed the door. Pushed the key into the ignition and started it.

"Nineteen seventy-six Cadillac Sedan DeVille." He pulled out of the parking lot. "Eight-banger. Automatic everything. Not a spot of rust. Bought her out in California from Jurassic Cadillac. Drove her back here. Check this out." He reached under the seat, fished out a fat tape and pushed it into the player.

"I don't believe it," she said. "It works?"

"Bet your ass." He turned up the volume. "*Small World* by Huey Lewis and the News. Nineteen eighty-eight. The last eight-track released by a major label."

"Why do you know that?"

"I don't know why I know that," he said as he piloted

the Cadillac north over the Wabasha Bridge. "I just do." He took a left at Kellogg Boulevard downtown. "What's the plan regarding the prints?"

"We'll keep our eyes open for an opportunity."

Duncan steered the car through downtown traffic. The streets and sidewalks were clogged with hockey fans. The Wild were playing the Red Wings at Xcel Energy Center. "This joint is down from the cathedral, right?"

"Yeah. Sits on a corner. Parking on Summit's a pain. You can probably find something on a side street. Might have to walk a ways."

The rain pattered on the windshield. "Good night for a walk," he said. He went up a hill and took a left onto John Ireland Boulevard, curved past the St. Paul Cathedral and got onto Summit.

"Thanks for doing this. Really. I wouldn't feel safe without someone watching my back."

"Yeah, yeah. Don't get all mushy on me." They drove past the hall. "Shit. Nothing on Summit."

"Keep going. We'll find something farther down. Here. Take the first right."

He turned down the narrow side street. "This isn't any good," he grumbled. "Parking isn't even allowed on this side. Trying to get me towed in my own town?"

"Hang a U-turn and park on the other side." They got to the end of the street. "Stop!" Murphy yelled. Duncan slammed on the brakes. Murphy opened the passenger's door and jumped out. Left the door open. Ducked her head back inside and pointed to a truck parked on the other side of the street. "This is Sweet's." She slammed the door and Duncan waited with the engine running. She looked up and down the block. Didn't see anyone coming. She ran across the street, stepped next to the truck and peeked inside the cab. Didn't see anything weird. Went around to the rear and looked through the topper window. "Shit. Can't see." She went back to the Cadillac, opened the passenger's door. Leaned inside. "Flashlight?"

Duncan reached under his seat, pulled one out and handed it to her. "What are you looking for?"

"I don't know," she said. She shut the car door, flicked on the light and went to the back of the Ford. Ran the beam around the inside of the truck bed. Jammed with stuff. Shirts. Boxes. A bunch of balled-up bed linen in that cowboy pattern the Trips favored. She flicked off the light and went back to the Cadillac. Pulled open the door, hopped inside and slammed it shut. "He's taking off, maybe right after the reunion." She opened the glove compartment and dropped in the flashlight. Shut it.

Duncan started driving slowly, searching for parking spots while he talked. "Suitcases?"

"Trunks. Boxes. Bedspreads. He's definitely taking a hike."

"What about Pappy?"

"Good question."

Duncan went around the block and got back on Summit. Saw a van pulling out of a space across the street from the hall. He did a U-turn and took it. "Guess some of your classmates did pretty good for themselves," he said, pulling into the spot between a Mercedes and a Range Rover.

"I'll bet there's not another car on the street with a working eight-track."

He turned off the car and pulled the keys out of the ignition. "Any other things we need to go over before we do this?"

"Don't eat or drink anything."

"You have got to be shitting me. I'm starving."

"He tried to dope me up at that restaurant in Moose Lake. He could try doing it again—to both of us."

348

He slipped the keys in his right pants pocket. Checked his left. Made sure he had his cell phone on him. "How about we keep an eye on our food and drinks? How about that?"

"Okay. But be careful. He's sneaky." She paused and then asked a question she knew he wouldn't want to hear. "When do we call for backup?"

"Not until we need it," he said.

"When's that?"

He put his hand on the driver's-side door. "When I say."

"Did you tell the bosses about this?"

He opened his door and set one foot on the street. "I am the boss."

37

Trip was on his third shot of whiskey by the time the two detectives crossed the street and entered the hall. By the time they paid the cover and hung up their coats and went down to the basement bar, he was on his fourth. Murphy asked for a glass of Chardonnay and Trip looked up. Recognized her from behind. The long, black hair. Like Snow White. The Snow White who'd been his dream. Who'd turned out to be his nightmare. The boyfriend had big shoulders. Big arms. Trip was sure they didn't see him; he was a shadow hunched in a dark corner. Still, he felt perspiration collecting above his lip and on his forehead. He took the bar napkin from under his glass and wiped his face. Dropped the napkin on the table. He reached into his pocket and pulled out the bottle. Keeping his hands under the table, he unscrewed the cap. Set the cap on his lap. Poured all the pills into his left hand and set the empty bottle on his lap. He couldn't see well in the dim light and with his hand under the table. He looked up. They'd already left with their drinks. He raised his cupped hand from under the table and poked around the tablets and capsules. They were sticking to his sweaty palm. With his right fingertips, he picked out eight Roofies and dropped them into his pants pocket. Four each would surely do the job. That still left him with six. No sense in wasting good pills. He dumped the remaining Roofies and the rest of the pills back in the bottle, screwed the cap back on, put the bottle back in his jacket pocket. He wanted to hang the jacket up after all. His mission might take a while and even in the cool basement, he was sweating like a pig.

Murphy and Duncan spoke in low voices as they walked upstairs from the bar.

"See him?" he asked.

"Yup. In the corner, hiding," she said. They reached the top of the stairs and stepped into a small side room. It contained one round dining table surrounded by chairs. No one else was there.

Duncan looked over his shoulder to make sure Trip wasn't coming up behind him. "Why didn't you go talk to him?"

"Sweet and his father are big boozers. Give him time and he'll get loose. We'll mingle and munch and keep an eye out for him. When he comes up from the bar, I'll back him into a corner. Get him talking about old times."

"Sounds like a plan." Duncan looked through the doorway into the dining room. "I'm hungry. Come on."

"Go ahead," she said. "I'm going to plant myself near the basement doorway."

They left the room, Murphy heading for her post and Duncan aiming for the food. A table filled with memorabilia caught her eye on the way. She picked up a framed eight-by-ten photo of Denny and his three buddies. The same picture they'd used on the memorial page in the yearbook. Arms around each other. They should be here, she thought. She set it down with an even stronger resolve to nail Trip.

"Paris. Where's Jack?"

She turned to see who was behind her. Father Leo, the priest who'd taught religion at the school for years and who officiated at her wedding. She smiled. "How's retirement treating you?" She extended her right hand. He took it in both of his. She'd run into him several times over the years and to her eyes, he never aged. He had the same thick gray hair. Same wire-rimmed glasses. Same tall, lean figure.

He laughed. "What retirement? The archdiocese has got me running from one parish to the other. Teaching was more relaxing."

"The priest shortage?"

He nodded and released her hand. "Back to my original question. Where's Jack?"

She hesitated and then answered. "We're split."

"Again?"

"This time for good."

"Want to talk?"

"Nothing to say."

"Bull." He pointed to his collar. "If this is the problem, I'll take it off. Meet you for beer."

"We'll see," she said.

"I'm shuffling between St. Luke's and Immaculate Heart of Mary. Hearing confessions and saying a few masses. Call either rectory."

She saw Duncan coming toward her; he was talking on his cell phone. He looked excited. "Gotta go," she said, touching the priest's arm.

Duncan pulled her back into the side room. "Interesting development." He shoved his cell phone back in his pants pocket. "That was Bergen. A home health-care nurse is missing. Keri Ingmar. Her employer just called it in. Last time they heard from her was Tuesday. She was supposed to check in Friday, see if they needed help for the weekend."

"So?"

"The last patient she visited was Frank Trip."

"Shit," she breathed. In her mind's eye, she saw Frank's hand resting on the white lid. "The freezer."

"Say again?"

"Remember that visit I made to their trailer? Last stop on the grand tour was a back bedroom with this huge chest freezer."

"You think Nurse Ingmar is cooling her heels in the freezer?"

"Maybe. Sweet's father was pulling some kind of crap while I was there. Egging Sweet on. Tormenting him. Taking his time showing me the place when it was obvious Sweet wanted me out of there. We get to this bedroom and Frank puts his hand on the freezer lid. I thought Sweet was going to have a heart attack."

"Pappy didn't actually open it?"

"No. I don't know if he really intended to open it. I think he was rattling Sweet's cage. Definitely some weird shit going on between father and son. I bolted before they sucked me into their family feud. Planned to get in there with a search warrant after the reunion. Figured we'd find a dope stash in the freezer since Sweet was a pothead in high school. At most, maybe some stolen money. Never thought of a body. Too bizarre."

"The thing was big enough to hold a body?"

"Hell yeah. Three bodies."

Duncan pulled his cell phone out again. "We've got to get into that trailer."

Murphy spotted Trip coming up from the basement. "I see Sweet." He started taking the stairs to the second floor, his jacket draped over his right arm. "I'm going to follow him. You stay down here, in case he gets past me."

Duncan nodded while holding the cell phone to his ear.

She let a few people get ahead of her on the stairs. She didn't want him to see her yet. She got to the top of the stairs and saw Trip go into the coatroom at the end of the hall. She ducked into the women's rest room off the hallway so he wouldn't see her. She stood on the other side of the door. Figured she'd give him a couple of minutes to hang up his jacket and go back downstairs. She waited. Opened the bathroom door. Ran her eyes up and down the hall. Saw Trip's back; he was headed back downstairs. He was hanging on to the rails. He was drunk. Good. She ran into the coatroom. Scanned the racks lining the walls. Saw his gray suede hanging toward the end of a rack. She looked behind her; no one was coming in. She stepped over to her own coat, took out her gloves and pulled them on. Went over to Trip's jacket. Slipped her right hand into the left pocket. Nothing. Slipped her hand into his right pocket. Felt something. A bottle. She pulled it out, read the label and gasped. The patient's name: "Ingmar, Keri M."

He killed her, Murphy thought. He killed her and took her pills. She looked at the prescription. "Prilosec." Common acid reducer. Half the people in the office were on it. She opened the jar and spilled some pills into her gloved hand. Saw more than the purple capsules. Couple of Valium. Tylenol with codeine. Some capsules she didn't recognize. Some scored white pills she recognized immediately. Rohypnol. She counted them. Six. Was this his entire supply or did he have more on him? She dumped all the pills back in the jar, screwed the cap on. Slipped it back in his pocket. She wanted to arrest him with Ingmar's prescription in his possession.

She heard music coming from downstairs. Pulled off the gloves and slipped them into her purse. Headed for the steps. She'd take a spin with Duncan. Then take a turn around the dance floor with a drunken murderer. Let him know what she knew. Get him to spill his guts. If he didn't, she'd still slap the cuffs on him.

Watching her glide across the wood floor. Her black hair shining in the dim room like it had a light source all its own. Seeing her smile at her boyfriend. Her handsome, golden boyfriend. Knowing she was happy and having a good time. It all freshened his hate for Paris Murphy. Reminded him of the time he was doing a sales demonstration and splashed cleaning solution on a scab. It burned his hand down to the bone. This reunion was the same thing. Solvent poured on an old wound. Making it worse was the setting. A party crowded with her old friends. His old enemies. Most of them had aged well. The men still had their hair. The women, their figures. One person from their class had died since they graduated. Breast cancer. He heard a knot of women talking about it in low, reverent voices. He recognized the dead woman's name. She'd been a class officer and a volleyball player. It wasn't as good as hearing about a former cheerleader or football player dying, but it still gave him a twinge of joy. He was sure any misery that any of them had suffered over the years was a fraction of what he had tolerated in his hellish years at St. Brice's. Their fucking school. It had never been his school. Never. He folded his arms over his chest and leaned against the wall and waited for an opportunity. Every so often he uncrossed his arms and

355

slipped his right hand into his pants pocket. Felt the pills resting alongside the straight-edge.

While they danced, Murphy told Duncan about finding the pill bottle. "Perfect," he said. He guided her around the floor during the old-fashioned waltz. "Sunrise, Sunset" from *Fiddler on the Roof*. At the same time, he monitored Trip. Didn't like what he saw. "The way he's glaring at you. He's gonna burn a hole right through you. Careful around him. Homicidal maniac."

"I know," she said.

"Sure it was that fight? It was high school, for God's sake. Wasn't even your fault."

"I think he's been stewing over it all these years, imagining I played some big role in the whole deal."

"Must have been quite a beating." He lifted her right hand over her head and spun her around once.

"It was bad enough that he killed those boys over it," she said as she finished the turn and returned her right hand to the palm of his left hand. She felt awkward doing the move with the purse over her shoulder.

Both his hands slid down to her waist and hers went to rest on his shoulders. "How sure are you of that?"

"My gut and the Flintstones coffee mug tell me I'm right," she said. "I need something to back it up."

"Forensic stuff after all these years? Hard to come by."

"I was hoping for something a little easier," she said.

"A confession?"

She nodded. The music stopped. They stood and clapped. Found themselves standing in front of the nearly empty punch bowl at the end of the banquet table. Duncan turned around, picked up a glass and ladled some of the dregs of the red drink into it. Handed it to her. She sipped.

So sugary it made her shudder, but she was thirsty. "You wore me out."

He poured a glass for himself. "You kept up. Very light on your feet." He gulped it. Set the empty glass on the table. The music started up again.

Murphy took another sip of punch. "Where's my other dance partner?" She stepped away from the table and looked across the room at where Trip had been standing. He was gone. "Shit."

Duncan ran his eyes around the room. "How'd we lose someone that big? Where'd he go?"

"His jacket," she said.

Duncan ran for the stairs. "I'll check the coatroom."

Murphy turned around and went back to the table to set her glass down. Saw Trip standing on the other side of the punch bowl in the narrow space between the back wall and the table. His right hand was over the punch. He was about to drop something into it. Only a glass or two left in the bowl and Murphy figured Trip was counting on her and Duncan drinking it. Murphy grabbed his right hand, digging her nails into his flesh. Put her open left palm underneath to catch the pills.

"Drop it," she said in a low voice. In the background, the band was playing "Unchained Melody."

He grimaced but didn't move. "Drop what? I g... got nothing."

At that moment, she figured she hated him even more than he hated her. "You've got a fistful of dope," she said. "Drop it."

He yanked his hand out of hers and dropped the pills on the floor. "Fuck you, b... bitch," he growled. With both hands, he grabbed the edge of the table and flipped it toward her, sending the bowl and glasses and platters of food crashing onto the wood floor. Murphy stumbled

357

backward to avoid getting hit. She felt herself bumping into other people. Heard gasps and screams from horrified dancers. The other end of the room didn't know what was going on. The band kept playing. Other partygoers continued dancing.

Trip dashed through the first opening he could find behind the table. The kitchen door. Murphy pulled out her gun and dropped her purse on the floor. She hopped around the table and the spilled food and broken plates and ran after him. Trip knocked over a young woman in a white apron and tipped an empty bread rack on its side to block Murphy's path. She jumped over it, slid on the kitchen floor but regained her balance. Trip pushed the back door open and ran outside. She was on his heels. As she clattered down the steps she heard another set of feet running behind her. She looked over her right shoulder and saw Duncan at her back. She wondered why his gun wasn't drawn.

The three running figures were illuminated by yard lights as they cut across the leaf-covered lawn. The drizzle had turned into a hard rain. Steam poured from the detectives' mouths as they hollered and ran.

Murphy: "He's going over the fence."

Duncan: "The fuck he is." In two strides, Duncan passed Murphy. "Stop, you dumb fuck," Duncan yelled. "I'm a cop."

Trip had his right leg over the fence and was about to throw the left one over when he saw Duncan racing toward him. He hesitated for an instant and then tried to pick up his left leg. The pant cuff was caught on the bottom of the fence. He reached down and pulled; it wouldn't budge. He thrust his right hand into his right pants pocket and pulled out the straight-edge. Opened it and reached down to slice his pant leg free. Too late. Duncan was almost on top of him. Trip straightened up, cranked his right arm back and took a swing. Duncan tried to dodge the blade, but it caught him on the chin and he stumbled backward. A shot rang out. Trip dropped the knife with a howl and clutched his left shoulder with his right hand. He saw Murphy bearing down on him, her gun raised. "Don't move!" she yelled. Trip pulled his left leg as hard as he could. The cuff ripped off. He threw his leg over the fence and ran down the alley, his right hand clutching his left shoulder.

Murphy shoved her gun into the waistband of her skirt and climbed over the fence. She landed on the other side, pulled her gun out. Duncan was right behind her. She eyed his face when he landed on the other side of the fence. Blood was oozing from his chin. They ran after Trip. By the glow cast from a streetlight, they saw him turn right when he hit the end of the alley. "His truck," she said.

"I'm getting my wheels," Duncan said, and ran ahead of her. At the end of the alley he took a left on the side street and ran toward Summit. He dug his keys out of his right pants pocket while he went and pulled his cell phone out of his left pocket. Called for backup while dripping blood down the front of his shirt.

Murphy got to the end of the alley and took a right. Followed Trip down the side street. She squinted through the rain and the night as she ran. She couldn't see Trip ahead of her. She looked for his truck at the end of the block. Gone. "Damn," she muttered. She stopped at the corner and looked up and down the side street. Up and down the street that crossed it. Nothing. She turned and jogged back toward Summit. She wanted to catch Duncan to tell him to call for backup. As she ran, she rubbed her arms and pushed the wet hair off her face. She was soaked and cold. Her sweater and skirt were matted against her like a second skin. She got to Summit and scanned the street.

An empty space between the Range Rover and the Mercedes. Duncan's Cadillac was gone.

She heard the squeal of tires. It had to be Duncan. She scanned the side street. Didn't see anything. Then Trip's truck came rumbling out of the alley, took a mad left onto the side street and headed for Summit. She stepped into the middle of the road to stop him. He kept coming. She raised her gun. He kept coming. She dove between two sedans parked on the side street and jumped on the trunk hood of one. Dropping to one knee, she aimed for Trip through the cab window on the passenger's side. As the truck roared by, she pulled the trigger. She heard the crackle of shattering glass but couldn't tell if she'd hit Trip. The truck kept heading for Summit. It would take Trip downtown. To the highways. To freedom.

As the truck rolled into the intersection, a black bullet shot down Summit and broadsided the driver's side. The thunder of metal slamming into metal. A hubcap rolled down Summit toward the reception house and another wobbled down the side street past Murphy. "Axel!" Murphy slid off the car trunk, shoved her gun in her waistband and ran to the intersection. Broken glass and bits of metal crunched under her shoes. She heard sirens in the distance and her own voice drowning them out. "Axel!"

She ran to the Cadillac. The front of the car was crumpled and the windshield was shattered. She tried to open the driver's door. Locked or jammed. She pulled with both hands and yanked it open. Duncan was lying back in the seat. He was wearing his seat belt; it saved his life.

His eyes opened. "Sorry I'm late."

She reached inside and wrapped her right hand around his left. She eyed his body but was afraid to touch him. "Where does it hurt?"

"Everywhere." He laughed. "Ouch. My poor Caddy."

"Don't move," she said. His eyes started to close. "Axel. No. Don't. Stay with me. Talk to me. Where were you? You dropped out of the sky."

His eyes fluttered but stayed open. "Drove to the end of the block and took a U-turn. I heard rubber burning. Figured he was coming out of the side street. Gunned it when I saw him."

"Why? We would have caught up with him."

"Couldn't risk a chase. The way he used his truck like a weapon, he could've taken out a bunch of people."

"You never drew your gun."

"Not a fair fight. He didn't have a gun." His eyes started to close again.

She squeezed his hand. "Axel. Stay with me."

Two squads pulled up. Then a third, followed by a fire rig and two paramedic units. She stepped aside so the paramedics could work on Duncan. She ran over to Trip's truck. The driver's side was punched in. Paramedics were crawling all over the cab. "How bad is it?" she yelled to one leaning in the driver's side. She looked past him into the truck. Didn't see evidence that airbags had gone off. She figured Trip had been in so many accidents, he'd stopped replacing the bags or disengaged them. "Is he conscious?" She had to know if he killed Denny and his friends. Wanted to ask how many others he'd murdered. "I'm a cop. Can I talk to him?"

The paramedic pulled his head out of the cab. "You the shooter?" She nodded. "Between that and the crash, he's gone."

She didn't know why she asked her next question: "Which finished him?"

"ME will have to sort that one out." He ducked his head back inside.

Another paramedic, a woman, came around to the cab from the back of the truck. She was shaking her head. "Never seen anything like it."

The impact of the collision had caused Trip's truck to jettison half its load. Curled up in the middle of Summit Avenue—amid a pile of cowboy linen and bloody towels and packaged dress shirts and Elvis memorabilia—were two bodies. A partially frozen old man. A frozen middle-aged woman. The man was clothed and had a sheet wrapped around his neck. The woman was nude. She had a plastic bag and duct tape wrapped around her neck and coins embedded in her eyes. A dime in one and a nickel in the other.

38

Searching for the perfect surface, Murphy turned the pumpkin around and around on her kitchen table. She stepped back, pointed to a flat spot. "How about here?"

Sitting at the table, Duncan pulled the pumpkin toward him. "Fine." He raised the small serrated knife to stab the top and start carving. He had to use his left hand; his right arm was in a sling.

"Wait," she said.

He sighed and set down the knife. "This is painful."

"I want it nice," she said. She walked to the refrigerator, pulled out two bottles of Grain Belt, shut the door and set the beers on the table. "I think some alcohol will improve my artistic vision." She took a chair on Duncan's left. The chair to his right was occupied by his crutches.

He tried to unscrew the cap by hugging the bottle with the sling and using his left hand. The bottle slipped and tipped.

"Let me. Stubborn." She took the bottle, unscrewed the cap and handed it to him. Unscrewed the cap off hers.

"No more St. Pauli Girl?" he asked.

She took a sip. "Fussy s.o.b."

"You should be nicer to me." He took a long drink, set the bottle down. "I had one broken foot in the grave."

She set down her bottle and turned the pumpkin around with both hands. It was sitting on sheets of newspaper. "A couple of busted bones, a few bruises. You didn't even have your big toe in the grave. You can thank your fat-ass Caddy for that."

"Don't speak ill of the dead," he said, and took another sip of beer.

A knock at the door. "Trick or treat!"

Murphy stood up. Grabbed the bowl of candy off the counter and went to the door. Pulled it open. Three boys dressed as bums in ratty clothes. She dropped a Hershey's bar into each sack. "Who do you guys belong to?" Only the relatives of yacht club members bothered hitting the houseboats.

"*The Commodore*'s our grandpa," said the tallest bum.

"Don't fall overboard," she said.

The shortest bum saluted. "Aye, aye." The trio tromped down the dock. She heard them greeting the barking Tripod next door. She shivered in her jeans and sweatshirt. Another cold night, she thought, but at least it wasn't raining on the kids. She closed the door.

While her back was turned to him, Duncan had picked up the knife and cut off the top of the pumpkin, sawing quickly and sloppily with his left hand. He steadied it by wedging it between his body and the sling. "Axel," said Murphy, coming back to the table. "That looks like shit."

He pulled off the top by the stem and thrust his left hand inside. Started pulling out gobs of seeds and string and dropping them onto the newspaper. "It's already seven o'clock. Halloween is almost over. Who cares how it looks? Get it done and get it out there so the kids have something to smash."

"We have a different tradition out here on the river." She sat back down. "My jack-o'-lantern ends up feeding the carp."

Duncan noticed something in the newspaper and scraped away some seeds with his knife. "Here's an ad for some GWPs." He tried ripping it off with one hand and tore the ad down the middle. "Damn."

She leaned over and ripped around the torn ad. Picked it up and read it. " 'German wire-haired pups'. I've been thinking about a dog, too. Same breed, as a matter of fact."

"Great for pheasant. When they're on point, nothing prettier."

She set the ad on a clean spot on the table. "You hunt?"

"You betcha. Missed the opener. I was hoping to get out before the season ends." He glanced at the crutches. "Maybe it won't happen."

"We could go out together." She took a sip of beer. "I could hold you up while you shoot."

"Thanks a bunch," he said dryly.

Her cell phone rang. She looked over at the kitchen counter. Wondered if it was Jack or Erik. She'd taken a break from them since the crash and concentrated on nursing Duncan. His injuries weren't life-threatening and the only permanent reminder he'd have of the case was the scar on his chin. Nevertheless, she felt guilty about what had happened and responsible for helping him heal. After his release from the hospital, she'd stayed with him and camped out on his couch. After a couple of days, they'd moved to her boat for his recuperation. She still took the couch.

The phone kept ringing. Duncan wiped his left hand on the edge of the newspaper. "Want me to get it?"

"Forget it, Speedy." She stood up and walked to the counter, took a breath and picked up the phone. "Yeah."

Amira: "How's your friend, honey?"

Murphy thought the way her mother asked that question made it sound like Duncan was a kid with a scraped knee. "He's much better, *Imma*." Murphy smiled at Duncan.

Then her mother asked a question Murphy had been trying to answer herself: "Gonna take that job he offered you?"

From his hospital bed, Duncan had asked Murphy to join him on a new five-state task force he was helping form with other homicide chiefs from around the Midwest. Police departments throughout Minnesota, Wisconsin, Iowa and the Dakotas were being tapped. The detectives would cross jurisdictions within their own states and even cross state lines to work on high-profile felonies. The states and feds would reimburse the home departments for hours spent working on the special cases. Duncan told her that assigning her to the Bunny Pederson case had been his way of auditioning her for the job.

"I don't know, Ma," Murphy said into the phone. With her personal life a mess, it didn't seem a good time to overextend herself on the job. "Thinking about it."

Duncan eyed Murphy. The minute she hung up the phone, he jumped on her. "I don't believe you. It's the opportunity of a lifetime for a cop. You get to skim off the cream. The most challenging homicide cases." He jabbed the knife into the middle of the pumpkin and started cutting out a triangle for the nose.

Murphy sat back down. Picked up her beer bottle. "Sweet's case was challenging, and I couldn't tie up all the loose ends. Maybe I'm not good enough."

"That's a load of crap." Duncan started carving a crooked smile below the nose.

The unanswered questions would always bother her. The bodies that bounced out of the truck were clearly Trip's handiwork. Evidence also credited him with the deaths of Pederson and Kermitt. The Eau Claire murder looked like his doing, but there was no forensic proof. How many others he'd killed while on the road would never be clear. Murphy was sure he'd murdered Denny and his buddies even though the only proof she had was the *Flintstones* mug. She got it back when they went through Trip's trailer. She kept it on her desk at the cop shop, a reminder of a high school love and a high school killer.

She took a long drink and set the bottle down. Picked at the label. "I couldn't answer the biggest question."

Duncan kept carving. "Motive."

"Why did he waste all those people? I know he hated Denny and his pals for beating him up. I get that. The ranger was in the park at the wrong time, saw Sweet burying Pederson or something. There's the motive for that. But why did he kill Pederson in the first place? To plant the finger and find it and play hero? Why did he kill Ingmar and that guy in Eau Claire and God knows how many others? His father. Why did he kill his father?"

Duncan managed to carve one fat tooth in the middle of the jack-o'-lantern's big grin. "Trip was a dope fiend with a fucked-up family life." He accidentally cut off the tooth. "Shit."

She took another sip of beer. "How fucked up did it have to be for him to slit his father's throat and stuff him in a freezer? What did his father do to deserve that?"

Duncan stabbed the pumpkin above the nose and started on the right eye. "Sweetie and his pappy were both pieces of shit. You couldn't even find anyone who liked them enough to claim their bodies, right?"

"I found a phone number for someone in Baton Rouge. I thought it was Trip's mother. Frank's ex. Anna. I told her Frank and Sweet were dead."

Duncan finished the right eye, a triangle the same size as the nose, and started on the left. "What'd she say?"

"She said, 'What goes around comes around.' Then she hung up on me."

He finished carving the second eye and popped out the triangle. "Sounds like a wrong number." He put the top on the jack-o'-lantern.

"No. That had to be his mother."

"Why do you think that?" He picked up his beer and finished it. The front of his sweatshirt and the sling were dotted with pumpkin string and seeds.

"Trip wrote that in my yearbook." Another knock at the door. Murphy got up from the table.

"Wrote what?"

"*What goes around comes around.*" She grabbed the candy bowl and headed for the door. "Must be their family motto or something."

CLEAN CUT

Theresa Monsour

Meet Paris Murphy: the Twin Cities detective with Lebanese good looks, Irish charm and double trouble on her plate.

Fionn 'Finch' Hennessy had been working the St Paul streets ever since she left Wisconsin and her abusive family past behind. Staying out in the rain for one last 'trick' was the worst decision of her life. Her killer was rough, brutal and, as Paris discovers on seeing the body, a man with a fetish: a large portion of the dead girl's hair has been removed.

As Paris and partner Gabe Nash start to piece the clues together, they soon realise that identifying the killer is only the beginning. For the murderer is a man with friends in high places, and unless they can put a watertight case together he's going to kill again . . .

'Paris Murphy, the heroine of this superb new novel, is a force to be reckoned with. So is Theresa Monsour'
Daniel Silva

'A great thriller debut . . . Think Michael Connelly or Sara Paretsky . . . scary and satisfying'
John Sandford

'Intuitive, gritty, and completely entertaining, Paris Murphy stakes a claim to the front rank of crime fiction heroines'
Chuck Logan

THE KILLS

Linda Fairstein

Prosecuting Andrew Tripping for the assault of Paige Vallis is already hard enough for Assistant District Attorney Alexandra Cooper. No evidence, no forensics, it is the classic 'he said-she said' scenario that is so difficult to prove. Which is why Alex is pinning her hopes on Kevin Bessemer, Tripping's cellmate at Rikers, and Dulles, Tripping's ten-year-old son, who was in the house on the night in question.

But on the way from Rikers to meet Alex, Bessemer uses the situation to make good his escape. And interviewing Dulles is proving equally difficult: first the social workers won't let her see him; and, when the judge does grant Alex permission, Dulles disappears.

Then, as the trial begins, a murder overtakes events in the courtroom, and Alex is plunged into a race against time to discover the truth: a terrifying journey that ends up in the Kills, the eerie waterways along the coastline of New York's harbour . . .

'One of America's most promising and exciting
crime novelists'
Patricia Cornwell

PARTS UNKNOWN

Lynne Heitman

Welcome to Miami – the city with the airport that never sleeps. The city where every crime is drug-related unless proven otherwise. The city where the vicious murder of an out-of-town airline employee just doesn't add up.

Alex Shanahan owes John McTavish everything from her time spent as General Manager for Majestic Airlines in Boston. So when she hears of his death, and the bizarre accusations of drug-dealing, unravelling the truth is the least she can do. Alex is sure the police are investigating a false trail, and her insticts are proved right. For what John had stumbled on was the illegal trade of airplane parts – the 'stripping and dipping' of old aeroplanes and selling the components as new. It's a market that offers lucrative profits, but turns any plane into a potential death-trap. Like the Air Sentinel flight that crashed in Peru, killing over two hundred people. An aircraft whose logbook John sent Alex shortly before he died . . .

Alex's investigation takes her deep into the corrupt underbelly of the airline industry – a world of embezzlement, laundering and drug-dealing, where the authorities are the last people you can trust, and where discovering the truth about a friend's death can cost you your life . . .

THE BEST REVENGE

Stephen White

Thirteen years ago, Tom Clone was convicted and sentenced to life imprisonment for the brutal murder of Ivy Campbell. Then the chance discovery of the murder weapon – and the subsequent DNA tests – proved what Tom had claimed from day one: someone else killed Ivy.

Arriving in Boulder, Colorado, to stay with his grandfather, Tom turns to clinical psychologist Alan Gregory to help him readjust to life outside prison. But psychological support isn't the only help Tom needs: the policemen who put Tom away make sure he knows they think he is still guilty; then his grandfather is attacked. And then, mysteriously, Tom disappears . . .

Alan's unravelling of the truth becomes a desperate race against time in the treacherous Colorado mountains. For what he discovers is the dark chaos of a disturbing past, the twisted logic of a tormented mind, and a thirst for revenge that knows no bounds . . .

'Stephen White writes thrillers of the first order'
Nelson DeMille

Other bestselling Time Warner Books titles available by mail:

☐ Clean Cut	Theresa Monsour	£6.99
☐ The Bone Vault	Linda Fairstein	£6.99
☐ The Kills	Linda Fairstein	£6.99
☐ Hard Landing	Lynne Heitman	£5.99
☐ Parts Unknown	Lynne Heitman	£6.99
☐ Warning Signs	Stephen White	£6.99
☐ The Best Revenge	Stephen White	£6.99

The prices shown above are correct at time of going to press. However, the publishers reserve the right to increase prices on covers from those previously advertised without further notice.

TIME WARNER
BOOKS

TIME WARNER BOOKS
PO Box 121, Kettering, Northants NN14 4ZQ
Tel: 01832 737525, Fax: 01832 733076
Email: aspenhouse@FSBDial.co.uk

POST AND PACKING:
Payments can be made as follows: cheque, postal order (payable to Time Warner Books), credit card or Switch Card. Do not send cash or currency.

All UK Orders   **FREE OF CHARGE**
EC & Overseas   25% of order value

Name (BLOCK LETTERS) . . . .

Address . . . .

. . . .

Post/zip code: . . . .

☐ Please keep me in touch with future Time Warner publications

☐ I enclose my remittance £ . . . .

☐ I wish to pay by Visa/Access/Mastercard/Eurocard/Switch Card

Card Expiry Date ☐☐☐☐   Switch Issue No. ☐☐